Pr...
Sebastian S...

P9-CEV-652

Where Serpents Sleep

"C. S. Harris' attention to historical detail and sense of adventure combine to make a ripping read. Sebastian St. Cyr's world of Georgian intrigue captivated me to the final page."
          —Will Thomas, author of the Barker & Llewelyn Novels

"Harris does a nice job of weaving the many plot strands together while exploring the complex character of her protagonist." —*Publishers Weekly* (starred review)

"[Sebastian and Hero] are a perfect hard-headed match, as they lead Harris' romping good story."
          —*The New Orleans Times-Picayune*

"The dashing Sebastian St. Cyr returns in *Where Serpents Sleep*, the appealing fourth installment of C. S. Harris' Regency mystery series. . . . Harris does an excellent job of interweaving the mystery in this book with the larger story arc of the series." —*St. Petersburg Times*

"The vividly described sights and sounds of Regency London, the stormy relationship between the well-developed main characters, and a complex mystery add to this fourth in the St. Cyr series." —*Booklist*

"C. S. Harris is a brilliant historical storyteller who brings to life the darker side of Regency London inside an intriguing mystery. . . . With a great plausible late twist to top off this strong early-nineteenth-century whodunit, Ms. Harris is at her bleakest best." —*Midwest Book Review*

"Harris gives her reluctant hero, Sebastian St. Cyr, the perfect foil in unorthodox feminist Hero. As Sebastian continues to fight his demons, they join forces to solve a horrendous crime, and their coupling is both humorous and fascinating. Harris delivers another spellbinding novel." —*Romantic Times*

Why Mermaids Sing

"Richly textured . . . rewarding."
          —*The New Orleans Times-Picayune*

"Harris captures the Regency era beautifully while providing the reader with a flawlessly constructed mystery."
          —*Library Journal*

continued . . .

What Angels Fear

"Perfect reading ... Harris crafts her story with the threat of danger, hints of humor, vivid sex scenes, and a conclusion that will make your pulse race. This is altogether an impressive debut." —*The New Orleans Times-Picayune*

"Appealing characters, authentic historical details, and sound plotting make this an amazing debut historical." —*Library Journal* (starred review)

"A stunning debut novel filled with suspense, intrigue, and plot twists galore. C. S. Harris artfully re-creates the contradictory world of Regency England as her marvelous characters move between the glittering ballrooms and the treacherous back alleys of London. Kat and Sebastian lead a cast of memorable characters you will want to meet again and again as they follow the twists and turns of the intricately woven plot." —Victoria Thompson, author of *Murder on Astor Place*

"An absorbing and accomplished debut that displays a mastery of the Regency period in all its elegance and barbarity ... [it] will grip the reader from its first pages and compel to the finish." —Stephanie Barron, author of the Jane Austen Mystery series

"*What Angels Fear* is a masterful blend of historical detail, page-turning suspense, and good old-fashioned romance. Move over, Nick and Nora, mystery fans have a new sleuthing duo to root for in Sebastian and Kat. I can't wait for the next installment." —Penelope Williamson, author of *Wages of Sin*

"The combined elements of historical fiction, romance, and mystery in this fog-enshrouded London puzzler will appeal to fans of Anne Perry and Will Thomas. Expect to hear more from Harris' troubling but compelling antihero." —*Booklist*

"Harris's riveting debut delivers a powerful blend of political intrigue and suspense ... this fresh, fast-paced historical is sure to be a hit." —*Publishers Weekly*

"A well-appointed debut." —*Kirkus Reviews*

"A masterful blend of history and suspense, character and plot, imagination and classic mystery. A thoroughly intriguing, enjoyable read." —Laura Joh Rowland, author of *The Secret Adventures of Charlotte Brontë* and the Sano Ichiro Mystery series

The Sebastian St. Cyr Mystery Series

WHERE SERPENTS SLEEP

A Sebastian St. Cyr Mystery

C. S. HARRIS

AN OBSIDIAN MYSTERY

OBSIDIAN

Published by New American Library, a division of
Penguin Group (USA) Inc., 375 Hudson Street,
New York, New York 10014, USA
Penguin Group (Canada), 90 Eglinton Avenue East, Suite 700, Toronto,
Ontario M4P 2Y3, Canada (a division of Pearson Penguin Canada Inc.)
Penguin Books Ltd., 80 Strand, London WC2R 0RL, England
Penguin Ireland, 25 St. Stephen's Green, Dublin 2,
Ireland (a division of Penguin Books Ltd.)
Penguin Group (Australia), 250 Camberwell Road, Camberwell, Victoria 3124,
Australia (a division of Pearson Australia Group Pty. Ltd.)
Penguin Books India Pvt. Ltd., 11 Community Centre, Panchsheel Park,
New Delhi - 110 017, India
Penguin Group (NZ), 67 Apollo Drive, Rosedale, North Shore 0632,
New Zealand (a division of Pearson New Zealand Ltd.)
Penguin Books (South Africa) (Pty.) Ltd., 24 Sturdee Avenue,
Rosebank, Johannesburg 2196, South Africa

Penguin Books Ltd., Registered Offices:
80 Strand, London WC2R 0RL, England

Published by Obsidian, an imprint of New American Library, a division of Penguin Group (USA) Inc. Previously published in an Obsidian hardcover edition.

First Obsidian Mass Market Printing, November 2009
10   9   8   7   6   5   4   3

In memory of
Dr. Robert D. Harris, December 1921–August 2007.
Scholar, mentor, friend.

"... who knows where serpents sleep?"
— Anonymous

Chapter 1

*T*he girl stared out the window, one hand sliding up and down her shawl-covered arm in a ceaseless, uneasy motion. Outside, a thick fog leached the light from the dying day and muffled the sounds of the surrounding city.

"You don't like the fog, do you?" Hero Jarvis asked, watching her.

They sat together in a pool of golden light thrown by the lamp on the plain tea table where Hero had laid out her notebook, pen and ink, and the standard list of questions she'd drawn up to ask. The girl jerked her gaze back to Hero's face. This one was older than some of the other prostitutes Hero had interviewed, but still young, her face still smooth, her skin clear, her green eyes sharp with intelligence. She said her name was Rose Jones, although in Hero's experience women in this business seldom gave their true names.

"Who does like fog?" said Rose. "You can never tell what's out there."

The girl's accent was disconcerting: pure Mayfair, without a trace of Cockney or any country inflection.

Studying the girl's fine bone structure and graceful bearing, Hero knew a flicker of interest mingled with something both more personal and less admirable that she didn't care to examine too closely. How had this girl—surely no more than eighteen or nineteen years old and so obviously gently born and bred—ended up here, at the Magdalene House, a refuge run by the Society of Friends for women who wished to leave prostitution?

Reaching for her pen, Hero dipped the tip into her inkwell and asked, "How long have you been in the business?"

A bitter smile touched Rose's lips. "You mean, how long have I been a whore? Less than a year."

It was said to shock. But Hero Jarvis was not the kind of woman who shocked easily. At twenty-five years of age, she considered herself immune to the excesses of sensibility that afflicted so many of her sex. She simply nodded and went on to her next question. "What sort of work did you do before?"

"Before? I didn't do anything before."

"You lived with your family?"

Rose tipped her head to one side, her gaze assessing the other woman in a way Hero did not like. "Why are you here, asking us these questions?"

Hero cleared her throat. "I'm researching a theory."

"What theory?"

"It is my belief that most women enter prostitution not because of some innate moral weakness but out of economic necessity."

A quiver of emotion crossed Rose's face, her voice coming out harsh. "What do you know about it? A woman like you?"

Hero set aside her pen and met Rose's gaze without flinching. "Are we so different?"

Rose didn't answer. In the silence that followed, Hero could hear the voices of the other women drifting up from downstairs, the clink of cutlery, a quick burst of laughter. It grew late; soon Hero's carriage would return to take her back to Berkeley Square, to the safety and comfort of her privileged world. Perhaps Rose was right, in a sense. Perhaps—

The sound of a fist pounding on the front door below reverberated through the house. Hero heard a woman's startled exclamation, mingled with a man's harsh growl. A cry of outrage turned suddenly to a scream of terror.

Rose leapt from her chair, her eyes wild. "Oh, God. They've found me."

Hero pushed to her feet. "What do you mean? What's happening?"

She could hear the voices of more men now, the crash of overturned furniture, the smashing of crockery. Women shrieked. Someone pleaded, tearful, her voice trailing off into a whimper that ended abruptly.

"They're here to kill me." Rose whirled around, her gaze sweeping the room to fix on an old walnut cupboard, which took up most of the near wall. "We must hide."

From below came the sound of running feet and a woman's scream transformed, hideously, into a throaty gurgle. Rose yanked open the cupboard door. Hero reached out a hand, stopping her. "No. That's the first place they'll search."

Crossing the room, Hero threw wide the casement window that overlooked the mist-swirled alley below. The window opened onto the sloping roof of what was probably the kitchen or a washroom. "This way," said Hero. She sucked in a quick breath, the damp, coal smoke–tinged air biting her lungs as she threw one leg over the low sill and ducked her head through the frame.

Covered with moss and condensation and soot, the slate roofing tiles felt treacherously slippery beneath the smooth leather soles of Hero's kid half boots. She moved cautiously, one hand braced against the rough brick of the house wall as she turned to help Rose through the narrow opening.

As she eased the window closed behind them, Hero heard a man shout from inside the house, "She's not here."

Another man answered, his voice lower pitched, his footsteps already heavy on the staircase. "She's here. She must be upstairs."

"They're coming," Hero whispered, and felt Rose's hand tighten around her upper arm in warning.

Following the direction of the girl's shaky, pointing finger, Hero discerned the figure of a man looming out of the fog below. A guard, stationed at the back door to make certain none of the women in the house escaped to the alley.

Hunkering low, Hero crab walked down the slippery slope of the roof to its edge. She watched the man below pace back and forth, his hat pulled over his eyes, his shoulders hunched against the dampness.

Moving as silently as she could, Hero swung her feet over the edge, her stocking-clad legs showing creamy white against the white of the mist as the hem of her fine blue alpaca carriage dress caught on the edge of the tiles and hiked up. She waited until the guard paused just below her. Then she pushed off from the eaves to drop straight down on him.

The force of the impact knocked him to his knees with a grunt and threw Hero to one side. She landed on her hip in the mud, hard enough to bring a small cry to her lips, but she scrambled quickly to her feet. The man was still on his hands and knees when Hero's heel caught him hard on the side of his head and sent him staggering back against the house wall to land in a slumped heap. He lay still.

Rose slid over the edge of the roof to come down in a rush of tearing petticoats and scraped skin. "Good heavens. Where did you learn to do that?"

"I used to play with my brother."

The sound of the upstairs window being thrown open brought both their heads up. A man's voice cut through the fog. "Drummond? You there?"

Rose grabbed Hero's hand and they ran.

They raced up an alleyway of mud and ancient half-buried cobbles hemmed in by soaring walls of soot-blackened brick. Breathing hard, her fingers gripping the other woman's hand tightly, Hero sprinted toward the square patch of white at the alley's mouth, where the silhouette of a carriage appeared out of the mist. They had almost reached the footpath when Hero heard the boom of a gun behind them. Beside her, Rose faltered.

Turning, Hero caught the girl as she began to crumple. The bullet had torn a gaping, oozing hole through her chest.

"Oh, no. No," Hero whispered.

Rose's lips parted, spilling dark red blood down her chin. Hero could feel the girl's blood running warm and wet over her hands, see the light in Rose's eyes ebb, dim.

"No!"

The boom of a second shot echoed up the alleyway. Hero imagined she could feel its passing like the whisper of a ghost beside her cheek.

"I'm sorry," she said, sobbing slightly as she eased Rose down into the mud and ran on.

Chapter 2

The morning dawned overcast and unseasonably cool, the air heavy with the scent of coal smoke and the last lingering wisps of the fog. Winding westward toward the City, a lady's yellow-bodied carriage persistently shadowed a gentleman's curricle as he wove around tumbledown hackneys and towering drays driven by men in smocks and leather aprons. When they reached the Strand, the curricle's driver reined in before the last in a row of small, bow-fronted shops, his pair of blood chestnuts snorting and throwing their heads, restless. Leaning forward, the lady signaled her own coachman to draw up.

"They were 'opin' fer a good run," said the gentleman's tiger from his perch at the curricle's rear, the sharp Cockney tones of his voice carrying clearly in the damp air.

"They'll get it soon enough," said the gentleman, handing the reins to the young groom.

The gentleman's name was Sebastian St. Cyr, Viscount Devlin. The fourth child and youngest of three sons born to the Earl of Hendon and his Countess, Sophia, he had only succeeded to the heir's title on the death of his two older brothers. Now nine-and-twenty, the Viscount was said to have been badly affected by his experiences in the Wars, although few in London seemed to know the exact nature of the circumstances that had led to his decision to sell his commission some two years before and return to England. Until the previous autumn, he had kept the famous actress Kat Boleyn as his mistress, but that liaison had ended abruptly for reasons also shrouded in mystery.

The lady in the carriage watched as the Viscount hopped down from his curricle, his multicaped driving coat swirling around him, his head falling back as he glanced up at the wooden sign with a dagger and a pair of crossed swords that swayed gently in the breeze. He was built tall and lean, with hair that was dark—darker even than that of his father in his prime. But whereas the father's eyes were a piercing blue, the son's were a feral yellow that brought to mind the howl of wolves in the night. Once, his lordship had made the apprehension of murderers his specialty. But for the past eight months, he had given himself over to drinking and gambling and riding to hounds with a reckless abandon that seemed calculated to get him killed sometime in the very near future.

The lady in the carriage watched as the Viscount entered the shop. "Wait here," she ordered her coachman, and signaled to the footman to let down the steps.

Sebastian balanced the dagger in his hand and carefully tested its heft. It was a splendid piece, its ebony hilt inlaid with silver and brass in a delicate Moorish design.

"It arrived just this week from Spain, my lord," said the shopkeeper, a short rounded man with full rosy cheeks and a balding pate who hovered behind the counter of his discreet little establishment in the Strand. "The finest Toledo steel. And the workmanship on the hilt is unusually exquisite, wouldn't you say?"

Nodding, Sebastian whirled to send the dagger flying toward the dartboard on the shop's back wall. The blade bit just left of center, quivered a moment, then stilled.

The shopkeeper's hands fluttered in dismay. Devlin never missed. "Obviously there is an unseen flaw. Let me show you another—"

"No. The blade flew true." Sebastian rubbed his eyes with a splayed thumb and forefinger, aware of a faint tremor in his hand born of too many sleepless nights, too many bottles of brandy, too many dinners left uneaten. "I'll take it." He was reaching for his purse when the bell on the door jangled and a gentlewoman in an ostrich-plumed hat and a hunter green pelisse entered the shop, bringing with her the scent of the cool spring morning.

She was a tall woman just past the first blush of youth, with light brown hair she wore pulled straight back in an unflattering style that accentuated the aquiline nose she had inherited from her father, Charles, Lord Jarvis, cousin to the King and the acknowledged power behind Prinny's fragile regency. She nodded in response to the shopkeeper's effusive greetings but turned her frank gray stare on Sebastian.

"I see your curricle is waiting outside. The one with the matched chestnuts and a tiger who looks no more than twelve."

Sebastian returned his attention to the business of counting out the requisite number of banknotes. "I believe Tom is thirteen. Why? Has he lifted your purse?"

She raised one eyebrow in an expression he found unpleasantly evocative of her father at his most arrogant and ruthless. "He's a pickpocket?"

"He used to be."

"How . . . original." She cleared her throat. "I would like to take a ride around the park."

Sebastian studied Hero Jarvis's hostile, determined face. He had no illusions about how this woman felt about him. She'd given it as her opinion on more than one occasion that he ought to be arrested—or else summarily shot. "I take it this is my cue to invite you for a drive?"

"Thank you." She swept toward the door. "I'll await you in your curricle."

His curiosity piqued, Sebastian walked out of the shop a few minutes later to find Miss Jarvis sitting on the high seat of his curricle, a furled parasol at her side, the reins in her own capable hands. Sebastian's tiger was nowhere in sight, although he could see Miss Jarvis's elegant town carriage waiting up near the corner. Its driver looked asleep.

"Where's Tom?" Sebastian demanded, leaping up beside her to take the reins.

"I told him he wasn't wanted."

"Two things," Sebastian said evenly, giving his chestnuts the office to start. "I don't like other people handling my horses, and I tolerate no one giving false orders to my servants."

"There was no falsehood involved. I didn't want him." She opened her parasol with a snap and tilted it toward the feeble sunshine. "And while I understand your sentiments about the horses, once I had eliminated your tiger, there really was no other option, now was there?"

"Miss Jarvis," he said, his voice coming out in a grating rasp, "in the last eighteen months, your father has attempted to have me killed and very nearly destroyed someone close to me. Why are we taking this drive?"

"*He* attempted to have *you* killed? It is my understanding that you threatened to kill him."

"Several times," Sebastian agreed, turning in through the gates to Hyde Park.

"And you kidnapped me," she reminded him.

"Along with your maid," he agreed. "But only briefly. Which brings us back to the question: Why are you here?"

"Last night, a group of unidentified men attacked the Magdalene House near Covent Garden. They killed over half a dozen women and set fire to the house."

The Magdalene House was not a subject generally discussed in mixed company. Sebastian cast her a quick glance before returning his gaze, deliberately, to his horses. "I knew the refuge had burned," he said. "But I don't recall hearing anything about the house being attacked."

"It is much easier for Bow Street to dismiss the fire as an accident." Her lip curled. "After all, the victims were only women of ill repute."

"How do you know the fire wasn't an accident?"

"Because I was there, in the house. One of the women and I escaped through a window and ran down the alley."

There was a moment's silence while he digested this. She said, "You haven't asked why I was there."

"Very well, Miss Jarvis: Why were you there?"

"I have been conducting research for a bill to be presented in Parliament at the next session, for the relief of indigent women. Centuries of sanctimonious moralists and ministers thundering from their pulpits have convinced society that women become prostitutes because they suffer from some innate moral depravity. I, on the other hand, believe that the unpalatable truth is most women enter the profession only as a last, desperate resort. Unable to earn a living wage by any of the other means our society makes available to them, they soon realize they can either steal, sell their bodies, or starve."

Sebastian glanced at her tightly held face. It seemed an unlikely subject to stir the passions of Lord Jarvis's daughter. But then, Sebastian really knew little about this woman. "What happened to the girl you say escaped with you?"

"She was shot and killed before we reached the street.

Fortunately, I'd left my maid in the carriage—she's so sour and censorious she tends to discourage the women from talking. Otherwise, I've no doubt she would have been killed, as well."

Sebastian stared off across the park, considering this. It was an unfashionable hour for a drive; except for a middle-aged man in a shabby gig teaching a half-grown boy to drive, the gravel road lay deserted in the fitful morning sunshine.

After a moment, Sebastian said, "You'll have to forgive me, Miss Jarvis, if I find all this rather difficult to believe. You see, it seems to me that if anyone had dared take a shot at Lord Jarvis's daughter last night, every magistrate and constable in England would be out, even as we speak, scouring the back alleys and flash houses of the city until those responsible were brought to justice."

She twitched her parasol back and forth in short, sharp jerks, a tinge of angry color touching her cheeks. "My father was disconcerted at the prospect my presence at the Magdalene House might become public knowledge—"

"Disconcerted?" said Sebastian, arching one eyebrow.

"Disconcerted," she said again, with emphasis.

"Given Lord Jarvis's attitude toward social reform, I suspect *dismayed* might be a more fitting description."

"My father understands that my politics are different from his."

Sebastian simply smiled.

"He has requested Sir William Hadley personally take charge of the investigation," she said.

"Then you may rest easy. As the chief magistrate of Bow Street, Sir William has proved himself to be crude, ruthless, and very effective."

"I fear I haven't made myself clear. Sir William has

been ordered to make certain that there is no official investigation, as any such inquiries would inevitably lead to my name being bandied about in connection with the incident. Instead, my father intends to take care of the men responsible himself. He wants it done quietly. Very quietly."

"Lord Jarvis is highly effective at 'taking care' of people quietly," said Sebastian. "I don't think you need concern yourself with the matter any further."

"My father's sole interest is in killing those who endangered my life."

"And that's not sufficient?"

She turned toward him, her gray eyes as intelligent—and inscrutable—as her father's. "One of the women I interviewed last night was called Rose. Rose Jones. She couldn't have been more than eighteen or nineteen years of age, tall and slender, with brown hair and green eyes. I would swear she was wellborn. Very wellborn."

"She may have been. Unfortunately, Miss Jarvis, gently born women are frequently reduced by circumstances to prostitution." Sebastian completed his second circuit of the park in silence, then turned back toward the Strand. "Clergymen's daughters, daughters of impoverished solicitors and doctors, the widows and orphans of officers killed in the war . . . all are far more common in Covent Garden than you obviously imagine."

"That may be. But when we first heard those men breaking into the Magdalene House last night, Rose said to me, *'Oh, God. They've found me. They're here to kill me.'* Then, later, I heard the men say, 'She's not here,' and, 'She must be upstairs.' I believe Rose Jones is the reason those women were killed. I want to know who she was and why those men were after her."

"Why?"

"Why?" The question appeared to surprise her.

"Yes. Why do you want to know? Vulgar curiosity?"

"*No.*"

"Then what?"

She was silent for a moment, the damp breeze ruffling her plain brown hair as she stared off across the misty parkland. She drew in a deep breath that flared her nostrils, then said, "I held that woman in my arms as she was dying. It could so easily have been me. I suppose I feel I owe her something."

It was a heartfelt performance, and if it had been delivered by anyone other than Jarvis's daughter, Sebastian probably would have believed it. He said, "So why, precisely, have you sought me out?"

She turned to face him, the hint of humanity he thought he'd momentarily glimpsed now gone. "It's the oddest thing, but I've realized that none of my acquaintances have much experience with murder. So naturally I thought of you."

Sebastian was startled into letting out a sharp laugh.

Something unpleasant gleamed in her eyes. "I amuse you, my lord?"

If truth were told, Hero Jarvis scared the hell out of him. Sebastian shook his head. But all he said was, "I may have been involved in several investigations in the past, Miss Jarvis, but apprehending murderers is not my hobby."

"What would you call it, then? Your avocation?"

Kat Boleyn had once called it his passion, his obsession, his self-imposed penance for sins she only half understood. But that seemed a lifetime ago now, and he slammed his mind shut against the thought. He said, "I haven't been involved in anything of that nature for a while now."

"I have heard something of how you've been spending your time these past months," she said drily. "Rest assured that I am not asking you to investigate personally. I am merely requesting guidance on how I should go about beginning such an investigation."

"It's your intention to investigate these murders *yourself*?"

"Are you implying that I am incapable?"

"I'm implying that women of your station generally hire Bow Street Runners to do their investigating."

"That's not possible in this situation."

"Because of Sir William?"

"Not exactly." A flush crept up her cheeks, and he wondered what she was not telling him. "I promised my father I would not approach the magistrates."

He studied her carefully composed features. "Yet Lord Jarvis has no objection to you pursuing your own inquiries?"

She turned her head away to study a passing row of shops, and Sebastian gave a low laugh. "You haven't told him, have you? He will find out." Lord Jarvis maintained an extensive network of spies and agents, which had earned the man a well-deserved reputation for omniscience.

She said, "I have no intention of denying my activities."

Sebastian knew a brief flicker of admiration. There weren't many with the courage to cross the King's powerful cousin. He said, "You also realize that I could use the information you've given me to hurt you."

"You mean, to hurt my father through me." She met his gaze and held it. "It has occurred to me. It's a risk I've decided I am willing to take."

"Discovering this woman's identity is that important to you?"

"I don't think anything has ever been this important to me," she said simply.

A tense silence fell between them. He had a dozen good reasons for avoiding this woman and very few incentives to help her. Yes, the temptation to annoy Jarvis was powerful. Yet that in itself might not have been enough to tempt him if he hadn't been aware of a vague, unexpected quickening of interest. He couldn't think of anything that had intrigued him—really intrigued him—for eight months now.

He reined in beside her carriage and said, "If it were me, Miss Jarvis, I'd begin by talking to the authorities. See what they have discovered so far."

For the first time since she had approached him that morning, he saw what looked like a slight faltering in her formidable composure. "But that's the one thing I can't do."

"No. But I can."

"You? But ... why would you involve yourself in this?"

"You know why."

She met his gaze. And in that moment he realized that she did, indeed, know why. She knew he would welcome any chance to discomfit her father. More than that: She had, in fact, been counting on it.

"Thank you, my lord," she said, allowing herself a slight smile as she turned to alight. "You will tell me if you discover anything?"

"Of course," said Sebastian, and went in search of his tiger.

Chapter 3

*S*ebastian found Tom waiting for him outside the cutler's shop. A small scrap of a boy with brown hair, a gap-toothed smile, and a usefully forgettable face, Tom served Sebastian as both a groom and a willing participant in some of Sebastian's less orthodox activities.

"She said I weren't wanted," the tiger exclaimed when Sebastian told him of Miss Jarvis's deception. " 'Ow was I to know a starchy gentlewoman like 'er was tellin' a bouncer?"

"Miss Jarvis would argue that, technically, it wasn't a bouncer, since *she* did not want your presence."

Tom's brows drew together in a dark frown that augured ill for any future encounters between the tiger and Lord Jarvis's formidable daughter.

Hiding a smile, Sebastian gathered his reins. "I want you to take a message to Dr. Gibson for me. You'll probably find him at the Chalk Street Almshouse—I think he volunteers there on Tuesday mornings. Ask him to meet me at the site of the Friends' Magdalene House in Covent Garden. I'll be there as soon as I've spoken to Sir Henry."

"The Magdalene House?" Tom's eyes danced with sudden interest. "Ain't that the place what burned last night?"

"That's right."

"You think there's somethin' not quite right about that fire?"

"Miss Jarvis claims it was murder."

Sebastian found Sir Henry Lovejoy, Chief Magistrate at Queen Square Public Office, sitting at his desk reading the *Hue and Cry*. "My lord," said Sir Henry, surging to his feet when the clerk, Collins, ushered Sebastian into the chamber. "Please, come in and sit down."

A small man with a bald head and reading glasses, Sir Henry had been a merchant before the deaths of his wife and daughter shifted his interest to the law. They were unlikely friends, Sebastian and this earnest magistrate, with his serious demeanor and steadfast adherence to a rigid moral code worthy of a preacher. But friends they were.

"What can you tell me about last night's fire at the Magdalene House?" Sebastian asked, taking the seat Sir Henry indicated.

Sir Henry peeled the small gold-framed spectacles from his face and rubbed the bridge of his nose. "Terrible business, that. Last I heard, they'd already pulled four bodies from the rubble and there are probably more. According to the Quakers who run the place, seven soiled doves were staying at the establishment at the time of the tragedy, in addition to the woman in charge of the day-to-day operation of the house—a matron named Margaret Crowley. She apparently took refuge with the Friends some ten years ago herself and recently came back to help. She's believed to be one of the victims."

"Any sign the women might have been killed before the fire was set?"

"You mean, murdered?" Sir Henry had an almost comically high voice, and it now rose even higher. "Good heavens, no."

Sebastian frowned. "How many survivors were there?"

"None that I know of."

"You don't find that strange? That none of the women managed to escape the fire? It was only—what?—five, six o'clock in the evening when the fire broke out."

Sir Henry lifted his thin shoulders in a shrug. "The house was old and its timbers dry. It would have burned quickly. People frequently assume they have more time to get out than they actually do. They become disoriented and they perish."

It was possible, Sebastian supposed. But he found it difficult to believe that none of those eight women had managed to stagger out of the smoke and flames into the night. "Bow Street is handling the investigation, I assume?" he asked casually.

Sir Henry nodded. "It's not far from their offices, after all. I believe Lord Jarvis has requested Sir William take charge of the incident personally."

"Lord Jarvis? What's his interest in this?" Sebastian asked, curious to hear what the magistrate would say.

Sir Henry looked mildly surprised, as if the question hadn't occurred to him. No one queried Lord Jarvis's activities. "That I do not know."

"And has Sir William ordered postmortems on the women?"

"I don't believe so, no. Last I'd heard the bodies were to be turned over to the Friends for burial." Sir Henry was looking troubled. After a moment, he said, "If I might be so bold as to inquire into your interest in this, my lord?"

Sebastian pushed to his feet. "I have no interest in it. I'm simply making inquiries on behalf of an acquaintance." He turned toward the door, but paused to look back and ask, "You haven't by any chance heard of a young prostitute named Rose Jones, have you? Eighteen, maybe nineteen years of age. Wellborn."

Sir Henry thought a moment, then shook his head. "No. You think she was one of the victims?"

"She might have been."

"Who was she?"

"That's the problem," said Sebastian. "I don't know."

Chapter 4

"We received reports this morning that the Luddites have burned another cotton mill in the West Riding," said the Right Honorable Spencer Perceval, Prime Minister of the United Kingdom. A small, thin man with a perpetually earnest expression, the Prime Minister paced nervously across the carpeted floor of the Carlton House chambers kept by Charles, Lord Jarvis.

"So I had heard," said Jarvis, going to stand beside the window overlooking the Mall. He was a big man in every sense of the word. Tall of stature and wide through the shoulders, he carried perhaps twice the weight of the Prime Minister. He was also easily twice as powerful and infinitely more cunning. The reports from Jarvis's own agents in Yorkshire had reached his desk the previous evening.

"Fortunately," continued Perceval, still pacing back and forth, "by some miracle the local militia arrived quickly enough to arrest some score or more of the participants. We believe they're the same men involved in smashing frames last month."

"It was no miracle. Merely the careful planting of agents provocateurs."

The Prime Minister spun to face him. "You have infiltrated the movement?"

"Did you think I would sit idly by while masked ruffians hamper the industrial production of this country and gather at night on the moors to practice drills and maneuvers like a bunch of bloodthirsty French revolutionaries? We have more troops fighting the Luddites here in England than we have against Napoleon in Iberia. I understand that the Prince is reluctant to move against his own people, but the time has come to put a stop to this nonsense."

"It's not just in Yorkshire," said Perceval. "There are also indications that some of the workers in Lancashire—"

Jarvis made a rough noise deep in his throat. "Execute a dozen of these Yorkshire lads and transport a few hundred to Botany Bay, and your Lancashire louts will think twice before they go smashing any more machines."

The Prime Minister looked troubled. "Yes. I suppose so. Still, agents provocateurs . . ."

"It's on my conscience, not yours," said Jarvis drily. "And if you are worried it will distress the Prince, we simply won't tell him."

"Yes, that might be for the best."

Jarvis turned back to the papers spread across his desk. "If there's nothing else?"

"What? Oh, no. Good day, my lord," said the Prime Minister, and bowed himself out.

Jarvis stood beside his desk, his thoughts drifting away from the Prime Minister and the Prince and the Luddites, to matters of a more personal nature. The descendant of an old and powerful family, Jarvis owned a large and prosperous estate, as well as a comfortable townhouse on Berkeley Square. But he generally avoided his own houses as much as possible, passing most of his time either in his clubs or in the chambers kept both here at Carlton House and in St. James's Palace. The Berkeley Square house was overrun with females, and Jarvis had little patience for members of the fair sex, least of all his half-witted wife or his grasping harridan of a mother. Once, Jarvis had had a son, David. The boy had seemed a disappointment at the time, although Jarvis had since come to realize he might have been able to make something of David had he lived. Instead, Jarvis had been left with only his daughter, Hero. The mere thought of her now was enough to bring a sour burn to his chest.

If she'd been born a boy, then he would have been proud of her, proud of her powerful will and her undeniable intelligence. But he'd left her too much in the care of her half-mad mother, who had exercised no control over the girl whatsoever. As a result, she'd grown up with a collection of ideas that could only be described as radical. As for this latest start of hers . . . well, at least she'd had the sense to come to him first, rather than bolting straight to Bow Street. He could handle Sir William. All that remained was to tidy up the loose ends.

Jarvis was very good at tidying up loose ends.

Jarvis might have owed his introduction to Court to his distant kinship to George III. But it was his incomparable intellect combined with the formidable strength of his will and his cunning that had made him indispensable first to the King, then to the Regent. The position of prime minister could have been his in an instant, had he wanted it. He did not want it, being content to leave the nominal governance of the country to men such as Spencer Perceval and the Earl of Hendon. None understood better than Jarvis the limitations of power politics. He found it far more satisfying—and lucrative—to exercise power from the shadows. There was no one more powerful in all of England than Jarvis. But then, there was no one in England more fiercely devoted to his King and his country. For the sake of England and the dynasty that ruled her, Jarvis would do anything.

A scratching at the door brought his head around. A

pale-faced clerk bowed and said, "Colonel Bryce Epson-Smith to see you, my lord."

"Send him in."

Hat in hand, the Colonel advanced halfway into the room and sketched a low bow. "You wished to see me, sir?"

The Colonel was a tall man. Not quite as tall as Jarvis, but superbly muscled, with dark hair and gray eyes. A former cavalry officer, Epson-Smith had now served Jarvis for more than three years. Of all Jarvis's agents, he was the most intelligent and the most ruthless.

Jarvis drew an enameled snuffbox from his pocket and opened it with one flick of his finger. "Last night, someone killed a half dozen whores at a house of refuge run by the Society of Friends near Covent Garden. I want you to find out who did it and kill them."

A flicker of surprise passed across the Colonel's normally impassive features. "The regent has an interest in the incident?"

Jarvis lifted a pinch of snuff to one nostril and sniffed. "It's a personal matter."

Colonel Epson-Smith inclined his head. "I'll get on it right away, sir."

"Discreetly, of course."

"Of course." Epson-Smith bowed again and withdrew.

Chapter 5

*L*ong before he reached what was left of the Magdalene House in Covent Garden, Sebastian could smell the fetid odor of old smoke hanging heavy in the cool air.

The house had collapsed in on itself, leaving only a smoldering, burned-out husk of blackened bricks and charred timbers. Three men with dampened hides wrapped around their boots and cloths covering the lower part of their faces were carefully raking their way through the ruins. A small crowd of ragged women and children had gathered at a nearby corner to watch, their faces drawn and solemn. Even the baker's boy was silent, his tray of cooling buns hanging forgotten from its band around his neck.

Sebastian spotted Paul Gibson crouched awkwardly beside a small body in a ripped, stained gown of yellow cotton. Six more bodies lay in a neat row along the footpath. Four of the bodies looked badly burned, their skin blistered and black, their faces charred beyond identification. But a couple of the women had obviously been sheltered by falling debris, their bodies battered and scorched but still recognizable.

Hunkering down beside his friend, Sebastian found himself staring at a young girl, her slim form relatively untouched by the fire. She couldn't have been more than thirteen or fourteen years of age, her face still full-cheeked and childlike, her cornsilk-fine fair hair fluttering gently in the smoke-tinged breeze. But what drew Sebastian's attention, and held it, was the ripped and bloodied bodice of her simple muslin gown. "Could that have been done by a falling timber?" he asked.

Paul Gibson shook his head. "No. She was stabbed with a knife. There, in the side"—he pointed—"and several times here, in the chest."

"Bloody hell," said Sebastian softly. "She was right."

"Who was right?" Gibson glanced up at him. "Did someone survive this?"

"So it would seem." Sebastian nodded toward that long, silent row. "What about the others?"

His lips compressing into a thin line, Paul Gibson turned his head to follow Sebastian's gaze. The Irishman had spent years as an army surgeon, dealing with all the unspeakable horrors of a battlefield's carnage. He now taught at St. Thomas's, in addition to keeping a small surgery near the Tower. But despite it all, Sebastian knew that any premature or violent death still troubled Gibson. It was why, late at night in the small, secluded building at the base of his unkempt garden, he could frequently be found exploring the mysteries of life and death with the help of a series of cadavers culled from the city's untended churchyards. No one in London could read a dead body better than Paul Gibson.

"The others are much the same," said Gibson. He lurched to his feet, stumbling slightly as his one remaining good leg took his weight; he'd lost the lower part of his other leg to a French cannonball. "Several are so badly burned it would be impossible to say how they died without a proper postmortem. But I've found at least one more that was stabbed, and another who had her throat slit."

"Could any of them have been shot?"

"Actually, yes. The woman at the far end was definitely shot. How did you know?"

Sebastian stared at that distant blackened form. "Is she identifiable?"

"Maybe by her mother. Although I wouldn't want her mother to have to remember her looking like this." Gibson glanced around as a hoarse shout went up from one of the men working through the smoldering ruins. "Looks like they've found another one," said Gibson. "That makes eight."

Sebastian blew out a long, slow breath. "Jesus." He watched as two men stumbled out of the ruins, a makeshift stretcher carried between them.

"This un 'ere's in bad shape," said one of the men as they eased their burden down on the footpath. "Please God it's the last."

Gibson hunkered down beside the charred, blackened form, but said, "This one's so burned that even with a proper autopsy—"

"Get away from that body!"

Sebastian looked up to find a tall, bearlike gentleman in an exaggerated top hat and red-and-white-striped silk waistcoat descending upon them from a lumbering dray. Sir William Hadley, one of Bow Street's three stipendiary magistrates, came puffing up to them, his jaw jutting forward like a man ready for a fight. "What do you think you're doing? Didn't you hear what I said? Get away from that body."

Gibson pushed slowly to his feet. "I'm a surgeon."

"A surgeon! Who gave you permission to examine these bodies? I've ordered no postmortem. And don't try to tell me one of the families requested it, because I won't believe it. Whores don't have families ... leastways, none that'll acknowledge them."

The Irishman's dark brows drew together in a frown.

"Nevertheless, a postmortem is called for, Sir William. These women were murdered."

"Murdered?" The Bow Street magistrate let out a harsh laugh. "What are you talking about? This wasn't murder. These women died in a fire. Someone left a candle too close to a curtain or let a hot ember fall from the hearth."

"And how do you explain the stab wounds?"

"Stab wounds? What stab wounds?"

"At least two of these women were stabbed, while one had her throat—"

Sir William swiped his massive arm through the air in a dismissive gesture. "Enough of this. I will not have my office's resources diverted to investigate the death of a bunch of strumpets. You think the good citizens of this city care if there are a half dozen or so fewer trollops walking the streets?"

Sebastian nodded toward the body of the fair-headed girl lying at the end of the row. "I think her mother might care."

"If she had a mother who cared, she wouldn't have become cash on the hoof." Sir William paused a moment, his eyes narrowing as he studied Sebastian. "I know you. You're Lord Hendon's son."

"That's right."

Hot color flooded the magistrate's big, fleshy face. "This is none of your affair—you hear me? I don't care if your father is Chancellor of the Exchequer. I won't have you meddling in this investigation."

Sebastian said, "I didn't realize there was an investigation for me to meddle in."

Sir William's face was so dark now it looked purple. He thrust a meaty finger inches from Sebastian's nose. "I'm warning you, my lord. Keep out of this or I'll have you arrested—peer's son or not."

The magistrate stomped away to go bark orders at the men searching the ruins. Gibson stared after him. But Sebastian was more interested in the elegant town carriage drawing up at the corner, its liveried footman hastening to open the carriage door.

"Who's that?" said Gibson, following his friend's gaze.

A tall gentlewoman in a smart pelisse had appeared in the open doorway, the ostrich plume in her hat waving in the cool breeze as she waited for the footman to let down the steps.

"That," said Sebastian, "is Miss Hero Jarvis."

"Lord Jarvis's daughter? Why is she here?"

"She's the woman who survived the fire."

"*Miss Jarvis?* What in God's name was she doing at the Magdalene House?"

"Research," said Sebastian, and went to hand the lady down from her carriage.

Chapter 6

"*I* expected I might find you here," said Miss Jarvis. She accepted Sebastian's assistance down, then released his hand immediately and took a step back. Within the shadowy interior of her carriage, he could see a maid waiting primly with hands clasped before her.

"That is Paul Gibson, is it not?" said Miss Jarvis, gazing beyond him to where Gibson stood beside the curricle talking to a glowering Tom. "The surgeon?"

"You know him?"

"I attended several of his lectures at St. Thomas's— on the circulatory system, and on human musculature."

It was the last thing Sebastian would have expected her to have done, but he kept the thought to himself.

"Frankly," she said, "I'm surprised to see him here. I didn't think Sir William planned to order autopsies."

"He hasn't. Gibson's here because he's a friend of mine."

She glanced up at him. "And has he discovered anything?"

"He says the women were murdered. Most were stabbed, although he thinks at least one was shot."

She opened her parasol and raised it against the feeble sun. "You doubted me, did you?"

"Yes."

She nodded, as if she had expected as much. In the street before the house, Sir William was now busy supervising the loading of that sad row of charred bodies into the back of the dray. She watched him for a moment, then said, "Has Dr. Gibson's opinion prompted Sir William to order the women autopsied?"

"No. I suspect we can thank your father for that."

She shook her head. "I doubt it would have happened, even without my father's interference. Sir William's attitude toward prostitutes is well-known. Last month, a costermonger came before the magistrates for beating a woman to death in St. Paul's Churchyard. Sir William let the man go with only a warning."

Sebastian studied her clear-skinned face. "Why are you here, Miss Jarvis?"

The breeze fluttered her hair across her face, but she pushed it back without a hint of artifice. "I've been talking to the Society of Friends. It seems a gentleman by the name of Joshua Walden was at the Magdalene House the night Rose first sought refuge with them. He lives in Hans Town. I thought he might be able to tell us more about her."

" 'Us'?" Sebastian crossed his arms at his chest and rocked back on his heels. "I was under the impression this was your investigation, Miss Jarvis. That my role was that of an adviser only and was rapidly coming to a conclusion."

She tilted her head back, one hand coming up to hold her hat as she stared up at the crumbling, smoke-darkened walls of the Magdalene House. Something quivered across her face, a breath of painful emotion that was there and then gone. "That was mere subterfuge and you know it. I want to find out who killed these women, Lord Devlin, and why, and I am not too vain to acknowledge that you are far more experienced in such matters than I. I was hoping that if you looked into the incident, even briefly, it would catch your interest."

When he made no response, she said, "Do you believe in justice?"

"As an abstract concept, yes. Although I fear there is little true justice in this world."

She nodded toward the blackened ruins of the Magdalene House. "In life, our society failed Rose—failed all these women. I don't want to fail them, in death."

"You are not responsible for society."

"Yes, I am. We all are, each in our own small way." She turned to fix him with a direct gaze. "Will you come with me to Hans Town?"

He started to say no. But as he looked into her fierce gray eyes, he realized that a part of her actually wanted him to say no, because it would give her an excuse to walk away from all of this, away from the fear and the horror that was that night.

Turning, he watched the workmen swing the body of the young fair-headed girl into the back of the dray. And in that moment, he wasn't thinking about Lord Jarvis, or Hero Jarvis. He was thinking about the life that child would never live, and the men who had taken it from her.

And so he surprised both himself and Hero Jarvis by saying, "Yes."

Chapter 7

Joshua Walden's home in Hans Town proved to be a modest house of red brick, with neatly painted white shutters, a shiny black door, and window boxes filled with well-tended masses of dianthus and saxifrage.

A tall, almost cadaverously thin man in his late forties or early fifties with a thick head of graying brown hair, he received them in a plainly furnished parlor. "I am honored by this visit, Hero Jarvis," he said, inviting them to sit. "Honored. I read thine article on the high rate of mortality amongst children sold by the parish as climbing boys to chimney sweeps. Fascinating work."

"Why, thank you," said Miss Jarvis, giving the Quaker a smile so wide it made Sebastian blink. "Although I must confess the methodology used was not my own."

From his seat beside the empty hearth, Sebastian listened, bemused, while Miss Jarvis worked, deliberately and adroitly, to insinuate herself in their host's good graces. The two crusaders rattled on at length about everything from laying-in hospitals to poor laws. Only gradually did she bring the conversation around, artfully, to the reason for their visit.

"I understand you were at the Magdalene House the night Rose Jones sought refuge there," she said.

"Yes. It was the third night."

"The third night?" said Sebastian.

Walden smiled. "What thou would call Wednesday. I remember it because the weather was dreadful—the rain was coming down in sheets, and it was quite cold. We haven't been having much of a spring, have we? The poor women were soaked through and dangerously chilled."

Sebastian sat forward. "Women?"

"Yes. There were two of them. I don't recall the other one's name. Helen, or Hannah ... something like that. She didn't stay long, I'm afraid. Our rules are not harsh but they are firm. We've discovered that some of the women who come to us don't really wish to leave the life. I'm afraid Helen, or Hannah, or whoever she was, fell into that category. She was frightened the night she came, but that soon wore off. She left after only a day or two."

Miss Jarvis nodded, neither embarrassed nor shocked by the nature of the conversation. "You say she was frightened?"

"Oh, yes. They both were. It's not unusual. Many of the women who come to us are fleeing dreadful situations—virtual slavery, you know. The brutes who keep them have either forced them to sign papers the poor simpletons believe are binding, or have contrived to reduce them to a state of hopeless indebtedness, even renting them the very clothes on their backs so that by fleeing they open themselves up to charges of theft."

"Did she give you any idea what kind of situation she'd fled?" Sebastian asked.

"We generally don't inquire too closely into such details. But from one or two things Hannah—yes, that was the other girl's name. Hannah, not Helen. At any rate, from one or two things she let slip, Margaret Crowley received the impression the women had been at a residential brothel." He paused, his thin chest rising on a sigh. "Margaret Crowley was the matron at the Magdalene House, you know."

Miss Jarvis leaned forward to pat his hand, where it lay on the chair's arm. "Yes. I'm so sorry."

"Any idea where the brothel may have been located?" Sebastian asked.

Walden cleared his throat. "The one girl—Hannah— was very talkative. I believe she mentioned Portman Square."

Sebastian nodded. Closed, stay-in brothels were rare in London. More common were lodging-house brothels, where the girls were—nominally, at least—independent. Picking up their customers from the pleasure gardens or the theater or even the streets of the city, they then brought them back to the lodging house where they kept a room. Other girls took their men to "accommodation houses" where they didn't actually live; they simply hired one of its rooms for the requisite number of hours—or minutes. Others made use of the numerous chop houses, cigar rooms, and coffeehouses that also had bedrooms available for use—their exclusively male clientele making them good hunting grounds, as well.

"I'm afraid there's really not much else I can tell you about Rose Jones," Walden was saying. "Many of the girls chafe at the restrictions we impose upon them, but Rose never did. She never left the house."

"Because she was still afraid?"

"Yes, I think so."

"Did she ever say anything about her life before she ..." Miss Jarvis hesitated.

Walden shook his head. "No. Although it was obvious she was gently born. We don't often see women quite like her. For some reason, many of the women who come to us claim to be clergymen's daughters, although I suspect few actually are. But I've no doubt Rose was very wellborn. Very wellborn indeed." He looked from

Miss Jarvis to Sebastian. "This has something to do with
the fire, doesn't it? Dost thou think it's possible the fire
was not an accident?"

"I think so, yes."

Joshua Walden nodded, his lips pressed together
tightly.

It was when he was escorting them to the door that
he said suddenly, "There is one more thing that might
help. We had a young girl in the house who called herself
Rachel. I don't think she could have been more than
thirteen—a lovely fair-haired child. One evening—just
by chance—I overheard Rose say to the child, 'I was
once called Rachel.' It stuck in my head because Rachel
laughed merrily and said, 'I was once called Rose.' "

He smiled gently at the memory, the smile rapidly
fading. "But it may mean nothing. Some girls change
their names frequently."

"Perhaps," said Sebastian, pausing in the Quaker's
simple entrance hall. "But it could also be Rose's real
name. Thank you."

"That was fortuitous," said Miss Jarvis as Sebastian
handed her up into her waiting carriage. "I hadn't expected to learn so much."

"You think we learned a great deal, do you?"

"You don't?" She turned to look at him in surprise. "How many brothels can there be near Portman
Square?"

He took a step back. "Believe it or not, Miss Jarvis,
I haven't the slightest idea. But I know someone who
will."

Chapter 8

*I*n addition to the modest estate in Hampshire bequeathed to him by a maiden great-aunt, Sebastian also kept a bow-fronted house in Brook Street. The establishment at Number 41 Brook Street was considerably smaller and less imposing than the Grosvenor Square townhouse of his father, Alistair St. Cyr, Chancellor of the Exchequer and Fifth Earl of Hendon. But Sebastian had not visited either his father's Grosvenor Square house or his ancestral estates in Cornwall since September of the previous year.

A distant rumble of thunder shook the cloudy afternoon as Sebastian took the short flight of stairs to his own front door. He handed his hat to his majordomo, Morey, and said, "Where is Calhoun?"

Jules Calhoun was Sebastian's valet. The less than orthodox nature of some of Sebastian's activities had in the past made it difficult for him to retain the services of a gentleman's gentleman. But it had been eight months now since Calhoun had joined the Brook Street household, and he'd never shown the least tendency to leave in horror or a fit of pique.

The majordomo, however, was not one of Calhoun's fans. He sniffed. "*Some* valets might have more sense than to invade the kitchen this close to the dinner hour," said Morey in sepulchral tones. "Unfortunately, Calhoun is not of their company."

Sebastian hid a smile. "Brewing boot polish, is he?"

A muscle bunched along Morey's tight jaw. "If Madame LeClerc should quit over this—"

"Madame LeClerc quit because Calhoun has chosen to spend some time in the kitchen?" Sebastian jerked off his gloves. "Not likely."

Madame LeClerc would have banished any other valet with a pot of boot polish to the stables. But the cook was called "Madame" solely out of courtesy; she was actually a young Frenchwoman in her late twenties, a softly rounded woman with black hair and laughing eyes and a short upper lip. And Jules Calhoun was a very dashing gentleman's gentleman.

Morey sniffed again. "Would you like me to have him wait upon you, my lord?"

Sebastian swung off his driving coat. "Good God, no." Boot polish was serious business. "I'll go to him."

Morey bowed in majestic silence and withdrew.

The descent of the Viscount into his own kitchens caused something of a flutter. The kitchen maid dropped a pot of half-shelled peas, while Madame LeClerc gasped and said, "Ees something wrong, my lord? You deed not like the sole I fixed for last night's dinner, perhaps?"

"The sole was wonderful," said Sebastian, carefully avoiding the cascade of rolling peas. "I've come to discuss boot polish with Calhoun. If you'll excuse us?"

Madame LeClerc threw a soulful glance at the small, lithe man stirring the contents of a heavy pot on the stove, and withdrew.

The air in the kitchen was redolent with the scent of hot beeswax and resin. In deference to the stove's heat, Jules Calhoun had removed his coat and rolled up his shirtsleeves, yet he still managed to convey a sense of punctilious neatness. Nothing about either his demeanor or his impressive skills as a gentleman's gentleman betrayed the fact that he had grown up in the most notorious flash house in London.

"As keen as your lordship is about the shine on his boots," said Calhoun, not looking around, "I can't see it luring you down into the kitchens."

Sebastian went to sprawl in one of the straight-backed chairs beside the scrubbed kitchen table. "I want to know what you can tell me about the residential brothels near Portman Square."

Calhoun glanced around, a lock of his straight flaxen hair falling across his high forehead. "Were you looking for anything in particular, my lord?"

"I'm looking for a house where one could hire an attractive, gently bred woman of some eighteen to twenty years of age. Dark hair. Slim. Educated."

Calhoun returned his concentration to the bubbling concoction on the stove. "Such a barque of frailty has caught your fancy, my lord?"

"Not exactly. Her name is Rose—or maybe Rachel—Jones and she was killed last night when someone attacked the Friends' Magdalene House in Covent Garden. I have reason to believe she fled a house near Portman Square."

"Ah. I see. Well, there are only three stay-in brothels in the Portman Square area." Calhoun poured a black mixture from a vial into his pot. Sebastian watched with interest. Like most valets, Calhoun kept his boot polish recipe a dark secret. "If your girl was slim and well-bred," said the valet, "then I doubt she'd have been at the Golden Calf. They go for the buxom milkmaid type. There's a house in Chalon Lane that sometimes has more refined girls, but they cater to those who like them young." A quiver of distaste passed over his features. "Very young. They're not all girls, either."

"And the third house?"

"I'd say it's probably your best bet. They call it the Orchard Street Academy. Most of the girls there are simply pretending to be ladies, but a few are the real thing. The abbess is a skinny, grasping harridan who was on the stage in her prime. Calls herself Miss Lil."

"She owns the place?"

"No. The actual owner is Ian Kane." Calhoun reached for a small bottle. "Now there's a crafty fellow."

Sebastian leaned forward. "Tell me about him."

Calhoun added a small measure of what looked like neat's-foot oil. "I've heard his father was a miner from Lincolnshire. Our Ian came up to London when he was but seventeen and married a widow who owned a grog shop on Newgate. Now he owns at least a dozen different establishments—everything from grog shops to pubs to places like the Orchard Street Academy. He's smart, and he's ruthless."

"Ruthless enough to kill a woman who fled his house?"

Calhoun raised his spoon to test the consistency of his mixture. "His wife died a year after the marriage. Fell down the stairs and broke her neck. There are those who claim Kane pushed her. But then, it could just be rumor."

Sebastian studied the valet's half-averted face. "What do you think?"

Calhoun moved the pot of boot polish off the fire. "I think people Ian Kane finds a danger or even just a nuisance seem to have a higher-than-average chance of ending up dead." He glanced around, his blue eyes somber. "You'd do well to remember that, my lord."

Chapter 9

*H*ero Jarvis considered herself a sensible woman not given to willfulness or foolish stubbornness. She came from an ancient, powerful family and understood well the obligations such a heritage entailed. Nevertheless, she did not subscribe to the oft-expressed belief that a woman's virtues were limited to chastity, humility, and obedience. She did strive for humility, although it was at times difficult. She was also a chaste woman and, at the age twenty-five, had resigned herself to a virginal old age. But that state of affairs came more from an unwillingness to submit herself to a husband's power than from anything else. And as for mindless obedience—well, in Hero's opinion, that was for children, servants, and dogs.

Her father tended to lump her in his mind with either the sentimentalists or the radicals, but in that, he erred. She was neither. She considered fervent democrats dangerously delusional, and while she supported charity work, she had no personal inclination to ladle porridge at a soup kitchen or volunteer in an orphanage. Her dedication to change and reform was more intellectual than emotional, and more legal than personal. She simply subscribed to a vastly different moral code from the one that governed her father—which did much to explain why he couldn't understand her.

Her decision to take it upon herself not to allow the Magdalene House murders to be forgotten had not been reached lightly. But once she had resolved not to fail the woman who had died in her arms, Hero pursued her goal with the same single-minded drive that characterized her father. Because she knew herself deficient in the experience and skills necessary to deal adequately with the task at hand, it was a logical step to solicit the assistance of someone such as Viscount Devlin. But Hero knew it would be both disingenuous and cowardly for her to convince herself that her obligation ended there. And Hero Jarvis was neither disingenuous nor cowardly.

Returning to the Jarvis townhouse on Berkeley Square, she exchanged her gown and matching pelisse of moss green for a more somber gray walking dress of fine alpaca and a small veiled hat. Then, accompanied reluctantly by her maid, she set forth in her carriage for Covent Garden.

Hero's research into the causes of the recent proliferation in the number of prostitutes in the metropolis had given her a familiarity with people and places unknown to most women of her station. She thought it made sense to use those contacts now, in an attempt to find the woman who had originally arrived at the Magdalene House with Rose Jones. Lord Devlin might be skilled in the arts of detection, but the fact remained that he was a man, and Hero knew well the attitudes toward men that characterized the fallen women of the demirep. They would be far more likely to open up to Hero, a woman, than to a member of a sex they both hated and scorned.

At this hour of the afternoon, the main square of Covent Garden was still given over to its market, the surrounding streets echoing with the shouts of fisherwives and the hawkers' cries of "fresh hot tea" and "fine ripe oranges sweet as sugar." The rouged and willing women

who would emerge later to prowl the darkening colon-
nades and the theaters could still be found huddled in
desultory conversation in the kitchens of their lodging
houses.

Hero directed her coachman to a discreet lodging
house in King Street run by an aged Irishwoman named
Molly O'Keefe. A large woman with an ample girth and
improbable red hair, Molly greeted her with hands on
hips, a broad smile crinkling the flesh beside her watery
gray eyes. Once, Molly had been a prostitute herself.
But she'd been shrewd enough to pull herself out of the
downward spiral that ended for most in disease and an
early death.

"I didn't expect to be seein' your ladyship agin," said
Molly, reaching out to pluck Hero off the small stoop.
"Come in, come in."

"I'm not a ladyship and you know it, Molly," said
Hero, pressing into Molly's hands the basket of fine
bread and fresh farm cheeses she had brought. "My father is a baron, not an earl."

Molly laughed, showing tobacco-stained teeth. "Sure.
But you're a lady, no gettin' around that. Besides, you
could be a ladyship if'n you wanted it. All you'd need
do is marry one o' them lords I've no doubt are courtin'
you."

"Now why would I want to do that?"

Molly laughed again. "Damned if I know."

Trailed by her sour-faced maid, Hero followed the
landlady down the shabby hall and into the kitchen,
which served as the lodging house's common room. The
center of the kitchen was taken up by an old and battered scrubbed table around which grouped the house's
various lodgers. Clothed in shabby dressing gowns and
slippers, a dozen or so women chattered with brutal
frankness about men and clothes and their own wildly
improbable schemes for the future. The close air smelled

of beer and gin and onions faintly underlain by another scent Hero had come to associate with such places, although its exact nature continued to elude her.

Molly O'Keefe's lodging house was not a brothel, although most of her lodgers were prostitutes. These were free-ranging prostitutes who preferred to keep their private lives separate from their trade. Scorning both the residential-style brothels and the lodging-house brothels, they lived here, in Molly O'Keefe's house, and took their pickups to an accommodation house to rent a room.

Hero had never been to a residential brothel or a lodging-house brothel, or to an accommodation house. It frustrated her, but because she was a young unmarried gentlewoman, there were still certain boundaries she did not dare cross, however impatient with convention she might be. Her contact with the women of the street she studied had therefore been limited to neutral territory such as this, or refuges such as the Magdalene House. But she'd learned enough about them to understand the ties that bound one segment of the underworld to the next. Through the residents of Molly O'Keefe's house, Hero would have access to virtually every prostitute in London.

"I would like to address your boarders, if I may," she said to Molly, and pushed back her veil.

Molly clapped her hands together. "Right then," she said loudly. "Listen up, ye drunken lot of worthless tarts. The lady here wants to talk to you."

Someone snickered, while perhaps half of the women around the table continued to talk. A woman with short blond hair and massive breasts visible at the gaping neck of her gown said, "And why the 'ell should we listen to 'er?"

"Because what I have to say could earn you twenty pounds," said Hero, stepping to the head of the table.

Twenty pounds were considerably more than a good housemaid could earn in a year. An immediate hush fell over the room. Now that she had their attention, Hero said, "Last Wednesday, two women fled a residential brothel near Portman Square. One called herself Rose. The other was named Hannah. Rose was one of the women killed at the Magdalene House last night. But Hannah left the refuge several days before the attack. She may be in danger, or she may know something about why the attack took place. I would like to speak to her."

A murmur of whispers and desultory comments swelled around the room. Hero raised her voice and continued speaking. "If you or one of your acquaintances provides me with information that enables me to find Hannah, that person will receive a reward of twenty pounds."

"Why, you must be lookin' fer me," said a tall, skeletally thin woman with long brown hair. "I'm Hannah. How'd you know I was here?"

The other women around the table laughed, while Molly growled and said, "Like hell. That's Jenna Kincaid."

"Please do not think," said Hero, letting her gaze travel around the assembled women, "that I will be so foolish as to pay for false information. I will know the woman I seek when I find her. Anyone stepping forward will receive a reward only if the information she provides proves accurate."

"How do we know you don't mean this Hannah no harm?" shouted one of the women at the far end of the table.

"I am not here as an instrument of the law," said Hero, again having to raise her voice above an undercurrent of murmurs. "The women at the Magdalene House were murdered. The authorities have shown no interest in discovering who was responsible. No one knows why these women were killed, which means that Hannah may not be the only one who is in danger. Whoever killed those women could do it again. You are all potentially in danger."

This statement provoked a predictable uproar. Hero waited a few moments, then said, "Anyone with the information I seek may meet me tomorrow morning at Bullock's Museum. I will be in the exhibition halls from ten to eleven a.m. I'll be wearing a navy blue walking dress and a hat with two ostrich plumes. But be warned: Anyone wasting my time with false information will have reason to regret their perfidy."

The women fell suddenly silent. Hero had a knack for sounding very much like her father when she wanted to.

Molly's face was unusually grim as she walked with Hero to the lodging house's front entrance. "I've heard talk them women at the Magdalene House was murdered, but didn't credit it."

"I'm afraid it's true," said Hero. She turned on the house's narrow stoop to take Molly's hand. "Thank you for your assistance."

Molly's sagging cheeks took on a reddish hue. She jerked her head toward the kitchen. "You think them strumpets really is in danger?"

"They could be. I honestly don't know."

Molly studied her with narrowed, unblinking eyes. "Most of the fine gentlemen and -women we see around here want to punish the whores—put them through a living hell so's they'll come out all pious and submissive. But you're not like that."

Hero gave a soft laugh. "Perhaps because I don't like pious, submissive women."

Molly didn't smile. She said, "This Hannah you're tryin' so hard to find . . . did it ever occur to you that if she's in danger, then you're putting yourself in danger, too, by lookin' for her?"

"I am far better protected than she."

"Maybe." Molly nodded toward the waiting coach with its two liveried and powdered footmen. "But if'n you're smart, the next time you come down here, you'll make certain that coachman of yours is carrying a blunderbuss. Nobody's completely safe."

Chapter 10

*T*reading cautiously over charred fallen timbers, blackened furniture, and shattered bricks, Sebastian worked his way through scorched rooms standing open to the joyless light of the cloudy afternoon. From the street came the rattle of a wagon and the cry of a scissors sharpener shouting, "Knives or scissors to grind today?" But here, all was unnaturally silent, brooding.

It had occurred to him that a visit to the Orchard Street Academy would be most productive in the hours after dark. And so he had returned here, to what had once been the Magdalene House, looking for answers to questions that hadn't yet occurred to him.

Pushing his way through a ruined doorway, he surveyed what had once been the kitchen. If Rose Jones had been shot in the alley as Miss Jarvis had said, then her killers must have dragged her body in here before setting the house aflame. They might even have kindled the blaze from the kitchen hearth.

A vague shuffling noise drew his gaze to the distant corner, where what he at first took for a dog rummaged for food. Only, this was no dog. At the sound of Sebastian's footfalls, a child's head reared up, his face darkened with dirt and soot, his hair matted. With a gasp, the ragged youngster bolted for the open doorway, bare feet kicking up little tufts of ash as he ran.

"Wait," called Sebastian, but the boy had already bolted off the back stoop and up the alley.

Sebastian followed him into a narrow, shadowed alleyway reeking of garbage and urine. To his left, the cobbled lane ended in a soaring brick wall. He turned right, retracing the steps Miss Jarvis must have taken the night before. The jumble of footprints in the muck could have belonged to anyone. But there, near the mouth of the alley, he found what he was looking for: a pool of dried blood smeared over the cobbles as if by a body being dragged.

He crouched down, alert for anything out of place amidst the rotting cabbage leaves and offal. He found nothing.

His head falling back, he stared up at the buildings around him. Surely someone had seen something—or heard something.

Pushing to his feet, he started with the tea dealer who occupied the premises on the corner. The proprietor turned out to be a stout middle-aged widow with heavy jowls and an uncompromising gray stare who flapped her apron and blustered at the first mention of the Magdalene House.

"Good riddance, I say," she grumbled. "This is a respectable street, it is. We didn't need those tarts here. It's the judgment of God, if you ask me, what happened."

"You didn't see anything suspicious? Before the fire, I mean. Some men watching the house, perhaps?"

The tea dealer swung away to lift a massive crate and shift it to one side with as much effort as if it had been a small sewing basket. "There were always men hanging around that place. It stands to reason, don't it? I mean, considering what those women were."

"Did you hear any gunshots last night?"

She swung to regard him with hard, unfriendly gray eyes. She had a large mole on the side of her nose from which protruded three hairs. The hairs quivered as she looked him up and down suspiciously, taking in the glory of Calhoun's painstakingly polished boots, the flawless fit of Sebastian's coat and the crisp white linen of his shirt and cravat. "What's it to you, anyway? A fine gentleman like yourself?"

"I'm making inquiries for a friend. There are suggestions the fire wasn't accidental. That it was murder."

"Suggestions?" The woman's meaty fists landed on her ample hips. "And who's making these suggestions, hmm? Them Quakers, I suppose. A lot of heathens, if you ask me, with their strange ways and outlandish ideas. Impugning the integrity of God-fearing Christians." She leaned forward. "It was a fire. Houses burn in London all the time. Especially the houses of the wicked."

"God's judgment?"

"Exactly."

Leaving the musty, redolent atmosphere of the tea dealer, Sebastian ranged up and down the street, talking to a chandler's apprentice and a haberdasher, a coal merchant and a woolen draper. It wasn't until he stepped into the cheesemonger's shop directly opposite the burned-out house that he found someone willing to admit to having seen or heard anything out of the ordinary the evening before.

The slim, brown-haired girl behind the simple wooden counter was young, no more than fourteen or fifteen, with the rosy cheeks and clear eyes of a country lass. "What you mean when you say did I notice anything out o' the ordinary before the fire last night?" she asked as she wrapped up the slice of blue cheese he had selected.

The dim light of the dreary day filtered in through aged windows that distorted the vision of a passing carriage. Standing here, Sebastian realized he had an unobstructed view of the blackened brick walls and broken chimneys across the street. "Someone who might have seemed out of place in the neighborhood, perhaps?" he suggested.

She glanced up, an impish smile curving her lips. "You mean, like you?"

Sebastian laughed. "Am I so out of place?"

"Well, we don't get the likes o' you in here often— that's for sure." She paused to lean forward, her elbows propped on the wooden counter, her smile fading as she dipped her voice. "But, yeah, I did see something struck me as kinda queer. I mentioned it to me da, but he told me to mind me own business. Said we don't need no more trouble."

The earthy odor of aged Cheddars and fresh farmers' cheeses rose up to scent the air around them. Sebastian found himself wondering what kind of trouble the cheesemonger and his family had already encountered. But all he said was, "What did you see?"

She threw a quick glance at the curtained alcove behind her, as if to make certain her da wasn't lurking there. "Men. Gentlemen. They was hanging around here for hours—wanderin' up and down the street, goin' in and outta shops but not buyin' nothin'."

"How many men?"

"I dunno exactly. Three. Maybe four. A couple of 'em come in here. They pretended like they was looking around, but mainly they was just keeping an eye on the house across the street."

"Were they dark haired? Or fair?"

She thought about it for a moment. "The two that come in here was dark. They was maybe a bit older than you, but not by much."

"Do you remember anything else about them?"

"We-ell . . ." She dragged out the syllable, screwing up her face with the effort of recollection. "They reminded me a bit of Mr. Nash."

"Mr. Nash?"

"The Nabob what used to buy all his cheese from me da. He died last year."

"In what way did the gentlemen remind you of Mr. Nash?"

She shrugged one shoulder. "I don't know. They just did."

Sebastian stared out the wavy-paned glass at what had been the Magdalene House's entrance. "Did you see those men go in the house?"

She shook her head. "It got so foggy I couldn't have seen the King himself if'n he'd been driving down the middle of the street."

"What about after the fire started? Did you see the men then, in the crowd?"

Again, she shook her head. Dropping her voice even lower, she said, "But I did hear gunshots. Two of them. Right before the fire started."

So many people in the area had denied hearing any shots that Sebastian would have begun to doubt Miss Jarvis's tale if it hadn't been backed up by Gibson's medical observations. He said, "No one else will admit to having heard a thing. Why would that be?"

Again, that quick look over the shoulder. "Nobody liked havin' that house here," she whispered. "They wanted it gone."

Sebastian studied the gentle lines of her young face, the baby-fine light brown hair that fell in artless disarray from beneath her mobcap. "So you're saying—what?"

She drew in a quick gasp, her eyes widening as she realized how he might have interpreted what she'd just said. "Don't get me wrong. I'm not sayin' I think anyone around here had anything to do with what happened. I'm just sayin' people complained about the house so much, maybe they're afraid somebody might blame them if the constables start lookin' into how that fire come about."

Sebastian reached for his wrapped cheese and laid a generous payment on the counter. "Then why did you tell me?"

"Pippa?" A querulous voice came from the back of the shop. "You still servin' that customer?"

Pippa began to back away.

"Why?" said Sebastian again. But the girl simply wheeled and disappeared through the curtained alcove.

He stepped out of the cheesemonger's into a street filled with lengthening shadows and buffeted by a cold wind. As he turned toward his carriage, the familiar figure of a man separated itself from the gloom cast by a nearby coal wagon and moved to block Sebastian's path.

"I'm surprised to see you here, Devlin," said Colonel Bryce Epson-Smith. "I was under the impression you'd given up this rather curious hobby of yours in favor of drinking yourself to death."

With deliberate slowness, Sebastian let his gaze travel over the former cavalry officer's tall, elegant person, from the smartly curled brim of his beaver hat to his shiny black Hessians. When Jarvis had threatened Kat Boleyn with a traitor's death, Epson-Smith had been his instrument. The man was smart, vicious, and lethal. "Which curious hobby were you referring to?"

"Your self-appointed role as avenger of fair maidens brought too early to the grave." Epson-Smith nodded toward the blackened walls of the burned-out house across the street. "Only, these weren't exactly maidens, now were they?"

"I take it you're here on Lord Jarvis's business."

Epson-Smith hooked a thumb casually in the pocket of his silk waistcoat. "I'd have said that in this instance, at least, we're about the same business."

"Are we? I'm interested in seeing justice done. Your involvement suggests Lord Jarvis is intent on something else entirely."

"Justice? For a half dozen worthless whores? What are they to you?"

"Eight," corrected Sebastian. "There are eight women dead. And if they're so worthless, why are you here?"

If the Colonel knew the real source of Jarvis's interest, he was too adroit to betray it. All he said was, "We could cooperate, you know."

"I don't think so."

His smile never slipping, Epson-Smith turned away. But he paused long enough to look back and say, "If you should change your mind, you know where to find me."

Chapter 11

The night fell unseasonably cold but clear, with a brisk wind off the distant North Sea that blew away the last of the lingering clouds and the coal smoke that could sometimes smother the city at this time of year.

Leaving his town carriage at the corner of Portman Square, Sebastian walked the short distance up Orchard Street, his footsteps echoing on the stone cobbles. This was a mixed section of the city, close to the fine mansions of Mayfair but with scattered older streets slowly fading with the passage of time. Laughter blending with snatches of a melody drifted from a nearby music hall, while the pungent aromas of freshly ground beans and Blue Ruin wafted from the coffeehouse and gin shop across the street. As he passed a doorway, a woman stirred from the shadows, a nearby oil lamp throwing wavering golden light across her bare blond hair and thin face.

"Looking for company?" she asked, her smile trembling. She couldn't have been more than fifteen, her eyes huge in a pale face. Sebastian shook his head and walked on.

The Orchard Street Academy was an ancient mansion set slightly back from the street. Flickering lamplight showed him a freshly blackened door and curtains drawn tightly at all the windows. But one of the gutters hung rotten and broken, and a musty smell of decay filled the air. He rapped sharply on the door, then stood, silent, while an unseen eye assessed his appearance. The guardians of such establishments were more skilled than any Bond Street beau at calculating in a glance the cost of a man's cape, buckskin breeches, and top boots.

He was expecting to be admitted by some aging heavy-weight from the Fancy. Instead, the door was opened by a thin middle-aged woman with a high-necked puce silk dress, brightly rouged cheeks, and dyed eyelashes. "Good evening, kind sir," she said in the stentorian tones of a woman who is always onstage. "Do come in."

From a secluded alcove came the sound of a harp gently plucked by skilled fingers. He stepped into a parlor with fading green silk curtains and striped settees that might have graced the drawing room of a countess down on her luck. Mildew bloomed in the once fine gilded mirror hanging over an empty hearth. The air smelled of wax candles and fine brandy only faintly underlain by the musky tang of sex and rising damp.

While most prostitutes in London picked up their men off the streets or from such traditional stomping grounds as the theater and Vauxhall, before taking them back to rooms, the residential brothels still had their place. They appealed to women who shied away from the rough and dangerous competition on the streets, and they appealed to men leery of venturing into back alleys or up the darkened stairs of an unknown house.

From the smoke-hazed room to Sebastian's right came the gentle murmur of voices and the whirl of cards. Glancing through the arched doorway, Sebastian recognized Sir Adam Broussard and Giles Axelrod among the half dozen or so gentlemen seated around a baize-covered table. Yet the flash cove disappearing up the far stairs with a bottle of wine and a buxom, golden-haired girl was obviously no gentleman. Despite its emphasis on pseudogentility, the Orchard Street Academy was not class conscious when it came to its customers. Its only criterion was the ability to pay, and to pay well.

"You've not visited us before, have you?" said Miss Lil, her blue eyes assessing the gold fob on his watch chain, the silver head of his walking stick.

Sebastian shook his head with a smile. "No. Your establishment was recommended to me by a friend."

Miss Lil spread her hand in an expansive gesture that took in the three Birds of Paradise who had appeared to lounge casually around the parlor. They were dressed in gowns of jewel-toned silks with plunging necklines from which spilled ripe breasts. The silk hugged every curve, leaving little to the imagination, while neat ankles peeked from beneath too-short hems. It had been eight months since Sebastian had known a woman's touch—years since he'd thought of having any woman except for Kat. He wasn't thinking of it now.

Something of his lack of interest must have shown on his face, because Miss Lil said, "Perhaps you would like to order a bottle of wine to share with the ladies. Get to know them some before making your selection?"

The three Cyprians stared back at him with the bold assessment of women for whom a man is just another customer, a mark. One, a tall, ebony-skinned woman with a regal neck, smiled at him and said in Jamaican-accented English, "I'm Tasmin." Beside her, a plump, heavily rouged Impure with the jet-black hair and pale skin of Ireland pursed her lips and blew him a kiss. The third, a dainty gamin with a riot of short flaxen curls, wrinkled her childlike nose and laughed merrily. The impression was one of youthful innocence. But looking into her rainwater gray eyes, Sebastian suspected she was considerably closer to twenty-five than to fifteen.

"A burgundy would be nice," said Sebastian.

Miss Lil nodded to the flaxen-headed Cyprian. "Becky will fetch it."

"I'm interested in a woman my friend was telling me about," said Sebastian, going to settle on one of the striped silk cushions. "A tall, thin woman with light brown hair and green eyes."

Becky, who had reappeared bearing a bottle of wine and glasses on a tarnished tray, faltered for one telling instant, her gaze flying to meet the Jamaican's startled stare.

"Oh?" said Miss Lil, calmly pouring the wine.

"I think he said her name was Rose," Sebastian continued, "although I could have that wrong." It had occurred to him that the woman might easily have made up a new name to give the Quakers at the Magdalene House. "My friend claims she is charming, with the manners and accent of a duchess."

From upstairs came a thump and a woman's startled scream, quickly cut off. None of the women in the room even turned her head.

"Your friend must have made the acquaintance of Rose Fletcher," said the abbess, handing him a glass of wine. Her fingers when they brushed his hand were unnaturally cold, as if the woman never saw the sun. "Unfortunately, Rose is not here this evening. But I think you'll find Becky an entertaining substitute."

Sebastian took a slow sip of the wine. It was surprisingly good. "If I come back tomorrow will Rose be here?"

Sebastian was aware of the dark-skinned woman, Tasmin, studying him with a fixed expression. But not a breath of emotion showed on the abbess's carefully made-up face. She stretched her lips into a smile. "I'm afraid Rose has left us. You know how restless some girls are: never content to stay in one place. If Becky doesn't capture your fancy, then I'm sure you'll enjoy Tasmin."

Sebastian raised his wine to his lips again. "Any idea where Rose might have gone?"

Miss Lil's smile stayed plastered across her face. "I'm afraid not." For one brief instant, the abbess's steely gaze flickered to the Jamaican. The girl rose gracefully to slip from the room.

"What a pity. I quite had my heart set on the girl." Sebastian cast a searching glance around the parlor. "My friend also asked me to give Mr. Kane his regards. Is he here?"

"Mr. Kane?"

"That's right. Mr. Ian Kane."

Miss Lil's pale blue eyes held his. The tension in the room had suddenly become palpable. She set aside her wineglass with a snap. She was no longer smiling. "It seems none of our girls strikes your fancy. I think the time has come for you to leave."

Sebastian stretched to his feet. From somewhere overhead came the sound of a door slamming and a woman's drunken laughter. "Thank you for joining me for a glass of wine," he said. He dropped a coin on the table to pay for the bottle and inclined his head to the two remaining Cyprians. "Ladies."

Outside, Sebastian paused at the top of the house's steps and let the cool breeze blow away the lingering, suffocating odors of the place. A couple of linkboys darted past, lighting the way for a carriage drawn by a nicely matched team of grays, their torches filling the air with the scent of hot pitch.

He had learned three things from his visit to the house. That Rose "Jones" had indeed practiced her métier at the Orchard Street Academy. That she had once called herself Rose Fletcher. And that the circumstances surrounding her precipitous departure from the house were of such a nature that the very mention of her name was enough to throw the house's remaining inhabitants into a state of consternation.

Idly swinging his walking stick, he descended the steps to the cobbled street. As he turned toward Portman Square, a large, burly man detached himself from the shadowy alley beside the house and walked right up to him.

"Why ye nosin' around 'ere, askin' all them questions?" the man demanded, his grizzled face shoved close enough that Sebastian breathed in raw gin fumes. "And what's yer business with Mr. Kane?"

The man had the look of an ex-prizefighter, with a broken nose and a cauliflower ear. In his late thirties or early forties now, he was beginning to run to fat. But he was still a powerful mountain of a man, standing a good half a head taller than Sebastian and with nearly half again his weight.

"I have a message for Mr. Kane from an old friend," said Sebastian, tightening his grip on his walking stick.

The man's lips pulled back to reveal broken brown teeth. "Mr. Kane don't associate with the clientele. What is it ye really want? If ye ain't 'ere to sample the merchandise, you've no business 'ere. It's my job to make sure there's no trouble in the 'ouse, and yer kind's always trouble." He reached out to crush Sebastian's lapel in one meaty fist. "Don't ye be comin' back, ye 'ear? We don't want yer kinda business 'ere."

"You are creasing my coat," said Sebastian.

"Yeah?" The man's smile widened. "Maybe I ought to crease yer skull instead."

Moving calmly and deliberately, Sebastian swung his walking stick back and then up, driving the full force of his body behind it. The ebony stick sliced up between the bouncer's legs to whack against his testicles. The thug's eyes bugged out, his breath *woosh*ing out of his body as he released his hold on Sebastian's coat to bend over and cradle his genitals in both hands. Reaching down,

Sebastian grabbed the man by the front of his greasy waistcoat and shoved him backward until his shoulder blades whacked up against the alley's brick wall. "Maybe you ought to consider answering a few questions."

Gritting his teeth, the bouncer groped his right hand toward a long blade sheathed in leather at his side. Sebastian whacked the man's wrist with the walking stick. The man howled and dropped the knife.

"That was not smart," said Sebastian, shoving the length of the walking stick against the man's throat, pinning him to the wall. "It's also not a very nice way to treat a customer. I've a good mind to complain to Mr. Kane." Sebastian tightened the pressure of the stick against the man's windpipe. "Where can I find him?"

The man's mouth hung open, slack with fear. "I cain't tell ye that!"

Sebastian withdrew the walking stick from the man's throat and swung it down to whack him across the right knee. The bouncer went down in a crooked, crumpled heap. "You might want to reconsider your reticence."

The man lay with one hand splayed over his knee, the other hand still cupped protectively around his genitals. "I tell you, I don't know!"

Sebastian lightly tapped the man's other knee with the stick's silver tip. "That's not a very clever answer."

The bouncer licked his lips. "He's at the Black Dragon. In Dyot Street, near Meux's Brewery."

"How will I know him?"

" 'E's a good-looking cove. Copper-colored 'air. Spends most o' 'is evenin's in 'is office on the 'alf landing, paintin'."

"Painting?"

"You know. Pictures. 'E likes paintin' pictures o' whores and o' the river and the city."

"I'd like my visit to Mr. Kane to be a surprise," said Sebastian. "Let's make a deal, shall we? You don't tell him I'm coming, and I won't tell him you're the one who spilled the information that enabled me to find him. Do we understand each other?"

The bouncer wiped the back of one hand across his loose lips. "You bloody bastard—"

Sebastian thrust the tip of his walking stick beneath the man's chin, forcing him to tilt his head back at an awkward angle. "Do we understand each other?"

"Aye, aye. Jist git that bloody stick away from me, will ye?"

Sebastian dropped the tip of his walking stick to the knife lying on the wet cobbles and, with a flick of his wrist, sent the blade clattering into the darkness of the alley. "Pull steel on me again and you're dead."

Chapter 12

Sebastian pushed his way through darkened streets crowded with ragged beggars and smocked workmen hurrying home to their suppers. The air was heavy with the scent of boiling cabbage and frying onions, and it occurred to him in passing that he hadn't eaten dinner himself. Appetite, like the desire for sleep, had eluded him for so long that he merely noted the passing of time without any accompanying urge to seek sustenance.

He was vaguely surprised to find himself involved, once again, in an investigation of murder. He'd survived the past eight months by tamping down all emotions— not just love and anger, but also curiosity and a desire for justice, even simple interest. He'd found lately that he could sometimes go as much as a day at a time without thinking about Kat, without remembering the scent that lingered on her pillow, without wanting her with an ache that left him ashamed and afraid.

But there was a reason he'd deadened himself with alcohol and sleeplessness these past months. It was as if one emotion were linked to the other. Open up to one, and the others came flooding back, out of control. He thought about the way he'd welcomed his encounter with the ex-pugilist of Orchard Street, and the realization troubled him. Violence could be seductive. He'd

seen too many men lose themselves in the heady embrace of death and destruction during war. He knew
what it could do to a man. What it had almost done to
him, once. What it could do again.

He smelled the brewery now, the pungent scent of
malt mixing with the ever-present odors of coal smoke
and horse dung. Dyot Street ran just to the northwest
of Covent Garden, in that part of London known as
St. Giles. A wizened, black-clad woman with a fire in
an old barrel was doing a good business selling roasted
potatoes on a corner just opposite the Black Dragon.
Sebastian paused to buy one as an excuse to linger for a
moment, his gaze on the tavern across the street.

It was a long, rambling place, built early in the last
century with a second story that overhung the first.
From the looks of things, its clientele was a mixture of
local tradesmen and riffraff from the nearby rookeries.
For a moment he considered returning to Brook Street
to change into a less conspicuous form of dress, then decided against it.

He became aware of a hollow-cheeked girl of eight or
ten standing in the shelter of a nearby doorway, her thin
hands clutching a ragged shawl about her shoulders, her
brown eyes fixed longingly on the potato in his hands.
"Here," he said, holding it out to her.

She hesitated a brief instant, then snatched the potato from him and took off, her heels kicking up the
torn hem of her dress as she ran. Sebastian waited for an
overloaded brewery wagon to rumble past, then crossed
the street toward the Black Dragon.

Halfway up the block he found a black-haired woman
with a brazen smile and a low-necked, threadbare yellow dress who would have retreated down the nearest
alley with him and done anything he asked of her for a
few shillings. She gasped when he pressed a crown into
her hand.

"No," he said when she would have led him into the beckoning darkness. "I've something else in mind."

Her dark eyes peered up at him with uneasy suspicion. She was probably no more than twenty-five, maybe thirty. Once she had been pretty, and traces of her youth still lingered. But she'd obviously had a hard life.

"What's your name?" he asked.

She sniffed. "Cherry. Why?"

"This is what I want you to do, Cherry. I want you to wait two minutes, then follow me into the Black Dragon. You'll see me standing in the back, near the stairs. Ignore me. All you need do is create some sort of ruckus. If you're successful there'll be another crown for you when I come out. Do you understand?"

"A ruckus?"

"That's right. Enough of a disturbance to attract and hold everyone's attention but not so much as to land you in the roundhouse."

"I can do that," said Cherry.

"Good. Now remember, wait two minutes."

Sebastian pushed open the tavern's door and walked into a murky, low-ceilinged common room that smelled of savory pies and warm ale and warm men. A crescendo of talk and laughter rolled from the leaded windows overlooking the street to the narrow wooden-railed staircase at the back that led up to the first floor. Sebastian could see a closed door on the half landing.

Heads turned as he threaded his way between men in blue work shirts and rough corduroy coats. He found a place at the end of the bar nearest the base of the stairs and ordered a half pint. Turning his back to the bar, he rested his elbows on the ancient boards and let his gaze wander over the scattered tables and darkened booths. Right on cue, Cherry walked into the room.

A gust of wind from the open door shuddered the flames in the tin lamps, sending dancing light across her black hair and pale round shoulders. She hesitated for a moment, her gaze scanning the crowd as he had done. Her eyes flicked over him without a hint of recognition, then settled on a potbellied, gray-whiskered man sprawled on his own at a table near the center of the room.

She planted her fists on her hips, her chin coming up in a display of fury that was utterly convincing. "There ye are, ye good-fer-nothin' mutton monger!" Her quavering, outraged tones cut across the murmur of male voices. The man with the gray whiskers paused in the act of raising his pint of ale to throw a quick glance behind him.

"No point lookin' behind ye like ye was expectin' to find St. Peter hisself standin' there. I'm talkin' to you, ye bloody belly bumper."

Gray Whiskers set down his ale with a thump and swallowed hard. "I don't know you."

"Don't know me!" She descended on him, her arms akimbo, her black eyes flashing. "Ye don't know me, ye say? I suppose ye don't know yer own ten poor wee bairns then, either?" Quivering with outrage, she stalked up to him. He was still pushing back his chair when she brought up her open hand and walloped him across the face.

The smack of flesh against flesh brought a sudden hush to the assembly. A gangly, half-grown lad with a tray of empty tankards quickly set aside his burden to grab her arm. "Now there ain't no call to—"

She wiggled free of his restraint. "Let go of me, ye bloody madge cull."

A bald-headed man with a broken nose reared up from a nearby table to collar the stripling with one beefy fist. "Hey. That's no way to treat a lady."

Gray Whiskers surged to his feet, one hand clamped to his stinging red cheek. "Lady? You callin' her a lady?"

The man with the bald head swung around and planted one of his meaty fists in Gray Whiskers's potbelly.

A cheer went up around the room. Someone threw a punch at the stripling, who ducked and fell back against a wooden chair, splintering it beneath him. Sebastian heard the door on the half landing jerk open and turned to see a burly man in a moleskin waistcoat come barreling down the stairs into the melee. "Here, here, what's this? We'll have none o' that at the Black Dragon."

Sebastian quietly slipped past him up the stairs and into the chamber on the half landing.

After the dim haze of the common room, the chamber's blaze of lights made Sebastian's eyes water. Two branches of wax candles burned on the mantelpiece, with three more scattered on the tabletops around the room. Ian Kane stood before an easel in the center of a good Chinese rug. Of medium height and build with hair the color of burnished copper, he was stripped down to his breeches, shirt, and waistcoat, and held a piece of charcoal in his hand. Some ten feet in front of him, a winsome young thing with soft white flesh and a halo of golden curls sprawled on a blue velvet divan. She wore pink slippers and a pearl necklace, and nothing else.

At Sebastian's entrance, Kane glanced around. The girl jerked, but Kane said, "Don't move," and she froze.

"Nicely done," said Sebastian, coming to look at a half-completed charcoal sketch somewhat in the style of Ingres.

From the room below came the sound of breaking glass and a man's hoarse shout. Kane reached for a rag and calmly wiped his fingers. "I presume you started that for a reason?"

The faint echo of a Lancashire burr was still there in the brothel owner's speech, but he'd obviously made considerable efforts to eradicate it in the ten or fifteen years that had passed since he'd fled the mines. His breeches, coat, and waistcoat could only have come from the best Bond Street tailors. Sebastian could easily see Pippa from the cheesemonger's shop taking this man for a gentleman. However nefarious the nature of his current businesses, Kane was working hard at obscuring his origins. But unless he'd dyed his hair, Pippa was unlikely to have described him as "dark."

"I thought our conversation would be more congenial without the presence of one of your gentlemen of the Fancy," said Sebastian. He wandered the room, his gaze roving over the series of canvases on the wall. Done in oils in much the same style as the charcoal sketch on the easel, the paintings included both London street scenes and views of ships on the Thames. One particularly striking image of the church of Allhallows Barking caught in a stream of sunlight was only half finished. But most of the paintings were of naked women in a variety of languid poses.

"I suppose that's one of the advantages of running a brothel," said Sebastian. "There can't be many artists with such ready access to a houseful of women who are more than willing to take off their clothes."

Kane merely set aside his rag and grunted.

"I wonder," said Sebastian, "did you ever paint Rose Fletcher?"

"Who?"

"Rose Fletcher. Up until last week she was one of the dashers at the Orchard Street Academy. I understand you're the proprietor."

Kane picked up a short piece of charcoal and traced a neat line along the hip of the figure in his sketch. "I have more than one house and employ scores of women. Do you think I know them all?"

From below stairs came a loud thump, followed by a bellow of rage. Sebastian said, "This woman left your house precipitously and went into hiding. I'm wondering if she was hiding from you."

"What do you think?" said Kane, keeping his attention on his work. "That I stock my houses with traffic from some nefarious white-slave ring?" He had a slickly handsome face and a wide mouth full of straight white teeth he showed in a smile. "Why would she hide from me? Every soiled dove on the street would have you think she was kidnapped and forced into the trade. It's all a fantasy. The girls in my houses are there because they choose to be, and they're free to leave whenever they want."

Sebastian glanced toward the Cyprian on the divan. She made a small movement, then lay still, her rosy-tipped breasts rising gently with each breath. A faint flush of color had spread across her cheeks. It was one thing, evidently, to pose naked for Ian Kane, but something else to do it in the presence of a stranger.

Sebastian said, "You weren't angry that she left?"

A muscle jumped along Kane's suddenly tight jaw. "Whores leave all the time. They usually come back. But even if they don't, do you think I care? There are always more where they came from." He jerked his head toward the street below. "You can't walk a block without tripping over half a dozen strumpets."

"Perhaps. Yet Rose Fletcher was undoubtedly afraid of someone."

"Most whores are afraid of someone. A husband maybe, or a boyfriend who's a little too handy with his fists." Kane cocked his head to one side, studying the sketch before him. "What I'm wondering," he said, carefully smudging the line he'd just drawn, "is why a fine gentleman like yourself would take an interest in a piece of Haymarket ware. Surely you don't fancy her for yourself?"

"Not exactly. She's dead. She was one of the eight women murdered at the Magdalene House last night."

The suggestion that the fire at the Magdalene House was no accident didn't seem to surprise Kane. But then, word traveled fast on the streets. Without looking up, he said, "You think I did that?"

"I think you're hiding something."

There was a pause, after which the brothel owner appeared to come to a decision. He reached for a finer piece of charcoal. "You're right. Rose Fletcher was at the Academy. She was there the better part of a year. I don't know why she left. She never gave any indication she was unhappy there."

"Rose Fletcher wasn't her real name, was it?"

"Probably not. They all take noms de guerre."

"Do you know where she came from?"

Kane gave a sharp bark of laughter. "Women like her are a commodity. You think I care where they come from? We're not talking fine wine here. The provenance is immaterial."

Sebastian glanced toward the naked woman on the divan. The flush in her cheeks had deepened.

"Did Rose ever have trouble with anyone at the Academy?"

"You mean customers?" Kane shook his head. "We're very careful with our clientele. Those who like it rough learn to go someplace else."

"Did she have any special customers?"

"She was a popular piece of merchandise." His eyes narrowed as he layered in defining detail to his sketch of the woman's breasts. "But as a matter of fact, there was one particular customer that I know of. He was so enamored of her that he offered to buy her away from the house."

"Buy her? I thought you said these women aren't slaves."

Kane shrugged. "She had some debts. Most whores do. They work to pay off what they owe."

It was the usual practice: Advance the women just enough money to keep them in a perpetual state of debt so that they couldn't leave even if they wanted to. It wasn't technically slavery, but that's what it amounted to.

Sebastian studied the man's smooth face. He had a faint blue line, like a tattoo, that ran across his forehead. Sebastian had seen marks like that before, on miners. Coal dust settled into healing cuts, leaving a mark that never disappeared. Kane had obviously spent some time in the mines himself as a lad, before fleeing to London. Sebastian said, "What was the name of the customer who tried to buy her?"

"O'Brian. Luke O'Brian."

"Who is he?"

Kane flashed his white smile. "You think I'm going to give you everything?"

"Actually, I'm wondering why you've told me as much as you have."

Kane laughed, his attention all for his sketch. Sebastian said, "And was Rose willing to be released to this O'Brian?"

Kane kept his gaze on his sketch. "Actually, no."

"Why not?"

"She didn't say."

"She didn't say, or you're not saying?"

They were both aware of a heavy tread on the stairs. A moment later, Kane's pet prizefighter came back into the chamber, the thug's eyes narrowing when he saw Sebastian. "Trouble here, Mr. Kane?"

"No trouble," said Sebastian, one hand slipping, significantly, to the small flintlock he kept in his coat pocket. "I was just leaving."

The henchman's gaze flicked to Sebastian's hand. He set his jaw, but stayed where he was.

Sebastian smiled. "Good evening, gentlemen." He bowed to the silent woman on the divan. "Madame."

*   *   *

Cherry was waiting for Sebastian on the footpath outside the Black Dragon.

"You didn't get hurt, did you?" he said, dropping a crown into her outstretched palm.

"Me? Nah. It was fun. Did yer little trick get ye what ye wanted?"

Sebastian glanced toward the tavern in time to see a bulky shadow jerk back away from the lamplight. "I'm not sure."

Chapter 13

*G*eorge, Prince Regent of the United Kingdom of Great Britain and Ireland, gripped a vial of smelling salts in one plump white hand and held it to his own nostrils.

"Perceval tells us there was another attack in Yorkshire," said the Prince. "Luddites!" He inhaled deeply and shuddered, although whether it was in reaction to the smelling salts or the thought of the Luddites, Jarvis couldn't be certain. "Carrying on like savages," continued the Prince. "Hiding their faces. Smashing machines. Something must be done about this!"

"A number of arrests have already been made," said Jarvis, privately consigning the Prime Minister to the devil. Whatever had possessed Perceval to regale the Regent with this tale? "Unfortunately, the lower orders are still infected by the events in France. They think they can remold society. Become uppity with their betters. But the more progress our armies make on the Continent, the sooner these Luddites and their ilk will see the error of their ways."

"Yes, but are we making progress on the Continent?"

"We will," said Jarvis resolutely.

The Regent shifted against his pillows, restless. A

giant platter of buttered crab and four bottles of port after dinner last night had brought on the most alarming of the Prince's symptoms—the bowel distress, the tingling in his hands and feet, the mental confusion. That episode—combined with a heavy bleeding by Dr. Heberden—had left George too exhausted to do more than totter between his bed and his dressing room couch. But not, unfortunately, too exhausted to receive his Prime Minister.

George said, "Perceval brought me a copy of his newest pamphlet. He seems to have discovered an alarming prophesy in the Bible. Something about a new satanic power rising in the west. The pamphlet is there, near the window." The Prince waved one fat, beringed hand in a vague gesture toward a small table.

Jarvis generally tried to ignore the Prime Minister's periodic attempts at elucidating godly intent. Religion had its place in society, reconciling the masses to their fate and assuring their docile acceptance of the rule of their betters. But this was taking things too far. "Don't tell me Perceval has equated our former American colonies with this new satanic threat?"

The Regent took another sniff of his salts. "He fears it may be so."

"Well, I'll be certain to read this new pamphlet with interest," said Jarvis. Tucking the offending publication beneath one arm, he bowed himself out of the royal presence.

A tall, muscular man had been leaning against the far wall of the Prince's antechamber. As Jarvis crossed the room toward the corridor, the man fell into step beside him.

"About the matter we discussed earlier," said Colonel Epson-Smith.

"Walk with me," said Jarvis, turning into the corridor.

The two men's footsteps echoed up and down the cavernous space. Epson-Smith kept his voice low. "It seems someone else has an interest in the event."

"Who?" said Jarvis without breaking stride.

"Devlin."

"Devlin? What is his interest in this?"

"He refuses to say. There's a woman making inquiries, as well."

"A woman?" Jarvis swung to face the man beside him, and whatever Epson-Smith saw in Jarvis's face caused the Colonel to take a step back.

"I'm not certain yet who she is, my lord. But word on the streets is that a gentlewoman has been asking questions at some of the lodging houses in Covent Garden and—"

"Forget about the woman," Jarvis snapped and continued walking.

Epson-Smith inclined his head and fell into step beside him. "As you wish, my lord. And Devlin?"

Jarvis paused at the entrance to his own chambers. A thin, nervous clerk leapt to attention. "My lord!"

Jarvis thrust the Prime Minister's pamphlet at the clerk and said curtly, "Burn this."

The clerk bobbed a frightened bow. "Yes, my lord."

To Epson-Smith, Jarvis said simply, "I'll deal with Devlin."

Chapter 14

*P*aul Gibson kept his surgery in an ancient sandstone building at the base of Tower Hill. Beside it stood his house, also of stone, but small and ill-kept, for Gibson was a bachelor with a housekeeper named Mrs. Federico who refused to set foot in any room containing human parts in glass jars—a prejudice that effectively limited her to the kitchen, dining room, and hallway.

"It's a pig's fetus," said Gibson, identifying the small purplish-pink curl floating in liquid in a jar on the parlor mantelpiece that had caught Sebastian's attention. "I was using it for comparative purposes in my anatomy class at St. Thomas's."

"Ah," said Sebastian, going to splash brandy into two glasses and carrying one to his friend.

"I told Mrs. Federico it was a pig," said Gibson, taking the glass with thanks. "But she still refused to clean in here."

Sebastian moved a pile of papers and books from the worn leather sofa to the floor and sat down. "One would think she'd be used to it by now."

"Some people never get used to it."

Sebastian wasn't sure he himself would ever get used to the body parts Gibson scattered so carelessly around his house, but he kept that observation to himself.

Gibson said, "Sir William turned all of the women's bodies over to the Friends for burial. The service is set for tomorrow evening. Unfortunately, the Friends refused to grant me permission to perform any postmortems. But they did allow me to examine the bodies more thoroughly."

"And?"

"I don't think any of those women died from the fire." Gibson propped the stump of his left leg up on a stool, his head bowed to hide the grimace of pain that contorted his features. There were times, Sebastian knew, when the pain grew so fierce that Gibson could abandon himself for days to the sweet relief of opium-induced oblivion. "They were all dead—or close to it—when the fire was set. At least," the doctor added, "I assume it was set. I have no evidence of that."

Sebastian raised his brandy to his nostrils and inhaled its heady scent.

"It's difficult to be certain," Gibson continued, "but I wouldn't say the killings were an act of passion. Whoever did it was very methodical. They must have killed each woman in turn, then simply moved on to the next. There was no superfluous hacking of the bodies."

Sebastian nodded silently. In the War, they'd both seen men caught in the grip of a killing frenzy hack at bodies over and over again, long after life had expired.

"What can you tell me about the woman who was shot?"

"Not a great deal, I'm afraid. The body was badly burned. From her teeth I'd say she was less than twenty. She was a slim, fairly tall woman. Does that sound like your Rose Jones?"

"When she was at the Academy she called herself Rose Fletcher."

Gibson raised one eyebrow. "You think that's her real name?"

"Probably not. Joshua Walden thinks her name might once have been Rachel."

Gibson grunted. "Not your standard Molly or Elizabeth."

"No. Whoever she was, she was well-bred. Everything I've found so far suggests that her presence at the Magdalene House was the reason for the slaughter."

Sebastian became aware of Gibson's eyes upon him, studying him intently. "Why have you involved yourself in this?" Gibson asked.

Sebastian took a slow sip of his drink. "Have you noticed anyone else interested in solving these murders?"

"Women are murdered on the streets of London all the time, Sebastian."

"Not like this."

Gibson was silent for another moment. Then he said, "It's because of Jarvis, isn't it? It's a way of sticking your finger in his eye."

A slow smile curved Sebastian's lips. "That's part of it, yes."

"Does Miss Jarvis know that your motives aren't entirely chivalrous?"

"Oh, she knows, all right. In fact, she's counting on it."

Gibson shifted his weight, seeking a more comfortable position for his mangled leg. "I saw Miss Boleyn today, when I was in Covent Garden. She stopped her carriage and spoke to me."

Sebastian took a long, slow swallow of his drink and said nothing.

"She asked about you," said Gibson. "She wanted to know how you are doing."

"What did you say?"

"I lied. I told her you're fine."

Sebastian took another drink. "She isn't Miss Boleyn anymore."

"She still uses it as a stage name, does she not?"

She did, of course. But Sebastian was careful never to let himself think of her in that way.

"I told her you'd involved yourself in another murder," said Gibson.

She wouldn't like that, Sebastian thought. In the past, she'd always fretted about what his involvement in the pursuit of murderers cost him. Then again, perhaps she no longer cared. Or cared in a different way . . . as a sister, rather than as the lover she'd once been.

To Sebastian's relief, Gibson changed the subject again. He said, "You think the brothel owner, this Kane, could be behind the killings?"

Sebastian blew out a long breath. He hadn't even realized he'd been holding it. "I think he's more than capable of it. The problem is, I'm not sure why he would do it."

"Rose Fletcher ran away from him, didn't she? She sounds as if she was a valuable commodity."

"Valuable, yes. But not exactly rare. This town is full of women ready to sell themselves to stay alive. And while Kane might have kept her in debt, you can be sure he never let the debt become excessively large."

"She could have been killed as an example to others," said Gibson.

"She could have been," Sebastian agreed. "But to kill seven women just to get to one?" He shook his head. "No, I think whoever did this was desperate."

"Or very angry," said Gibson. "How do you intend to find this man O'Brian?"

Sebastian drained his brandy. "I'll set Tom on it tomorrow."

Gibson lurched to his feet and reached for his friend's empty glass. "A girl like that—educated, wellborn—how could she have come to such an end?"

"Someone betrayed her," said Sebastian, "and I'm not talking about whoever killed her. She was betrayed before that, by those whose duty it was to love her and care for her."

"I wonder if her family even know she's dead."

Sebastian raised his gaze to the pig fetus on the mantelpiece. "I'd say that depends on whether or not they're the ones who killed her."

Chapter 15

*S*ebastian stood beside his bedroom window, his gaze on the still-sleeping city streets below, on the gleam of dew on the cobbles and the pigeons fluttering on the ridge of a nearby roofline. In the pale blush of early dawn, the chimneys of London loomed thick and dark, the spires of the city's churches thrusting up against a slowly lightening sky. It was that hour between night and day when time seemed suspended and a man could get lost in the past, if he let himself.

Grasping the sash, he thrust up the window and let the frigid air of the dying night bite his naked flesh. He'd been driven here from his bed by the dreams that still crept upon him far too often in the undefended hours of sleep. During the day, he could control his thoughts, even control the yearnings that still came upon him. But sleep made him vulnerable. Which is why he avoided it as much as possible.

Some men could spend a lifetime in a soft, brandy-tinged blur, squinting through a smoky haze at cards that meant nothing. Win or lose, the deadness inside remained. But it was all an illusion, Sebastian had decided—both the sensation of inner deadness and the comfort of the blur. A trick a man played on himself.

No one else was fooled.

The day broke warm and sunny with all the golden promise of the long-delayed spring. Sebastian breakfasted early, then called his tiger, Tom, into the library.

Tom came in dragging his feet. "I didn't mean to do it," he blurted out.

Sebastian looked up from the estate agent's report he'd been reading and frowned. "You didn't mean to do what?"

Tom hung his head, his tiger's cap twisted between his hands. "I'm that sorry, gov'nor. Truly I am."

"If you set fire to the tails of Morey's coat again—"

Tom's head jerked up. "I didn't!"

"Thank God for that, at least." For all his disapproving ways, Morey ran Sebastian's decidedly irregular household with the competence and efficiency of the gunnery sergeant he'd once been. Sebastian would be hard put to replace him. "Out with it then," he said, his gaze steady on the tiger. "What have you been doing?"

"I was down in the kitchen, see? Me and Adam—he's the new footman. We was just playin' around and—"

Sebastian became aware of a disturbance emanating from the lower regions of the house, Madame LeClerc's outraged cries punctuated by Calhoun's soothing tones. "Explain it to me later. I want you to find someone for me. A man named Luke O'Brian."

Tom's eyes flashed with anticipation. "You think 'e might 'ave somethin' to do with the murder of them women?"

"I think he might."

"What manner o' man is 'e?"

"I haven't the slightest idea. The only thing I know about him is that he frequents a brothel near Portman Square called the Orchard Street Academy."

Tom jammed his cap back on his head. "I'll find 'im, ne'er you fear."

"Oh, and, Tom—"

Tom turned at the door.

"Be careful."

Tom flashed a gap-toothed grin and took off.

The noise level from the kitchen increased. Sebastian set aside his estate agent's report and stood up. He was crossing toward the entry hall when he became aware of the sounds of a carriage drawing up outside his door. Glancing out the library's bowed front window, he saw a smartly dressed young woman appear in the carriage's open door.

She was tall and striking, with glossy dark hair and a wide, laughing mouth. She stood for a moment, the sunlight soft on her face, and just the sight of her was enough to make his breath catch. He watched as she extended one hand elegantly gloved in yellow kid and accepted her footman's assistance down the carriage steps. Memories of last night's dreams came to him in a wash of shame, memories and desires that had driven him from his bed last night and that haunted him still.

For eight months now she'd called herself Mrs. Russell Yates. But once, her name had been Kat Boleyn and she'd been the love of Sebastian's life.

Now he called her sister.

Chapter 16

Sebastian waited with his back to the empty hearth and let Morey usher his visitor into the library. She came in smelling of the cold morning air and herself, and the assault on his self-control was so great that he could only stand there with his hands gripped together behind his back and watch her.

She paused just inside the door, her head turning as Morey bowed himself out. For a long moment, her gaze met Sebastian's across the room. She said, "I didn't expect you to be glad to see me."

His voice was a rusty, grating sound. "You shouldn't have come."

She searched his face, her blue St. Cyr eyes narrowed with worry and her own pain. "You know I wouldn't be here without good reason."

"Something's wrong. What is it?"

He watched her jerk off her fine kid gloves and loosen the velvet strings of her hat. Once, she had been the center of his existence, the only woman he'd ever wanted to take to wife. Then, eight months ago, his life had come tumbling down around him in a series of brutal revelations.

The discovery that his father, the Earl of Hendon, once kept a beautiful Irish actress named Arabella as his mistress had come as no surprise. Many men of their station did so. Nor was it unusual that Hendon had fathered a child upon his mistress. Such matters were typically handled discreetly. After birth, the child would be taken from its mother and dispatched to some "good farm family" in the country, never to be seen or heard from again. Except in this instance, the mother of Hendon's love child had balked at his determination to separate her from her baby and fled back to Ireland.

That should have been the end of the story. Instead, Arabella's child had, in her turn, come to London. Calling herself Kat Boleyn, she had become one of the most acclaimed actresses of the London stage and mistress to a young viscount—Hendon's son, Sebastian.

She stood before him now, her fine kid gloves held in a tight grip, her carefully schooled face inscrutable. She said, "Do you know Hendon is not well?"

Sebastian shook his head. "He has said nothing to me."

"Well, he wouldn't, would he? You don't speak to him."

"You make it sound as if I cut him. I don't."

"Of course not. That would be too vulgar, wouldn't it? Odd that a curt hello in passing should wound more than the cut direct. That at least would betray some emotion."

"Has he sent you here to plead his case?"

"You should know better than that."

She was right, of course; he did know better. "I beg your pardon." He swung away to the collection of carafes and glasses that rested on a table near the window. "A glass of ratafia?"

He glanced over to see a wry smile curve her lips. "I think we both need something stronger, don't you?"

He reached for the brandy. "Something stronger, definitely."

The tension in the room—the awareness of what had once been between them and could never be again—

stretched taut. She said, "Hendon is not to blame for what happened. He did nothing that men of his station haven't done for a thousand years or more. He took a mistress and begat a child upon her. How could he have foreseen what we would become to each other?"

Sebastian glanced up from splashing brandy into two glasses. "You defend him? He would have taken you from your mother if she hadn't fled him."

"He meant it for the best."

"For whom?"

She didn't answer him. Hendon always did what was best for the St. Cyr lineage and the St. Cyr legacy. Anything and anyone else was expendable. She said, "You're not angry with Hendon because of what he would have done to my mother."

"I've been angry with Hendon for years. This is just one more lie on top of so many others."

"Not a lie, exactly, Sebastian. He didn't know I was his child. None of us did."

"Yet he knew you existed, and he never said a word. It rather begs the question, doesn't it? What else hasn't he told me?"

Sebastian held out her glass. She took it, being very careful not to allow her fingertips to brush his. She said, "You haven't found your mother yet?"

For half his life, Sebastian had believed his mother dead, the victim of a boating accident the summer he was eleven. In truth, she had merely fled her loveless marriage—and abandoned Sebastian, her only surviving son. Another lie his father had told him. He said, "I believe she's in France somewhere. The war makes searching for her ... awkward." He took a slow sip of his brandy and felt it burn all the way down. "You have forgiven Hendon for what he did to your mother?"

"I was angry with him at first. Yet I've come to believe his love for Arabella was genuine. I see it in his face when he speaks of her. His voice softens. His eyes come alive."

Some flicker of emotion must have shown on Sebastian's own face because she said, "I'm sorry. I shouldn't have said that," and he knew she'd misunderstood entirely the pain and envy she'd glimpsed.

"I've known most of my life that there was no love in my parents' marriage," he said. She went to stand beside the bowed window overlooking Brook Street, her head turned away, and for one stolen moment he lost himself in looking at her. "Do you see Hendon much?" he asked.

She swung to face him again. "He comes to the theater. Sometimes we go for a drive in the park."

"I don't imagine Amanda likes that," said Sebastian. Amanda, Lady Wilcox, was Sebastian's other sister—his legitimate sister.

"She knows the truth," said Kat.

"And acknowledges you no more than he."

"How can either of them acknowledge the truth when all the world knows I was your mistress?"

Painful words. Words that brought back the shame of all they had once done together. Yet with the shame came such a rush of every feeling Sebastian had spent the last eight months trying to ignore that he shuddered.

She set aside her brandy untouched. "I can understand your anger. You think I am not angry? But to blame Hendon for it is not right. He did not do this to us."

He drained his own glass and set it down with a snap. "Yet he somehow managed to get what he wanted, didn't he?" Sebastian had loved Kat since he was twenty-one and she just sixteen. For all those years Hendon had fought and schemed to prevent his son and heir from marrying beneath him. In a sense it was ironic that the key to the destruction of their love had been there all along, if only he'd known. "You think the fact that it is—" Sebastian realized what he'd been about to say and began again. "You think the fact that it *was* wrong for me to want you should somehow make the loss of you easier to bear? Well, it doesn't."

He was surprised to see a sad smile light up her eyes. "Oh, Sebastian. You always think you should be able to change things, to make them right."

"Are you telling me I'm arrogant?"

"You know you are."

They shared a smile that faded slowly. He said, "How are you? Truthfully?"

"Truthfully?" She raised her chin in a gesture he remembered all too well. "Yates is not a demanding husband. We deal well together. He has his life and I have mine."

Sebastian had heard something of Russell Yates's activities, the unorthodox but discreet liaisons that had continued since his marriage. He'd heard no such tales of Kat. "Do you?" he said.

She twitched one shoulder in a shrug. "I have my work at the theater. It's enough."

He walked up to her, close enough that he could have touched her although he did not. "More than I want anything else," he said, "I want you to be happy."

She gazed up at him. "True happiness is rare."

"It shouldn't be."

"Paul Gibson tells me you've involved yourself in the death of these women in Covent Garden."

"Yes."

He was aware of her searching his face, and he wondered what she saw there. The sleepless nights? The months of drinking and dissipation that had brought oblivion if no relief? She said, "In the past, I always worried whenever you found yourself drawn into murder investigations. But I suppose it's preferable to watching you break your neck on a hunting field or drink yourself to death."

He swung abruptly away. "You say Hendon is not well. What is wrong with him?"

"The doctors say it's his heart. He eats too much, drinks too much."

"That's not likely to stop."

"He's been worse these last months. He misses you, Sebastian. The estrangement between you causes him much grief."

Sebastian paused beside his desk and looked back at her. It was a moment before he could answer. "I'm sorry. I'm not ready to speak to him yet."

She nodded briskly, then retied her bonnet strings and pulled on her fine kid gloves. "Just don't wait until it's too late, Sebastian."

Chapter 17

$\mathcal{A}$t the highly unfashionable hour of half past nine in the morning, Miss Hero Jarvis was drinking a cup of tea in the morning room when her father came upon her. "You're up early," she said.

He sank into the chair opposite hers. "I wanted to catch you before you left the house."

"Oh? Would you like a cup of tea?" she asked, reaching for the teapot.

"Yes, thank you." He leaned forward, his frowning gaze hard on her face. "I thought we had an agreement."

She poured a measure of milk into his cup with a steady hand, then added the tea. "I haven't violated it. I agreed not to approach the magistrates, and I have not done so." Of course, their agreement had been more along the lines of an edict, to which she'd had little choice but to concur. He'd warned her that if she did attempt to approach the magistrates about the killings, he would let it be known that her claims to have been present in the house at the time of the attack were motivated by nothing more than a desire to draw attention to the plight of such women and should therefore be disregarded.

She handed him the cup. "I take it you've received a report from one or more of your minions?"

"You knew I would."

"Yes."

He pressed his lips together in a sour line. "It is you, isn't it? The gentlewoman who has been asking questions about the Magdalene House?"

"Did you think I would not?" When he didn't answer, she said, "I know your main concern in all this is that my name not be bandied about in connection with the incident. You needn't fear that I've been anything other than discreet. There is nothing to link my name to what happened that night."

Lord Jarvis pushed aside his tea untasted, his gaze still on her face. "If I ordered you to stop, would you obey me?"

She met his stare without flinching. "Yes. But I would resent it."

Jarvis nodded. "Then I won't ask it of you."

Hero didn't realize she'd been holding her breath until she felt it easing out of her in a long sigh.

He pushed to his feet. "It goes without saying that you will be cautious."

"I will be cautious."

He nodded again and left the room.

She stared after him in surprise. She had expected him to ask her about Devlin's involvement, as well, for she had no doubt that by now her father had also learned of the Viscount's interest in the murders. Jarvis's reticence puzzled her, but only for a moment. She did not know all the details of the animosity between the two men, but she knew it ran deep. And she realized it doubtless had never occurred to Lord Jarvis that Devlin had involved himself in the Magdalene House murders at her specific request.

At just before ten o'clock that morning, Hero's carriage drew up before the pylon-shaped facade of Bullock's

Museum at 22 Piccadilly. Giant twelve-foot statues of Isis and Osiris, nearly naked and bewigged *à la égyptien*, stared down at her. She paid her shilling fee and passed through a papyrus-columned portico styled to resemble the entrance to an Egyptian temple.

For an extra sixpence she was able to acquire a small booklet detailing the wonders of the various exhibition halls. She wandered for a time, studying first the collection of carvings in wood and ivory, then the curiosities brought back from the South Seas by Captain Cook. In the western wing she came upon the Pantherion, which contained—according to her booklet—"all the known Quadrupeds of the Earth." Stuffed, of course. The Pantherion was reached by way of a basaltic cavern said to be modeled on the Giant's Causeway of the Isle of Staffa—although her guidebook neglected to mention precisely where that might be.

In the distance, Hero could hear a progression of church bells chiming the quarter hour. It was nearly eleven o'clock. She studied an Indian hut set against the background of a tropical forest complete with glassy-eyed elephants and roaring tigers and a large, coiled snake, and felt a sense of frustration well within her. It had been a mistake, she realized, to set the rendezvous for this morning. She'd been driven by a sense of urgency, but she should have allowed more time for news of her reward to spread. More time for the women of Covent Garden to summon up the courage to step forward.

She climbed the steps to the first floor, where a room styled to resemble a medieval hall displayed an exhibit of historic arms and armor. Here she found a young woman seated by herself on a bench beneath the domed ceiling. Hero eyed the woman with a renewed surge of expectation. She was obviously waiting for someone. She sat with her reticule clutched in both hands, her gaze darting warily around the room. With her demur pink muslin and round bonnet, she looked more like a young debutante than Haymarket ware, but perhaps she had deliberately dressed in a way that would not draw attention to herself. Hero had just made up her mind to approach the young woman when she jumped up from her seat and rushed across the hall toward the stairs.

Looking around, Hero noticed the gentleman in buff-colored breeches and an olive drab coat who had followed her up the steps. *Of course,* thought Hero; *a secret assignation.*

Blowing out an ungenteel breath of disappointment, Hero was about to turn back toward the stairs herself when a woman's lightly accented voice said, "You're the one, aren't you? The gentry mort who was at Molly O'Keefe's, asking questions about Rose and Hannah?"

Hero turned as a tall Jamaican with a long regal neck and an elegant carriage stepped out of the shadows. Hero felt a frisson of anticipation. "Do you have information for me?"

"For a price," said the Jamaican.

"You'll be paid your twenty pounds when and if the information you provide proves to be correct."

The woman's almond-shaped eyes narrowed. "How do I know you'll deliver?"

Hero's head jerked up. No one had ever before questioned her honor. "You have my word."

The woman simply laughed.

Hero said, "What's your name?"

"Tasmin. Tasmin Poole."

"You know where I can find Hannah?"

Tasmin Poole shook her head. "I don't know where Hannah Green is. But I've got this." She held up a delicate silver chain bracelet from which dangled a shield embossed with a coat of arms.

Hero reached out her hand, but the Cyprian closed

her fist tight around the bracelet, hiding it from view. "Uh-uh. You want t'see it, you pay for it."

"Where did you get it?"

"Rose gave it t'me."

"*Gave* it to you?"

Tasmin Poole smiled. "Let's call it a payment."

"How do I know you're telling the truth? How do I know this bracelet was Rose's?"

A sly smile curved the Jamaican Cyprian's wide mouth. "You have my word."

Hero's fingers tightened around the strings of her reticule. "I'll give you ten guineas for the bracelet."

"Fifteen," said the Jamaican.

"Twelve."

"Thirteen."

"Thirteen, then." Hero reached into her reticule for the money. She'd have paid twice that. "Now what can you tell me about Rose?"

In one deft motion, Tasmin Poole handed over the bracelet and scooped up the payment. "That'll cost you extra."

Chapter 18

*I*n an effort to humor his volatile French cook, Sebastian was picking at an elegant nuncheon of cold salmon in his dining room, when Tom returned with the information that Luke O'Brian, the man named by Ian Kane as Rose's particular customer, was a purchasing agent with clients who ranged from India to the West Indies and Canada.

"He buys 'em everything from kegs o' nails and plows to furniture and rugs and stuff for their 'ouses—whatever they need. I couldn't find anyone what 'ad anything to say to 'is discredit. They say 'e's 'onest as can be with 'is clients, yet 'e don't seem to put the squeeze on the merchants, neither."

"A regular paragon." Sebastian folded his napkin and set it aside. Catching Morey's eye, he said, "Tell Calhoun I'll be needing him right away."

The majordomo bowed and withdrew.

Tom frowned. "A para-what?"

"A paragon. A model of excellence and perfection."

"That sounds like 'im all right."

Sebastian pushed up from the table. "Which begs the question, doesn't it? What's this paragon doing frequenting someplace like the Orchard Street Academy?"

*   *   *

"The brown corduroy, don't you think?" said Calhoun, sorting through that portion of Sebastian's wardrobe culled from the secondhand-clothing dealers of Rosemary Lane and Monmouth Street. "It will clash hideously with the red waistcoat, but Bow Street Runners seem to have a strong predilection for brown corduroy. And you'll like this—" The valet turned, a black neckcloth held delicately between two extended fingers. "The individual who sold it to me assured me one could wear it for a month without washing it."

Sebastian looked around from rubbing powder into his hair. Between the powder and some judiciously applied theatrical makeup, he had already added twenty years to his appearance. A bolster around his torso would add twenty pounds. "Only a month?"

Calhoun laughed. "Two, in a pinch."

A few simple questions asked along the riverfront soon brought Sebastian to the outward-bound West Indian docks at the Isle of Dogs, where he found Luke O'Brian overseeing the loading of a shipment of canvas and hemp bound for Barbados. For a moment Sebastian simply watched him from a distance. The purchasing agent was a well-made man of perhaps thirty or thirty-five, expensively if quietly dressed, his manner easy toward ship's captain and sailor alike.

Most of the Bow Street Runners Sebastian had met were gruff, bullying men. That was the demeanor Sebastian assumed now, sinking further into the persona as he walked the length of the wind-buffeted dock so that even his posture and manner of movement altered. It was a trick Kat had taught him when they were both young and in love and fatally unaware of the common blood that coursed through their veins.

"You're O'Brian, aren't you?" said Sebastian brusquely. "Luke O'Brian?"

The purchasing agent turned. He had light brown

hair and hazel eyes that flashed with a lively intelligence. "That's right. May I help you?"

"My name is Taylor." Sebastian clasped the lapels of his corduroy coat and threw out his chest. "Simon Taylor. We're looking into the death of Rose Fletcher." He'd learned he never actually had to *say* he was from Bow Street; as long as he looked and acted the part, the assumption simply followed.

Sebastian watched as the guarded smile slid away from O'Brian's face and his lips parted on a quick, silent intake of breath. "Dead? Rose is dead? You're certain?"

"We believe she was one of the residents of the Magdalene House when it burned Monday night."

O'Brian turned toward the canal, one hand coming up to cover his mouth, his eyes squeezing shut. He was either devastated or a very, very good actor. It was a moment before he managed to say, "You're certain there's no mistake?"

The smell of hot tar and dead fish pinched Sebastian's nostrils. "We don't think so. When was the last time you saw her?"

O'Brian shook his head, his face still half averted, his voice a torn whisper. "I don't know. . . . Ten days ago, maybe. She didn't tell me she was leaving Orchard Street. I just went there one day and they said she was gone." He looked around suddenly. "You're quite certain she was at the Magdalene House?"

"It's difficult to know anything with these women, isn't it? Did she ever tell you her real name?"

"No. She didn't like to talk about her life . . . before."

"She never told you anything?"

O'Brian fiddled thoughtfully with the fob at the end of his watch chain. It was of gold, Sebastian noticed, discreet but well-fashioned. The cuffs and collar of his shirt were carefully laundered, his cravat snowy-white. No black neckcloths for this agent. "Only that her mother was dead," said O'Brian, staring out over the masts of the ships rocking at anchor off the docks. "From one or two things she let slip, I gathered the family lived in Northamptonshire. She may have had a couple of sisters—and a brother. I believe he was in the Army. But she didn't like to talk about them."

"Northamptonshire? Do you know why she left home?"

O'Brian shook his head. "No."

"And you've no idea why she fled Orchard Street?"

"No. She knew how I felt about her. If she had trouble, why didn't she come to me?"

Sebastian said, "You think her trouble was with Kane?"

O'Brian's jaw hardened. "Maybe. More likely that bloody magistrate."

"What magistrate?"

O'Brian's nostrils flared on a quickly indrawn breath. "Sir William. The bastard knocked her around pretty bad a couple of times."

"Ian Kane says he keeps rough customers away from his girls."

"Usually." O'Brian stared against the sun peeking out from behind a cloud to set the wind-ruffled surface of the water to sparkling and flashing. "But you can't exactly keep a Bow Street magistrate away, now can you?"

"Bow Street? You mean Sir William *Hadley*?"

O'Brian cast him a sideways glance, an unexpectedly hard smile curling his lips. "That's right. Sir William Hadley himself. So what are you going to do about that? Hmmm, Mr. Bow Street Runner?"

Chapter 19

Since Bow Street Runners did not in general drive around London in their own carriages, Sebastian had arrived at the Isle of Dogs in a broken-down hackney driven by a gnarled old jarvey who refused to nudge his mule out of a slow trot. But Sebastian had better luck on the return journey, the hackney swaying along at a satisfying clip as they bounced over the bridge spanning the Limehouse Cut and swung into the long, straight stretch of the new Commercial Road.

It was only by chance that Sebastian glanced back in time to glimpse the dark-coated man astride a raw-boned gray trotting along behind them. Sebastian had noticed the man before, lounging in the door of a coffeehouse near the wharf.

It could be a coincidence, of course. Anyone wishing to return to London from the West India Company docks would inevitably travel this same route. Leaning forward, Sebastian spoke to the driver. "Turn left here. Just wind your way down toward the river."

"Aye, gov'nor," said the jarvey in surprise.

They swung into a narrow lane bordered on one side by an open field, on the other by a long row of new houses. This was a part of the city that was expanding rapidly, transformed by the massive new construction of docks and warehouses that had accompanied the war. They ran past the long rope walks of Sun Tavern Fields and, beyond that, the spicy fragrance of a cooperage and the blasting heat of a foundry.

The dark-coated man on the raw-boned gray kept pace behind them.

"Where now, gov'nor?" called the jarvey.

"Pull up at that tavern halfway down the lane."

The tavern was a new two-story brick structure with twin bay windows. As Sebastian paid off the jarvey, the dark-coated man trotted past, then reined in at the base of the hill overlooking the quay and the warehouses that bordered it.

Sebastian entered the tavern and ordered a glass of daffy. The tavern was crowded with dockers and day laborers who filled the small public room with their voices and the smoke of their pipes and the pungent scent of their hardworking, unwashed bodies. Gin in hand, Sebastian took a seat at an empty table near one of the windows overlooking the street.

At the mouth of an alley directly opposite the tavern stood Dark Coat. As Sebastian watched, he lit a white clay pipe, the blue smoke wafting about his face as he drew hard on the stem. He looked to be in his early thirties, a medium-sized man with a crooked nose and a powerful jaw shaded blue by a day's growth of beard. He sucked on his pipe, one shoulder propped against the brick wall of the shop beside him, his eyes narrowed against the smoke and the inevitable reek of the alley.

Sebastian set his drink on the table untasted and walked out of the tavern. He had to check for a moment and wait while a dray piled high with coal rumbled past. Then he stepped off the footpath into the churned mud of the unpaved lane. Dark Coat turned his head away, his attention seemingly all for the forest of masts that filled this part of the Thames.

Sebastian planted himself directly in the man's line of vision. "Who set you to follow me?"

The man's eyes widened, but he otherwise managed to keep his face admirably blank as he pushed away from the wall. "I don't know what the bloody hell yer talkin' about."

Experience had taught Sebastian to watch a man's hands. He saw the flash of the knife the instant before it slashed up toward his face. Flinging up his left fist, Sebastian knocked the man's forearm with his own in a sweeping block as he took a quick step backward.

Too late, Sebastian felt his boot come down on a trampled sludge of rotten cabbage leaves and mud. The leather of his sole skidding dangerously, he slid sideways, one leg shooting out at an awkward angle.

Dark Coat pivoted and ran.

"Shit." Catching his balance, Sebastian raced after him, past smashed hogsheads and broken crates and dustbins of refuse that reeked of fish guts and offal. They erupted out of the end of the alley through an open gate and into a coal yard. Sebastian heard a hoarse shout from one of the workmen as they pelted past, dodging between towering mountains of gleaming, blue-black coal, their feet kicking up foul clouds of fine coal dust.

The man ahead of Sebastian swerved sideways. Scrambling over the yard wall, he darted out into the traffic of the quay. Dodging lumbering drays and the cracking whip of a bellowing teamster, Sebastian pelted after him.

The dark mouth of a warehouse yawned before them, a vast vaulted chamber whose dank air breathed the heady, forbidden fumes of the Bordeaux and the Côte d'Azure. Dark Coat plunged down the stone steps, the string of lamps above flickering with his passing. Sebastian raced after him. Racks of wine casks towered over them, threw long shadows across a cobbled floor gleaming damp in the wavering lamplight. Somewhere, moisture dripped—wine, or a residue of last night's rain—a slow *drip-drip* that formed a counterpoint to the slap of boot leather and the rasp of gasping breath.

"What the hell do you want from me?" shouted the man, his voice echoing back as he took the stairs at the far end of the wine cave two at a time.

"Who hired you?"

"Go to hell!"

At the top of the steps, the man veered right. Wary of an ambush, Sebastian slowed. By the time he emerged into the blinding light of the afternoon, the man had disappeared.

Breathing hard, Sebastian let his gaze travel over the darkened warehouses around him. A couple of drunken flaxen-haired sailors stumbled past warbling a German sea song. From the distance came the sound of coopers hammering at casks on the quay, the rattle of chains flying up on a crane ... and, from the warehouse to his right, a *thump*, like the sound of a body careening into an unseen obstacle.

This storeroom was dark, without the string of lanterns that had turned the wine warehouse into a long cavern of dancing shadows. Sebastian entered cautiously, giving his eyes time to adjust. With each step, his feet stuck to the floor as if it were newly tarred. It took him a moment to realize what it was: years and years of sugar that had leaked through casks to cover the floor, then half melted in the damp air. From up ahead came that same furtive sucking sound. Then it stopped.

Away from the open doorway, the darkness of the warehouse was nearly complete. But Sebastian's senses of sight and sound had always been acute. Wolflike, Kat used to say. Trying to still his own breathing, he listened, his gaze raking the towering rows of casks.

It was the barest hint of sound—cloth brushing

against wood. Sebastian whirled just as Dark Coat leapt toward him from atop the nearest stack of kegs.

The sudden movement dislodged the casks, toppling them in an avalanche of crushed staves and cascading sugar that swept Sebastian off his feet. He went down hard, his hand scooping up a fistful of sugar he threw in Dark Coat's face as the man lunged toward him, knife in hand. The man swore and staggered back, buying Sebastian enough time to roll to one side and come up onto his knees, a broken stave clutched in both hands.

"Ye son of a bitch," swore the man, charging again.

Swinging the stave like a curving club, Sebastian slammed the jagged edge into the man's wrist, sending the knife skittering away into the darkness. "Who hired you?" shouted Sebastian.

Whirling, the man took off toward the distant rectangle of light, his boots sliding and sucking in the sugar.

Shoving to his feet, Sebastian tore after him. They erupted into the sunlight covered in a fine dusting of sparkling white crystals.

"Englishes," said one of the German sailors, laughing as Sebastian ran past.

He could hear the bleating of a goat from a ship out on the river, the raucous cries of the seagulls circling over the docks. Heads turned as, one after the other, the sugar-encrusted men raced up the hill and into the lane. Dark Coat had a good hundred-foot lead, and Sebastian couldn't close it.

Snatching up his gray's reins on the fly, Dark Coat threw himself into the saddle, the horse shying violently as the man's weight came down hard and he set his spurs into the animal's sides.

"Son of a bitch," said Sebastian. Breathing hard, he leaned forward, his hands on his sugar-dusted knees as he watched the gray's tail disappear with a shivering swish up the lane.

*   *   *

Sebastian was in his dressing room brushing the sugar out of his hair when Jules Calhoun came in. "A bath is on the way, my lord." He held out a sealed missive on a silver tray. "This arrived while you were out. Delivered by a liveried footman."

Sebastian reached for the letter and studied the masculine-looking handwriting of the address. He flipped it over, frowning at the sight of the familiar coat of arms on the seal. The handwriting might be masculine, but it obviously belonged to Miss Hero Jarvis. He broke the seal and unfolded the heavy white page.

> *My lord,*
> *I have new information concerning Rose's identity. I will be visiting the Orangery in Kensington Gardens at two o'clock this afternoon. Please be prompt.*
> *Miss Jarvis*

"Please be prompt," repeated Sebastian, dropping the missive back on the silver tray. *Bloody hell,* he thought. *That acorn didn't fall far from its tree.*

Calhoun moved about the room gathering up the Viscount's sugar-dusted disguise. "You think the man who followed you was working for Ian Kane?"

"It's possible. Kane is the one who sent me after O'Brian in the first place." Sebastian glanced over at his valet. "But there may well be more to Mr. O'Brian than meets the eye."

"Would you like me to look into the gentleman, my lord?"

"It might prove interesting."

Calhoun bowed and turned toward the door.

"Oh, and, Calhoun—tell Tom to bring my curricle around in half an hour. I think it's time I paid a little visit to Bow Street."

Chapter 20

*D*ressed once more in his own exquisitely tailored dark blue coat and buckskin breeches, Sebastian drove his curricle to the Brown Bear, the aging inn in Bow Street that was essentially treated as an extension of the Bow Street magistrate's office.

"Walk 'em," he told Tom, handing the boy the reins. "We'll be leaving for Kensington as soon as I'm finished here."

Pushing through the inn's smoky public room, Sebastian found Sir William Hadley seated at a booth near the rear, a plate of cold roast beef and a tankard of ale on the worn, stained boards before him. "You might be interested to know I've discovered the identity of one of the women who was killed Monday night at the Magdalene House," said Sebastian, sliding into the bench opposite the Bow Street magistrate.

Sir William raised his tankard to his lips and drank deeply. "Now why the bloody hell would I be interested in that?" he said, drawing the back of one meaty hand across his wet mouth.

"Because it's someone you know. Rose Fletcher, from the Orchard Street Academy."

Sir William went suddenly still. "What the bloody hell makes you think I knew her?"

Sebastian gave the man a slow, mean smile. "Your frequent visits to the Academy are hardly a secret. She was a favorite of yours, was she not?"

Sir William bowed his head over his plate and gave his attention to his beef, shoving a large forkful into his mouth.

"There are those," said Sebastian, "who think you might be the reason Rose fled Orchard Street. You've a nasty reputation for roughing up women, Sir William."

The magistrate's head came up as he swallowed slowly. Eyes narrowing dangerously, he raised one thick finger to point at Sebastian. "I told you to keep out of this, Devlin. I meant it."

"Under the circumstances, I'm not surprised my interest has made you a trifle—shall we say, nervous?" Sebastian leaned his back against the panel behind him and crossed his arms at his chest. "In fact, I find myself wondering where you were on Monday night."

The magistrate's knife clattered against the thick edge of his white ironware plate. "Not that it's any of your bloody business, but as it happens I was with the Prime Minister. Next I know you'll be accusing Perceval himself."

Sebastian studied the magistrate's fleshy red face. "Since you obviously knew the young lady, perhaps you can tell me more about her."

Sir William's lip curled. *"Young lady?"* He pushed his plate away and stood up. "She was a whore, just like all the others, for all her airs and graces. You think I've nothing better to do than waste the afternoon nattering on about some worthless trollop? I've merchants breathing fire because someone's cleaned out a warehouse of prime Russian sables, and a loyal officer of His Majesty's Army who seems to have vanished into thin air, and a Member of Parliament assaulted in broad daylight on the Strand. Believe me, any one of those incidents is more important than a thousand dead strumpets."

Sebastian pushed to his feet. "Not to me."

Sir William tore away the napkin he'd tucked into his shirtfront and slammed it on the table beside his half-eaten meal. "I warned you to cease this interference in Bow Street's affairs, and I meant it. You might be thick with Sir Henry Lovejoy, but this is Bow Street, not Queen Square. Good day, my lord."

Sebastian watched the portly magistrate push his way toward the tavern's door just as Bow's bell chimed once, then again. It was two o'clock.

Kensington Gardens lay to the west of Hyde Park in an area of town unfashionable enough to ensure that no one of any consequence would be likely to observe the encounter between Miss Jarvis and Viscount Devlin.

Leaving Tom walking the chestnuts up and down the lane, Sebastian nodded to the attendant at the gate and continued on foot to where the redbrick and glass walls of the Orangery rose at the end of an avenue lined with high yew hedges. He found Miss Jarvis smartly dressed in a navy blue walking dress topped by a dashing hat with not one but two ostrich plumes. She stood as if enraptured by the study of an ornamental planting of lilies, but Sebastian was not deceived. A tall, thin maid, her face tight with discomfort, hovered nearby.

"You're late," said Miss Jarvis, twirling her parasol with impatience as he walked up to her.

Sebastian opened his eyes wide in mock dismay. "I am?"

To his surprise, a hint of a smile touched her lips. She swung her head away to stare out over a nearby open lawn interspersed with groves of shade trees. "Point taken," she said, and turned to walk along the broad avenue.

Sebastian fell into step beside her, the tight-faced maid trailing at a respectful distance. "So tell me, Miss Jarvis, what have you discovered that is of such vital importance that you felt compelled to arrange this assignation?"

She held her head high, her features remarkably composed. "This is not an assignation, my lord. This is an exchange of information. I have discovered that the woman who gave her name at the Magdalene House as Rose Jones was previously known as Rose Fletcher. She fled a house on Orchard Street."

"The Orchard Street Academy," said Sebastian.

Miss Jarvis swung to look directly at him. "How did you know that?"

"I went there."

She turned her head as if to study a green damsel-fly hovering about a nearby wisteria, but not before he saw the shadow of annoyance that flitted across her features. "Oh. And did you discover anything else of significance?"

He wasn't about to regale her with the sordid details of his encounters with either Ian Kane or Luke O'Brian. "It opened up one or two avenues of inquiry. But nothing of any significance yet." He turned their steps toward the east, where the Long Water shimmered blue and sun-dazzled in the distance. "How precisely did you come to know about the Orchard Street Academy?"

"I spoke to a woman named Tasmin Poole."

Sebastian drew up abruptly. *"You what?"* He remembered the tall, long-necked Jamaican he'd encountered in the Academy's tawdry parlor. "How in the name of all that's holy did you meet her?"

Miss Jarvis continued walking. "I put out word that I was willing to pay for information that would lead me to the woman who originally took refuge at the Magdalene House with Rose. According to Tasmin Poole, Rose fled the Orchard Street Academy with a woman named Hannah Green. Unfortunately, Tasmin is unaware of the woman's current whereabouts."

Sebastian stayed where he was. "Hang on. Exactly how did you put out word?"

She turned to face him, impatient and impervious. "I spoke to some women at a lodging house in Covent Garden. I'd met with them before in the course of my research."

Sebastian watched as the cold breeze plucked a strand of Miss Jarvis's rigidly controlled brown hair and blew it across her cheek. He said, "You don't even realize what you've done, do you?"

"What I've done? I've discovered the identity of the woman—"

"Yes. But at what cost? The men who killed those women at the Magdalene House saw two people running away. They shot one in the alley, but they knew one escaped. If they were watching your rendezvous with Tasmin Poole this morning, they now have a good idea who that second woman was. Not only that, but they know you're pursuing an inquiry into what happened and they're going to think Rose Jones, or Rose Fletcher, or whoever she was, told you something."

A slow heat moved up into her cheeks, but otherwise she remained perfectly composed. "I am well protected."

"I hope so. Because the type of people we're dealing with won't take kindly to too close a scrutiny. They've already killed eight women and burned a house to the ground. You think they won't hesitate to kill you?"

He continued up the path toward the Long Water, and after a moment, she fell in beside him again. She said, "Had you discovered the name of the woman who fled with Rose?"

"No," he admitted, glancing sideways at her. "Did Tasmin Poole tell you why the two women ran away from Orchard Street?"

"She said she didn't know. But she had this—" Reaching into her reticule, Miss Jarvis held up a short length of silver chain. "She said Rose gave it to her as payment for something."

Sebastian reached out to take the chain and cradle it in his gloved palm. It was a bracelet, small and delicate, with a single round medallion. He remembered his sister, Amanda, having something similar as a child. "It's a child's bracelet," he said, glancing up at the woman beside him. "How do you know this really belonged to Rose Fletcher?"

"I recognized the coat of arms on the medallion."

He flipped over the small medallion to study the helm with three eagles' heads. "The Fairchilds," he said. He looked up to find her watching him. "You do realize that either Tasmin Poole or Rose Fletcher could have acquired this bracelet in any one of a hundred different ways?"

"Of course I realize that," she said with ill-disguised indignation. "But the coincidences are more than intriguing."

"Coincidences?"

"Lord Fairchild has a daughter named Rachel, who made her Come Out just last Season. Her betrothal was announced in May, not long before she supposedly retired to the family estates in Northamptonshire for health reasons. But there are rumors that Miss Fairchild is not in Northamptonshire. There are rumors that she ran away."

Sebastian rubbed the pad of his thumb over the bracelet's delicate silver links. According to Luke O'Brian, Rose's family was from Northamptonshire. He said, "Why would she take this with her, of all things? It can't be worth much."

"Perhaps it was given to her by someone she loved. I don't know. But Tasmin told me something else significant. She said Rose—or Rachel, or whatever her name is—was terrified someone would find her. Tasmin thought it might have been her family, but she wasn't certain."

Sebastian said, "If Rose was Rachel Fairchild and she came out last Season, then why didn't you recognize her when you met her at the Magdalene House?"

Miss Jarvis shrugged. "I may have seen her at a ball, but if so I don't recall it. She wasn't the type of young woman one would notice in a crush, and I seldom attend Almack's Assemblies these days." At twenty-five, Miss Jarvis was virtually an ape leader.

He held up the bracelet. "You bought this?"

"Yes. With the promise of twenty pounds if Tasmin Poole should discover the current whereabouts of Hannah Green." When he remained silent, she said with some impatience, "At least we've a new avenue of inquiry to pursue."

Sebastian raised one eyebrow. "We, Miss Jarvis?"

She stared back at him. "That's right."

"What precisely do you intend to do? Go to Almack's and offer twenty pounds to anyone who can furnish you with the whereabouts of Miss Rachel Fairchild?"

The color was back in her cheeks, only this time he suspected it was a flush of annoyance. Miss Jarvis wasn't yet as good at controlling her emotions as her father. "No," she said evenly. "But I can make a call upon Lady Sewell."

"Who?"

"Georgina, Lady Sewell. Before her marriage she was Miss Fairchild—Rachel Fairchild's elder sister. I can't help but wonder if Rachel ran away from the Fairchilds' house on Curzon Street, why didn't she seek refuge with her sister?"

"Rather than in a brothel? It is an interesting question." Sebastian frowned, remembering what Luke O'Brian had told him about "Rose's" family. *I think*

*she might have had two sisters, and a brother in the
Army....* Sebastian knew that Lord Fairchild had at
least one son, Cedric; he'd served with Sebastian in the
Peninsula. "Is there a younger sister, as well?" he asked
aloud.

"I don't know," said Miss Jarvis, shifting her parasol
to keep the faint sun off her face.

Sebastian stared off across the sparkling surface of
the Long Water toward Hyde Park. What he needed, he
realized, was someone intimately familiar with every
hint of gossip and scandal attached to the Fairchilds in
the last fifty years. Someone like his aunt—

"I think the information we've gained was worth
whatever minimal risk I might have incurred," said Miss
Jarvis, reaching to take the bracelet from his hand.

Sebastian closed his fist around the chain. "I might be
able to use this," he said. "Leave it with me."

He expected her to argue with him, but she did not.
Looking into her frank, intelligent gray eyes, he had the
disconcerting realization that she didn't argue because
she knew precisely what he planned. She knew that as
soon as he'd visited his gossipy aunt Henrietta, he meant
to confront Lord Fairchild himself.

In fact, she was counting on it.

Chapter 21

Sebastian's aunt Henrietta, the Dowager Duchess of Claiborne, lived in an enormous pile on Park Street. Technically the house belonged to her eldest son, the current Duke of Claiborne, although the current Duke—who took after his father—was no match for the former Lady Henrietta St. Cyr. He'd long ago retired with his wife and growing young family to a smaller house on Half Moon Street and left his mother to reign supreme in the house she'd first entered as a bride some fifty-four years before.

But the Dowager Duchess of Claiborne was not at her Park Street residence. Trailing his aunt through silk warehouses and Pall Mall haberdasheries, Sebastian finally ran her to ground at the shop of a fashionable milliner on Bond Street.

He was aware of speculative eyes following him as he wound his way toward her through clusters of exquisitely gowned ladies peering at their reflections, past glass-topped counters and rows of gleaming mahogany drawers that reached to the ceiling. "Good heavens. Devlin," she said, groping for the quizzing glass she wore on a riband around her neck. "Whatever are you doing here?"

"Searching for you." He eyed the puce and flamingo

pink plumed turban she held in her hands. "You're not seriously considering that, are you?"

Henrietta had never been a tall woman, but she had the same stout build and large head as Hendon, with the piercingly blue St. Cyr eyes so conspicuously lacking in Sebastian. She fixed those eyes upon him now and slammed the turban on her head. "Yes, you unnatural child, I am. Now tell me what you want and go away."

He gave a soft laugh. "Dear Aunt Henrietta. I want to know what you can tell me about Rachel Fairchild."

Henrietta's plump cheeks sagged. "Lord Fairchild's middle daughter? Whatever is your interest in her? Nothing against the girl, mind you, but I don't like the stable."

Sebastian raised one eyebrow. "Tell me about the stable."

Henrietta studied her reflection in the mirror, her lips curving downward. The effect of the flamingo pink was not a happy one. "Basil Fairchild," she said in accents of strong distaste.

"I don't recall hearing anything to his discredit."

"Probably not. If I remember correctly, you were off at war trying to get yourself killed at the time. His first wife died seven or eight years ago, and he remarried just two years later to a young chit barely out of the schoolroom. Fairchild himself was in his forties at the time. Most unseemly."

"I knew Cedric Fairchild in the Army. Are there other sons?"

Henrietta removed the offending turban and reached for one done up in puce and navy blue silk. "No. This new marriage has been childless. But there is an older daughter, Georgina. She married Sir Anthony Sewell. . . . It was the year Pitt died, if I remember correctly. I understand there's a younger girl, as well, but she's still in the schoolroom."

Sebastian stared out the shop window at a red-and-green brewer's dray lumbering up the street. A brother in the Army, one older sister, one younger. It fit only too well. He said, "Rachel came out last year?"

"That's right." Henrietta settled the puce-and-navy confection on her iron gray curls. "But let me tell you right now, Sebastian, that if you've developed a *tendre* in that direction—"

"I've never met the girl." Sebastian studied his aunt's latest venture. "The navy is definitely an improvement," he said, then added, "What does she look like? Rachel, I mean."

Henrietta stared at her reflection in the counter's round glass, her chin sinking back against her chest in a way that emphasized her heavy jowls. "Her mother was Lady Charlotte, one of the Duke of Hereford's daughters. Rachel takes after her. She's pretty enough, I suppose. I myself have never cared much for that rather nondescript shade of brown hair, but she has good skin and teeth, and her green eyes are lovely. Still, she never exactly *took*, if you know what I mean. She always simply faded into the background. It was as if she were going through the motions of her Come Out because it was what was required of her rather than because it was something she wanted to do." Henrietta looked over at him. "If you've never even met the girl, then what is your interest in her?"

Sebastian simply ignored the question. "You say she didn't take?"

"Well, she was certainly far from being all the rage. But she did manage to contract a respectable alliance. Tristan Ramsey, if I remember correctly. No title, of course. But the Ramseys are quite warm."

"They married?" said Sebastian in surprise.

"The engagement was announced. Then the child supposedly took ill and retired to the country."

"Supposedly?"

"That's right. Rumor has it she's not there."

"Were there other suitors?"

His aunt thought a moment, then shook her head. "Not that I recall."

"What do you know of Tristan Ramsey?"

The Duchess fixed Sebastian with a dark glare. "He's steady and boring—quite appallingly so, actually, considering he's only twenty-four or twenty-five. He has a younger sister—Elizabeth or something like that. She's making her Come Out this Season, and he's being quite the dutiful son and brother, squiring his mother and sister all over town. He came into his inheritance as a child, you know. Sometimes that has disastrous effects on the development of a young man's character. But not Ramsey's. He keeps his estates in order, he doesn't gamble to excess, and if he keeps a mistress, he must be very discreet about it because I've never heard tell of it. In many ways he reminds me of Lord Fairchild."

"Yet despite this list of virtues, you don't care for either one. Why?"

"If I liked steady, virtuous, boring men, I'd have lost patience with you years ago, now wouldn't I?" She removed the puce-and-navy silk confection and nodded to the demure shop assistant hovering nearby. "I'll take this one." To Sebastian, Henrietta said, "Now, not another word until you explain your interest in the child."

"I'll explain later," said Sebastian, leaning forward to kiss her cheek. "Thank you, Aunt."

Henrietta reached out to snag his arm. "Oh, no, you don't. You can carry my package to the carriage."

Sebastian glanced at the Duchess's liveried footman waiting patiently beside the shop door, then silently scooped up her purchase and followed her out of the milliner's into the fitful May sunshine. Once on the footpath, she fixed him with a critical eye that made him suddenly uncomfortable. "I've been hearing disturbing reports about your activities these past months, Sebastian. Most disturbing reports. And from what I can see, they're all true. You look like the very devil."

"Why, thank you, Aunt."

"Don't get me wrong. I can understand drowning your sorrows in a few bottles of brandy and wild nights on the town. It was a shock, obviously. A shock to us all. But eight months, Sebastian? Don't you think that's a trifle excessive?"

"Obviously not."

She grunted. "At any rate, that's not what I wished to speak to you about. I'm worried about Hendon."

"Aunt—"

"No. Hear me out. I said I understand it was a shock, learning of the connection between Hendon and Miss Boleyn. But to allow the consequences of something that occurred more than twenty years ago to poison your relationship with Hendon now is worse than illogical. It's mean-spirited. And that's something I've never known you to be."

"You think I should be able to accept with equanimity the discovery that my father is also the father of the woman I planned to marry?"

"Equanimity, no. Understanding and forbearance, yes." She tightened her hold on his arm, her fingers digging into his flesh through the fine cloth of his coat and shirtsleeve. "This estrangement grieves him, Sebastian. More than you'll ever know. Nothing means more to him than you."

They had reached the carriage. The footman let down the steps and stood waiting woodenly. Sebastian passed him the package, then took his aunt's hand to help her negotiate the passage through the narrow door. "Good day, Aunt," he said, stepping back.

Swinging away, he had taken two strides toward his own waiting curricle when her voice stopped him. "By the way, Sebastian," she called maliciously through the carriage's open window, "I hear you were driving Miss Jarvis in Hyde Park yesterday."

He whirled back around. "Good God, wherever did you hear that?"

But his aunt simply smiled and nodded to her coachman to drive on.

Chapter 22

Lord Fairchild's residence in Curzon Street was impressively large and stylishly decorated by its new young mistress, with striped silk drapes and rich Oriental carpets and Egyptian-inspired settees. As Sebastian followed the solemn-faced butler across a polished marble entry, he knew a moment of misgivings. Silver gleamed; the wood of the balustrade and hall tables glowed with wax. How could the granddaughter of a duke, born to such a genteel, rarified atmosphere, possibly have fallen so low as to grace the tawdry parlor of a brothel like the Orchard Street Academy?

Still solid and straight-backed despite his fiftysomething years, Basil, Lord Fairchild had the silver-laced dark hair and sallow skin more typically seen in a Spaniard or a Frenchman from the Côte d'Azure. Receiving the Viscount in a red-velvet-draped library, he fixed Sebastian with a heavy scowl and said, "If Hendon sent you here to talk to me about these damnable Orders in Council, you're wasting your time."

The Orders in Council were part of Britain's tit-for-tat economic war with Napoleon. But one of the system's unintended consequences had been a heating up of tensions with the Americans. Lord Fairchild was one of those pushing for the Orders' repeal, whereas

Sebastian's father was a strong supporter of the Prime Minister's determination to stand tough against the Americans' belligerence. "It's not that I'm soft on the defense of Canada or British shipping interests," Fairchild was saying. "But Britain needs to stay focused on defeating the French."

"I'm not my father's envoy," said Sebastian, and left it at that.

Lord Fairchild looked surprised for a moment, then gave a gruff laugh. "Well, then. Have a seat, Lord Devlin. My son, Cedric, has told me much of your exploits on the Continent. If we had a few more men like you, maybe Boney'd be on his way to hell by now, rather than riding roughshod over all of Europe."

As far as Sebastian was concerned, his activities in the Army were something to be atoned for and, hopefully, someday forgotten—not glorified. But he merely inclined his head and said, "Thank you. I'd rather stand."

"But you will take a drink," said Fairchild with a smile. There was nothing in either the man's manner or his demeanor to suggest the grieving father.

Sebastian said, "I'm afraid I may have some unfortunate news for you."

"News?" Lord Fairchild's smile faded. "What news?"

"It's about your daughter Rachel."

Lord Fairchild went to splash brandy into two glasses, his movements controlled, methodical. After a moment, he said, "Rachel? Unfortunate news? I don't know what you can mean. My daughter is in the country." Turning, he held out one of the brandies. And in that moment Sebastian knew, unequivocally, that the man was lying.

Rather than taking the glass, Sebastian reached into his pocket and drew out the delicate silver bracelet. It landed with a soft clatter on the polished surface of the table between them. "I think not."

Lord Fairchild stared at the bracelet. Carefully set-

ting aside the brandies, he stretched out a hand that was
not quite steady to pick it up. He studied the medallion's
crest, then raised his gaze to Sebastian's face. "Where
did you get this?"

"Two days ago the young woman who owned that
bracelet was murdered. She had brown hair and green
eyes, and said her name had once been Rachel—
although she'd lately taken to calling herself 'Rose.' "

"I told you," said Lord Fairchild, setting the bracelet
down again, "my daughter is in Northamptonshire."

"When did you last see her?"

"Why—Easter, I suppose." The man stared back at
Sebastian as if daring him to contradict it. "Yes, that was
it. Easter."

"I don't think so," said Sebastian. "I think she's
missing. I think she's been missing for some time. Now
she's dead, and in a few hours, she'll be given a pau-
per's funeral by the Society of Friends. Is that what you
want? For your daughter to be buried in an unmarked
grave?"

Lord Fairchild's cheeks darkened with rage, his eyes
narrowing down to two small slits. "Get out," he said
through tight, twisted lips. "Get out of my house."

Lord Fairchild thrust out his hand, reaching again
for the bracelet. Sebastian got there first, his fist closing
over the delicate silver chain and the medallion with its
damning crest. "It's not your daughter's, remember?" he
said.

For a moment, the two men's eyes clashed, Lord
Fairchild's full of fury and fear, Sebastian's sending a
steady promise of intent. Then Sebastian turned on his
heel and strode from the house.

Sending Tom and the curricle ahead of him, Sebastian
walked the footpaths of Mayfair, a deep disquiet blooming within him. *Why?* he kept wondering. Why would

a young, gently bred woman raised in the comfort and splendor of Curzon Street run from her family's protection to seek a bleak refuge on the streets? What had she seen? Heard? Learned? What did she fear?

He was turning his steps toward St. James's when a gentleman's carriage swung around the corner and pulled in close to the curb, the coachman dropping the horses to a walk. Sebastian glanced at the well-known crest on the panel and didn't alter his stride.

The King's cousin, Charles, Lord Jarvis, let down the near window and said, "Ride with me a ways, Devlin."

Sebastian turned to face him. "If you're planning to do away with me, I'd like to point out that there are rather a lot of witnesses about."

Jarvis said drily, "You of all people ought to know I never do my own dirty work."

Sebastian laughed and leapt up into the carriage without waiting for the steps to be let down.

Jarvis signaled to the coachman to drive on. "It's been brought to my attention that you've been asking questions about Monday night's fire."

There was a pause. When Sebastian made no attempt to fill the silence, Jarvis shifted his considerable weight and said, "What precisely is your interest in the matter?"

Sebastian studied the Baron's impassive features. "I don't like murder. Especially when no one wants to acknowledge that it has taken place."

Jarvis drew a delicately enameled snuffbox from his pocket. "People are murdered in London all the time."

"So I've been told."

Jarvis flipped open the snuffbox and lifted a pinch to one nostril. They were playing a game, a delicate verbal dance in which Jarvis was attempting to discover if his daughter's presence at the murder scene was known without in the process betraying it. "There's a reason you've interested yourself in these murders," said Jarvis. "Do you have a connection with someone who was there?"

"I didn't know any of the victims," said Sebastian, choosing his words with equal care.

Jarvis snapped his snuffbox closed. "A witness, perhaps?"

"Sir William says there were no witnesses. But then, Sir William says there was no crime."

"And have you discovered anything of interest?" asked Jarvis, dusting his fingers.

"Not yet." Sebastian paused, then asked maliciously, "And what is your interest in this, my lord?"

A slow smile spread across the big man's face. "I take an interest in the welfare of all the King's subjects."

The two men's eyes met and clashed, the air charged with the memory of all that had passed between them. "Of course," said Sebastian, and signaled the coachman to pull up.

Sebastian was striding away when Jarvis called after him, "I saw Miss Boleyn at Covent Garden Theater last Saturday. She's as lovely as ever. But then, she's not Miss Boleyn anymore, is she?"

Sebastian stiffened a moment, but kept walking.

Dropping into Gentleman Jackson's salon, Sebastian glanced around, passed a few minutes chatting with acquaintances, then left again. He was looking for Tristan Ramsey, the man who was to have wed Rachel Fairchild before she disappeared forever into the suppurating world of the city's streets. Sebastian had no doubt that Lord Fairchild would deny his daughter's disappearance to the grave. Her betrothed might be more forthcoming.

Tristan Ramsey proved elusive. But in the Blue Room of the Cocoa-Tree Club, Sebastian ran across Rachel's brother. A sporting young buck in doeskin breeches and topboots, Cedric Fairchild sat sprawled beside another man in one of the bell chairs clustered around the room's empty hearth, one leg thrown carelessly over the chair's arm, a glass of brandy cradled in his right hand. The man beside him was unfamiliar, although he wore the yellow-frogged blue tunic of a captain in the 20th Hussars.

Sebastian's acquaintance with the younger Fairchild was slight. They'd served together, briefly, in Lisbon. But Sebastian had been a captain at the time while Cedric had been a cornet some four or five years his junior. Sebastian remembered him as a likable young officer, open-faced and guileless and quick to laugh.

"Devlin," said the younger man, his leg sliding off the chair's arm when Sebastian walked up to him. "Good God, I haven't seen you in an age."

"When did you sell out?" asked Sebastian.

Cedric Fairchild had his father's almost black hair, with his sister's fair skin and green eyes. "Just after Albuera." He motioned to the hussar captain at his side. "You know Patrick Somerville?"

"No," said Sebastian, shaking the man's hand. "But I've heard of you. You're General Somerville's son, aren't you?"

"That's right," said the captain. He was tall and gaunt, with swooping blond side-whiskers and the shiny pale skin suggestive of both malaria and a too-frequent recourse to the relief to be found in quinine and arsenic. "You know m'father?"

"I served with him as a young lieutenant." Sebastian settled into a nearby chair. "I hear he's retired now."

"Nominally." A smile crinkled the skin beside the hussar's pale blue eyes. "He spends his days preparing for a possible French invasion by marching every able-bodied cottager of Northamptonshire back and forth with pitchforks and shovels."

"Only the able-bodied ones?"

Somerville laughed. "Well, the ones with two legs at any rate."

Cedric leaned forward. "I say, Devlin, did you ever serve with Max Ludlow?"

"I don't believe so. Why?"

"Somerville here has just been telling me he's gone missing."

Sebastian turned toward the captain. "Since when?"

"Last Wednesday night," said Somerville, draining his porter.

Wednesday? Sebastian knew a quickening of interest. "Precisely what do you mean when you say he's gone missing?"

"We thought at first he must be with some wench. But six days and six nights?" Somerville shook his head. "Ludlow doesn't have that kind of stamina—or interest, for that matter."

Sebastian studied the hussar's troubled, sweat-sheened face. "Is Ludlow from Northamptonshire, as well?"

"Ludlow? No, Devonshire. We sent word to his brother's country seat, but they haven't seen him in months." Somerville lifted his empty glass and stretched to his feet. "I need a refill." Nodding to Sebastian, he told Cedric, "Let me know if you hear anything."

Sebastian waited until the sandy-haired captain was out of earshot, then said bluntly, "I just had a conversation with your father. About your sister Rachel."

Cedric Fairchild stiffened, his pleasant smile fading away. "What about my sister?"

"Two nights ago a woman answering your sister's description was murdered in Covent Garden. I'm told this bracelet was hers." Sebastian drew the silver bracelet from his inner pocket and held it out in his palm.

Cedric made no move to touch it. "Oh, God," he whispered, his face going slack.

"Your father insists she's in Northamptonshire. But it's not true, is it?"

Sebastian expected the man to deny it. Cedric sat for a moment, his gaze fixed on the crested medallion. Then he covered his face with his hands and drew a ragged breath.

"When did she run away?" Sebastian asked.

Cedric drew in another deep breath. "Last summer," he said, his voice muffled.

"She never went to Northamptonshire?"

"No—I don't know. She was already gone by the time I got back from Spain."

"Do you know why she left?"

Cedric shook his head, his splayed fingertips digging into his forehead. "Father said she quarreled with Ramsey."

"Her betrothed?"

Cedric scrubbed his hands down his face, drawing them together before his mouth. "That's right."

"But you don't think so?"

"I don't know." He looked up, a desperate hope kindling his features. "Are you quite certain this dead woman— I mean, it might not be Rachel. Someone could have stolen her bracelet, right?"

"The woman was described as young and pretty, with green eyes and brown hair. Tall. Slender."

Cedric collapsed back in silence. It was as if he were slowly drawing into himself, trying to absorb the unbelievable. After a moment he said, "What happened?"

"She was at the Magdalene House when it burned."

"Rachel?" He threw a quick glance around and leaned in closer to lower his voice. "At the Magdalene House?" Anger flared, brittle and blustering. "What the devil are you suggesting? That my sister was a—a—"

"I'm saying that a woman who fit your sister's description died in that fire."

Doubt and determination hardened Cedric's face. "I want to see her body."

"You won't be able to recognize her. Most of the women were badly burned."

"I don't care. I want to see her."

Sebastian hesitated. But after four years of war, there would be little in the way of horrors Cedric Fairchild hadn't seen. He said, "The Society of Friends is planning to bury the women this evening. If we hurry, we should make it."

Chapter 23

The Friends' Meeting House in Pentonville stood at the corner of Collier Street and Horseshoe Lane, just beyond where the last straggling houses of the village gave way to fields of green growing barley and small garden plots. Roofed in thatch, it was a simple structure of coursed stone, with a small cemetery stretching out beyond it. Sebastian drew up his curricle in the lee of a spreading elm tree and turned to the silent man beside him.

"I can wait here, if you like."

A cold wind blew over them, bringing with it the earthy scents of the surrounding fields and the song of a robin from somewhere in the distance. Cedric Fairchild sat with his shoulders hunched, his eyes narrowing as he stared at the small knot of drab-gowned women and plainly dressed men in collarless coats and broad-brimmed black hats gathered on the flagged walkway leading to the meetinghouse's simple stoop. "No. Please, come in."

"Walk 'em," said Sebastian, handing the reins to Tom. As he jumped down, one of the men near the meetinghouse door detached himself from the small group and came toward them, his body tall and gaunt.

"Sebastian St. Cyr," said Joshua Walden, "it is good of thou to come." The Quaker nodded to Fairchild. "And thou, friend, welcome."

"This is Cedric Fairchild," said Sebastian. "It's possible one of the women killed at the Magdalene House was his sister. He would like to see her body." Sebastian paused, then added, "It's the woman who was shot."

Cedric cast Sebastian a look of surprise, while Joshua Walden's smile faltered. "That body is badly burned. Very badly burned."

"I'd still like to see her," said Cedric, his jaw rigid.

Walden studied the younger man's tightly held face, then nodded. "Very well. Come this way."

He led them through the meetinghouse's simple door into a large, plain room filled with benches and the softly glowing light of evening. The room smelled of freshly planed wood underlain faintly by the sweet stench of decay. Eight crude wooden coffins stood in a row in the center of the meeting hall. "The woman thou seeks is the second from the end on the left," said Walden, pausing respectfully just inside the door. "The lids have not yet been nailed down."

Cedric hesitated. When he finally walked forward, it was with the measured tread of a man who dreads what he is forcing himself to do. At the side of the coffin, he hesitated again, and Sebastian thought for a moment his courage had failed him. Then he grasped the edge of the plain wooden lid with both hands and thrust it up.

From where he stood beside the Quaker, Sebastian watched Cedric's face blanch. He watched the man's hands tighten around the edge of the lid, saw the quiver of revulsion and horror that swept across his face. Then Fairchild dropped the coffin's lid back in place and bolted for the door.

Sebastian caught up with him just beyond the stoop. He stood hunched over, his hands on his knees, his body heaving with each successive shudder of dry retching. "Here," said Sebastian, holding out his handkerchief.

Cedric straightened, his fist closing convulsively around

the handkerchief. A cold sweat beaded the pallid flesh of his forehead and upper lip, and he dabbed at it. "You were right," he said, his breath coming in strained gasps. "She was beyond recognizing. But I had to—" He broke off.

"I understand." Sebastian studied the shaken man beside him. "You knew Rachel was in Covent Garden, didn't you?"

Hot color flooded his pale face. "Good God, of course not. How can you even suggest such a thing?"

The denial rang untrue, but Sebastian let it slide. He said, "Tell me about your sister. What was she like?"

Cedric stared up the lane, to where a milkmaid in a white apron and a large-brimmed bonnet was hazing a cow toward home. The evening breeze ruffled his dark hair and his features softened with memory. "When she was a child, she was the sweetest little creature imaginable. Always bubbling with laughter and joy, yet so tender and loving. Whenever something happened—if Georgina or I were upset about something—Rachel would always come and put her arms around us and sing us a song." A deep breath shuddered his chest. "She used to love to sing. She'd sing to her dolls, to our father's hounds, to the stable cats."

Sebastian tried to reconcile the laughing, loving child of Cedric's memory with the cynical Cyprian Hero Jarvis had described. The two images refused to blend. "You said she used to love to sing. That changed?"

Cedric nodded. "Around the time our mother died. It was as if . . . I don't know. As if all the joy within her just leached away. She quit singing, and then she—" He broke off.

"And then what?" prodded Sebastian.

Cedric looked down at the handkerchief he held crumpled in his fist. "I found her one day digging a row of graves in a meadow in the park. She'd borrowed a shovel from one of the gardeners. The graves were for her dolls. She said they were all dead. And she buried them."

"How old was she?"

"Ten. Eleven."

Sebastian's mother had died the summer he was eleven . . . or rather, he'd been told she died. He stared off across fields lit now by the soft golden light of evening. The breeze brought them the scent of ripening grain and the bawling of a goat tethered somewhere out of sight. "Did she write to you, when you were in the Army?"

"Sometimes."

"Did she write about Tristan Ramsey?"

"She told me of the betrothal. I honestly thought she was pleased with it. She sounded . . . happy."

"She didn't normally sound happy?"

Cedric's eyes narrowed. Instead of answering, he said, "Why have you involved yourself in this?"

Sebastian chose his words carefully. "There was a woman at the Magdalene House who survived the attack. She asked for my help."

From somewhere down the lane came the sweet tolling of a church bell. Cedric brought up a hand to rub his temples. "I don't understand. What's this about an attack, about Rachel being shot? I thought the Magdalene House was simply destroyed by fire."

"The fire was deliberately set to cover up the women's murders."

Cedric's hand dropped. "I've heard nothing of this."

"You won't."

Sebastian turned as Joshua Walden walked up behind them, his hands folded in front of him, and cleared his throat. "We are about to begin. You are welcome to attend."

Cedric pressed the handkerchief to his lips. "I've never attended a Quaker service before."

"We believe that true religion is a personal encounter

with God rather than a matter of ritual and ceremony, and that all aspects of life are sacramental. Therefore, no one day or place or activity is any more spiritual than any other. But we gather together at such times to discover in stillness a deeper sense of God's presence."

Cedric lifted his gaze to the small cemetery that stretched away from the road, a plain grassed area surrounded by trees and shrubs and enclosed by a mortared low rubble wall. "You will bury her there?" he said hoarsely. "Despite what she'd become?"

"There is a spark of God in every human being," said Walden, following his gaze. "And all ground is God's ground." He put out a hand to grip the younger man's shoulder. "Come. Thy sister is at peace. Let us bid her farewell."

Chapter 24

That night, Sebastian dressed in black velvet knee breeches and black pumps with silver buckles, and set forth for Almack's Assembly Rooms.

Known as the Seventh Heaven of the Fashionable World, Almack's was a private club that provided its male and female members with a dance and supper every Wednesday night for the twelve weeks of the Season. But unlike the men's clubs of St. James's, Almack's was a club controlled by women. The mere possession of vulgar wealth was not enough to enable one to penetrate these carefully guarded portals; the Patronesses of Almack's were very careful to exclude rich Cits, crass country nobodies, and even titled, gently bred ladies whose indiscretions had carried them beyond the pale. For above all else, Almack's served as a safe haven where society's marriageable young women could be introduced to society's marriageable young men. Which was why Sebastian had no doubt that Tristan Ramsey, whose young sister was making her debut that Season, would be in attendance.

Arriving at the long, Palladian-styled building on King Street well before the fatal hour of eleven o'clock—after which time absolutely no one was allowed admittance—Sebastian paused just inside the club's ballroom. Adorned with gilt columns and pilasters, the room was lit by scores and scores of candles clustered in multitiered chandeliers suspended overhead. The club was crowded, for the Season was now at its height and Almack's was as popular with the wives of aging Parliamentarians and select foreign ministers as with the younger set. The air was heavy with the scent of hot candles, French perfume, and well-dressed, perspiring bodies.

He was standing beneath the semicircular balcony for the musicians and watching the progress of Tristan Ramsey down a line of the country dance when a woman's voice behind him said coldly, "Whatever are you doing here?"

Sebastian swung around to find his sister, Amanda, studying him through narrowed blue eyes. She wore an elegant gown of silver-gray satin simply adorned with puffed sleeves, for she was still less than eighteen months widowed.

"Did you hope the Patronesses had blackballed me?" he said.

Amanda let out her breath in a scornful huff. "Don't be ridiculous. You're the heir to an earldom. You could murder half a dozen virgins in the middle of Bond Street, and they'd still let you in."

Sebastian returned his gaze to Tristan Ramsey. A small but well-formed man in his midtwenties, he had curly auburn hair and pleasant, even features. But he moved with distracted clumsiness, his face as haggard and pale as a man with the ague . . . or a man who'd just learned that the woman he'd once planned to make his wife was dead. He partnered a dainty young thing with the exact same auburn hair and a scattering of freckles across her small, upturned nose. This, obviously, was the young Miss Ramsey making her debut.

"We got on far more comfortably when you were still on the Continent," said Amanda.

"Not to mention the exciting possibility that I might at any moment get myself killed." Sebastian let his gaze wander over the other dancers until he spied his eighteen-year-old niece, Miss Stephanie Wilcox, going down the line with Lord Ivins, the rakish young heir to a Marquis. "Would it make you feel better if I pledged to endeavor not to irretrievably disgrace the family before my niece goes off?"

He watched as Stephanie executed a neat pirouette. She had grown into a ravishing young woman, with a tumble of golden curls and the vivid blue St. Cyr eyes. Along with her mother's coloring, she had Amanda's tall, slim elegance. But unlike Amanda, Stephanie had escaped the rather blunt features Amanda had inherited from Hendon. In fact, Stephanie looked startlingly like Sebastian's own mother, Sophia.

"How is Stephanie doing on the Marriage Mart, by the way?" he asked. "Any bidders yet?"

Amanda also watched her daughter. "Don't be vulgar."

"I wouldn't go with Ivins if I were you. He's rather too fond of faro."

"We have hopes for Smallbone."

"Has he come up to scratch yet?" Sebastian watched his niece throw a provocative, laughing gaze up at the admiring Lord Ivins. Stephanie not only looked like the errant Countess, Sebastian realized, but she acted like her, as well.

"Not yet."

"Best hope he does so soon," said Sebastian. "My niece looks dangerously fond of Ivins."

The dance was ending. Sebastian watched Tristan Ramsey lead his glowing sister back to a matronly woman in puce, then disappear toward the supper room. "Excuse me," said Sebastian, and left Amanda glaring after him with icy dislike.

He came upon Ramsey in the supper room. The tables were spread with the usual Almack's fare, which was simply thinly sliced bread and butter, plain cakes, lemonade, and tea. Ramsey had passed up the tea in favor of a glass of lemonade, but the bread and cakes didn't appear to tempt him. He stood turned half away, the glass of lemonade seemingly forgotten in one hand, the fingers of his other hand sliding up and down his watch chain as he stared into space.

Sebastian's acquaintance with the man was slight. They might belong to the same clubs and at times frequent the same routs and balls, but they were separated by some four or five years and by a world of interests. Yet when Sebastian entered the supper room, Ramsey left the table and walked right up to him. "The woman whose body you showed Cedric Fairchild . . ." Ramsey threw a quick glance around and lowered his voice. "You're quite certain it was Rachel?"

"Fairly certain, yes."

Ramsey swallowed hard, his face going slack. He had even features and a pleasant enough face only slightly marred by a weak chin.

Sebastian said, "You knew she was missing?"

Ramsey nodded. From the ballroom came the beginning strains of a Scottish reel.

"Then you also know, presumably, why she ran away."

"No." The man's gaze had wandered, but he now brought it back to Sebastian's face. "I went to Curzon Street one day, planning to take her for a drive in the park, and Lady Fairchild told me Rachel was ill. They kept fobbing me off with one tale or another. Then they said she'd gone to Northamptonshire to recuperate."

"So how did you realize she wasn't there?"

"She never wrote to me. I finally went up to Fairchild Hall myself." His lips flattened into a straight line.

"When the servants told me they hadn't seen her since shortly after Christmas, I drove straight back to Curzon Street and demanded the truth."

"And?"

"Lord Fairchild admitted she'd run away."

"You had quarreled?"

Ramsey's eyes widened, his jaw sagging in denial. "No. Never."

"Then how do you explain her behavior?"

"I don't know. I looked for her everywhere. It was as if she just . . . disappeared."

Sebastian studied the other man's ashen face. He had not, obviously, thought to search the alleyways and brothels of Covent Garden. But then, who would?

Ramsey dropped his voice even lower. "Cedric says you've involved yourself in this at the request of a woman who survived the fire."

"That's right."

"One of the whores?"

"I'd rather not say."

For some reason, the answer seemed to trouble Ramsey. He stood with the glass of lemonade still untasted, the fingers of his free hand fiddling now with the gold locket he wore at the end of his watch chain. Sebastian said, "People typically run away because they're angry, or because they're miserable, or because they're afraid. Was Rachel afraid of marriage?"

A hint of color touched the other man's pale cheeks. "Of course not. She couldn't wait to be married."

"She was anxious to get away from her stepmother? The new Lady Fairchild?"

Ramsey gave a surprised laugh. "Don't be ridiculous. The woman's a cipher, a shadow."

"What about her father? How did Rachel get along with him?"

"Lord Fairchild?" Ramsey shrugged. "I don't think

she saw much of him, frankly. From what I understand he's pretty much devoted himself to affairs of state. At least, since his first wife's death."

Sebastian studied the other man's pale, haggard face. "It's curious, don't you think, that a gently born woman would flee her home and seek refuge in Covent Garden, only to run away again in fear less than a year later?"

"What makes you think she ran away in fear?"

It struck Sebastian as a curious question. "Can you think of another reason she would run away? Twice?"

"I told you. I don't know." His gaze drifted back to the ballroom. "Now you'll have to excuse me. I promised my sister this lemonade," he said, and brushed past Sebastian into the ballroom without a backward glance.

Chapter 25

*I*t was when Sebastian was leaving Almack's Assembly Rooms that he fell in with a small party that included Mr. Spencer Perceval, the Prime Minister. "Devlin," said the Prime Minister, excusing himself from his party. "Walk with me a ways. I've been wanting to speak to you."

The night was cold and clear, the bells of the city's churches chiming the hour as the two men turned their steps toward St. James's. In his fiftieth year, the Prime Minister was a small, slender man with a thin, smiling mouth, protuberant light eyes, and a rapidly receding hairline. "I'm concerned about your father," he said. "He doesn't look well these days."

"Hendon eats too much, drinks too much, and smokes too much," said Sebastian, wondering how many times in one day he could have this same conversation.

Perceval laughed. "Don't we all."

Sebastian kept his peace, although in truth, Spencer Perceval was a temperate family man who spent whatever free time the affairs of state left him either playing games with his children or searching the Bible for prophecies that he then wrote up and published in a series of religious pamphlets. "And how is Lady Perceval? And the children?" Sebastian asked, deliberately changing the subject.

"Lady Perceval is well, thank you. And as for the children ... well, they're growing up too fast," said the Prime Minister with that special smile that always lit his face when he spoke of his six sons and six daughters. "My eldest son will be heading off for Trinity College in the autumn."

Sebastian eyed the tattered hackney carriage that had pulled in close to the curb ahead of them. A man wearing an evening cloak stepped down, but the hackney didn't move on and the man stayed in the shadows. "I remember when Spence was off to Harrow."

The Prime Minister smiled. "Makes one feel one's age, does it not?" The smile faded, and he worked his square jaw back and forth in a way that reminded Sebastian of Hendon. "My Jane tells me I'm worse than a nosy old woman, but here it is. I don't know what's happened between you and Hendon, but I do know it grieves him. Grieves him badly. There. That's all I've got to say on the matter. Just thought you ought to know. Before it's too late."

Sebastian swallowed a spurt of annoyance and said evenly, "I understand you dined with Sir William Hadley on Monday."

"That's right. At Long's," said the Prime Minister with a rush of heartiness, as if this time he were thankful for the shift in topic. "The food was appalling. I've a good mind to quit going there."

"What time did the evening break up?"

"Not until midnight at least. You know how it is. A roomful of men with a steady supply of port and a dozen different opinions as to why the country is going to rack and ruin."

"Ah. I thought I saw Sir William that evening at Covent Garden, but I must have been mistaken."

"I don't know about that," said Perceval. "You might have. Sir William arrived late—close on to nine o'clock, if I remember correctly. Said something about—" He broke off as a man lurched toward them from out of the shadow of the waiting hackney.

"There you are!" said the gentleman, planting himself in the center of the footpath with his hands clenched into fists at his side, the light from the nearest streetlamp limning the side of his face. "Thought to avoid me again, did you?"

A spasm of embarrassment passed over the Prime Minister's features. Like all well-bred Englishmen, Perceval found public scenes mortifying. "Mr. Bellingham, I did not attend Almack's Assembly in an effort to avoid you."

The man was small and dark haired, with a long face that looked prematurely aged. He might have been fifty or sixty, but the blackness of his hair suggested an age nearer to forty. "All I demand is what is the birthright and privilege of every Englishman," said Bellingham, shoving his face up against Perceval's. "How would your wife and family feel if you were torn from them for years? Robbed of all your property and everything that makes life valuable?"

Perceval drew back, putting distance between them again. "You still have your wife and family, sir. And that is what makes life valuable."

"Easy for you to say," sneered Bellingham, pivoting as Perceval brushed past him. "You haven't been robbed of your liberty for years. Years!"

"My good man." Perceval swung to face him again. "I am sorry for your predicament. But it is not the place of the government to compensate you. Bring suit against this Israelite if you will, but your business with me is done."

Perceval turned on his heel and continued walking, Sebastian at his side. Bellingham shouted after them, "You think you can shelter behind the imagined security of your status, but you can't. Do you hear me? You can't!"

Perceval kept walking, his lips pressed into a tight line, the click of their bootheels on the flagstones sounding unnaturally loud in the sudden stillness of the night.

Sebastian said, "Who the devil was that?"

"John Bellingham." Perceval drew his handkerchief and pressed the neatly folded cloth against his upper lip with a hand that was not quite steady. "The poor man was imprisoned for years under the most dreadful conditions in Archangel. He had accused a shyster by the name of Solomon Van Brieman of insurance fraud over a scuttled ship, and Van Brieman retaliated by scheming to have the Russians ruin him. Truly, the poor man has been most grievously wronged, but he seems to think he's entitled to a hundred thousand pounds' compensation from His Majesty's government, and that he is not."

"He sounds mad."

"He may very well be. I fear his sufferings have turned his mind."

"You would do well to be careful," said Sebastian.

Perceval huffed a laugh. "Of Bellingham? I deal with his ilk most every day."

Sebastian threw a glance over his shoulder. Bellingham still stood in the center of the footpath, his small body rigid with rage and frustration, his dark head thrown back against the soft glow of the nearest oil lamp. "He might attempt to do you harm."

"What would you have me do? Surround myself with bodyguards? Never venture forth in public or mingle with the people? What sort of leader would I be then?"

"A live one?" suggested Sebastian.

But Perceval only laughed again and shook his head.

Chapter 26

*H*ero's plans to pay a call on Rachel Fairchild's older sister, Lady Sewell, were frustrated by Lady Jarvis, who insisted upon her daughter's company on a protracted shopping expedition that afternoon. As this was followed by an early departure for a dinner party being held that evening at the country house of one of Lady Jarvis's childhood friends, Hero resigned herself to putting off the visit to the next day.

The estate of Sally, the Duchess of Laleham, lay only on the outskirts of Richmond, but Lord Jarvis insisted that both the footmen and the coachman be armed since they were traveling outside of London. At the end of the evening, as the carriage started on the long drive back to Berkeley Square shortly after midnight, Hero found herself unusually grateful for her father's precautions.

"It's the arsenic powder," Lady Jarvis was saying as mother and daughter sat side by side, gently rocking with the motion of the carriage. "Or so I've heard. It utterly ruined her health. Which is a pity, because Sally was quite lovely when she was young. But vain."

"Hence the too-liberal use of the arsenic powder," said Hero.

"Yes." Lady Jarvis settled more comfortably against the plush seat and sighed. In contrast to her daughter's

Junoesque proportions, Lady Jarvis was a tiny woman, small of bone, with a head of once golden curls now fading gently to gray. "Yes," she said again. "But there's no denying it does give one the whitest skin. Sally was so lovely when she was young."

It was one of Lady Jarvis's more irritating habits, this tendency to repeat nuggets of her conversation. Or at least, it irritated her husband, Charles, Lord Jarvis, to the point he could rarely tolerate her company. But Hero remembered a time when her mother had been different, when Lady Jarvis had been high-strung and emotional but not half mad and childlike.

The light thrown by the carriage lamps bounced and swayed with the action of the horses and the bowling dips of the well-sprung chaise. Through the window, Hero caught a glimpse of a copse of birch trees, a flash of white trunks and darkly massed leaves against a black sky. The crisp evening air was heavy with the scent of plowed fields and damp grass and the lush fecundity of the countryside. Normally this was a journey Hero enjoyed. But tonight she found herself scanning the shadows and listening to the drumming of the horses' hooves on the deserted road. An inexplicable shiver coursed up her spine.

"Are you cold, dear?" asked Lady Jarvis, leaning forward solicitously. "Would you like the rug?"

"No. Thank you," said Hero, annoyed with herself. The road might be deserted, but she was not one to imagine highwaymen behind every wall or stand of trees. "I'm fine."

"The cream silk was a good choice," said Lady Jarvis, casting an approving eye over Hero's gown. "Better, I think, than the white I wanted you to wear."

"Cream is always a better choice than white," said Hero with a light laugh, her gaze still scanning the horizon. "White makes me look like a cadaver."

Her mother shuddered. "Hero! The things you say! But you do look lovely tonight. You should crimp your hair more often."

Hero swung her head to look at her mother and smile. "If you had any maternal feelings at all, you would have found some way to ensure that your daughter inherited all your lovely curls."

Lady Jarvis looked troubled for a moment. Then her brow cleared. "Oh. You're funning me. As if I had anything to say about it!"

Hero felt a pain pull across her chest and turned her head to stare out the window again. She loved her mother dearly, but there were times when the contrast between the way Lady Jarvis was now and the way Hero remembered her was enough to bring the sting of tears to her eyes.

The carriage lurched and swayed down a long hill, hemmed in on both sides by stands of dark trees undergrown with shrubs and gorse that pressed so close Hero fancied she could reach out and touch their branches. She became aware of the carriage slowing as the horses dropped down to a trot, then came to a shuddering halt as Coachman John reined in hard.

"Why are we stopping?" demanded Lady Jarvis, sitting upright.

Hero peered out the window at the horse and gig slewed across the road. "There appears to be a carriage in the way." A man stood at the horse's head, his voice a gentle murmur as he stroked the animal's neck and said soothingly, "Easy, girl. Easy."

"What's the trouble there?" shouted Coachman John.

"A broken trace," said the man, walking toward the carriage. By the pale light of the carriage lamps, Hero could see him quite clearly. He looked to be somewhere in his midthirties, rawboned and darkened as if from years under a tropical sun. But his accent was good, and he wore a neat round hat and a gentleman's driving cape, which swirled around a fine pair of high-topped boots.

As he paused near the box, she became aware of the sound of hoofbeats coming down the hill behind them. One horse, ridden fast. Her gaze traveled from the man in the road to the double-barreled carriage pistol in a holster beside the door.

The gentleman in the cape said, "If one of your footmen could help me move the gig out of the road, you can be on your way."

Reaching out, Hero slowly eased the carriage pistol from its holster.

Lady Jarvis said, "What on earth are you—"

Hero put out a hand, hushing her.

Hero couldn't see the man who'd ridden up behind them, but she heard his horse snort. "Need some help?" he called.

"I think everything's under control," said the man in the road. Reaching beneath his cape, he drew out a pistol and extended his arm so the muzzle pointed up at the box. "Don't move."

"What the bloody hell?" blustered the coachman.

The man in the road said, "You'll notice my friend here has a gun, as well. Throw down your weapons. We know you've got them."

Lady Jarvis's eyes went wide. "Oh, my goodness," she said in a panicked, high-pitched whisper. "*Highwaymen.* Hero, put that thing away. We must give them everything! Thank heavens I didn't wear the sapphires tonight. But there are your pearls—"

Hero put her hand over her mother's mouth. "Hush, Mama."

She heard muffled thuds as the two footmen threw down their guns. The man in the road said, "You, too, Coachman."

The carriage shuddered as the big coachman shifted his weight. His blunderbuss landed with a *thump* in the grassy verge. Hero tightened her grip on the handle of the pistol and carefully eased back both hammers.

"You didn't tell me we was stoppin' a lord's rig," said the second man, nudging his horse forward into the lamplight. "Two ladies in a carriage like this oughta be sportin' some nice baubles." Hero watched him swing down from his horse. He was younger than the man in the cape, and more coarsely dressed. She steadied the heavy carriage pistol with both hands and pointed the barrel at the door.

"That's not what we're here for," snapped the caped man, shifting his stance so he could cover both the footmen and Coachman John. "Just make it quick before someone comes along. And make bloody sure you shoot the right woman."

The younger man laughed. "I can tell a young'un from an old'un," he said, jerking open the carriage door.

Hero squeezed the first trigger and discharged the pistol straight in his face.

The man's face dissolved in a bloody red shattering of skin and bone. The percussion was deafening, the carriage filling with a blue flash of flame and smoke and the acrid smell of burned powder. Lady Jarvis screamed and kept screaming as the impact of the shot blew the man out of the carriage and flopped him back into the dirt of the road.

"Drummond!" The gentleman in the cape whirled, the barrel of his gun leveling on the carriage door. Half falling to her knees on the carriage floor, Hero leaned out the carriage door and squeezed the second trigger.

She shot higher than she'd meant to, and wilder, so that instead of hitting the man square in the chest her bullet smashed into his right shoulder, spinning him around and sending his pistol flying out of his hand.

"Quick," Hero shouted to the servants. "Get his pistol." She shoved up, only to sag slightly against the side of the open door. Now that it was over, her knees were shaking so badly she could hardly stand. "Is he dead?"

"Naw," said Coachman John, turning the caped gentleman over. "But he's bleedin' pretty bad, and he 'pears to have gone off in a swoon."

"This one's done for," said one of the footmen, Richard, bending over the first man she'd shot. "My Gawd, look at that. He don't have a face no more."

"Get that gig out of the middle of the road so we can drive on," said Hero, turning back to deal with her now hysterical mother. "Lady Jarvis has sustained a terrible fright."

"It would appear," said Paul Gibson, studying the chessboard before him, "that Sir William has his own reasons for discouraging any investigation of the Magdalene House fire."

Sebastian and the Irishman sat beside the empty hearth in the surgeon's parlor, the chessboard, a bottle of good French brandy, and two glasses on the table between them. The neighborhood had long since settled into quiet, and only an occasional footfall could be heard passing in the street outside. From the distance came the cry of a night watchman making his rounds. *"One o'clock on a fine night and all is well."*

Sebastian said, "Just because he knew Rachel when she called herself Rose and entertained gentlemen in Orchard Street doesn't mean he knew she'd taken refuge at the Magdalene House." He watched his friend move his rook to b3.

"Check," said Gibson, sitting back in his seat and reaching for the brandy bottle. "But it is highly suggestive."

Sebastian crossed his arms at his chest and studied the

board before him. "In the Levant, if a young woman disgraces her family by loose, immoral conduct, the only way the family can regain their honor is to kill her. Some people think it's a Muslim custom, but it's not. All the religions of the area do it—Christians, Jews, Muslims, Druze. It's not religious. It's tribal, and it goes back to prebiblical days when the Jews were just another Semitic tribe wandering the deserts of the Arabian peninsula."

Gibson refilled their glasses and set the brandy bottle aside with a light *thump*. "This isn't the Levant."

"No," said Sebastian, moving his queen to e7. "But Englishmen have also been known to kill unfaithful wives and wayward daughters."

Gibson frowned down at the board. "You think that's why Rachel fled Orchard Street and took refuge at the Magdalene House? Because her father discovered where she was?"

"Her father or her brother. I'd say Cedric Fairchild knew his sister was in Covent Garden."

"But why? That's what doesn't make sense about any of this. How did she end up there in the first place? *A lord's daughter?*"

"That I haven't figured out yet."

Gibson leaned forward suddenly, his two hands coming up together. "She could have had a secret lover. Someone her father considered unsuitable. Rather than marry Ramsey, she fled to her lover, who then abandoned her and left her on the streets. Too ashamed to go home, she was forced into prostitution to survive."

Sebastian sat back in his chair and laughed. "If you ever decide to give up medicine, you could make a fortune writing lurid romances."

"It's possible," insisted Gibson.

"I suppose it is." Sebastian watched his friend move his queen to d5. "The fact remains that however she came to be in Covent Garden, all three men have a motive for killing her. Both Lord Fairchild and Cedric Fairchild might well have wanted her dead for disgracing the family name, while Tristan Ramsey would hardly be the first man to kill a woman who rejected him."

Gibson reached for his brandy glass. "What about the other man you were telling me about? This purchasing agent."

"Luke O'Brian? His motive is roughly the same as Ramsey's. He wanted her enough to try to buy her out of the Academy. According to Kane, she rejected him."

"So he flew into a rage and threatened to kill her? That sounds logical. She fled Orchard Street to get away from him."

"There's just one little detail that doesn't fit with any of these scenarios."

Gibson frowned. "What's that?"

"According to both Joshua Walden and Tasmin Poole, two women fled the Orchard Street Academy last Wednesday night—Rachel, and another Cyprian named Hannah Green." Sebastian made his final move, and smiled. "Checkmate."

Gibson stared at the board. "Bloody hell. Why didn't I see that coming?"

Sebastian raised his head, his attention caught by the sound of a team driven at a fast clip up the street. There was a jingle of harness and the clatter of wheels over uneven cobbles as the carriage was reined in hard before the surgery. An instant later, a fist beat a lively tattoo on the street door.

"What the devil?" Gibson lurched awkwardly upright.

"I'll get it," said Sebastian, grabbing a brace of candles as he headed up the narrow hall.

The pounding came again, accompanied by a man's shouted "Halloooo."

Sebastian jerked back the bolt and yanked open the door. A liveried footman, his tricorner hat askew on his powdered hair, one fist raised to knock again, was caught off balance and practically fell into the hall. Sebastian gazed beyond him to the team of blood bays sidling nervously in the street, their plumed heads shaking. His eyes narrowing, Sebastian was studying the crest emblazoned on the carriage panel when the door was thrust open and an imperious female voice said, "Don't just stand there. Help me."

It took Sebastian a moment to realize she spoke not to him but to a second footman, who now scrambled to let down the carriage steps.

"George," snapped the woman's voice, recalling the first footman. "Come take the man's shoulders while Richard takes his feet. Careful. He's bleeding quite dreadfully."

"Bleeding?" Gibson limped toward the unconscious man the two footmen were easing through the carriage door. "No, don't lay him down in the street! Take him straight into the surgery. This way," said Gibson, hurrying before them.

"Who is he?" asked Sebastian.

"A would-be assassin," said Miss Hero Jarvis, appearing in the open carriage door. A picture in a demure cream silk confection with a high waist and a skirt sodden dark with blood, she held a beaded reticule in one hand and what looked like a carriage pistol in the other. "We left one dead on the road from Richmond, but this one's still living. I'm hoping he'll survive long enough to tell us who hired him."

Sebastian stepped forward to offer her his hand down. "Who shot him?"

She handed him the carriage pistol as if somewhat surprised to find she was still clutching it. It was a double-barreled French flintlock, and he saw that both barrels had been fired.

"I did."

Chapter 27

*S*tripped to the waist, his face ashen in the flickering candlelight, the man lay on a table in the front room of Paul Gibson's surgery. The room was silent except for a trickle of water as Gibson squeezed out a sponge in a pan of bloody water, the tin ringing as he knocked its edge.

"Will he live?" asked Miss Jarvis from where she stood in the doorway.

"I don't know," said Gibson, not looking up. "The bullet shattered the right shoulder blade and nicked a major artery. He's lost a lot of blood."

"I tried to keep pressure on the wound."

Gibson nodded. "It's probably the only reason he's alive as it is."

Sebastian reached for the wounded man's torn and bloody cloak lying amid his hastily discarded shirt, waistcoat, and coat. "Exceptionally fine tailoring for a highwayman."

"He's not a highwayman," said Miss Jarvis, watching him. "He called the man we left dead on the road Drummond. I remember hearing that name the night the Magdalene House was attacked."

Without commenting, Sebastian began going through the injured man's pockets.

"There's a purse with forty guineas, but no identification," said Miss Jarvis. "I already checked."

Sebastian glanced over at her. "Did you check the man you left on the road?"

"No. My mother was hysterical. I took her home even before coming here. I'm afraid her nerves were quite overset by the incident."

Sebastian finished going through the man's pockets. She was right; there was nothing to tell them who he was.

"This one," she said, nodding to the silent man on the table, "was in charge. He spoke well, like a gentleman."

Gibson made a pad of bandages to apply to the man's chest. "He's certainly groomed like a gentleman. Cleanly shaven, hair neatly trimmed, fingernails manicured. Although from the looks of him, I'd say he's spent a fair amount of time in the sun."

Miss Jarvis watched with interest as the surgeon went about his task. "The other man was a rougher sort. He may be a hireling."

"With orders to kill you?"

"That's right." When he kept silent, a faint touch of color darkened her cheekbones. She said crisply, "You don't need to tell me I brought this on myself."

Sebastian tossed aside the assassin's garments and walked up to her. She stood tall and elegant and perfectly composed, despite her blood-drenched gown and the fact that she'd just fought off two assassins and killed a man. She was an incredible woman. He said, "The men who attacked the Magdalene House last Monday killed seven innocent women to get to one because they intended to leave no witnesses. Now they obviously know who you are."

"But I don't know who they are," she said, and for the first time he caught an echo of fear in her voice.

"Whoever they are," said Gibson, tying off his bandages, "they're either incredibly courageous or incredibly foolhardy, to go after the daughter of Lord Jarvis."

Sebastian shook his head. "At this point, I suspect they realize they've no choice."

He watched her glance out the darkened window to where her carriage and footmen awaited. She said, "I must get back to my mother. If he regains consciousness—if he says anything—"

"We'll let you know."

She brought her gaze back to Sebastian's face. "Have you discovered anything yet?"

"Only that you were right. The woman you met at the Magdalene House was in all likelihood Rachel Fairchild."

She nodded. He was only confirming what she'd already suspected. He noticed the way exhaustion had sharpened her features, making her eyes huge in a pale face.

He said, "It's what you wanted to know, isn't it? Who she was. Now you know. You can go back to writing petitions to Parliament, or however you spend your time. Let your father deal with these people. God knows he's capable."

"Have you discovered how Rachel Fairchild came to be there, in Covent Garden?"

"No."

"Then I can't stop." She looked beyond him to Gibson. "You will send the bill for the man's care to me."

"As you wish," said Gibson.

She nodded again, and left.

Gibson stared after her. They could hear the jingle of harness, the clatter of hooves on cobbles as the carriage moved off. "Jesus, Mary, Joseph, and all the saints," he said softly, then went back to work on the mangled man before him.

Thursday, 7 May 1812

The next morning, Sebastian received some interesting intelligence from Jules Calhoun.

"I've learned a wee bit more about your Mr. O'Brian," said Calhoun, putting away Sebastian's razor.

Sebastian finished buttoning his shirt and glanced around. "Oh?"

"Not only is he held in the utmost esteem by the city's tradesmen, but he's trusted implicitly by his clients," said the valet, holding out a crisply laundered cravat. "His commissions are reasonable, he never demands compensation from merchants, and he's a regular contributor to the Orphans' Fund."

Sebastian carefully wound the cravat's folds around his neck. "So how does he afford all the expensive pleasures of life?"

"It's quite simple, actually. He's one of the biggest thieves working the Thames."

Sebastian looked around. "Now that is interesting."

"It's a very clever arrangement, when you think about it," said the valet. "His activities as a procurement agent mean he's constantly down on the docks dealing with shipments and going in and out of warehouses. From what I understand, the man's meticulous—plans his operations to the most exacting detail, then executes them flawlessly. He's really quite brilliant. They say he's been behind every big job on the river in the past five years. His last enterprise cleaned out an entire warehouse full of Russian sables from just off the Ratcliff highway."

Sebastian shrugged into his coat. "Russian sables? Sir William mentioned something about Russian sables. When was this?"

"Monday night," said Calhoun, holding out Sebastian's hat. "Just hours after the attack on the Magdalene House."

Chapter 28

 $\mathcal{L}$ uke O'Brian kept rooms in a well-tended stone house not far from the ancient pitched slate roofs and towering chimneys of St. Katherine's Hospital below the Tower.

A few simple inquiries in the area brought Sebastian to a small eating house squeezed in between a ship's chandler and a biscuit baker, for this was a part of the city that made its living from the docks and the river that linked London with the sea and the world beyond. The eating house was simple but wholesome, the air filled with the smell of sizzling bacon and fresh bread and boisterous conversations rising up from tables filled with ships' officers, customs men, and clerks. Luke O'Brian sat by himself at a small table near the front window. Sebastian nodded to a middle-aged woman with rosy cheeks and an apron tied over her expansive middle, and went to slide into the seat opposite the agent.

"I understand congratulations are in order," said Sebastian, keeping his voice low. "That was quite a successful enterprise you managed to pull off."

O'Brian glanced up from his plate and frowned. "Do I know you?"

"We've met."

O'Brian gave Sebastian a hard look, then grunted.

"So we have. You've lost twenty years and a good two stone in twenty-four hours. Quite a feat."

Sebastian smiled. "It turns out that neither one of us is exactly what we first portrayed ourselves to be. You, for instance, are not just a purchasing agent."

O'Brian carefully cut a piece of bacon. "And I take it you're not really a Bow Street Runner."

"No." Sebastian paused while the apple-cheeked woman bustled up to take his order. "Just tea, please," he told her with a smile. After she'd gone, he brought his gaze back to the agent and said quietly, "Nor am I interested in what happened to a certain warehouse full of Russian sables."

O'Brian chewed slowly, and swallowed. "So what are you interested in?"

"The death of a young woman."

"We went over all that."

"Did we? I've learned a few things since then. For instance, did you know Rose was really Rachel Fairchild, daughter of Basil, Lord Fairchild?"

The man's face gave nothing away. "Who told you that?"

"This," said Sebastian, laying the silver bracelet on the table. "Have you ever seen it?"

O'Brian's fork clattered against the side of his plate. He stared at the bracelet a moment, then lifted his gaze to Sebastian's. "You obviously know it's hers. Where did you get it?"

"From one of the whores at the Academy. It used to belong to Rose?"

"Yes." Picking up the bracelet, O'Brian studied the medallion with its crested helm and three eagle heads. "You say she was a Fairchild?"

"You didn't know?"

"No."

If the man was lying, he was bloody good at it. But

then, of course he was good at it. His life depended upon it. Sebastian said, "I understand Russian sables are very valuable."

O'Brian gave a slow smile. "So they say."

"A man with that much to lose could be dangerous," said Sebastian, "if someone found out about his plans." He paused while the plump-faced woman put his tea on the table before him. O'Brian said nothing.

"If he realized a woman knew what he did for a living, such a man might well intimidate her—bully her— just to keep her quiet. Except, I can see a woman like Rachel—or Rose—getting scared. So scared she ran away. In which case then, she'd really be a threat. A threat that needed to be tracked down and silenced before she ruined everything."

O'Brian tore off a piece of bread and used it to wipe up the egg yolk on his plate. "A man doesn't stay in this business long if he doesn't learn to keep his mouth shut. I'm not that careless." He popped the bread in his mouth, chewed, and swallowed. "If I was, I'd be in Botany Bay. Or dead."

"Mistakes happen."

"Not if you're careful. I'm very careful. I'm also not a violent man. Ask around the docks; anyone will tell you. Sure, I have a temper. My father was Irish, after all." He leaned forward. "But a body'd have to be sick to kill all those women."

"Or very afraid."

O'Brian met Sebastian's gaze, and held it. "There's nothing I'm that afraid of."

Sebastian took a long sip of his tea. "Kane tells me you wanted to buy Rose out of the house, but she refused."

"He said that?"

"Are you saying it's not true?"

"Are you kidding? Of course she was willing. She hated Kane, and she hated that house."

"Do you think that's why she ran away? Because of Kane?"

"What would be the sense in that? I was getting her out of there." O'Brian leaned his elbows on the table, his linked hands coming up to tap against his chin. "The only thing I can figure is something must have happened. Something that scared her. She just bolted."

"So why didn't she bolt to you?"

"Maybe she figured she'd be too easy to trace." A wry smile tightened the flesh beside his eyes. "Didn't take you long to find me, now did it?"

Sebastian studied the agent's dark, handsome face. "Ian Kane says her departure meant nothing to him. That she was easily replaced."

O'Brian huffed a humorless laugh. "What do you think? I was about to pay him two hundred pounds for her." He leaned forward. He was no longer smiling. "It sets a bad example for the other girls, now doesn't it? Her taking off like that. I don't know what he told you. But the truth is, he was livid when he found out she'd run away. Said if he ever got his hands on her again, he'd kill her."

Chapter 29

Ian Kane sat on a folding stool amidst the tumbledown tombs and overgrown headstones of the churchyard of Allhallows Barking, a paintbrush in one hand, a flat palette smeared with paint in the other. Balanced on the easel before him stood the canvas on which the north face of the church was beginning to emerge in a glory of sun-washed golds and blues and reds. Sebastian squinted up at the billowing clouds building overhead and said, "You're about to lose your sun."

"This is England," said Kane, his gaze on the church before him. "I always lose my sun."

Sebastian watched the brothel owner load his paintbrush with gold. "I'd have thought a gloomy day more suited to your subject."

"You would," said Kane.

Sebastian gave a sharp laugh. The church was a curious blend of styles and materials, the massive round pillars and Gothic arches of the west end dating back to the thirteenth century, while the eastern end was much more recent, with a brick steeple that had been added only a hundred fifty years before.

"I was eight when I started in the mines," said Kane, squinting at the point where the church's old staircase turret wound toward a roof badly in need of replacement. "I was lucky. Most lads go down when they're only six—some as young as four. I was a pony boy. Did you know that they keep those poor beasts down in the mines until they die? Their hooves turn green. It's unnatural, stabling horses a mile underground so they never see the sun." He added a fleck of light to the painted turret on the canvas. "I like the sun."

The air filled with a gentle cooing from the pigeons roosting on the steeple. Kane painted for a few moments, then said, "What brings you sniffing around me again?"

Sebastian leaned against the edge of a nearby lichen-covered tomb. "I found Luke O'Brian."

"That didn't take long. Did he confess to the murders?"

"No. But he provided me with some interesting information. He says Rose Fletcher was more than happy to let him buy her out of your house."

Kane added a touch of blue to a clerestory window. "I don't buy and sell women. You make me sound like some bloody Yank."

Sebastian crossed his arms at his chest and leaned back. "Right. You were simply going to let O'Brian pay the woman's debts—with a handsome commission for you, of course."

"It's the English way, isn't it—commissions?"

"He also said you weren't as sanguine as you would have me believe about her precipitous departure. He says you were furious that she'd left. Furious enough to threaten to kill her if you found her."

Kane shrugged. "It's an easy thing to say, isn't it? *I'd like to kill him.* Or, *I could kill her.* People say it all the time. Not many follow through on it."

"Some do."

"I had no reason to kill her. Rose was a good source of revenue but she wasn't irreplaceable. What good would killing her do me?"

Sebastian said, "She was about to be sold—excuse me, *released*—to O'Brian. So why would she run?"

"You tell me."

"Maybe she saw something she wasn't supposed to see."

Kane threw him a sideways glance. "What are you imagining? Murder? Treason? Satanic rituals?"

Sebastian met his gaze and held it. "I hadn't thought about the satanic rituals."

Kane swung back to his painting. After a moment, he said, "A gentleman came to the house a couple of weeks ago. He was quite surprised to find Rose at the Academy. Only, he didn't call her Rose. He called her 'Rachel.' "

"A gentleman?"

"Most definitely a gentleman. Not a scrambling functionary or schoolteacher or vicar, but a real gentleman." Kane gave him a mean smile. "Like you. Only smaller, thinner. Reddish brown hair. Good-looking enough, I suppose, but he had a weak chin."

The church bells began to peal, startling the pigeons roosting on the tower so that they flew up, their wings beating the air with a soft whirling sound quickly lost amid the distant rattle of harness and the crunch of iron-bound wheels over cobbles, and the cry of a chimney sweep's boy shouting, " 'Weep, 'weep."

"Sound like anyone you know?" said Kane, one eyebrow raised in mocking inquiry. He waited a beat, then added, "My lord Devlin?"

Sebastian studied the clouds building overhead. "You had me followed," he said.

Kane squinted up at the sky. "There goes the sun."

"How's your man's arm?" Sebastian pushed away from the tomb as Kane flipped open a leather-bound wooden box littered with paint-stained bottles and old rags at his feet. "An injury like that can incapacitate a man for a spell."

"I heard you'd tangled with a cadger near the docks yesterday," said Kane, thrusting his palette and brushes into the box. "I don't know who the fellow was." He closed the lid on the box and snapped the fastenings before straightening. "But I do know this: It wasn't one of my lads."

"Now why should I believe you?" said Sebastian.

"Believe me or not, as you choose. But your questions are obviously making someone uneasy." Kane smiled and reached for his easel. In the pale light, the blue scar left across his forehead by his early years in the coal mines looked even darker. "Uneasy enough to want to kill you."

In his surgery near Tower Hill, Paul Gibson shifted on the hard wooden seat of his chair, his head tipped to one side as he listened to the wounded man's ragged breathing. Hero Jarvis's assailant had passed a restless night drifting in and out of consciousness. Once, he had startled awake, his gray eyes open wide, his lips parting as if on a gasp. Gibson had leaned forward to say softly, "What's your name?" But the man had only closed his eyes and turned his head away.

Pushing to his feet, Gibson left the man's bedside and limped down the hall. The stump of his left leg was aching badly, giving him a slow, awkward gait. He answered a call of nature, then splashed water on his face and roughly toweled it dry. He was pouring himself a morning ale when he thought he heard a step in the hall.

"Anyone there?" he called.

The stillness of the surgery stretched out around him, raising a sudden, inexplicable length of gooseflesh on his arms.

"Who's there?" he called again, setting aside the ale.

He lurched toward the front room, torn between surging alarm and a feeling of profound foolishness.

From the street outside came the shuffling hoofbeats of a passing horse and the voice of a hawker crying, " 'Ere I am with me rabbits hangin' from me pole. Who'll buy me rabbits?"

At the doorway, Gibson hesitated. The wounded man appeared to be sleeping peacefully, the sheet pulled up over his chest. It wasn't until Gibson limped over to the bedside that he saw the man's eyes staring wide-open and sightless. Gibson put out one hand, touching the man's slack jaw and watching the head loll.

Someone had broken his neck.

Chapter 30

*P*arting from Ian Kane outside the churchyard of Allhallows Barking, Sebastian went in search of Rachel Fairchild's onetime betrothed, Tristan Ramsey.

He found him drinking Blue Ruin with Lord Alvin and Mr. Peter Dimsey at the Thatched House Tavern in St. James's. Walking up behind Ramsey's chair, Sebastian laid a heavy hand on the younger man's shoulder. "We have something to discuss," said Sebastian, fixing his gaze on the other two men in a way that made both gentlemen shift uncomfortably in their seats. "You gentlemen will excuse us?"

Ramsey froze. "My friends and I are having a drink," he said with a nervous laugh. "Surely this can wait?"

Sebastian kept his hand on Ramsey's shoulder. "I think not."

Ramsey's gaze went from Sebastian to his friends. If he was hoping for any succor from either Alvin or Dimsey, he misjudged his friends. Both gentlemen had suddenly become wholly absorbed in the study of their drinks. "Perhaps for a moment," he said, and thrust back his chair.

They pushed through the crowded tavern to a narrow passage that led to a door opening onto a cobbled lane at the rear. Ramsey closed the door behind him with a snap and said, "Now see here, Devlin—"

Moving calmly and deliberately, Sebastian whacked the back of his gloved hand across the man's face. He was in no mood for any more of Ramsey's bluster and lies.

A different kind of man might have called Sebastian out for such an offense. Not Ramsey. "Bloody hell!" Both hands cupped protectively over his nose, he doubled over as if he'd been gut-punched. "You've drawn my cork."

Picking up the man by his lapels, Sebastian slung Ramsey back against the brick wall behind him. "We're going to have a conversation. Only, this time, you're going to be very careful not to lie to me."

"What? What the hell is wrong with you? I didn't lie to you!"

"You did. You knew Rachel Fairchild was in Covent Garden. More than that—you knew exactly which house she was in."

A tiny trickle of blood ran from Ramsey's left nostril. "What? I don't know what you're talking about. I—"

"You went there." Sebastian grabbed the man's shoulders and thumped his back against the wall again. "You like paying for it, do you, Ramsey? You like it when women have to do exactly what you tell them to do? When they moan on cue whether you're really bringing them pleasure or not? Must have been quite a shock to find your own fiancée lined up there with all the other soiled doves offering her charms to any man with the money to pay for them."

"Why you—" Ramsey bucked against Sebastian's hold, his lips twisting with rage.

"What I don't understand is how the hell you walked away and left her there."

"I tried to get her to leave!" said Ramsey, his breath blowing bloody bubbles out his nostril. "She wouldn't come with me. I had to pay for her just to talk to her!

She took me upstairs to one of those awful rooms." His upper lip curled at the memory. "The bed reeked of stale sweat and sex. *She* reeked of sex—of men. I begged her to come with me. But she just stood there listening to me with her arms crossed and a bored look on her face. Then she said I only had three minutes left, so if I wanted to fuck her, then I'd better hurry up and do it."

Sebastian studied the younger man's trembling chin as full understanding dawned on a tide of rage and revulsion. "And so you did, didn't you?" Sebastian let Ramsey go and took a step back before the urge to plant the bastard a facer grew overwhelming. "Mother of God. What manner of man are you?"

Ramsey wiped his sleeve across his bloody upper lip. "You don't understand. She *taunted* me. She wanted it!"

"Is that what you told yourself? So you—what? Fucked her there? In the upstairs room of a Covent Garden brothel? *And then you just left her?*"

"What else was I supposed to do?"

"You could have told her father where she was."

"Lord Fairchild?" Ramsey looked appalled. "You think I wanted to kill him? The man has a weak heart."

Sebastian studied Ramsey's blood-smeared features. "Did you find out how Rachel ended up in Covent Garden?"

"No."

"You did ask, didn't you?"

"Of course I asked!"

"And she told you nothing? Nothing at all?"

"She told me to go away and leave her alone."

"Did you ever go back there?"

Revulsion spread across the man's face. "Good God, what do you think I am?"

"You don't want to know." Sebastian stooped to

scoop up Ramsey's hat from the cobbles, where it had been knocked in the scuffle. "Here," he said, slamming it against the man's chest.

Ramsey's hands jerked up to close on the hat's brim. "Anyone would have done the same in my place," he said, clutching the hat to his chest.

Sebastian studied the man's heightened color and shifting, restless gaze. "You didn't try to talk her into leaving with you," said Sebastian, suddenly knowing it for the truth. "Oh, I've no doubt you ranted at her. Demanded to know why she'd left you and how she could have done such a thing to you. But you didn't try to talk her into leaving. After all, what if she had said *yes*? What would you have done with her then? Taken her to wife?"

Ramsey's head snapped back. "You say that as if you would have done any differently. What man would have wanted her after that? She was a whore!"

He must have seen something flare in Sebastian's eyes, because he took a hasty step back. "All right," said Ramsey, breathing heavily enough to shudder his chest. "It's true. I didn't beg her to leave with me. But it isn't as if she asked me to take her away from there."

"And that surprises you?"

Ramsey raked the back of one hand across his upper lip. The bleeding was stopping now. "You don't know the way she treated me. The way she just stood there swearing at me, talking to me like a—" He broke off.

"Like?" prompted Sebastian.

Ramsey sniffed and shook his head.

"When was this?" Sebastian demanded.

"Two weeks ago." Ramsey sniffed again. "Something like that. I don't remember for certain."

"Two weeks ago? And you did nothing?"

Ramsey carefully set his hat on his head. The crown

was dented, giving him a rakish air. "I said I didn't tell Lord Fairchild. That doesn't mean I did nothing."

"You astound me," said Sebastian. "What did you do?"

Ramsey twitched his lapels and adjusted his cuffs. "I told her brother."

Chapter 31

Sebastian sat for a time on the terrace of the gardens overlooking Whitehall Stairs. The patches of blue sky and intermittent sunshine of that morning had vanished behind thickening piles of gray clouds that shaded to black in the distance. The river flowed dark and choppy before him, whipped by the wind into white-flecked waves. A wherryman halfway across the Thames worked his oars with a strong, steady rhythm, the plash of his paddles hitting the water carrying clearly in the strengthening breeze.

Sebastian kept remembering the expression on Cedric Fairchild's face when first told of his sister's death in Covent Garden. The shock of denial had been all too readily apparent—that natural human tendency to disconnect when first confronted with the death of a loved one, the wailing mental *No!* that is common to all. Yet Fairchild had displayed neither disbelief nor confusion when told of his sister's presence in Covent Garden. That brief bristling at the mention of the Magdalene House had all been for effect, because Cedric Fairchild had known only too well what his sister had become.

Tristan Ramsey had told him.

Sebastian slid off the low wall, his gaze lifting to the dark thunderclouds churning overhead. He understood why Cedric would attempt to keep the truth of his sister's disgrace to himself, even after her death. What he couldn't understand was why Rachel's brother, like her betrothed before her, had simply walked away and abandoned her to her fate.

Rachel's brother was cupping wafers at Menton's, his right arm extended, steady and true, when Sebastian walked up to him. "One would think you'd have had all the target practice you needed in Spain," said Sebastian when Cedric Fairchild turned away from the firing range.

"It doesn't hurt to keep one's hand in," said Cedric. He had stripped down to his shirtsleeves and waistcoat to shoot. Now, handing his pistol to the attendant, he reached for his dark blue coat.

"You sold out and came back to London because of Rachel, didn't you?" said Sebastian, watching the former lieutenant shrug into his coat. "Who told you she was missing? Ramsey?"

Cedric straightened his collar, his eyes narrowing. "Actually, it was our sister Lady Sewell." A sudden burst of laughter from a group of men entering the room brought his head around.

"Walk with me," said Sebastian.

Buffeted by a cool wind, they strolled up the Mall toward Cockspur Street, with the rolling green swath of St. James's Park stretching away to their right behind Carlton House and its gardens. "There used to be a leper hospital there," said Cedric, looking across the park toward the river. "Did you know? It was a pretty insalubrious place at the time, all swamps and marshland. They say a fair number of lepers from the hospital are still buried there. Every now and then the royal gardeners dig up some poor bastard's skull or thighbone."

Sebastian stared out across the carefully tended

greens and clipped hedges of the gardens and the park beyond it. Beneath the cloudy afternoon sky, the park had assumed a cold, somber aspect.

"They were outcasts," said Cedric. "Shunned even by their families. Some were tradesmen, peasants, and laborers. But there were also noblemen, scholars . . . artists. It didn't matter. What they had been was superseded by what they'd become. Something diseased and rotting. A threat to society."

Sebastian shifted his gaze to the man beside him. "Is that how you thought of your sister?"

Cedric let out his breath in a harsh grating sound. "No. But it's how she thought of herself."

"You went to see her after Tristan Ramsey told you where he'd found her?"

Cedric's face was ashen. "I tried to get her to come away with me." His lips flattened. "She refused." Tristan Ramsey had said much the same thing; but in Cedric's case, Sebastian was inclined to believe it was true. "She said she was where she belonged. That house—" He broke off, swallowed. "It was horrible seeing her there."

"Did she tell you why she ran away?"

Cedric shook his head. "I asked. She refused to say."

They turned their steps toward Charing Cross and Northumberland House and Gardens beyond it. "I still don't understand how she ended up there," said Cedric. He threw a sideways glance at Sebastian, pale features suddenly flushing dark with anger. "But I swear to God, if you breathe a word of this to anyone, I'll kill you."

Sebastian said, "Do you think it's possible she was in love with another man? I mean someone other than Ramsey. Someone who lured her away from home, then abandoned her?"

Cedric thrust his hands into the pockets of his coat, his shoulders hunched. "I admit I thought it possible. When I pressed her to leave with me, she just threw back her head and laughed. She said she was in love with that Lincolnshire fellow. The one who owns the house."

Sebastian cast Cedric a sharp sideways glance. "You believed her?"

He shook his head. "She didn't look like a woman in love to me. If anything, I'd say she was afraid."

"Of Kane?"

"I think she was afraid he'd kill her if she tried to leave. She said he'd killed before—other women who had tried to leave him. I told her she was being irrational. That we could protect her from the likes of some Covent Garden thug." He paused. "She just told me to go away and not come back."

"And so you did?"

"What else could I do? She refused to talk to me anymore. When I went back last Saturday, they told me she was no longer there." He brought up both hands to scrub them across his face, his shoulders hunched. "I thought they were lying—that she just didn't want to see me again. But a part of me was terrified something must have happened to her."

"What made you think that?"

Cedric knotted the fingers of his hands together, as if he were in prayer. "I don't know. It was just a feeling I had." He hesitated. "I remember this one time in Spain, just before Ciudad Rodrigo. A fellow by the name of Hobbs took out a patrol. They were late coming back. We'd had one of those bloody awful rains that can come up out of nowhere in the Peninsula. Everyone was convinced they'd just used the storm as an excuse to spend the afternoon in a bodega somewhere."

"But you didn't think so?"

"No." Cedric stared off across the gardens. "They'd been ambushed. We found them not two miles outside camp. They'd been set upon by peasants with pitchforks and scythes." His face contorted with the memory. "They were literally ripped apart."

Both men were silent for a moment, lost in visions of the past, of men bloodied and torn by cannon fire and bayonets as well as by pitchforks and scythes. Sebastian said, "Did you tell Lord Fairchild that you'd found your sister?"

Cedric let out a sound that was like a laugh, only devoid of all humor. "My father?" He shook his head. "My father isn't well. It would kill him, if he knew what had happened to Rachel."

"Sometimes not knowing is worse than knowing."

"Not this time."

Chapter 32

*H*ero gently closed the door to her mother's room and paused in the hall for a moment, her hand still on the knob, a weight of sadness pressing down on her. Lady Jarvis had reacted badly to last night's incident. Sometimes she worked herself up into such a state that it lasted for weeks.

Her hand slipping off the knob, Hero was just turning away when her father came up to her. "How is your mother?" he asked. There was neither warmth nor caring in the question.

"Resting. Dr. Ross has dosed her liberally with laudanum. She should sleep the rest of the day."

Lord Jarvis's lips thinned into the pained expression he inevitably assumed whenever the topic under discussion was his wife. "That's a relief." His eyes narrowed as he studied Hero's face. "You're certain you're all right?"

"Thanks to you teaching me to keep a steady finger on the trigger."

Father and daughter shared a private smile. His smile faded quickly. "I've dismissed the two footmen you and your mother had with you last night."

"It wasn't their fault."

"Of course it was their fault," said Lord Jarvis. "I

didn't send you into the country with three armed men to have you come back covered in some highwayman's gore."

Hero opened her mouth, then shut it.

"Coachman John tells me you took the injured highwayman to Paul Gibson's surgery near Tower Hill. Why?"

"I doubted the practitioners of Harley Street would appreciate the delivery of a bloody highwayman at midnight. And if I'd simply taken him to Bow Street, he'd have died."

"The man still lives?"

"Last I heard, yes."

"Good. Then he can be made to talk."

Hero felt a chill prickle down her spine. She'd heard dark rumors of the methods employed by Lord Jarvis's henchmen to make people talk. "Papa—"

Jarvis raised his hand, stopping her. "These men are connected to what happened last Monday, aren't they?"

"It would seem so, yes."

He was so good at hiding his thoughts and feelings that even Hero often had a difficult time reading him. She was both shocked and touched when he suddenly said, "I'm concerned about you, Hero. You're all I have left."

"I'll be careful," she promised. Reaching up, she brushed her father's cheek with a kiss and turned toward the stairs.

But she was aware of him still standing in the hall, watching her.

Jarvis was in the small chamber he reserved for mixing snuff when his butler ushered Colonel Epson-Smith into the room.

"You wanted to see me, my lord?" asked the Colonel.

"What I want is to see this unpleasantness brought to

an end. Quickly." Jarvis added a pinch of macouba to his mortar and began to grind it with a pestle. "You've had two days. What have you learned?"

Epson-Smith stood in the center of the room, his legs braced wide, his hands clasped behind his back. "Indications so far are that we're dealing with a simple tussle over merchandise. It's not clear yet precisely who is involved, but we're working on it."

Jarvis grunted. "Work faster." Reaching for a small vial, he added three drops to his mixture. "You've heard of last night's incident?"

"Yes, my lord. I'm not convinced, however, that it's related to Monday night's—"

"It is. The surviving individual is at a surgery near Tower Hill. Use whatever means necessary, but make him talk."

"Yes, my lord."

Jarvis looked up from shaking his mixture out over the sheet of parchment that he'd spread across the room's table. "I also want one of your men watching over Miss Jarvis from now on. Discreetly, of course."

The Colonel kept his face perfectly composed. If he'd learned yet of Hero's presence at the Magdalene House the night of the attack, he had more sense than to mention it. He bowed, said, "Yes, my lord," and withdrew.

Chapter 33

Sebastian arrived at Paul Gibson's surgery near the Tower to find Miss Jarvis's town carriage drawn up in the street outside. The wind had turned cold, the team of matched off-white horses shifting restlessly in their traces, tails flicking away an endless buzz of flies.

Tom studied the elegant equipage through narrowed eyes. "That's 'er, ain't it? The gentry mort what fooled me into leavin' the chestnuts."

Sebastian handed him the reins. "I'd advise you to get over it, Tom. Miss Jarvis is like her father: brilliant and deadly. You don't want to tangle with her."

But Tom simply thrust out his lower lip in a mulish scowl and stared straight ahead.

Sebastian jumped down from the curricle and was halfway across the footpath when the door to the surgery was yanked open. "Oh. It's you," said Miss Jarvis, standing on the threshold, a formidable presence in a burgundy driving gown and matching velvet hat.

Sebastian paused in midstride. "Whom were you expecting?"

"The constables." She stepped back to allow him to enter. "Dr. Gibson sent for them shortly before I arrived."

"Is he all right?"

"No. He's dead."

Sebastian knew a curious sensation, as if the blood had suddenly drained away from his head. It was only the appearance of Paul Gibson himself at the entrance to his front room that brought the blood pounding back to Sebastian's temples when he realized she had spoken not of his friend but of her assailant from the night before.

"I'm sorry," said Gibson, drying his hands on a rough towel. "I was with him all night. I just stepped into the back to wash my face and grab something to eat. I couldn't have been gone five minutes."

"It's not your fault," said Sebastian, glancing at the silent, shrouded form on the bed. "He was gravely wounded."

"True. But it wasn't his wound that killed him." Gibson went to flip back the sheet covering the dead man's face and shoulders. "Someone came in here and broke his neck."

Sebastian stared down at the dead man's pale features. "Bloody hell. Did he ever say anything?"

"Nothing of any significance. He was delirious. In and out of consciousness. I couldn't even get him to tell me his name."

"Bloody hell," said Sebastian again, only softly this time, for he'd remembered Miss Jarvis's presence.

She said, "Your arrival here is fortuitous."

He looked around to find her still standing in the narrow hallway. "How is that, Miss Jarvis?"

She retied the fluttering burgundy velvet ribbons of her hat with crisp, no-nonsense movements. The woman had been born without an ounce of coquetry or flirtation, Sebastian thought, just intellect and lethal purposefulness. She said, "I've arranged to meet the Cyprian from the Orchard Street Academy, Tasmin Poole, at Billingsgate this morning. It is my hope that she might have discovered something else of interest."

"Billingsgate? Why Billingsgate?"

She raised one eyebrow in a gesture so reminiscent of Lord Jarvis himself that Sebastian felt a chill. "You think Berkeley Square would have been more appropriate?"

Paul Gibson made a strangling noise in his throat and turned away.

She looked Sebastian square in the eye and said, "It occurs to me that you may have questions you'd like to ask her yourself."

Sebastian met Miss Jarvis's frank gaze and saw there a faint hint of mockery lightly tinged with resentment. She obviously knew full well he was not telling her all the sordid details he was learning of Rachel Fairchild's life, and so she'd decided to listen to the questions he asked Tasmin Poole and learn from them.

He smiled. "I have indeed, Miss Jarvis."

"Good." She turned toward the door. "We'll take your curricle." To her maid she said, "Jenna, you will await me in the carriage."

The maid's eyes widened, but she simply dropped a meek courtesy. "Yes, miss."

Gibson let out a half-smothered laugh he turned into an improbable cough. Sebastian said softly to his friend, "If I should disappear, you'll know where to tell them to search for my body," and followed Lord Jarvis's daughter out into the blustery afternoon.

"There's a reason we're taking my curricle," said Sebastian, helping Miss Jarvis up into his carriage's high seat. "Care to tell me what it is?"

"You are very perceptive, aren't you?" she said, arranging her burgundy skirts around her.

Ignoring Tom's fierce scowl, Sebastian hopped up beside her and gathered the reins. "I do occasionally have these rare moments of blinding insight."

A smile played about her lips. She opened her parasol.

He said, "There's no sun."

"It's there. It's just behind the clouds."

He hesitated a moment, his gaze on her aquiline profile, then gave his horses the office to start. "It's your father, isn't it?" he said when it was obvious she had no intention of answering his question. "Someone has tried to kill you twice in the past week, and so Lord Jarvis has set one of his men to watching you."

She turned her head to look at him. "How did you know?"

"I know Lord Jarvis." Sebastian deliberately swung his horses away from Billingsgate and the river. Over his shoulder, he said to Tom, "Anyone following us?"

"Aye. There's a cove on a neat bay."

"Can you lose him?" she asked.

"Probably," said Sebastian. "Where precisely in Billingsgate are we going?"

"St. Magnus."

Sebastian gave a sharp laugh. "No wonder you wished for me to accompany you." The church was on the edge of the rough-and-tumble fish market that had made Billingsgate famous. It wouldn't be as boisterous now as, say, at five o'clock on a Friday morning, but it was hardly the place for a lady. He glanced down at her fine burgundy skirt. "People generally wear their oldest clothes to Billingsgate."

"Then we're both overdressed, aren't we?" She threw a quick glance over her shoulder. "How do you intend to lose him?"

Sebastian kept his attention on his horses. "Ever visit St. Olave's in Seething Lane?"

"St. Olave's?" she repeated, not understanding.

"The wife of Samuel Pepys is buried there. I think," said Sebastian, guiding his horses between the vast warehouses of the East India Company, "that you've just been seized with an overwhelming desire to visit it."

The church and its neglected churchyard lay in the shadow of one East India Company warehouse and across the street from another. Sebastian drew up outside a gate adorned with five skulls.

"Cheerful," said Miss Jarvis, eyeing the ancient, moss-covered gateway.

"More cheerful now than when Pepys described it overflowing with the high graves of hundreds of new plague victims." He handed the reins to Tom. "There's a cold wind blowing, so you'd best walk them. But don't go far."

"Aye, gov'nor."

Sebastian helped Miss Jarvis to alight, and noticed approvingly that she was careful not to let her gaze stray toward the dark-haired man reining in his bay at the end of the lane.

"Now what?" she asked, walking beside him into the churchyard.

"I will discourse at length on windows and corbels and the quaint gallery that once adorned the south side of the church, and you will look fascinated."

"I'll try."

They took a tour of the overgrown graveyard with its broken, lichen-covered tombstones and leaning iron picket fence, then entered the church through a squeaky transept door. Miss Jarvis admired the organ gallery, and the altar tomb of some obscure Elizabethan knight named Sir John Radcliffe, who lay recumbent with his dutiful wife kneeling beside him for all time.

"I wonder where she is buried," said Miss Jarvis, eyeing that devoted spouse. "Sir John seems to have forgotten to provide for her."

"Perhaps she remarried some gallant courtier who didn't expect her to spend the rest of eternity praying on her knees."

Miss Jarvis fixed her gaze upon him. "I'm impressed with your knowledge of London's obscure churches, but I must confess to a certain amount of confusion. What precisely have we accomplished by coming in here?"

"That depends upon how close a watch your shadow was ordered to keep."

The sound of the church door opening echoed through the nave. A gust of wind entered the church, stirring up the scent of old incense and dank stones and long-dead knights.

Miss Jarvis's watchdog entered the church with his hat in his hands, his head turned away as he affected an intense study of the church's peculiar flat-topped windows. Sebastian touched Miss Jarvis's elbow, glanced toward the door, and whispered, "Quickly."

Side by side, they strode through the porch and down the church's ancient, worn stone steps. The watchdog had left the reins of his horse looped over the iron railing of the churchyard. Walking up to the bay, Sebastian reached down and slipped his knife from the sheath in his boot.

"Good heavens," said Miss Jarvis, watching him.

Throwing back the stirrup leather, Sebastian calmly sliced through the bay's cinch as the horse nickered softly and swung its head to nose at Miss Jarvis's reticule.

A shout arose from the church porch. "Bloody 'ell! What the bloody 'ell ye think yer doin'?"

"I don't like being followed," said Sebastian as Tom drew the curricle in beside them.

"Bloody 'ell," said the shadow again, hopping from one foot to the other, his face a study of anger and chagrin mingling now with a touch of consternation.

Sebastian handed Miss Jarvis into the curricle and

scrambled up behind her. "Your father will hear of this," he warned her, giving his horses the office to start.

The chestnuts sprang forward. Miss Jarvis unfurled her parasol and held it aloft. "I can deal with my father."

Sebastian steadied his horses. He was beginning to acquire a measure of sympathy for the King's powerful cousin.

Chapter 34

Sebastian smelled the fish market long before he could see it. As they neared the steps, an increasingly sharp odor like seaweed filled the damp air, the cries of gulls mingling with a buzz of raucous voices and the shouts of white-aproned salesmen standing on their tables and roaring their prices.

"There she is," said Miss Jarvis, nodding to the long-necked Jamaican, who stood on the footpath. With the fingers of one hand, the Cyprian clutched together a drab cloak she wore to cover her Covent Garden finery. She glanced around nervously, her brown eyes open wide enough to show a rim of the dusky-blue whites surrounding her irises.

"Walk 'em," said Sebastian, handing the reins to Tom.

The tiger threw Miss Jarvis a malevolent glare. "Aye, gov'nor."

"Was he really a pickpocket?" asked Miss Jarvis, accepting Sebastian's arm to cross the raucous width of Lower Thames Street.

"It was either that or starve," said Sebastian.

She released his arm the instant they reached the far footpath. "It's a curious conceit," she said, "hiring a pickpocket as your tiger."

"Tom's good with horses." The boy had also saved Sebastian's life, but he saw no reason to add that.

"I didn't think ye was gonna come," said Tasmin Poole as Hero walked up to her. Since the last time Sebastian had seen the Cyprian, someone had obviously worked her over with his fists, leaving her with a discolored cheek and a split lip. She threw a narrowed glance at Sebastian. "What's he doin' here?"

"He is also interested in what happened to Rose."

The Cyprian sniffed and held out her hand, palm up, fingers crooked. "You said you'd give me five pounds, just for showing up here."

"With the promise of more," said Miss Jarvis, passing the woman a small cloth purse, "if you can provide me with the information I seek."

The purse disappeared quickly amidst the woman's clothes. Most whores cleared little or nothing from the long lines of customers they labored every night to service. These were earnings the girl wouldn't need to share with her keepers. Precious indeed.

Miss Jarvis said, "Have you learned anything more about Hannah Green?"

"People are lookin' at us queer," said Tasmin, turning toward the fish market. "We need t' keep moving."

Miss Jarvis plunged after her into a malodorous crowd of men in shiny corduroy jackets and greasy caps. A woman with the limp tails of codfish dangling from her apron brushed past with a sibilant hiss, her elbows clearing a path as she went. A porter bent nearly double beneath a huge dripping hamper that had soaked the shoulders and back of his canvas coat barked, "Move on, there! Move on."

Miss Jarvis whisked her skirts out of the way and kept going. "*Have* you learned more about Hannah Green?"

Tasmin Poole said, "I got one or two ideas about where she might be, but I ain't had time t'go there yet."

"Where?" asked Sebastian.

The woman glanced over at him. "If I tell you and you find her, then she"—here Tasmin jerked her head toward Miss Jarvis—"won't give me my money."

Miss Jarvis said, "You'll be paid for any information that enables us to find Hannah Green. I've told you that."

Tasmin Poole stared out at the tangled rigging of the oyster boats moored along the wharf, each with its own black signboard and milling crowd of men and women massed around a white-aproned salesman. She bit her lip, obviously weighing the odds of being given a chance to track down the missing Hannah Green herself against the risk of divulging her information here and now. At last she said, "Hannah used t'work the Haymarket before she come to the Academy. She might have bolted back there."

Sebastian said, "I've been told Rose was in love with Ian Kane. Is that true?"

Tasmin Poole's laugh was a melodious peal of merriment that brought to mind palm trees swaying in a soft tropical breeze. "That's rich, all right."

Miss Jarvis cast Sebastian a sharp look. He knew it was only with effort that she kept from demanding, *And who is Ian Kane?*

To Tasmin, Sebastian said, "I take it Rose wasn't particularly fond of Mr. Kane?"

"She despised him," said Tasmin Poole. She'd caught the eye of a red-capped fisherman in a striped jersey sitting on the side of his boat and smoking a clay pipe. The fisherman smiled, and Tasmin smiled back.

Sebastian said, "For any particular reason?"

Tasmin brought her gaze back to Sebastian's face. "You mean, apart from the fact Kane's a mean son of a bitch? Yeah. He's hard on all his girls, but he was hardest of all on Rose. It was like he was tryin' t'break her. Never did, though."

"She was afraid of him?" said Miss Jarvis.

Tasmin threw her a scornful look. "We're all afraid of him. But Rose—" She broke off.

"Yes?" prompted Miss Jarvis.

"Rose was afraid of someone else. She come to the Academy afraid."

"Any idea who she was afraid of?" asked Sebastian.

The Jamaican twitched one thin shoulder. "She never was one to talk t'the rest of us." She tipped her head to one side, her gaze thoughtful as she glanced from Miss Jarvis to Sebastian, then back. "You keep talking about Rose and Hannah, but you never ask nothin' about Hessy."

Sebastian sidestepped a barrel piled high with black oyster sacks. "Who?"

"Hessy Abrahams. She was another girl at the house. She left the same night as the other two."

"Why didn't you tell me about her before?" said Miss Jarvis, sounding ever so slightly aggrieved.

Again that faint twitch of the shoulder. "I didn't think you was interested. You only asked about Rose and Hannah."

"You're certain this Hessy Abrahams left with the other two women?" asked Sebastian.

"Well, she sure ain't been seen since."

For one startled moment, Sebastian's gaze met Miss Jarvis's. The air filled with the cries of the fish salesmen shouting, "Ha-a-ndsome cod! All alive! Alive! Alive, oh!" and "Here! This way for a splendid skate."

Tasmin Poole's fingers crept up to touch her split lip. Then she must have realized what she was doing, because her hand fluttered away and she stared off across the shed with its piles of reddish brown shrimp and white-bellied turbots gleaming like mother-of-pearl in the gloom.

"Looks like someone worked you over pretty good," said Sebastian.

The Cyprian's palm cupped her bruised cheek, her lip curling. "Bloody magistrate."

"Sir William?" said Sebastian.

She lifted her brown gaze to his. "That's right." She spit the words out contemptuously. "He likes it rough. Sometimes he gets carried away. This is nothin'. You should've seen what he did t' Sarah once. Broke two of her ribs. She couldn't work for near a month."

"Did he come to the house last week?" Sebastian asked suddenly.

"Maybe. I don't know," said the Jamaican warily.

"Which night?"

"I tell you, I don't know." Suddenly frightened, she gripped the folds of her cloak more tightly around her. "I need t'be gettin' back." She threw an avaricious glance at Miss Jarvis. "You find Hannah Green in Haymarket, I get my money." It wasn't a question.

Miss Jarvis said, "Just tell me where to meet you, and when."

"I'll contact you."

"You don't know who I am."

The Cyprian laughed. "I know who you are," she said, and slipped away through the crowd gathered around an oak-sided Dutch eel boat.

Sebastian stared down at the pierced, coffin-shaped barges floating at the eel boat's stern. He'd never liked eels, ever since he'd watched as a boy when the half-eaten body of a drowned wherryman was pulled from the river, a dozen long black eels sliding sinuously away from it.

Miss Jarvis said, "You've heard of this Sir William before. Who is he?"

Sebastian swung his head to look at her. "Sir William Hadley."

"From Bow Street?"

"The very one."

To his surprise, she let out a sharp laugh. "And my father pressured him not to investigate the fire. Now that's rich."

Thunder rumbled in the distance. Sebastian squinted up at the sky. "We should have brought your carriage. It's going to rain."

They turned their steps back toward the bridge. She said, "I gather Ian Kane is the man who owns the Orchard Street Academy?"

"That's right."

"Lord Devlin." She swung to face him, oblivious to the red-cheeked fishmonger at her side shouting, "Who'll buy brill, oh? Brill, oh!" She said, "What else do you know that you're not telling me?"

He met her indignant stare with a bland smile. "Miss Jarvis, I am not some Bow Street Runner you hired to give you daily reports."

She was an inch or two shorter than he, but she still managed to look down her nose at him. "I would think that common courtesy—"

"Courtesy?" He jerked her out of the way just as the fishmonger in the nearest stall slopped a bucket of water across his marble slab. "Believe me, Miss Jarvis, it is courtesy that prevents me from regaling you with the sordid details of this murder."

"If I were a man, or if I'd asked for your assistance in discovering the facts surrounding the murder of a cleric of impeccable character, you would tell me?"

"Probably," he said slowly, not sure where she was going with this.

"Then I would like to point out to you that in this

case, ignorance is not bliss. Last night, two men tried to kill me because of what I do not know."

They had reached that part of Billingsgate known colloquially as Oyster Street from all the oyster boats drawn up at the wharf. Sebastian stared at the bobbing red cap of a man in the hold of the nearest boat, his spade rattling over the gray mass of sand and shells at his feet. "Believe me, Miss Jarvis, you don't want to hear about this."

"On the contrary, my lord Devlin. I do."

He studied her squarely held shoulders, the contemptuous twist of her lips. "Very well, Miss Jarvis. I will tell you. Ian Kane is an ex-miner from Lancashire who enjoys painting nude women and sunlit buildings. He also in all likelihood murdered his first wife. Whether or not he murdered Rachel Fairchild I do not know, but he certainly expressed a desire to do so, seeing as how when she ran away from his house last Wednesday, he was on the verge of selling her to a customer for two hundred pounds."

"Selling her?"

"That's right. We don't quite put our women and children up on the auction block like the Americans, but we still sell four-year-olds to chimney sweeps and nubile young women to anyone with the coin to buy them."

He hesitated. She stared back at him, tight lipped, and said, "Go on."

"Very well. The customer in question—let's just call him Luke, shall we? It seems that Luke is a thief. A very successful thief who, incidentally, had an ambitious project scheduled for Monday night, just hours after the murders in Covent Garden. Is that significant? I don't know."

Her face was quite pale, but all she said was, "What else?"

"Well, then there's Rachel's betrothed, the inappro-

priately named Tristan Ramsey. It seems Mr. Ramsey
was very well aware of the fact that his future bride was
not in Northamptonshire recuperating her health. In
fact, he knew she was at the Orchard Street Academy."

"How did he know that?"

"He went there as a customer." He left it at that. Hero
Jarvis might bring out the worst in Sebastian, but he
wasn't so ignoble as to tell her what Ramsey had done
to Rachel there, on the stained sheets of that Covent
Garden brothel. He said instead, "Ramsey told Rachel's
brother, Cedric Fairchild, where she was. According to
Cedric Fairchild, he went to see her last week, but she
refused to leave with him. Both men claim they don't
know why she ran away from home, or how she ended
up in Covent Garden."

Miss Jarvis sucked in a deep breath that stirred the
once-jaunty ribbons of her hat, now wet and limp. Two
tiny lines appeared between her brows as she studied his
face. He wondered what she saw there. "But you know,
don't you?" she said. "Or at least, you have some idea."

He stared out over the stairs of Billingsgate, to the
wind-whipped, choppy brown river. He was thinking
about the leper colony that had once stood in the marshes
of what had since become St. James's Park, and what Rachel had told her brother about the diseased and rotting
outcasts who threatened society.

"Tell me," said Miss Jarvis.

He swung his head to look at her, at her windblown
brown hair and her once fine burgundy carriage dress
now ruined by the slime and muck of the fish market.
She was brilliant and well-educated and more aware of
the harsh realities of the world than most women of her
station. But the explanation that was beginning to take
shape in his mind was too raw, too ugly to be spoken
aloud.

He shook his head. "I honestly don't know."

She didn't believe him, of course. She remained uncharacteristically silent, her lips pressed into a thin, straight line, her shoulders stiff as he guided her to where Tom was walking the chestnuts up and down the lane. He handed her up into the curricle. She remained withdrawn, lost in her own thoughts, until he swung the horses out into traffic and headed upriver, away from where she'd left her own carriage awaiting her outside Paul Gibson's surgery.

"This isn't the way to the Tower," she said suddenly, looking around.

Sebastian set his horses at a brisk trot toward Upper Thames Street. "I thought you might enjoy coming with me to pay a call on Sir William."

She cast him a withering glance. "No, you didn't. You want me there for some other reason. What is it?"

He gave her a wry smile. "You're quite right, Miss Jarvis. My motives are entirely disreputable. I'm simply looking forward to watching Sir William explain to Lord Jarvis's daughter his own involvement in the murder Lord Jarvis ordered him not to investigate."

Chapter 35

"Keep 'em warm," said Sebastian, pulling up in front of the Bow Street Public Office and handing Tom the reins.

Tom blew out a long breath through the gap in his front teeth and tried to look nonchalant. "I reckon maybe I'll walk 'em around the block," he said, casting an uneasy glance at the bustling entrance to the public office.

"One might almost imagine," observed Miss Jarvis as Sebastian ushered her into the smoky, pungent din of the public office, "that your tiger finds the prospect of lingering too close to Bow Street a decidedly uncomfortable proposition."

"One might," Sebastian agreed. The public office was crowded with the usual assortment of beggars and pickpockets, constables and barristers. He collared a harried, bucktoothed clerk who tried to brush past them. "Miss Hero Jarvis and Lord Devlin to see Sir William."

The clerk cast a dubious eye over their slime-smeared clothes, his thin nose twitching as the smell of oysters and hake and brill engulfed him. "I'm afraid Sir William has left strict instructions that he never be disturbed for an hour after—"

"If you think," said Sebastian with that icy self-composure only the son and heir of an earl could achieve, "that Sir William will thank you for leaving Lord Jarvis's daughter waiting in the common lobby of a public office, you obviously have not considered the matter."

The clerk was a pale-skinned man with protuberant eyes and a short upper lip that refused to cover his pronounced front teeth. He swallowed convulsively, his Adam's apple bouncing up and down above his modest cravat. "Lord Jarvis's d—" He broke off, his eyes bulging even more. "Please follow me," he said, tripping over his own feet in his haste to lead them up the stairs to the private apartments overhead.

He escorted them to a small anteroom, then paused. "If you'll just wait here," he whispered, extending both hands out palm flat in a gesture reminiscent of someone quieting a congregation. The man should have been a cleric, Sebastian thought, instead of a clerk. "I'll tell Sir William you're here."

"Why do I get the impression Sir William makes it a habit of slipping away from his duties every afternoon for an hour's nap?" said Miss Jarvis as she watched the clerk creep through the door to their left.

"I suspect you're—" He broke off as a wailing shriek arose from the far side of the door. "What the devil?"

Miss Jarvis reached the door before him, pushing it open without ceremony. The room was small, a cross between an office and a storage room overflowing with untidy files. The clerk stood just inside the door, his mouth now opening and closing silently on his large front teeth.

Sir William half sat, half lay in an awkward pose in a padded chair behind a battered oak desk, his eyes wide and staring, his jaw slack, his head lolling at an unnatural angle.

Sebastian expected Miss Jarvis to scream. Instead she said calmly, "Good heavens, someone's broken his neck."

*   *   *

Jules Calhoun's nose twitched. "What is that smell?"

"Fish." Sebastian tossed his coat to one side and stripped off his waistcoat. "I need a bath."

"It's coming, my lord," said the valet, picking up the offending coat with one crooked finger and heading for the door.

"Oh, and, Calhoun?"

The valet turned. "My lord?"

"Somewhere in this city are two whores who formerly graced the parlor of the Orchard Street Academy. One, named Hessy Abrahams, hasn't been seen since Wednesday of last week. The other, Hannah Green, arrived at the Magdalene House with Rose Fletcher but fled before the fire. She may or may not have gone to ground in the Haymarket. I need to talk to both of them—if they're still alive."

"If they're alive, I'll find them, my lord," said Calhoun, and bowed himself out.

Scrubbed clean of the last lingering traces of Billingsgate, Sebastian prowled the West End, from the clubs of St. James's to the pleasure haunts of Covent Garden. He was looking for the malaria-plagued hussar captain from Northamptonshire named Patrick Somerville, and finally ran him to ground in the Crown and Thorn, a tavern near Whitehall popular with both military men and sporting young men from the country.

"Any luck yet locating your missing friend?" asked Sebastian, pausing beside Somerville's table, where he sat with his chin sunk against his chest and shoulders hunched as if against the cold.

Somerville looked up and shook his head. "We haven't found a trace of him."

Pulling out a chair, Sebastian signaled a passing waiter and ordered two more pints. "I understand you served in Africa," he said casually.

"Yes, Egypt," said Somerville. "As well as the Sudan and Cape Town."

"I spent some time in Egypt myself, but I never went below the Sahara."

They spoke for a time of Africa and the Americas, slipping easily into that camaraderie known to soldiers everywhere. Sebastian took his time bringing the conversation around to the Fairchilds. "You grew up in Northamptonshire, I take it?" he asked casually.

"Wansford." Reaching into his pocket, Somerville tipped the contents of a rice-paper packet of white powder into one palm. He licked it clean, then gulped his beer as a chaser. "Quinine," he said when he became aware of Sebastian watching him.

"With a little added kick of arsenic?"

The man gave a wry grin. "It's a winning combination. Africa would be lost to us without it."

Sebastian said, "Was Cedric Fairchild with you in Africa?"

"Cedric? No. We've known each other since we were in leading strings. My father's land marches with Lord Fairchild's estate."

"Then you know his sister Rachel." Sebastian deliberately kept the sentence in the present tense.

Somerville nodded. "She used to come over and play with m'sisters when she was little."

Sebastian smiled. "How many sisters do you have?"

Somerville gave a mock groan. "Five. M'father claims buying a pair of colors is nothing compared to the cost of a London Season."

"How many still left to go off?"

"Four. Fortunately Mary—the eldest—managed to do quite well for herself. Married Lord Berridge, you know. She's promised to sponsor her younger sisters, when the time comes. M'father's relieved, I can tell you. He always hoped Cedric would take a fancy to one of them, but I'm afraid Cedric always looked upon my sisters as if they were his sisters, too."

"I imagine they were often at Fairchild Hall."

"Well, no," said Somerville. His eyes were bright, feverish with a deadly combination of sickness and arsenic. "As a matter of fact, m'father would never let any of 'em go over there." The captain hesitated, then leaned forward to add softly, "He always said Lord Fairchild was a tad too fond of little girls, if you know what I mean?"

Sebastian took a slow sip of his beer. *A tad too fond of little girls.* It was a polite, euphemistic expression for something so ugly and bestial most Englishmen found it difficult to admit it actually existed in their oh so proper and painfully civil society. If Somerville hadn't imbibed so many beers, Sebastian doubted the man would even have mentioned it.

Had there been rumors around the village of Wansford? Sebastian wondered. Tales of frightened little girls? Servants who caught glimpses of what was meant to be hidden? Sebastian couldn't even say exactly what had first raised the suspicion in his head. There couldn't be that many reasons a gently bred young woman would flee her home to end her days on the streets.

Yet Rachel Fairchild had run away twice. Once from the Fairchild townhouse in Curzon Street, then again from the Academy in Covent Garden. Were the two flights linked? Or had the first flight merely exposed her to the danger that had led to the second—and, ultimately, to her death?

Sebastian regarded the young man beside him. "Tell me about the first Lady Fairchild."

"Lady Fairchild?" Somerville looked surprised. "She was French, you know. An émigrée. I remember she always wore a red velvet band around her neck, in memory of some relative or other who'd been guillotined." He brought up one hand to touch his throat. "It fascinated me when I was a lad. But I don't recall much else about her. I was still at Eton when she died."

"Was she ill for long?"

"Ill? Hardly. She was shot."

"Shot?"

Somerville nodded. "Lord Fairchild himself found her in the Pavilion—you know, one of those follies built like a Greek temple. By the lake. The inquest decided it was some poacher's shot gone wild, but, well"—Somerville shrugged—"people will talk."

"They thought it was murder?"

"Murder? Oh, no." Somerville drained his tankard. "They thought it was suicide. But then, what were they going to do? Bury her ladyship at the crossroads with a stake through her heart? They returned a verdict of death by misadventure, and Lady Fairchild now sleeps peacefully in the family tomb."

"Buy you another beer?" offered Sebastian.

The captain looked at his tankard as if startled to discover it empty. "I thank you, but no." He set the tankard aside and rose to his feet. "I promised m'sister Mary I'd take her for a drive around the park this afternoon. Since I've been posted back here to London, she's decided to make good use of me—she's lined me up for everything from Lady Melbourne's famous picnic this Saturday to some grand ball or t'other I can't remember when. It's enough to make a man look upon forced marches and monthlong sieges with something approaching fondness." Smiling faintly, Somerville gave a casual salute and turned toward the door.

It was when Sebastian was leaving the Crown and Thorn that he very nearly walked straight into the Earl of Hendon. Both father and son took a startled, awkward step back, and for one blazing moment their gazes met and held.

They had encountered each other in this manner a

dozen times or more over the past eight months. And each time Sebastian had felt the same shaking rush of anger and betrayal, the same brutal reminder of all he was trying to forget. He thought that, in time, he might be able to forgive Hendon for the lies, for the wretched coil Sebastian knew was not intentional, even if it was of Hendon's making. But Sebastian wasn't sure how he was ever going to forgive Hendon for the triumphant joy Sebastian had glimpsed in his father's face the day Sebastian's world had come crashing down around him.

He was aware of the leap of hope in his father's eyes. Saw, too, when hope faded into hurt. With painful politeness, Sebastian executed a short bow, said, "Good evening, sir," and withdrew.

Chapter 36

*H*aving bathed and exchanged her ruined burgundy carriage dress for a walking dress of soft fawn alpaca, Hero sallied forth again, this time to pay her long-delayed call on Rachel's sister Lady Sewell.

The former Georgina Fairchild had married a middle-aged baronet named Sir Anthony Sewell. Sewell was comfortably rather than excessively wealthy, his house on Hanover Square well appointed but modest. The match had surprised many, for Georgina Fairchild was both attractive and well dowered, yet she had contracted this unspectacular alliance just halfway through her first Season. Hero Jarvis was not the type of female to interest herself in such gossip and speculation, but she nevertheless found herself contemplating possible explanations as she followed Lady Sewell's butler up the stairs to the Sewells' drawing room.

She discovered Lady Sewell already entertaining visitors. One, a flaxen-haired, plump-faced young woman in pink muslin, Hero recognized as Lady Jane Collins. She sat on a red damask sofa beside a sprightly older woman introduced to Hero as Miss More. Miss More was the well-known author of numerous bestselling tracts on Christian piety, and it soon became obvious to Hero that Lady Sewell, too, was something of an Evangelical.

"We've just been discussing this dreadful new poem that has taken the ton by storm," said Lady Jane, shaking her head and *tut-tut*ting in a way one might expect of a woman thirty years older. "Shocking. Positively shocking."

Hero glanced at Lady Sewell. Tall and slim, wearing a high-necked crimson gown of figured muslin, she sat in a chair covered in the same red-and-gold-striped silk that hung at the windows. The room was dramatically yet tastefully done. The vibrant palette became its owner, for she was dark of hair and pale of skin, with exquisite high cheekbones and enormous green eyes. Except for the tall, slender nature of her build and those green eyes, there was nothing about this intense, self-contained woman to remind Hero of the frightened Cyprian she had met in Covent Garden.

"Lady Jane is referring to *Childe Harold's Pilgrimage*, of course," said Lady Sewell. "Have you read it, Miss Jarvis?"

Hero was torn between her natural tendency for blunt honesty and the need not to alienate Rachel's sister. Whatever she thought of the absurd posturing of Lord Byron himself, Hero found his poem both lyrically written and profoundly emotionally evocative. She compromised by simply saying, "I have read it, yes."

"The profane, too, have their place in God's plan," intoned Miss More with all the moral authority of a woman who'd spent the last thirty years of her life writing improving religious tracts. "They serve to confirm the truths they mean to oppose."

"Vice enhancing virtue by contrast?" said Hero drily.

Miss More's pinched lips stretched into a smile. "Exactly."

Hero suppressed the urge to shift restlessly in her striped silk chair. She could hardly bring up Rachel with the two Evangelical ladies present. Yet propriety limited

Hero's own visit to fifteen minutes. If they didn't leave soon—

As if on cue, Miss More and Lady Jane rose to their feet and, after reassuring themselves of Lady Sewell's plans to attend the next meeting of the London Society for the Promotion of Christianity Among the Jews, took their leave. Hero waited until she heard their footsteps descending the stairs, then said, "I met your sister Rachel the other day."

Lady Sewell sat very still. "My sister?"

Hero pushed on. "You are very different from each other, are you not?"

Lady Sewell smoothed her skirt over her knee with a hand that was not quite steady. "That's right. Rachel takes after our mother."

Hero studied the other woman's composed features. Either Lady Sewell was an incredibly cold woman, or she had no idea where Hero was going. She said more gently, "You haven't been told, have you?"

"Been told? Been told what?"

How did you tell a woman her little sister had been murdered? Hero had never been very good at this sort of thing. She said bluntly, "I'm sorry. Rachel is dead."

Lady Sewell's mouth sagged open, then closed, the muscles jumping along her tight jaw. "There must be some mistake."

"I was with her when she died." Hero leaned forward. "When was the last time you saw her?"

Lady Sewell rose very slowly and walked across the room to stare out the window, one hand clutching into a fist around the striped silk of the curtain at her side. Instead of answering, she said, "You say you were with Rachel when she died. When did this happen?"

"Last Monday. At the Magdalene House."

Lady Sewell whirled to face her. "At the *what*?"

"The Magdalene House. It was a refuge for women wishing to leave their life on the streets."

"I know what it was." Hero watched as horror and disbelief flickered through those beautiful green eyes. "You can't be serious."

"Where did you think she's been all this time?" said Hero. "You knew she wasn't in Northamptonshire."

"I'd hoped..." Lady Sewell's voice caught. She swallowed, her throat working convulsively. "You said you were with Rachel. What were you doing at this refuge?"

"I've been conducting research for a bill to be introduced to Parliament. I've discovered that women tend to enter prostitution for two reasons. For some, it's quite straightforward; they simply can't earn enough money to stay alive any other way. The second reason is more complicated. It's as if for some women life on the streets becomes a form of never-ending penance. It's as if they see themselves as ruined and give up any hope of ever leading a respectable life."

Lady Sewell stood stiffly, her chest jerking with each convulsively indrawn breath.

Hero pushed on. "If Rachel needed money or a refuge, surely she could have come to you. Couldn't she?" When the woman remained silent, Hero said again, "Couldn't she?"

Lady Sewell reached out one hand to grip the back of a nearby chair.

Hating herself for what she was doing, Hero said, "Why did your sister leave home?"

Lady Sewell swallowed again, then shook her head and said in a hoarse whisper, "I don't know. She was happy with her betrothal. At least, I thought she was."

"Did she quarrel with your father, perhaps?"

Sudden fury flared in the other woman's eyes, bringing a flush of hot color to her pale cheeks. "What do you mean by that?" She pushed away from the chair, then drew herself up short. "If you're suggesting—" She broke off.

Hero stared at the other woman in confusion. "Suggesting—what?"

Lady Sewell brought one hand to her forehead in a distracted gesture and turned half away. "Why are you here? Asking these questions? Involving yourself in this?"

"Because your sister died in my arms. She was shot."

Rachel's sister spun back around, all trace of color leaving her face again. "But . . . the Magdalene House burned."

"The fire at the Magdalene House wasn't an accident. Those women were murdered, although because of what they were, no one seems to care."

For one telling moment, Lady Sewell's gaze met hers, then wavered away. "I . . . I'd like to be alone now."

Hero rose to her feet. She discovered that her hands were tingling, and tightened her hold on the strings of her reticule. "If you're interested, Rachel was buried by the Society of Friends, at their meetinghouse in Pentonville."

"Please, just . . . go."

Hero inclined her head and turned toward the door. Lady Sewell still stood tall and rigid beside the windows.

But when Hero glanced back at the woman's mask-like face, she saw the glistening of silent tears.

Charles, Lord Jarvis was in the courtyard of Carlton House, preparing for the arrival of the Spanish minister, when Colonel Bryce Epson-Smith walked up to him, the heels of his boots tapping a military-like staccato as he crossed the paving.

"There have been some developments," said Epson-Smith, his voice pitched low.

Jarvis swung his head to study the Colonel's lean, sun-darkened features. "Not here."

They walked away from the turmoil of the reception area, into the lee of the portico. "Now what?" snapped Jarvis as the cool shadows of the coming evening closed around them.

"The assailant who survived last night's attack is dead."

"Did you learn anything from him?"

"Unfortunately, he died before we could reach him." Epson-Smith stared off across the courtyard entrance of the palace. "There's more."

"What else?"

"This afternoon, one of our men—Farley—was following Miss Jarvis when she met up with Lord Devlin. Farley . . . lost them."

Jarvis was silent long enough that a muscle jumped along the Colonel's jaw. "Where did this happen?"

"Near the Tower. Miss Jarvis initially encountered Devlin at the surgery of an Irishman, Paul Gibson. Farley trailed them from there to the church of St. Olave on Seething Lane."

"What? What on earth were they doing there?"

"I don't know, sir. But I suspect it was merely a stratagem. When Farley followed them into the church, Devlin backtracked and cut the cinch on Farley's saddle. Our man didn't catch up with them until some time later, at Bow Street."

"Bow Street?"

"Yes, my lord. Sir William has been murdered. I'm afraid Miss Jarvis was there when the body was discovered."

"Is she all right?"

"Miss Jarvis?" The question seemed to surprise the Colonel. "Of course, my lord."

Out on Pall Mall, the new gas lamps had been lit, their flares feeble flickers just visible in the last gasps of daylight. "Your man's an idiot," said Jarvis.

"Yes, sir. But I thought you should know that it is evidently Miss Jarvis's intent to elude our protection."

Jarvis drew out his snuffbox and flipped it open with one expert flick of his finger. He didn't look at Epson-Smith, although he was aware of the man beside him. Epson-Smith was coldly efficient and utterly ruthless. He didn't usually fail. Jarvis lifted a pinch of snuff to one nostril, sniffed, and said, "I don't care if you need to set a regiment to follow Miss Jarvis through the streets of London. This is not to happen again. Understood?"

Something flickered in the other man's eyes, then was gone. "Yes, sir. And Lord Devlin?"

Jarvis snapped his snuffbox closed and turned back toward the Colonel. "I told you, I'll deal with Devlin."

Chapter 37

*S*ebastian was crossing Margaret Street, headed toward a meeting with Sir Henry at Queen Square, when he heard himself hailed by an imperious voice.

"Lord Devlin."

Sebastian turned.

Attired in evening dress and a silk-lined cape that fluttered open with each angry step, Lord Fairchild strode purposely toward him across New Palace Yard. "This must stop," the Baron blustered as he came up to Sebastian. "Do you hear me, sir? It must stop."

"I beg your pardon?"

Lord Fairchild's face darkened to a hue somewhere between magenta and purple. "Don't play me for a fool." He spat the words out like bullets. "You know full well of what I speak."

"If you mean my investigation into the murder of your d—"

Lord Fairchild made a low growling sound deep in his throat. "Not here, for God's sake," he snapped, drawing Sebastian farther up the pavement. "Is that what this is all about?" His voice dropped to an acid whisper. "Do you seek to damage me by attacking my daughter's reputation?"

"What this is about," said Sebastian, his gaze search-

ing the other man's mottled, distorted features, "is justice. Justice for a murdered woman lying in an unmarked
grave."

The Baron clenched his teeth together so tightly his
jaw quivered. "My daughter is in Northamptonshire. You
hear me? Northamptonshire. If you persist in insinuat-
ing otherwise, I swear to God, I'll call you out for it."

Sebastian studied the beefy, red-faced lord before
him. He thought about the short, tragic life of Rachel
Fairchild, and about Lord Fairchild's "fondness" for little girls, and he knew a revulsion so swift and profound
it turned his stomach.

Once, Sebastian had thought the link between father and child one of the closest bonds in nature, second only to that between a mother and her children.
Sebastian's relationship with his own father had never
been an easy one; he'd always known he both baffled
and disappointed Hendon. There had even been a time,
in the dark days after the death of the last of Sebastian's brothers, that Sebastian would have said Hendon
hated him—hated him for living when Hendon's other
sons had died. Yet through it all, Hendon's devotion to
the preservation of his remaining son—and the pledge
he represented to the future—had endured. Sebastian
had always believed it must be so for all fathers. It was
only in the past year that he had come to realize just
how fragile—and secondary—paternal devotion could
sometimes be.

The bells of Westminster began to chime the hour, the
melodious notes echoing out over the city. "I understand
there's an important debate this evening on the Orders
in Council," said Sebastian evenly. "You're missing it."

Lord Fairchild opened his mouth and closed it, then
swung away, his jaw held tight, his head thrust forward
like a bull's.

Sebastian waited until the Baron had taken several strides before calling after him, "I hear you're the one who discovered your wife's body. How . . . tragic."

The Baron swung back around, his massive frame quivering with fury. "If you mean to insinuate—"

"I insinuate nothing," said Sebastian, and continued on his way to Queen Square.

"It's quite an innovation," said Sir Henry Lovejoy, nodding to the rows of flickering gas lamps that bathed the interior of McCleod's Coffee Shop in a soft golden glow. Gas lamps had already replaced the oil lamps along Pall Mall and in the surrounding streets, but few shop owners were as innovative—or as courageous—as the proprietors of McCleod's. The sputtering gas jets and occasional explosions and asphyxiations generally limited the introduction of gas to the outdoors. "I've heard it said that someday, not only every street in London, but every house in London will be lit by the gasworks."

Sebastian shifted his weight against the booth's unpadded back. "I've heard it said that the runoff from the gasworks is what's killing the fish in the Thames."

Sir Henry brushed away the suggestion of pollution with an impatient hand. Apart from the law, the only other passion in the little magistrate's life was science, and he brooked no criticism of it. "There are always naysayers."

Sebastian simply smiled and raised his coffee to his lips.

Sir Henry cleared his throat. "I understand it was your misfortune to discover Sir William this afternoon. It's why you've sought me out, isn't it, and bought me this coffee?"

Sebastian laughed. "I'd have bought you a brandy but I know you don't imbibe."

A fervently devout man, Sir Henry had secret lean-
ings toward the Reformist Church, although he generally kept his views to himself. Being anything other than
High Church wasn't good for one's career. He said, "I
take it you think this death is somehow linked to what
happened at the Magdalene House on Monday." The
barest hint of a smile tugged the edges of the Queen
Square magistrate's mouth. "I know you have continued
to involve yourself in the investigation."

Sebastian took another sip of coffee. "It was my understanding there was no investigation."

"Not officially. But according to Sir William's clerk,
Sir William was intrigued by what happened."

Sebastian knew a flicker of surprise, although when he
thought about it, he realized it made sense. By instruct-
ing Sir William to shut down any speculation about the
fire, Lord Jarvis had obviously sparked the magistrate's
curiosity.

"Officially," Lovejoy was saying, "the fire was just a
fire. But Sir William was nevertheless pursuing a few discreet inquiries."

"Obviously not discreet enough."

"You think it's why he was killed?"

"Yes."

Sir Henry cleared his throat again. "It's rather embar-
rassing, you know. Having the chief magistrate of Bow
Street murdered in his own public office."

"Is that why it's been released that Sir William died
of an apoplectic fit?"

"There will be rumors, of course. But then, there
would have been rumors even if he *had* died of an apoplectic fit."

"Very true."

Lovejoy fixed him with an uncompromising stare.
"Tell me about the Magdalene House fire."

Sebastian gave the magistrate a carefully edited version of what he had so far discovered. He left out all mention of Russian sables and Irish thieves, but the tale he wove was still sordid—and utterly inconclusive. In the end, the magistrate removed his wire-framed glasses and rubbed the bridge of his nose. "It is all rather complicated. It's as if it goes off in six different directions at once."

Sebastian said, "I'm obviously missing something. Something important."

Sir Henry fit his glasses back on his face and cleared his throat again. "I've been offered the position of Bow Street magistrate."

Sebastian raised one eyebrow. "Congratulations."

"It is an honor, of course. I wouldn't be chief magistrate—Sir James will replace Sir William in that capacity. But . . . well, if truth were told, I suspect I might somewhat miss Queen Square."

"So you haven't decided yet whether or not to accept?"

"No. The prestige means nothing to me. But . . ." The magistrate hesitated, and Sebastian knew he was remembering certain incidents in the past, when Bow Street had interfered in Sir Henry's own investigations in a high-handed and contemptuous manner.

"It is tempting," said Sebastian.

"Yes."

The door to the coffee shop swung inward to admit another customer, who brought with him the smell of coming rain and a great gust of wind that snuffed out three of the gas lamps on the nearest wall.

"The fault's in the design of the gas jets," said Sir Henry as the proprietor bustled forward with a taper to relight them. "With a better design, that wouldn't have happened." When Sebastian remained silent, he added,

"Imagine the reduction in crime the city will experience once every street is illuminated by gas."

"As long as there's no wind," said Sebastian.

"I tell you, the fault's in the design of the jets," insisted Sir Henry.

But Sebastian only laughed.

Chapter 38

That evening shortly before dinner, Hero was working in the library when her father entered the room. Lord Jarvis rarely dined at his own home. Looking up, she had little doubt as to why he was here, now.

He stared at the books she had scattered across the library table and frowned. "What is all this?"

Hero laid down her pen and sat back. "Some research I'm doing."

Lord Jarvis grunted. "Why can't you arrange flowers and embroider seat covers like other women?"

"Because I'm your daughter," she said, gathering the books into a neat stack.

He didn't even smile. Pressing both hands flat on the tabletop, he leaned into them, his gaze hard on her face. "What exactly is Devlin's interest in the deaths of the Magdalene House women?"

Hero stared up at him without flinching. His lackey had obviously wasted no time reporting back to him. "The same as mine. To see justice done."

Pushing away from the table, he swiped one big hand through the air, like someone brushing aside an annoying gnat. "There is no justice in this world. There are only the strong and the weak. Those women were weak."

"Which is why it is the obligation of the strong to fight for them."

Lord Jarvis let out his breath in a scornful huff. "I told you I would deal with those responsible."

Hero pushed to her feet. "Because of me. Not because of them."

"What difference does that make?"

She found herself oddly reluctant to explain to him the effect her meeting with Rachel Fairchild had had upon her, or the guilt that drove her to try to understand what had gone wrong in the young woman's life. She said instead, "Has your Colonel Epson-Smith discovered those responsible?"

"Not yet. But he will." He turned away to pour himself a glass of brandy. "You broke our agreement. You went to Bow Street."

"On a slightly different errand. You heard Sir William is dead."

"Yes."

"Did you know he was involved with one of the women killed?"

Jarvis looked over at her. "Who told you that? Devlin?"

"No. Someone else."

Jarvis grunted. "You brought Devlin into this?"

"Yes."

"How much does he know?" he asked, decanter in hand.

"You mean, does he know I was at the Magdalene House when it was attacked? Yes."

Lord Jarvis poured himself a measure of brandy, then replaced the stopper in the decanter and set it aside without looking at her. She knew he was choosing his words carefully. "Devlin wouldn't hesitate to hurt you to get at me. You know that, don't you?"

She chose her words with equal care. "I know he is your enemy. But I do not believe he would hurt me to get at you. He's not"—she started to say, *like you*, then changed it to—"like that."

She expected him to laugh at her again. Instead, he merely looked thoughtful. He took a slow sip of his drink, his gaze turned now to study her face in a way that made her uncomfortable. He said, "Why Devlin?"

Because he's the one man in this country who isn't afraid of you, she thought. But again, she didn't say it. She said, "He has achieved good results in the past, in similar situations."

"And did you ask yourself why he agreed to help?"

"I know why he agreed. To get back at you."

"Yet you say he wouldn't hurt you."

"That's right."

He went to sit in one of the upholstered chairs near the empty hearth, his glass cradled in his palm. "I set Farley to follow you this afternoon for your own protection. You knew that. Yet you evaded him. Why?"

"I know something of your Colonel's methods. The last thing I would ever want to do is unwittingly furnish him with a few more hapless victims."

Lord Jarvis pressed his lips together in a frown. "That's not the intent here."

She met his gaze squarely. "It's not a risk I'm willing to take."

He glared right back at her. "And your exposing yourself to danger is a risk I'm not willing to take."

"Papa." She went to lean over the back of his chair, her arms looped around his neck. "I was never in any danger this afternoon and you know it."

He brought up one of his big hands to cover hers. With anyone else, he would have been overbearing and coldly threatening, but he'd learned long ago that didn't work with Hero. She was too much like him. He said, "Where did you go this afternoon?"

"To meet a woman I hoped would help me make some sense of what happened at the Magdalene House."

He took a long swallow of his brandy. "With Devlin?"

"Yes."

"I suppose it's better than going on your own." He shifted his hand to lightly grasp her wrist and tug her around so that he could see her face. "Finding out about this woman is so important to you?"

"Yes."

He shook his head. "I don't understand it."

"I know."

He hesitated, and she knew again the fear that he would forbid her to continue her inquiries. But all he said was, "I would ask you to be careful."

"I will. I promise."

He nodded. "You are unusually sensible for a woman . . . however ill advised your political ideas are."

She knew he had said it to provoke her. But she only smiled and refused to rise to the bait.

That night, Hero and her mother were descending the steps of their Berkeley Square house toward the carriage that had been ordered to take them to a fashionable soiree when a malodorous little boy came pelting down the footpath toward them.

"My goodness," gasped Lady Jarvis, shrinking back in a cloud of pale azure satin as the boy slammed right into Hero.

"You there," shouted the butler, starting forward, "watch where you're going."

But the boy was already off, feet flying, one hand held up to clamp his cap to his head as he disappeared around the corner.

"Brazen guttersnipes," muttered Grisham, staring after him. "Whatever is the world coming to? I trust you suffered no harm, Miss Jarvis?"

"I'm fine," said Hero, the folded missive slipped her by the boy carefully tucked out of sight.

Chapter 39

*T*he next day Hero dressed in her plainest riding gown topped by a particularly ugly hat with a dense veil that made her grandmother *tut-tut* and prophesy she was destined to end her days as an old maid.

"I sincerely hope so," said Hero, then prudently whisked herself out of the room to avoid being sucked into an old and well-worn argument.

She evaded the watchdog set by her father simply by descending into the kitchens to confer with the housekeeper and then slipping out by the area steps. Walking briskly to the corner of Davies Street, she caught a hackney and directed the driver to Number 41 Brook Street.

It was most unseemly for a young unmarried woman to visit the house of an unmarried gentleman—particularly without her maid. Hero had given the situation considerable thought, but in the end decided there was no avoiding it. She had promised her father she would not put herself in danger, and Hero Jarvis kept her promises. Her major concern was that she might find Lord Devlin already gone from home.

Paying off the hackney, she rang an imperious peal on the Viscount's door. It was opened almost at once by a military-looking majordomo who regarded her with unconcealed suspicion.

"Pray inform Lord Devlin that I am here to see him," she said loftily.

"And whom shall I say is calling?"

"My good man," said Hero at her most condescending, "if I wanted you to know my name, I would have given it to you."

The majordomo hesitated. Fear of giving offense to a veiled noblewoman warred with the horror of ushering some grasping harpy into his master's presence. Fear of giving offense won. He bowed and let her in. "One moment while I see if his lordship is receiving."

He achieved a measure of revenge by leaving her in the hall rather than ushering her into a receiving room. He returned in a moment, his face giving nothing away, to lead her upstairs to the drawing room. "Tea will arrive shortly," drawled the majordomo, and withdrew.

Pushing back her veil, Hero prowled the room. She studied the curious, intricately incised brass platter on one wall, the carved wooden head that looked as if it had come from Africa on another. A tea tray arrived along with a plate of bread and butter, but she ignored it, her attention caught by a painting over the mantel. It was by Gainsborough, of a laughing young woman with unpowdered golden hair and a braid-trimmed riding costume in the style of the last century. Hero could trace the resemblance to the Viscount in the flare of the woman's cheekbones, the curve of the lips. So this was Devlin's mother, Hero thought. They still talked about the long-dead Countess of Hendon in scandalized whispers.

She was so absorbed in her study of the painting that she failed to hear the door open behind her.

"I suspected it was you," said an amused voice, "from

my majordomo's description. I don't know that many tall, haughty gentlewomen with the manner of a Turkish pasha."

She swung to face him. "I don't know any Turkish pashas."

"Which is probably a good thing," he said, leaving the door open behind him. "They like their women obsequious and agreeable."

"Like most Englishmen."

"Like most men," he agreed, advancing into the room.

He was dressed in doeskin breeches and a well-tailored dark coat, but his hair still curled damply away from his face. She said, "I've caught you at your bath."

"Actually, you caught me still abed." He glanced at the tea, which she hadn't touched. "Join me?" he asked, pouring a cup.

She took it from his outstretched hand. "You haven't asked why I'm here."

He poured himself a cup and lifted one of the pieces of buttered bread from the plate. "I have no doubt it is your intention to enlighten me."

He had a nearly limitless capacity for irritating her, and it did no good to remind herself that he provoked her intentionally. The urge to simply set down her tea and leave was overcome with difficulty; a promise was a promise. She said, "I've received a note from Tasmin Poole. A boy passed it to me as I was about to enter my carriage last night."

He selected another slice of buttered bread. "She has located the missing Hannah Green?"

"So it seems. The woman is hiding in a cottage just off Strand Lane, and she has agreed to meet me there."

The Viscount swallowed his bread and took a sip of tea. "You're suspicious. Why?"

"I am to go there at midday with only one servant to accompany me. According to the note, these precautions are necessary because Hannah Green is frightened. I believe the note to be genuine, but I am aware of the possibility that it could be a trap."

"It certainly sounds like one to me."

"Yet if it's not and I fail to go, the chance to meet Hannah Green will be lost."

He reached for another slice of bread. "Are you certain you don't want some of this?" he asked, nudging the plate toward her. "It's really quite good."

"Thank you, but I breakfasted hours ago."

"Is that an insult? I wonder."

"Yes."

He laughed and finished the last of the bread. "I think I begin to understand. If you were anyone else, I might assume you had come to ask for my advice. On the strength of our limited acquaintance, however, I suspect you have already made up your mind to go and have simply come here to request that I accompany you"— his gaze took in her riding costume—"posing, I take it, as your groom?"

"And to beg the loan of a horse. I was forced to slip out the basement to avoid my watchdog."

"We could take a hackney."

"Then I would need a lady's maid, not a groom," she pointed out.

"True. Unfortunately, I don't own any ladies' horses."

"Neither do I." She glanced at the ormolu clock on the mantel. "If you have finished your tea and bread?"

"It's a trap, you know," he said, suddenly serious.

"Will you do it?"

"Drink your tea," he told her, "while I transfer myself into a more humble attire."

Lying just to the west of St. Clements, Strand Lane proved to be a narrow cobbled passage that wound a torturous path down toward the river.

The day was overcast and cold, with the kind of biting wind more typical of March than May. Pausing his gelding at the head of the lane, Sebastian let his gaze flick to the watch house and church of St. Mary's that had been left marooned in the center of the Strand by the widening of the street. "It seems an unlikely place for a frightened prostitute to go to ground," he said.

"Perhaps she grew up around here," said Miss Jarvis, reining in her mount beside him.

He kneed his horse forward between aged gabled houses of timber and whitewashed daub that nearly met overhead. The buildings might be old, but they were well kept, the cobbles and worn doorsteps swept clean. A little girl dashed past, laughing as she chased a kitten through flowers tumbling out of green-painted window boxes. They passed a ramshackle old inn, the Cock and Magpie, and a livery. But within a hundred yards or so, the lane unexpectedly opened up to their right and Sebastian found himself staring out over a tumbledown stone wall at a stretch of open land.

"It's a curious place for a meeting," he said, reining in. He could see, scattered amidst rioting wisteria and lilacs, the broken, ivy-covered statues and rusted iron gates of an abandoned garden that stretched all the way to the terrace and neoclassical side elevation of Somerset House in the distance.

"It's the ruins of the eastern gardens of the original Somerset House," said Miss Jarvis. "When they tore down the old palace, the plan was to construct an eastern wing on the new building that would stretch nearly to Surrey Street. But the government ran out of money. My father is always raging about it. He thinks the capital of a great nation needs impressive government buildings, and London is woefully lacking in anything majestic or monumental."

Sebastian narrowed his eyes against the glint of the

light reflected off the Thames. Down near the river's edge, to their left, stood a lumberyard, its great stacks of drying timber towering twenty to thirty feet in the air. But a strange air of quiet hung over the area. "I don't like it," he said, thankful for the weight of the small, double-barreled flintlock pistol he'd slipped into the pocket of his groom's coat before leaving Brook Street.

"Surely if it were a trap," she said, "the rendezvous would have been set for tonight. What are they going to do? Cosh me—and my servant—over the head in broad daylight? It's not exactly a disreputable neighborhood."

"Would you have come here at night?"

"Of course not."

Sebastian studied the expanse of overgrown gravel paths and untamed shrubbery. "Where exactly is this Hannah Green supposed to be?"

"There," said Miss Jarvis, nodding to what looked like a caretaker's cottage at the base of the garden near the water's edge.

Sebastian swung out of the saddle. "Wait here," he told her. "Your groom is going to knock on the door."

He expected her to argue. Instead, she took his reins in her strong gloved hand, a frown line forming between her eyes as she studied the small stone house.

The original Somerset House had been built in the mid–sixteenth century by the Duke of Somerset, uncle and Lord Protector of the boy king Edward VI. A vast Renaissance palace, it had been pulled down late in the previous century and replaced by the current Somerset House, now used by various Royal societies and government offices. Only this stretch of the old gardens had survived. Once, the sandstone cottage near the river might have been a part of the ancient Tudor palace itself. A retainer's lodge, perhaps, or a delightful garden retreat for the dowager queens who had once used the old palace as their Dower House. The echoes of the original house's renaissance glory were there, in the crumbling stone steps, in the sweet-scented damask rose blooming stubbornly from amidst a thicket of thistles.

Sebastian walked up the neglected path, the gravel crunching beneath his feet, his senses alert to any movement, any sound. The garden appeared deserted.

Studying the cobwebs draping the delicately carved tracery of the windows and the leaded panes, Sebastian knocked on the warped old door and listened to the sound fade away into nothing. He was raising his fist to knock again when he heard a furtive whisper of sound from the far side of the thick panels. The scrape of a slipper over stone flagging, perhaps, or the brush of cloth against cloth.

He waited, aware of a sense of being watched. Tilting back his head, he scanned the crenulated decoration at the wall's edge, then heard the rasp of a bolt being drawn back.

The door creaked inward a foot and stopped. He had a glimpse of a young woman's pale face, her brown eyes widening in fear. Behind her stretched an empty stone-flagged passageway with thick whitewashed walls.

"Miss Jarvis sent me to inquire—" he began, only to have the woman let out a little mewl of terror. Her hands slipping off the door's latch, she whirled, her fists clenching in her skirts, her brown hair flying as she pelted back down the passageway.

Thrusting open the door with one outflung hand, Sebastian sprinted after her. He took two steps, three, then felt a blinding pain that crashed down upon the back of his head and brought with it the bright darkness of oblivion.

Chapter 40

*T*he pain was still there.

He realized he was lying on something cold and hard. That confused him. He considered opening his eyes to investigate, but at the moment, that seemed more effort than it was worth. He lay still, trying to recall where he was and what he was doing here. He remembered handing the reins of his horse to Hero Jarvis. He remembered walking through the abandoned garden. Stone steps. A warped door. A brown-eyed woman running.

He shifted his weight, wincing as a jagged agony arced around the side of his head. From somewhere quite close, he heard Miss Jarvis say, "You were right. It was a trap."

He opened his eyes.

He found himself staring at a stone groined vault high above where he lay. The stones were old and worn, and stained with damp. Turning his head ever so carefully, he was able to make out a row of thick, crude pillars holding up the roof, and to see the no-nonsense face of Miss Jarvis.

He groaned again and closed his eyes. "Where the hell are we?"

"I'm not entirely certain what this place was originally. At first I thought it might be the crypt of one of the churches or chapels Somerset pulled down to build his palace. But more likely it's simply a storeroom or cellar from one of the medieval bishops' palaces he also tore down."

Sebastian brought up a hand to probe gingerly at the back of his head. "And why precisely are we here?"

"I am told the vault floods when the tide comes in."

He opened his eyes again, his hand falling. He realized he was lying on a wide, elevated stone ledge some three feet off the ground that ran along as much of the crypt wall as he could see. She sat perched on the edge of the ledge beside him. She was hunched forward, her arms crossed at her waist, her hands hugging her elbows in close. From the way she had her jaw set, he suspected she was having to try very, very hard to keep control of herself. He realized her veiled hat was gone, her sleeve torn. However she had come to be here with him, she obviously had not come without a fight.

"What happened?" he asked.

She rocked gently back and forth in a movement so subtle he doubted that she even knew she was doing it. "I waited for you for about five minutes, but you never came back. Just as I was trying to decide what to do, a gentleman walked out of the Cock and Magpie and asked if I needed help."

"A gentleman?"

"Most definitely a gentleman. He was both well dressed and well spoken. Just like the gentleman with the gig on the road from Richmond."

"And?" he prompted.

"I wheeled my horse, meaning to flee. But he reached up and grabbed my reins just above the bit. And then he pulled a pistol on me."

"In a respectable neighborhood in broad daylight."

"Quite," she said evenly. "I freely admit to deserving any and all reproaches you care to heap upon my head. It was a trap."

He might not like Hero Jarvis, but there was much that he found he did, reluctantly, admire about her. And so he surprised himself by saying gently, "We all make mistakes."

She raised her head to look at him. "When they dragged me down here—"

"They?"

"Yes. Another man joined us in the garden. They had simply dumped you at the foot of the steps. I thought you were dead."

"What steps?" he said, trying to sit up.

She turned to help him. "Do you think that's wise?"

"What time does the tide come in? Any idea?"

"It's been running at about half past five, I think."

"And what time is it now?"

"You can hear the bells of St. Clements down here. They just tolled three."

Sebastian had aborted his attempt to stand and contented himself with sitting, slumped, while he regained his breath. He said, "If I was on the floor, how did I end up on the ledge?"

"I requested they pick you up and put you on the ledge. They ridiculed me for it, but in the end they did it."

He could imagine her high-handed orders to her captors, the men's laughing compliance. She said, "They also left the lantern at my request. I told them I was afraid of rats."

His gaze fell to the simple tin lantern with horn windows at their feet, its single tallow candle spilling a faint golden glow that left the farthest reaches of the chamber in darkness. "Are there rats?"

"I haven't seen any."

The giddiness was beginning to recede. He said, "Tell me about the steps."

"They're there, just to our right. They're barred by

an iron gate at the base and a stout wooden door at the top."

He could see them now, worn shadowy steps disappearing upward. He lurched to his feet and reached for the lantern. She got to it first.

"If you insist on inspecting the gate, I'll carry the lantern. If you drop it, I've no way to rekindle the candle and neither do you."

"How do you know I've no tinderbox?"

"I checked your pockets."

He clapped a hand to the capacious pocket of his groom's coat. His pistol was gone. With difficulty, he overcame the impulse to swear long and crudely.

The gate covered an arched opening some four feet wide. Built of iron, with thick vertical bars braced top and bottom by stout crosspieces, it looked newly installed, without a trace of rust. A thick chain had been wrapped around the bars twice, then secured by a heavy padlock well beyond his reach. He clasped both hands around one of the iron bars and pushed. Its solidity mocked him.

She said, "I did check it. It's quite strong."

He tested each bar and crosspiece himself, just to be certain, but he doubted even the strength of ten men could dislodge them. Breathing heavily again, he leaned against the gate, his gaze on the stairwell it protected. From here he could see that the steps led up to a stout wooden door set into a corbeled arch at the top. He said, "There was a woman in the house. A young woman. Did you see her?"

Miss Jarvis shook her head. "They never took me into the house. These steps lead down from an alcove in the garden wall near the river."

He could see a point, some ten or twelve steps up, where the stonework used for the steps changed, became darker, less worn, as if it were of more recent

construction. He'd heard tales of the building of the old
Somerset House by Edward Seymour, about how he'd
appropriated land occupied by the inns of the Bishops
of Chester and Lichfield, Coventry and Worcester. The
old bishops' palaces had been pulled down, their building materials either reused or dumped as fill to raise the
height of the garden for a terrace.

"Let me see the lantern," he said, reaching for it.

"Are you quite certain you're—"

"I'm fine." Holding the lantern aloft, he explored the
crypt. Built of worked sandstone blocks, it was a space
some forty-five to fifty feet long and five bays wide, the
ceiling vaults supported on rows of squat, plain pillars.
One end was neatly walled off with a darker sandstone
that reminded him of the upper steps. At the other end,
the far reaches of the chamber disappeared beneath a
cascade of rubble.

He played the lantern light over the jumble of stones,
some rough, others shaped but broken. Here and there
he saw glimpses of carvings, of scrollwork and carefully
incised patterns.

"That's where the river is," she said, coming to stand
beside him.

"How far?"

"Some ten or twelve feet, I'd say."

So much for any wild schemes of digging through the
rubble to freedom.

"I've seen engravings of the Thames from the days
when the bishops' palaces stretched from the river to the
Strand," she said. "Some of them were constructed over
arches that opened to the river. Barges used to come up
the river and then pull in under the arches to unload. It
could be that's what this is from."

"So maybe it won't flood completely," he said, his
head falling back as he studied the worn stone of the
ceiling vaults.

"I suspect they tested the theory before they left us down here to die," she said drily.

He glanced over at her. She'd kept pace with him as he prowled the crypt, her hands still clutching her elbows in close to her sides. He said, "Why leave us down here? Why not simply kill us outright?"

She squared her shoulders. "As I understand it, their intention is to throw our bodies in the river. Make it look as if we suffered an accident. Any autopsy would simply show that we'd drowned, wouldn't it?"

"Why would they care whether or not it was obvious we were murdered?"

"That I don't know."

He met her gaze. Her eyes were dilated so wide they looked black. "I don't intend to drown," he said, turning back toward the steps.

She trailed after him—or, more exactly, after the light. "Well, that's reassuring."

He laughed softly, the lantern making a chink as he set it down on the stone paving. "We could try shouting."

"I did. Do you have any idea how much earth there is on top of us?"

He was trying not to think about that.

"Where are you going?" she asked as he headed back toward the rubble wall.

He selected a massive chunk of what looked like a broken ionic capital from some long-ago despoiled church. Bending his knees and grunting, he hoisted it to his chest, his head swimming sickeningly. She watched, silent, as he staggered back toward the gate and heaved it at the padlocked chain. It clattered against the iron, then crashed to the stone floor. The chained gate held firm.

Swearing, he heaved the stone at the gate again and again, until he was sweating and his hands were bleeding from the stone's jagged edges. After perhaps the tenth try, she said calmly, "Stop it. It isn't doing any good and you're only hurting yourself."

He swung to face her, his breath shuddering his chest. "Do you have a better idea?"

"We could try to set fire to the door. Someone might see the smoke and come to investigate."

It was a crazy idea, but not without merit. He eyed the distance to the door at the top of the stairs. "And how do you propose we do that?"

"I don't know."

Still breathing hard, he went back to select a fist-sized chunk of rock from the rubble. "Here, hold this," he said, handing her the rock. He stripped off his groom's coat and waistcoat, then pulled his shirt off over his head. The damp chill of the subterranean vault sent a shiver through him. He hadn't thought to check his boot to see if they'd missed his knife. They had.

"Do you always carry that?" she asked, watching him slip the knife from its hidden sheath.

"Always." He flashed her a smile that showed his teeth. "I even threw it at your father once."

Using the blade, he sliced his shirt into strips and began to plait them. Her mind was quick. She said, "Let me help."

He wrapped the plaited shirt around the rock like a long wick, then opened the hinged tin and horn door of the lantern.

"Don't put out the candle," she warned.

Grunting, he kindled the torn edge of the shirt, watched it flare and catch. Thrusting his arms through the iron bars of the gate, he held the burning, weighted shirt as long as he could. Then he hurled it at the door above.

It flew through the air, a flaming catapult that illuminated the shadowy stairwell and hit the stout door with a solid thud. Falling to the stone lintel in a shower of sparks, it burned up bright for one shining moment and went out.

"Hell and the devil confound it," he whispered, then added, "I beg your pardon, Miss Jarvis."

She stood beside him, her hands, like his, gripping the bars of the gate. "That's quite all right."

He swung to look at her, assessing the sturdy cloth of her riding habit. It wouldn't burn any better than his coat or waistcoat.

She said, "Why are you looking at me like that?"

"Your petticoats."

"My—" She broke off. He thought for a moment that she meant to refuse him. But what she said was, "Turn around."

He went to select more rocks from the rubble. She said, "I'm finished."

He threw his coat up to the door first, followed by his rough waistcoat, not even bothering to try to light them first. "Why?" she asked as he set to work ripping the first of her fine petticoats.

"They're fodder. The lawn of the petticoats will burn fast, but the wool coat will smolder."

"We hope."

"We hope," he agreed.

He threw the first petticoat-wrapped rock short, so that it burned in a bright, useless heap on the second step. The second try landed square.

"Thank goodness," she whispered, pressing against the gate, her gaze on the small fire above.

It burned for a time, long enough to fill the air with smoke and the pungent odor of singed wool. Coughing, she said, "Will it kill us, do you think? The smoke, I mean."

"Probably not if we go to the far end of the chamber, near the rubble. I could feel air coming in there."

But in the end they had no need to retreat. Once

again, the fire sputtered and went out. They had part of one petticoat left.

"It isn't going to work," he said.

"It has to work." She pushed away from the gate. "Start ripping up the last petticoat," she said, setting to work on the brass buttons of her riding habit. "Your coat was wet from lying on the stone."

"You'll be cold," he said.

She stripped off her habit with angry, purposeful jerks, the white flesh of her arms bathed in gold by the dim light of the flickering lantern. "Just hit the door."

Both parts of the riding habit landed with satisfying plops atop his coat and waistcoat. He'd have added his breeches, too, but they were of buckskin and would never burn. Clad only in her short, lightweight stays, a thin chemise, boots and stockings, she watched him carefully kindle the last petticoat. He let it flare up until it was almost burning his hand, then lobbed it at the pile of clothes above.

This time, the cloth beneath the burning missile caught, blazing up hot and fast. The air filled with the crackle of flames, the smell of singed wood. They stood and watched it burn, the big bell of St. Clements tolling four times in the distance. Then, as the small bell began to toll again for those who might have miscounted the first bell, this fire, too, hissed softly and went out.

Chapter 41

"I'm sorry I involved you in this," she said.

They sat side by side on the ledge that ran along the near wall of the stone vaulted chamber. She had her knees drawn up to her chest, her arms wrapped around her legs so that she could hug them close. He had set the lantern next to her on the ledge, but its feeble warmth provided a pitiful defense against the cold gloom of the subterranean room.

He turned his head to look at her. She'd lost most of her pins. Her hair was coming down, falling in artless disarray about her face. It made her look uncharacteristically approachable. He said, "I involved myself."

"Why?" That frown line appeared again between her eyes as she studied his face. "Why do you involve yourself in the investigation of murder?"

He tilted back his head, his gaze on the ancient vaulting above. "I've been told it's a form of arrogance, thinking I can solve a mystery that baffles others."

"But that's not why you do it."

He felt a smile curve his lips. "No."

"It's the victims, isn't it? That's why you do it. For them."

He said, "It's why you involved yourself in this mess, isn't it? For the woman who died in your arms?"

She was silent for a moment. He could hear the distant drip of water, feel the weight of a thousand tons of earth pressing down on them. She said, "I'd like to think so. But I have the most lowering reflection that I've been doing it for myself."

"Yourself?"

She shifted restlessly, edging ever so slightly closer to him. If she'd been any other woman, he would have offered her the warmth of his body—for his sake as well as hers. But one did not offer to hold Lord Jarvis's daughter, even if she was freezing and about to die. She said, "My father thinks I involve myself in reform because I have a maudlin attraction to good works."

"He doesn't know you well, does he?"

She surprised him by letting out a soft huff of laughter. "In that way, no. I'm not a charitable person. I work for reform out of a sense of what's right, a conviction that things ought to be different. It's far more intellectual than emotional."

"I think you're being too severe with yourself."

"No. I concern myself with the fate of the poor women and children of London the way I might concern myself with the well-being of cart horses. I empathize with them as fellow creatures, but I certainly never imagined I could ever find myself in their position. But then—"

She broke off, swallowed, and tried again. "Then I met Rose—Rachel Fairchild. And I realized . . . there was a woman like me. A woman born into wealth and privilege who had danced at Almack's and driven in her carriage in Hyde Park. And yet somehow she had ended up there, at the Magdalene House. That's when I think for the first time I truly understood . . . *there but for the grace of God go I.*"

He swung his head to look at her. The light from the lantern limned the proud lines of her face with a soft glow, touched her hair with a fire it lacked by the light of day. He said, "So that's why you set yourself to discover who she was and why she was killed? Out of guilt? Because your life remained privileged and safe while hers . . . fell apart?"

A trembling smile touched her lips. "I'm not exactly safe now, am I?" She shivered, and he reached awkwardly out to draw her against the heat of his body. He expected her to resist, but all she said was, "I am so scared."

He chaffed his hands up and down the cold flesh of her arms, rested his chin on the top of her head, and held her close. "So am I."

At one point, she said, "Tell me about your time in the Army."

And so he talked to her about the places he'd been, and about the War. He found himself telling her things he'd never told anyone, not even Kat. He talked to her about the things he'd seen, and the things he'd done, and why in the end he'd realized he had to leave it all behind or lose himself in a world where everything he believed in could be sacrificed for a chimera. When he fell silent after a time, she said, "Don't stop. Please. Just . . . talk."

And so he did.

She said to him, "If we die here today, what will you regret never having done?"

He tightened his arms around her, holding her so that her back was against his bare chest. Holding her that way, he couldn't see her face and she couldn't see him. After a moment's thought, he said, "I suppose I regret having failed my father. The one thing above all else he wanted of me was that I marry and sire an heir. I didn't do that." He hesitated. "Why? What do you regret?"

She leaned her head back against his shoulder. "So many things. I've always wanted to travel. Sail up the

Nile. Explore the jungles of Africa. Cross the deserts of Mesopotamia to the land of the Hindu Kush."

He found himself smiling. "I can see you doing that. What else?"

She, too, was quiet for a moment. He felt her chest rise with a deeply drawn breath, then fall. "I regret never having known what it's like to have a child of my own. Which is an odd thing to realize, since I never intended to marry."

"You didn't? Why not?"

"A woman who marries in England today consigns herself to a legal status little different from that occupied by slaves in America."

"Ah. You're a student of Mary Wollstonecraft."

She twisted around to look up at him. "You know of her work?"

"That surprises you?"

"Yes."

He said, "She married."

"I know. I've never been able to figure out why."

He smiled against her hair. "You wouldn't."

A silence stretched out, filled with awareness of things said and unsaid. And then the big bell of St. Clements began to toll the hour, followed by its echo. Five o'clock.

"Oh, God." She pushed away from him, thrusting up from the ledge to stalk across the shadowy chamber to where the pile of rubble separated them from the river. She stood with her back to him, her hands coming up to rake the loose hair from her face, her fingers clenching together behind her neck. When the chimes of St. Clements began to play "Lass o' Glowrie," she shifted her hands to cover her ears, as if to block out the sound. "I don't want to die. Not yet. Not here. Not like this."

He went to her, drawing her back into the comfort of his arms. She turned toward him, her face lifting to his.

Her kiss was a maiden's kiss, driven by fear and despera-
tion rather than lust. And he clung to her as fervently
as she clung to him, because he knew her horror, and
shared it.

He heard her breath catch, felt her body arch against
his as the bells of St. Clements echoed away into stillness. He knew a strange sense of wonder, like a man
awakening from a long, drugged sleep. And he thought,
This is what life feels like. This is what a woman feels like.
Skin soft, heart pounding against his, her hand guiding
his to all the secret places she'd never been touched. No
restraints now. No strictures of society that could stand
in the face of looming death.

Picking her up, he carried her back to where the
lantern cast a pool of golden warmth. He felt her eyes
watching him as he eased her down beneath him. He
said, "Tell me this is what you want."

In answer, she slid her hands up to his neck and
wrapped her legs around his waist.

She kept her eyes wide-open when he entered her.
She cried out once, sharply, her breath coming in quick
little pants. He tasted the tears spilling wetly down her
cheeks. He said, "I can stop."

She said, "Don't stop," and closed her eyes.

Fiercely, she held him to her as if she could in this last
act of defiance and by sheer force of will hold on to life
itself. He'd thought himself dead within. Had at times
found himself wishing for death. Ironic that he should
be so aware of the life coursing through him now, when
he was about to lose it.

"Hold me," she whispered, her breath warm against
his ear, her fingers curling into his shoulders.

He'd known somehow that she would taste like this,
feel like this. As he loomed over her in the flickering
darkness, she said, "The French call it *le petit mort*. I've
always wondered why."

And he said, "What could be more intimate than to die together?"

Afterward, he smoothed the damp hair away from her high forehead. His hand shook, his breath still coming hard and fast. Then he stilled, his attention caught by a distant sound.

She seemed to sense his tension. "What is it?" she asked, or started to ask. Except by then the sound was unmistakable. It was the relentless surge of rushing water.

Chapter 42

*T*hrusting up from the ledge where they had lain together, Sebastian scrambled into his breeches and
reached for the lantern. The candle was nearly gone
now, guttering in its socket as he held the lantern high.
For a moment the light dimmed and almost went out.

The water was a black torrent seeping through the
rubble fill. He grabbed Hero's hand, dragging her with
him to the iron gate. Already he could feel the water
cold against his feet. "Climb up onto the crosspiece of
the gate," he shouted.

She clung to the iron bars, her eyes huge in a pale
face, her hair loose around her. She said, "Throw the
lantern."

His gaze met hers.

"Throw it," she said. "It might ignite the clothes."

It was one last crazy gesture of defiance. He eased the
battered tin and horn cylinder between the bars, trans-
ferring his grip to the base. It was awkward, throwing
it that way, the hot metal burning his fingers. The lantern soared up the stair shaft, the light flickering over
stone coffers and worn steps. Then it slammed against
the wooden door in a rending of tin and horn and they
were plunged into darkness.

He moved to stand behind her, his body close to hers.

The water was already lapping at their ankles. He said, "When the water gets too high, you must stand on my shoulders."

Her teeth were clenched so tightly against the numbing strain of cold and fear that she could barely push out the words. "To buy myself an extra minute? No."

He rested his cheek against her hair, his body bracketing hers, his grip on the iron bars tightening as he felt the tug of the water swirling around his legs.

She said, "I never liked you. What an irony that we should die together." And he laughed.

The water was at his hips when he heard the scraping of a bolt being drawn back above. He stiffened, anger surging through him. "It seems our murderers have misjudged the tide," he said softly against her ear.

Her head came up, her body jerking as sunlight flooded in from above and a man's puzzled voice echoed down to them. "Wot the bloody 'ell? There's a pile o' burned clothes 'ere! That musta been wot started the fire. Only wot the bloody 'ell—"

"Help!" she screamed. "Help us, quickly!"

Sebastian added his voice to hers. "We're trapped down here behind a gate and the tide is coming in. Get a crowbar to break the padlocked chain. *Quickly!*"

The stairwell filled with gruff voices and the clomp of heavy boots tramping down the steps to splash through the water that crept ever higher. A giant of a man with red hair and a full blond beard eased one end of a crowbar into the loops of the padlocked chain, his face purpling with strain as he broke the links.

"Wot the 'ell ye doin' down 'ere?" he asked as Hero Jarvis, her wet shift clinging to her skin, fell against him.

Helping hands reached out to grip them, drag them up to light and fresh air and the blessed, unexpected warmth of the late-afternoon sun. A blanket appeared, passed from hand to hand. Miss Jarvis clenched it around

her like a cloak, her face so pinched with cold her lips
were blue.

Sebastian took a deep gulp from a brandy flask
pressed into his hands and said, "How did you know?"

One of their rescuers—the red-haired giant with the
bushy beard—said, "We smelled smoke. Ain't nothing
a lumberman fears more'n fire. So we come to investigate."

Sebastian's gaze fell to the charred vegetation at his
feet. And he realized some of the clothes they'd thrown
to the top of the stairs must have wedged into the gap
between the bottom of the old door and the worn lintel
beneath. The fire might have gone out in the stairwell,
but at some point it had obviously burned beneath the
door enough to catch the long lank grass of the Duke of
Somerset's ruined, forgotten garden and set it alight.

The crowd around them was growing. Smocked workmen from the timber wharf and ostlers from the livery
jostled with barmaids from the Crow and Magpie. Sebastian noticed Miss Jarvis studying the sea of curious faces,
searching the assembly for their would-be murderers.

"Are they here?" he whispered, leaning in close to
her. But she only shivered and shook her head.

He found his purse in the pocket of his ruined coat
amid the pile of charred clothes at the top of the stairs
and stood for a round of drinks at the Crow and Magpie.
A cheer went up as the crowd surged toward the inn.
A strapping barmaid eyed the coins in Sebastian's hand
and offered to sell "the lady" her best spare dress.

"An' I got me a good stout cloak, too," said the barmaid, "what you could buy."

"Get the lady out of this," said Sebastian, pressing another coin into her hand. "And see that she has some hot
water to wash."

The barmaid's eyes widened. "We got a real nice
chamber upstairs where she can clean up," said the bar-

maid, shepherding Miss Jarvis toward the stairs. For one instant, Lord Jarvis's daughter turned, her gaze meeting his over the heads of the noisy throng. Then she was gone.

Half an hour later, he put her into a hackney carriage and gave the driver an address a block from her own home. It was the first private moment Sebastian had had with her, and before he shut the door on her, he managed to say, "I am prepared to do the honorable thing—"

She snapped, "Don't be ridiculous," and told the jarvey to drive on.

Alighting from the hackney a block from Berkeley Square, Hero drew the hood of her barmaid's rough cloak up around her face and walked briskly toward her house.

She expected to be stared at. Instead, no one paid her any heed. She was just one more cheaply dressed woman amidst a stream of housemaids and dairymaids, shopkeepers and traders' wives. And she realized she'd caught a glimpse of the anonymity that Viscount Devlin sometimes employed so effectively in the course of his investigations. She'd never before understood what a heady sense of freedom it entailed.

Her knock was answered by Grisham, the butler, his condescending attempts to redirect her to the area entrance cut short when she shoved back her hood and brushed past him. "Miss Jarvis!" he said with a gasp. "I do beg your par—"

"That's quite all right," said Hero, heading for the stairs.

She had the misfortune to meet her mother on the first-floor landing. But Lady Jarvis simply smiled at her vaguely and said, "I don't recall that cloak, Hero." The smile faded, her eyebrows puckering together. "We really must consider changing your modiste."

Hero gave a startled laugh. "I'm simply trying it on for a costume ball. I was thinking of going as a common barmaid."

Lady Jarvis pulled her chin back against her neck. "I suppose you could if you wanted to, dear. But don't you think it's rather, well, common?"

"Perhaps you're right," said Hero, as if much struck. "Perhaps I'll go as Jane Seymour."

She was halfway up the stairs to the second floor before Lady Jarvis said, "Is there a fancy-dress ball soon? I don't recall hearing about it. Goodness, I've given no thought to a costume myself."

"Perhaps I simply heard someone talk about the possibility of giving one," said Hero, terrified by a sudden vision of Lady Jarvis bringing up the topic of the nonexistent masquerade at her next soiree.

"Oh," said Lady Jarvis, and continued on her way down the stairs.

Gaining the refuge of her own bedroom, Hero tore off her ragged clothes, and rang for her maid and a hot bath. She realized she was shivering again. Wrapped in a dressing gown, she went to sit on the window seat overlooking the Square below.

The dying light of the day drenched the garden's plane trees and yew hedges with a golden richness they usually lacked. Yet the scene was otherwise unaltered from the tableau she'd seen every other evening of her life in London. She could see milkmaids heading toward home, their empty pails swinging from their shoulder yokes. A lady's carriage whirled up the street toward the east, the *clip-clop* of its horses' hooves echoing up between the tall houses. Everything was the same as it had been before.

Only Hero was different.

Chapter 43

"It's fortunate you made your visit to Strand Lane dressed as a groom," said Calhoun, picking up one sodden boot between a carefully extended thumb and forefinger. "From the looks of it, this lot's good for naught else but the dustman." His nose wrinkled. "And from the smell of it. Is it my imagination, or is the dressing room beginning to acquire a fishy odor?"

Sebastian settled back in his copper hip bath and closed his eyes. "I've noticed I'm becoming decidedly popular with the stable cats."

"Tom tells me the horses are still missing."

"I've set the constables to scouring every livery in the area. They may yet turn up."

"What was your assailants' plan, do you think?"

Sebastian tipped his head forward so he could probe the tender area near the base of his skull with careful fingers. "They probably would have waited until after dark to remove our bodies and dump us in the river someplace. Make it look as if we'd drowned when a wherry boat overturned or some such thing."

Calhoun bundled the ruined boots and breeches together, then hesitated. "And would you still be interested in the whereabouts of Hessy Abrahams from the Orchard Street Academy?"

Sebastian glanced around. "You've found her?"

The valet was looking unusually serious. "Not exactly. But I've someone you'll want to be talking to."

"Oh?"

"A woman named Maggie McQueen. Until two nights ago she was a charwoman at the Academy. She left when she decided the atmosphere of the place was becoming unhealthy."

"Unhealthy?"

"Lethal."

"She knows what happened to Hessy Abrahams?"

"According to Maggie McQueen, Hessy is dead."

Sebastian decided to take his town carriage. His head ached, and despite the hot bath, he was still occasionally racked by chills.

"If you don't mind my saying so, my lord, you look like the devil," commented Calhoun, taking the forward seat.

Sebastian sneezed. "I feel like the devil."

Darkness had fallen, enveloping the city in a starless black blanket. They rode through streets lit by the flickering light of carriage lamps and the torches of running linkboys. A light rain had begun to fall, glazing the paving stones with a slick wetness and driving indoors the throngs that usually crowded around the city's grogshops.

Their destination proved to be an unsavory flash house in a back alley in Stepney called the Blue Anchor, owned by Calhoun's notorious mother. The timbers of the jutting upper story were gray with age. Passing drays had knocked bricks off the corners of the ground floor so that the building gave the appearance of an old man missing half his teeth. But inside, the Blue Anchor was warm and snug. Its ancient bar, booths, and wainscoting might be black with age, but the public room smelled pleasantly of beeswax mingled with ale and gin.

Sebastian sneezed again. "This is the infamous Blue Anchor?"

"Not what you were expecting, my lord?" said Calhoun. He led the way to a cabinet behind the stairs. "I won't be a moment."

Sebastian subsided into one of the comfortably worn chairs beside the fire, closed his eyes, and listened to the pounding in his head. Calhoun was back all too soon with a glass of hot rum punch for Sebastian and a wizened little woman with lank gray hair, a broad nose, and unexpectedly bright black eyes.

"Your lordship, this is Maggie McQueen," said Calhoun, steering her toward the seat opposite Sebastian. "Now, Maggie, I want you to tell his lordship everything you told me."

Maggie ran her shrewd gaze over Sebastian and evidently found him wanting. "What the bloooody hell happened to you?" she demanded in a thick Geordie accent.

"I suppose you could say I fell in the river." It wasn't strictly true, of course, since the river had come to him. But he didn't feel up to explaining it.

Maggie grunted. "Harebrained thing to have done. Were you foxed, then?"

"I'm afraid I don't have that excuse."

She grunted again. "The boy here, he tells uz you're interested in what happened at the Academy a week ago Wednesday night."

It took Sebastian a moment to realize that by "the boy" she meant Jules Calhoun. "Very interested," said Sebastian, taking a sip of his hot rum punch. A tingling warmth began to spread through his body.

"Mind you, Aa never could make sense of it all," said Maggie, extracting a white clay pipe from some hidden pocket and beginning to pack it with tobacco. "But then Aa divint think anyone could, 'cept maybe them two whores, and they're long gone now, aren't they?"

As long as he remembered that "Aa" meant "I" and that Geordies liked to put as many vowels as possible into a word, Sebastian figured he might be able to get through the conversation. He said, "You mean Rose Fletcher and Hannah Green?"

"That's right. It wasnit until after we'd found the bodies that anyone even noticed they'd up and disappeared."

"Bodies?" said Sebastian.

Maggie kindled a spill and held the glowing end to her pipe, her cheeks hollowing as she sucked. Sebastian waited with mounting impatience until the tobacco caught and she drew on it several times, blowing out a stream of fragrant smoke. "Bodies," she said. Only, the way she said it, it came out sounding like "booodies."

"Men, or women?"

"One man, one woman."

Sebastian sat forward, the rum punch clasped in both hands. He breathed in the fragrant fumes of all-spice, cinnamon, and hot rum, and felt the pounding in his head begin to ease. "Do you know who they were?"

"Aa divint know nothing aboooot the man, 'cept that he was a cooostomer. But the dead girl, she was Hessy Abrahams."

"They were found together?"

"Ach. No. The man, he was in the Chinese room, while our Hessy was in the peep room near the back stairs."

"The peep room?"

"For them that likes to watch," said Maggie without a trace of embarrassment or coquetry.

Sebastian exchanged glances with Calhoun. They had started out investigating the death of one young woman shot down in an alley, but the number of dead just kept multiplying. He said, "The dead man in the Chinese room . . . whose customer was he?"

"Why, he was Rose's."

Sebastian took a long, thoughtful sip of his punch. "Can you tell me what he looked like?"

Maggie drew on her pipe, her eyes half closing in thought. "He was young." She subjected Sebastian to a moment's scrutiny, then said, "Abooot your age, Aa'd say. Maybe a mite older, maybe a mite younger. But fair, like the boy here." She glanced at Calhoun. "Can't remember anything remarkable abooot him, 'cept he had a scar across his belly. Like this." She drew a diagonal line across her stomach.

"He was naked?"

Maggie nodded. "Some men just drop their breeches and get dooon to it, but this 'un, he'd paid for a whole hour."

"How did he die? Do you know?"

Maggie shrugged. "Stabbed, Aa suppose. Leastways, he was sure bleeding all over the place. Took uz forever to clean it all ooooop." She hesitated. "Didint see a chir, though."

"A what?"

"A knife," supplied Calhoun.

"Ah." Sebastian fortified himself with more punch. "What about the man who was with Hannah Green?" he asked. "Did you see him?"

"No. But Aa heard him, all right. He raised quite a ruckus on account of her going off and leaving him like that. Miss Lil had to give him his money back."

"Ian Kane wasn't there?"

"Not then, no. Miss Lil sent for him, after she found the bodies."

"What did Kane do with them?" Sebastian asked, intrigued. "The bodies, I mean."

Maggie McQueen narrowed her eyes against the smoke of her pipe. "You ask a powerful lot of questions for a lord." She cast a sideways glance at Calhoun. "You sure he's a real lord?"

"The bona fide article," said Calhoun solemnly.

"The bodies," prompted Sebastian. "What did Kane do with them?"

She shrugged. "Dumped 'em someplace. Aa divint knaa wair. What else was he gonna do with 'em? Call in the magistrates?" She gave a low, earthy chuckle.

Sebastian glanced at his valet. " 'Aa divint knaa wair'?"

Calhoun leaned forward to whisper, "I don't know where."

"Oh," said Sebastian. Tipping back his head, he drained his glass. The movement made him vaguely dizzy so that it was a moment before he could say, "The man who was with Hessy Abrahams—her customer. Did you see him?"

"Nah. Aa s'pose he walked ooot the house alive. Aa only seen the dead man because Aa helped wrap him in a length of canvas so's Thackery could carry him oooot the house," she added by way of explanation.

"Thackery?"

"He used t'be a gentleman of the Fancy."

"Ah, yes," said Sebastian, remembering the pugilist with the broken nose and cauliflower ear. "I believe I met Mr. Thackery."

Maggie McQueen squinted at him through a cloud of tobacco smoke. "You don't look so good. Too many late nights'll do that to you."

"Indeed they will," agreed Sebastian. "How well did you know Rose Fletcher?"

"Know her?" Maggie gave a harsh laugh that ended in a cough. "Aa'm a charwoman. You think them whores had aught t'do with the likes of uz?"

"But you knew who she was."

Maggie sucked on her pipe. "Aye. She was the one who cried all the time. When she thought no one was looking, of course. But Maggie sees more than most."

"Why do you think she cried?"

"Why do *you* think she cried?" said Maggie scornfully. "Why does any woman cry?"

Sebastian studied Maggie McQueen's bright dark eyes, age-worn face, and work-gnarled hands. "Do they cry much?" he asked quietly. "The women of the Orchard Street Academy?"

Maggie shook her head. "Not most o'm. Most o'm have more'n they ever dreamed of—plenty of food, a roof o'er their heads, nice clothes."

"But Rose?"

"That one . . ." Maggie hesitated, the smoke from her pipe drifting up to waft around her head. "She grew up dreaming of other things."

Yet still she stayed, Sebastian thought, *caught in a purgatory of her own making, trapped by self-loathing and misplaced guilt and suffering for the sins of others.* Aloud, he said, "Why did you leave the Academy?"

Maggie knocked the ashes out of her pipe against the hearth and prepared to stand up. "You come around asking questions. They got nervous."

"They?"

She shrugged. "Mr. Kane. Miss Lil. Thackery. Aa seen 'em loooking at uz. Wondering if Aa'd squawk. Old woman like uz, who'd notice if Aa disappeared one day? So Aa disappeared meself. Afore they could make uz disappear." She hawked up a mouthful of phlegm and shot it at a nearby spittoon with flawless accuracy.

"Did you see Hessy Abrahams's body?" asked Sebastian.

" 'Course Aa did. Aa wrapped it in canvas, too."

"Was she stabbed, as well?"

Maggie pushed to her feet. "Nawh. Twern't no blooood on her. Somebody'd gone and snapped her neck. Just like a chicken ready for the pot."

Chapter 44

Saturday, 9 May 1812

*T*he Black Dragon lay somber and quiet in the cold light of early dawn, a dark lair for the shadowy prince of an underground realm of sin and despair. Ian Kane might not have all the answers to what had happened at the Orchard Street Academy on that fateful Wednesday night, but Sebastian had no doubt the Lancashire man knew more about those events than his charwoman. The problem would be getting close enough to the man to question him.

Sebastian watched the tavern for a time from across the street, where a scattering of ashes and a black scorch mark on the broken paving stones marked the spot once occupied by the hot potato seller. A few men turned to stare at him as they passed, their jaws unshaven, their eyes sunken. But the streets were largely empty. This was a district that really only came to life in the afternoon and evening.

A noisome alley ran along the south side of the tavern. Crossing the street, Sebastian took a deep breath and ducked down the passageway, his bootheels crunching the debris of broken bottles and oyster shells and rain-sodden playbills that fluttered halfheartedly in the breeze. Like most alleys in London, this one served the area's residents as an outdoor chamber pot. It made a change from the smell of fish, but he doubted Calhoun would consider it an improvement.

After his last visit to the Black Dragon, Sebastian suspected his chances of simply strolling in the front door unmolested were limited. He needed a less direct entrance.

He found the door that opened onto the alley from the tavern's kitchens and, just beyond it, a flight of rickety wooden steps that led up to the first floor. Beyond that the alley ended abruptly in a high brick wall. Sebastian was standing at the base of the stairs and considering his options when the kitchen door opened behind him.

He swung around to see a burly man wearing a brown corduroy coat back into the alley as he wrestled with an overflowing dustbin. He was followed by a second man with a broken nose and cauliflower ear who dumped an armload of broken-up crates to the side of the door, then straightened. Sebastian recognized Thackery, the ex-pugilist from the Orchard Street Academy.

"Well, well," said Thackery, his small black eyes lighting up at the sight of Sebastian. "Look what we got here." His smile widened to show his broken brown teeth. "I see ye forgot yer bloody walking stick."

With a brick wall behind him and two thugs in front of him, Sebastian's options had suddenly become limited. He took a step forward and slammed his bootheel into the pugilist's right knee. "That is the one I hit before, isn't it?" he said as the ex-fighter went down with a howl.

"Wot the 'ell?" The burly man in brown corduroy set down his dustbin with a thump and reached inside it to pull out a broken bottle. "Ye know this cove, Thackery?" Moving into the center of the passageway, he crouched down into a street fighters' stance, the broken bottle held like a knife. "Looks like ye wandered down the wrong alley," he said to Sebastian.

One hand clamped to his knee, Thackery staggered up to lean against the soot-stained brick wall behind him, his breath coming hard and fast. Sebastian kicked again, this time aiming at the dustbin. It toppled over with a cascading crash of broken glass and animal bones that knocked the other man off his feet in a swill of stinking refuse. Leaping over the strewn garbage, Sebastian managed to take two steps toward the mouth of the alley before Thackery came off the wall at him.

Big and enraged, the man caught Sebastian in a rush that carried him across the alley to slam him up against the far wall. The impact sent the breath whooshing out of Sebastian. He was dimly aware of light spilling down the steps as the door to the first floor opened above them. Then Thackery picked Sebastian up bodily and pinned him to the bricks.

Gripping his hands together, Sebastian pyramided his forearms and drove them up, intending to break the pugilist's grip on his jacket. It didn't work. Nonplussed, he hammered his doubled fist down into the man's face. Thackery grunted but stood firm.

His hands still locked together, Sebastian swung his doubled fists back, then slammed them into the side of Thackery's head. He still didn't budge.

"That's enough," said Ian Kane from the top of the steps. "Let him go."

Thackery hesitated.

"You heard me. Let him go."

Breathing heavily, his face red, Thackery took a step back and let Sebastian slide down the wall.

Sebastian straightened his lapels and adjusted the folds of his cravat.

"Since you're here, you might as well come up," said

Ian Kane, resplendent in buckskin breeches and a silk paisley dressing gown in swirls of red and blue.

"Thank you," said Sebastian, aware of Thackery's angry gaze following him as he picked up his hat and mounted the steps.

"Some ale?" asked Kane, leading the way into a comfortable old parlor with gleaming wainscoting and an elaborately carved stone hearth.

"Please," said Sebastian, his gaze on the carved caryatids holding up the mantel. "Lovely piece."

"Yes, it is, isn't it?"

Sebastian surveyed the damage to his hat. "I've been hearing some interesting tales about the Academy."

"You know what they say," said Kane, going to pour two glasses of ale. "You don't want t'be believing everything you hear."

"No denying that," agreed Sebastian. "For instance, I heard there were only two women missing from your house—Rose Fletcher and Hannah Green. Now I discover there's actually a third. Hessy Abrahams."

Kane's head came up just a shade too fast. But otherwise, he gave nothing away. He held out one of the glasses of ale. "It seems you know more about my establishment than I do."

"Do I?" said Sebastian, taking the ale. "It's my understanding Hessy Abrahams didn't run away like the others. She was murdered."

Kane raised his own glass to his lips. "You must have been talking to one of my competitors. They're always spreading dastardly tales about me."

"Actually, I've been talking to Maggie McQueen."

"Ah. Dear Maggie. I wondered where she'd taken herself off to."

Sebastian held his ale without tasting it. "Something rather spectacular happened in your house on Wednesday of last week, Kane. What was it?"

Kane shrugged. "I wasn't there."

"Maybe. But nothing happens in one of your houses that you don't know about."

A smile lit up the other man's eyes. "I heard that Bow Street magistrate—Sir William—died of an apoplectic fit in his own public office."

"Well, you can't believe everything you hear."

Kane gave a short bark of laughter and went to stretch out in an upholstered seat near the fire. "Very well. You like stories, Lord Devlin? I'll tell you a story. Once upon a time there were three gentlemen out on the town. Like most young men, they had a perennial itch in their pants. As ill luck would have it, they chose to scratch their itch at the Orchard Street Academy. They selected three Cyprians and disappeared up the stairs with them. After that, I'm afraid, the tale becomes rather murky. The next thing we know, one of the gentlemen is raising a dust because his particular Bird of Paradise has flown—without, it seems, performing the services for which he had already handed over a substantial sum. Prime articles in my establishment do not come cheap, you understand."

"And his lady of choice was?"

"Hannah Green. Miss Lil was still looking for dear Hannah when she discovered Hessy."

"With her neck broken."

"You've heard this tale before."

"Not in its entirety," said Sebastian. "And the gentleman who had selected Hessy?"

"Disappeared."

"Like Hannah Green," said Sebastian.

"That's right."

"What about Rose Fletcher?"

"Rose, too, had simply vanished."

"Leaving a dead customer in her bed?"

"Unfortunately, yes." Kane leaned back in his chair. "I'm sure you understand my position. Dead bodies are not good for business. They attract all sorts of unwelcome attention from the local constabulary and scare away customers."

"So you—what? Dumped the bodies in the river? Buried them in Bethnal Green?"

Kane gave a slow smile. "Something like that."

"It's an interesting story. There's just one small problem."

"What's that?"

"It doesn't make any sense."

Kane pressed his splayed hands to his chest in mock astonishment. "Stories need to make sense?" His hands fell. "I'll be frank with you, my lord. I don't understand what happened that night. All I know is that a few more nights like that and the Academy will be out of business."

"Had you ever seen any of the three men before?"

Kane's lips curved up into a slow smile. "You forget, my lord, I wasn't there."

"The dead man, then. You saw him. Did you recognize him?"

"Believe me, Lord Devlin, I don't have the slightest idea who he was."

"Believe you, Mr. Kane? Now why should I believe you?"

Ian Kane was no longer smiling. "I could have let Thackery and Johnson kill you in the alley."

Sebastian set aside his ale untouched. If the confrontation hadn't occurred in uncomfortable proximity to the Black Dragon, Sebastian doubted the brothel owner would have felt compelled to interfere. As the man said, dead bodies weren't good for business. "That wasn't a matter of altruism. That was just . . . geography."

Kane stayed where he was, his head falling back as he watched Sebastian turn toward the door. "Then I suggest that in the future you choose your locales wisely."

Chapter 45

Sebastian sat on the scorched, crumbling remnant of a wall and breathed in the pungent smell of wet burned wood and old ash. He'd come here to what was left of the Magdalene House after leaving the Black Dragon in St. Giles. A journeyman glazier passing in the street threw him a sharp look, but kept walking. Sebastian stared out over the charred jumble of debris and wondered why he hadn't seen it before.

What manner of men would kill seven unknown women just to get at one? The answer was only too obvious. *Men who were accustomed to killing.* And no one was more accustomed to killing than military men.

He thought about the girl from the cheesemonger's shop, Pippa. She'd given him a clue that first day, when she'd told him the gentlemen she'd seen watching the Magdalene House had reminded her of some old Nabob. One could always tell a Nabob by his sun-darkened skin, just as one could tell the military men who had spent years under the fierce suns of India and the Sudan, Egypt and the West Indies.

The sound of boot leather scraping over fallen timbers brought Sebastian's head around. "What are you doing here?" asked Cedric Fairchild, picking his way toward him.

"Trying to make sense of all this." He studied the younger man's haggard face. "What brings you here?"

"I don't know." Cedric stood with his hands thrust into the pockets of his coat, his shoulders hunched against the dampness as he stared out over the house's shattered walls and twisted, burned contents. "I can't believe she died here. I keep thinking that if I'd only managed to talk her into leaving—"

"Don't," said Sebastian. "It's not your fault."

Cedric swung his head to look at him. "Yes, it is." He sucked in a breath that seemed to shudder his entire frame. "I was talking to Georgina—Lady Sewell. My sister. She'd heard about Rachel's death and came to see me. She told me something I didn't know. It seems that last summer—before I came home—Rachel did quarrel with Ramsey. So maybe my father was right. That is why she ran away."

Sebastian's brows drew together. "Would Lord Fairchild have forced her to marry Ramsey even if she had changed her mind?"

"I don't know. I never thought about it. I suppose he might. He's a stickler for the proprieties, you know. And if she'd broken off her betrothal, there would doubtless have been a scandal."

Sebastian watched as Pippa from the cheesemonger's across the street came and stood in her shop's doorway, a frown on her face as she narrowed her eyes, watching them.

Cedric said, "I don't understand why you're poking into the past, asking these questions about Rachel. About my family. What's any of it got to do with this?" He swept his arm in a wide arc that took in the fallen, blackened beams, the crumbling chimney of what was once a fireplace.

"I'm not certain it has anything to do with it," Sebastian admitted.

Cedric's arm dropped to his side. "My father's not well, you know. The news about Rachel hit him hard."

"You told him it was true?"

"My sister told him."

"And he believed it? He accepted that she is dead?"

Cedric's gaze shifted away. "I don't know. He said he didn't. I mean, it's hard to believe, isn't it, with her body burned like that? But he's—he's not himself. I'm worried about him."

Sebastian felt his lips curl into a wry smile. "You want me to stop asking questions about Rachel. Is that what you're saying?"

"She's dead! Dead and buried. Knowing what happened to her isn't going to bring her back, but it could very well kill our father." Cedric jerked his head toward the back of the burned-out house. "You want to find out what happened to the women in this house, fine. But leave my family out of it!"

In the sudden silence that followed his outburst, Sebastian could hear the rattle of a shutter being thrust up. He glanced down at his clasped hands, then up at the other man's tight-lipped face. Cedric Fairchild might have been to war, but he suddenly looked very, very young. Sebastian said, "This man who's missing . . . Max Ludlow. Did you know him well?"

Cedric frowned, as if confused by the shift in subject. "I've met him a few times. But I don't know him well, no. I never served with him."

"He was in the hussars?"

"Until he sold out, yes."

"Was he ever wounded?"

"In Argentina, I believe." Cedric's eyes narrowed. "Why?"

Sebastian was thinking about a dead man in a brothel room with an old scar like a saber slash running diagonally across his belly. But all he said was, "Just wondering." He glanced across the street at the cheesemonger's shop.

Pippa had disappeared.

"It don't make no sense," said Tom from his perch at the rear of Sebastian's curricle. "It's near three o'clock. 'Ow can this Lady Melbourne be 'avin' a picnic breakfast?"

Sebastian neatly featheredged a corner. They were passing through Putney on their way to Kew, the site of Lady Melbourne's highly anticipated breakfast. "Breakfasts are like morning calls, which is to say they take place in the afternoon. When you don't generally get up before midday, it shifts things a bit."

"You reckon this Mr. Ramsey will be there?"

"He has a sister he's launching into society. Lady Melbourne's picnic breakfast is one of the most important events of the Season. He'll be there."

They arrived at Kew to find the wildflower-strewn hillside near the pagoda crowded with linen-draped tables set with gleaming silver and crystal. "Gor," said Tom, practically falling off his perch as he craned around to stare. " 'Ow'd they get all this out 'ere?"

"The servants brought the tables and trimmings in wagons and set it up before her ladyship's guests arrived."

The tiger cast a thoughtful eye toward the clouds above. "And if'n it rains?"

"On Lady Melbourne's picnic?" Sebastian handed over the reins and jumped down. "It wouldn't dare."

Winding his way through liveried servants and ladies with parasols, Sebastian was aware of his sister, Amanda, glaring at him from near the towering, dragon-roofed pagoda. He deliberately avoided her, only to fall into the clutches of the Prime Minister, Spencer Perceval.

"I'm surprised to see you here, Devlin," said Perceval, hailing him. "Not usually your type of scene, is it?"

"Nor yours, I'd have said."

The Prime Minister raised his wineglass with a wry grimace. "I have six daughters, which means I'll be fighting flies and ants for my food for many years to come, I'm afraid. What is it about the concept of alfresco dining that so captivates the fair sex?"

Sebastian nodded to where the Prime Minister's daughter—a vision in white muslin and chip straw— stood laughing with a friend. "It does show them to advantage, don't you agree?"

"There is that," agreed Perceval. He took another sip of his wine and said with feigned nonchalance, "Your father tells me you've no interest in politics."

"No."

The Prime Minister looked nonplussed. "We could use a man like you in the House of Commons."

Sebastian hid a smile. "I doubt it."

"There's trouble brewing over the Orders in Council, you know. Bloody Americans. They've had their sights set on annexing Canada for thirty years now. There are reports they're planning an invasion and using the Orders in Council as an excuse."

"You're expecting a revolt in the Commons, are you?"

"There's a formal Inquiry scheduled for Monday evening's session. But it's not just the Commons. It's the Lords, too. Fairchild is leading the pack. He's saying we ought to rescind the Orders. Appease the Americans."

"There's no doubt the timing would be bad for another war," said Sebastian. "We're already rather occupied with Napoleon."

"Hence the Americans' bellicosity. It's bloody opportunism."

"They're learning, aren't they?" said Sebastian, scanning the open hillside. He spotted Tristan Ramsey's young sister first, then the widowed Mrs. Ramsey. Tristan

Ramsey himself was rapidly disappearing down a path hemmed in by rhododendrons and lilacs. "Excuse me, sir," said Sebastian before the Prime Minister had a chance to launch into an impassioned defense of his much-maligned Orders in Council.

By striking a diagonal course through the shrubbery, Sebastian came out onto the path leading toward the distant pond just as Ramsey was casting an anxious glance back over his shoulder.

"If I didn't know better, Ramsey, I'd suspect you of trying to avoid me," said Sebastian, stepping out from behind a cascading wisteria in full bloom.

Ramsey's head snapped back around, his weak jaw sagging. "Of course I'm trying to avoid you. The last time I saw you, you nearly broke my nose. Any sane man would try to avoid you."

Sebastian smiled. "If you didn't want to risk having your cork drawn again, you shouldn't have left the ladies."

Ramsey threw a wild glance around, his mouth opening and shutting soundlessly as he realized the shrubbery effectively hid them from the view of the others.

Sebastian crossed his arms at his chest and said, "Tell me about the quarrel you had last summer with Rachel Fairchild."

"Quarrel? We didn't—"

"You did, Ramsey. Tell me. What was it about?"

The man's shoulders sagged, the air leaving his chest in a long, ragged exhalation. "Someone told her things about me. I don't know who. She wouldn't say."

"Told her . . . what?"

Ramsey's jaw tightened mulishly. "A man has appetites."

"She discovered you kept a mistress."

"A mistress? No." The man seemed indignant at the thought. "Nothing like that. Just every once in a while . . . You know what it's like. I can't imagine what she expected. She was always so skittish. Never wanting me to do more than kiss her hand, even after we were betrothed. What was I supposed to do? A man needs some relief."

"Someone told her you were in the habit of picking up prostitutes?"

Righteous indignation flared in Ramsey's eyes. "She followed me. Can you imagine such a thing? She followed me and watched me pick up some strumpet in the Haymarket."

"She confronted you?"

"Not there on the street, thank God. But the next day, when I came to take her for a drive. She said the most outlandish things, about how she'd thought I was different from other men." He gave a ragged laugh. "Like I was supposed to be a monk or something."

Sebastian stared out over a hillside covered with Turkish hazel and American sweet gum, and tried very, very hard to control his temper.

"I was pretty indignant, I can tell you." Ramsey's chest swelled with remembered pique. "I told her all men had appetites, and while I might be content to leave her alone while we were betrothed, I expected things to be different after the wedding."

Sebastian considered how a young woman like Rachel Fairchild, already traumatized by years of her father's unwanted attentions, must have reacted to a speech such as that. "And so she ran away," he said softly.

Ramsey bit his lip and nodded. "I went back the next day to try to reason with her—maybe moderate some of the things I'd said. But she was gone."

"When you saw her later, in Orchard Street, did she tell you how she had ended up there?"

Ramsey swallowed hard enough to bob his Adam's apple up and down. "She said she met an old woman who was kind to her—or at least that's what she thought at first. Turned out the old hag was a procuress."

It was an all too familiar story. Young women fallen on hard times or newly arrived from the country, befriended by helpful old women whose business it was to keep the brothels and whoremasters of the city supplied with fresh goods. Sebastian said, "But she had family—friends. She could have escaped."

Ramsey sniffed. "I asked her why she didn't leave."

"And?"

"She said the strangest thing. She said she'd spent the last ten years of her life fighting it, only now she realized there was no use. I didn't understand. It made no sense. But when I asked what she meant . . . that's when she told me I only had three minutes left."

His body swept by raw fury, Sebastian felt his hands curl into fists at his sides.

Tristan Ramsey's eyes widened and he took a prudent step back, his arms thrust out in front as if to ward off a malevolent spirit. "I told you everything. You've no call to hit me again!"

It wasn't the fear in Ramsey's eyes that gave Sebastian pause. What stopped him was the sweetness of that rush of anger, the ease with which the old familiar bloodlust of the battlefield could return to beguile a man. He'd seen where the seductive power of violence could lead a man.

Taking a deep breath, and then another, he forced himself to uncurl his fists and walk away.

Pleading a headache she didn't have, Hero begged off from accompanying her mother to Lady Melbourne's picnic and spent the afternoon curled up on the window seat in her room with a book open on her lap.

The irony of Hero Jarvis, determined spinster, succumbing to the lures of the flesh in a moment of frightened weakness was not lost on her. She kept telling herself that, with time, she would come to terms with the cascade of embarrassment and consternation in which she now floundered. Resolutely putting all thought of the incident out of her head, she'd just picked up her book again for perhaps the tenth time when the butler, Grisham, appeared to scratch at her door. "There is a personage here to see you, miss."

Hero looked around. "A *personage*?"

"Yes, miss. I hope I haven't done wrong to admit her, but I know your ... er ... activities do sometimes bring you into contact with a certain class of female which you would otherwise be—"

Hero cut him off. "Where is she?"

"I left her in the entrance hall with one of the footmen watching her."

"Watching her? What do you think she's going to do? Make off with the silver?"

"The thought had occurred to me."

Hero closed her book and hurried downstairs.

James the footman stood at the base of the steps, his back pressed against the paneled wall, his arms crossed at his chest, his gaze never wavering from the auburn-haired woman who sat perched on the edge of one of the Queen Anne chairs lined up along the hall. She wore a spangled pink dress striped à la Polonaise, with a blatantly low décolletage decorated with burgundy-colored ribbons. A saucy hat sporting three burgundy plumes completed the stunning ensemble. Once, the effect might have been jaunty. But the plumes drooped, the Cyprian's shoulders slumped, and she had one hand up to her mouth so that she could gnaw nervously on her thumbnail. Hero had never seen her before in her life.

"I understand you wished to see me?" said Hero.

The woman leapt up, her eyes wide. Now that Hero

was closer, she realized that beneath the plumes and rouge, the Cyprian was no more than a girl. Sixteen, perhaps, seventeen at the most. She was so small she barely came up to Hero's shoulder. She was visibly shaking with fear, but she notched her chin up, determined to brazen it out. "You're Miss Jarvis?"

"That's right," said Hero.

The girl cast a scornful glance at the footman. "I ain't here to prig yer bloody silver."

"Then why precisely are you here, Miss—?"

"I'm Hannah," said the girl. "Hannah Green."

Chapter 46

"Indeed?" said Hero, lifting one eyebrow. She'd wondered how long it would be before hordes of tawdry "Hannahs" started showing up at her door.

The girl frowned in confusion. "Aye," she said slowly.

Hero crossed her arms. "Prove it."

The girl's mouth sagged. "What? Ye don't believe me? Ye can ask anybody. They'll tell ye."

"Anybody such as . . . whom?"

The girl put her hand to her forehead. "Aw," she wailed, half turning away. "Now what the bloody 'ell am I supposed to do?"

"You could go back where you came from," suggested Hero, torn between annoyance and amusement.

"What? An' get me neck snapped like poor Tasmin?"

Amusement and annoyance both fled, chased by a cold chill. "Come in here." Hero put her hand on the girl's arm, plucked her into the morning room, and closed the door on the interested footman.

"Where precisely have you been?" Hero demanded.

The girl's eyes slid away, going round as they assessed the room with its yellow silk hangings and damask chairs, its gilt framed paintings and tall mirrors. "Gor," she breathed. "I ain't never seen nothin' like this. It makes the Academy's parlor look downright shabby, it does."

Hero spared a thought for her grandmother's reaction, were she to be told that her morning room compared favorably to a brothel. "After you left the Academy," said Hero, still unconvinced this ingenue really was Hannah Green, "what did you do?"

Hannah wandered the room. Hero kept an eye on Hannah's hands. Hannah said, "Rose drug me to that bloody Magdalene 'Ouse. She said we'd be safe there, that no one would think t'look for us there." Hannah's lips thinned with remembered outrage. "Six o'clock in the bloody morning!"

Understanding dawned. "They made you get up at six?"

"Not just get up. Get up and *pray*. For a whole bloody hour!"

"Every day?" said Hero.

"Aye! The first time, I thought it was just some mean trick they was playin' on us, but when they done it again the next day, I knew we were in for it."

"Rose didn't mind?"

"No," said Hannah in a voice tinged with mingled awe and exasperation. "I think she actually liked it. It was scary."

"So what did you do?"

"I left. I was afraid they might try to stop me, but if truth were told, I think them Quakers was glad to see the back of me."

"You weren't afraid to leave?"

"Nah. I mean, I was scared when we left the Academy, but after a couple of days, I started thinking it was all a hum, that Rose had made it all up." She reconsidered. "Well, most of it."

"Surely you didn't go back to the Academy?" Hero asked, stunned.

The girl looked at her as if she were daft. "Ye take me fer a flat or something? No. I got me a room off the

Haymarket." She paused. " 'Course, when I heard what happened at the Magdalene 'Ouse last Monday, I got scared all over again. I tried to lay low but, well, a body's got t'eat."

Hero studied the girl's animated face. If she really was Hannah Green, the girl was living proof that God takes care of idiots. "Tell me about Tasmin," said Hero.

The girl sniffed. "I was working the stretch between Norris Street and the George when she found me. She said there was a gentry mort willin' to pay ten pounds t'talk to me, but if'n we was smart, we could maybe figure out a way to get more."

Hero had actually offered twenty pounds to anyone who could put her in touch with Hannah Green. But Tasmin Poole had obviously been less than honest with her former coworker. "Go on."

The girl's eyes slid away. "Tasmin was gonna write ye—Tasmin was clever, ye know. She could read and write like nothin' you ever saw. She came up to m'room to work on writin' the note while I went to get us some sausage rolls. It's when I was comin' back that I saw that cove going into the lodging house."

"A man?" said Hero. "What man?"

"What do you mean, what man?" said Hannah scornfully. "Don't you know nothin'? The same man what killed Hessy."

Lady Jarvis's querulous voice could be heard raised in annoyance somewhere above stairs. Hero looked at Hannah's burgundy-plumed hat, the plunging décolletage, the glory of spangles and pink-and-white Polonaise stripes and said, "Wait here."

Yanking open the door, she found James standing patiently in the hall. "Watch her," Hero told him, then hurried upstairs to furnish herself with the reticule, hat, gloves, and parasol without which no respectable lady would be seen out of doors in London—no matter how nefarious her errand.

Hannah Green sat in the hackney pulled up across from Paul Gibson's surgery, her body rigid with mulish obstinacy. "I ain't goin' in there," she said with all a prostitute's loathing of the medical profession. "I don't need no doctor."

With difficulty, Hero resisted the urge to shake the girl. "That's not why we're here. You need someplace safe to stay. There isn't anyplace else." Not that Paul Gibson's surgery was exactly safe either, Hero thought, remembering the fate of the wounded assailant she'd brought here. But she kept that information to herself.

Hannah Green cast her a doubtful glance. "No medical exam?"

"No exam," promised Hero.

The girl consented to get out of the hackney. Hero paid off the driver, then had to practically pull the girl across the road.

"Good God," said Paul Gibson, his eyes widening when he opened the door to Hero's knock.

"Dr. Gibson, meet Hannah Green. I think," she added as Hannah glared at the surgeon and Gibson continued to stare in awe at the lady's burgundy plumed hat and spangled pink-and-white stripes. "I'm sorry, but I had no place else to take her," said Hero, putting her hand in the small of the girl's back and giving her a push that propelled her over the threshold and into the hall.

Chapter 47

Sebastian arrived back at his house in Brook Street to find a note from Paul Gibson awaiting him. The Irishman had written cryptically:

> I have an interesting guest I'm convinced you'll want to meet. Do come. Quickly.

The word "quickly" was heavily underscored three times.

"Why all the mystery?" Sebastian demanded when Gibson opened the door to him.

"I was concerned my message might fall into the wrong hands," said Gibson, turning to lead the way back down the hall.

"So who's your guest?"

"I have two, actually."

Sebastian stopped on the threshold of Gibson's parlor. Miss Jarvis stood beside the empty hearth, her gaze on the pickled pig's fetus on the mantel. She was turned half away from him, her spine as rigid and uncompromising as ever, her brown hair once again pulled back as neatly as a schoolteacher's, her forehead faintly crinkling as she stared with apparent fascination at the blob of purple-pink flesh in the jar. She looked as she had always looked and he wondered why that surprised him. As if that brief, desperate coupling in the dark should have transformed her and made her—what? Soft and winsome? *Hero Jarvis?* What an absurd conceit.

She turned then and he had the satisfaction of seeing her lips part on a quickly indrawn breath. And he knew in that moment she, too, was remembering the touch of flesh against flesh, the taste of salt on a questing tongue. Then a woman's voice said, "Bloody 'ell. You gonna make me say it all *again*?"

Looking around, he beheld a vision in spangled pink-and-white stripes that made him blink.

He was aware of Miss Jarvis's lips curling into that malicious smile that was so much like her father's. She said, "Lord Devlin, meet Hannah Green."

Sebastian studied the girl's button nose and scattering of freckles. Whatever he'd been expecting, it wasn't this—this exuberant bundle of irreverence. "Are you certain she really is Hannah Green?"

"Are you bamming me?" said the girl. "I'd have to be daft to be claimin' t'be me if'n I wasn't me. I don't want to be me right now."

"According to Hannah here, Tasmin Poole is dead," said Miss Jarvis by way of explanation. "Someone snapped her neck two nights ago."

"It was the same cove," said Hannah. "The one what come to the Academy and done for Hessy."

Sebastian went to pour himself a brandy. "Do you know who this cove is?" he asked, reaching for Gibson's decanter.

"Not exactly." She threw a questioning glance toward Miss Jarvis.

"Tell Lord Devlin what you told me. About the three men who hired you out of the house last week."

Sebastian looked up. "When was this?"

"Tuesday," said Hannah. "They was havin' a party,

you see. It was one of the coves' birthday, and they hired
Hessy, Rose, and me fer the whole night."

"Go on," said Sebastian, splashing brandy into a glass.
He silently offered some to Miss Jarvis and Gibson, but
only Gibson took him up on it.

"We'd done it before. I don't mean fer them three,"
Hannah hastened to add, her gaze on the brandy. "But
fer other coves." Her face shone with saucy glee. "It
can get a bit naughty, if you know what I mean. But
it's a lot less work than spending the night traipsing up
and down the stairs at the Academy."

Sebastian glanced at Miss Jarvis, with her primly
knotted spinster's hair and rigidly held spine. Did she
have any inkling of the wild Dionysian scene conjured
by Hannah Green's words? Of the kinds of things three
young men could demand of the compliant women
they'd bought for the night? And then it occurred to him
that she probably had a better idea now than she would
have twenty-four hours ago.

"What manner of men were they?" he asked.

"Gentlemen," said Hannah Green, as if that said
it all.

"Old? Young? Fat? Thin?"

"Pretty old," she said. Sebastian was picturing pon-
derous men with graying pates and drooping bellies
until she added, " 'Bout yer age."

"I'm twenty-nine." He glanced over at Miss Jarvis in
time to see her bring up her hand to hide a smile. He
said, "Did they take you to a house, or to rooms?"

"Rooms. Right fancy they were, too." She cast a dis-
paraging glance around Gibson's unpretentious parlor.
"More swell than this."

"Where were these rooms?"

Hannah frowned in thought. "I don't rightly know.
They took us there in a carriage."

"A gentleman's carriage?"

"No. A hackney." Then she frowned and added, "I think."

Sebastian blew out his breath in a long sigh. "Do you remember anything from that night at all?"

She grinned. "Not much. I was that foxed, I was."

"But you say you saw one of them again?"

"All three of 'em. They come to the Academy the very next night. Asked fer Rose, Hessy, and me again. Only, this time they weren't hirin' us off the floor. Just fer an hour."

"So what happened?"

Hannah Green's gaze returned again to Sebastian's brandy. She licked her lips. "Can I 'ave one of them?"

"When you've remembered everything. I want you clearheaded. Tell me what happened Wednesday night. Exactly."

"Exactly?" She screwed up her face with the effort of memory. "Well . . . I was takin' off me dress when Rose comes bangin' on me door, sayin' she needs to talk to me. So I goes out into the hall to tell her to go away, and she grabs me arm and says them three gentlemen had come to kill us. At first I thought she was bamming me, but then she drags me down the hall and shows me poor Hessy layin' there with her eyes wide-open and her neck bent all funny. *And* she tells me that she's done gone and stabbed the gent what had paid fer her. I can tell you, we was that spooked. Rose give Tasmin Poole her bracelet to distract Thackery while we nipped down the back stairs and took off."

Sebastian studied the girl's animated face, unsure how much—if any—of this wild tale to believe. "The man you say you saw going into your lodging house in Haymarket right before Tasmin Poole was killed—was he the man you were with Wednesday night?"

Hannah shook her head, her eyes wide. "He's the one went with Hessy."

"What did he look like?"

"I told you, he was a gentleman! Now can I have that drink?"

Sebastian poured her a brandy and held it out. "Dark hair, or light?"

She took the brandy in both hands and gulped it. "Dark. I think. At least, pretty dark."

Paul Gibson made an incoherent sound, while Sebastian asked, "Tall or short?"

Hannah's eyes narrowed. "Neither."

"You don't remember anything about him at all, do you?"

" 'Course I do. What I'm sayin' is, he were an ordinary-lookin' cove. I'd recognize 'im in a minute if'n I was to see 'im again. I recognized 'im when I seen 'im in the Haymarket, didn't I?"

"What about the gentleman you were with that Wednesday night. What did he look like?"

"He were the same. Just an ordinary-lookin' gentleman." She twisted her mouth sideways in a thoughtful frown. "Though I think maybe he weren't as dark. He was the birthday cove."

Sebastian moved to refill her glass. "Do you remember any of their names?"

"I don't pay no attention to names. In my experience, most men just make up the names they give me anyway."

"Yet that night of the birthday party, surely the men called one another by name?"

She frowned. "Maybe. I don't know. Like I said, I don't pay no attention to names."

"Was one of them named Max?"

She nibbled on a fingernail. "Coulda been. I can't say fer sure, though."

He was aware of Miss Jarvis's gaze upon him. He knew she was bursting to ask, *And who is Max?*

"Do you have any idea at all," Sebastian said to Hannah Green, "why those men came back to the Academy to kill you?"

Hannah downed her second brandy in a long pull. "Rose said it was because she knew they was plannin' to murder someone."

Sebastian was aware of Paul Gibson's arrested expression, of Miss Jarvis sitting forward. This was evidently one part of her tale Hannah Green had not yet told. Sebastian said, "She knew but you didn't? Why?"

Hannah gave a ringing laugh. "Go on wit' you. I don't speak French!"

Sebastian's gaze met Miss Jarvis's. "They were speaking French?"

"Amongst themselves, yeah," said Hannah. "At first. Till the other cove come."

Sebastian frowned. "The other cove? There were four men?"

"No. Just the three. The birthday cove come later."

"Did Rose tell you exactly who they were planning to kill?"

"Sure. But it didn't mean nothing to me. Some guy named Perceval, or something like that."

Miss Jarvis's eyes widened. "Spencer Perceval?"

Hannah swung her head to look at Lord Jarvis's daughter and say, "Who's he?"

Chapter 48

*M*iss Jarvis pushed up from her chair. "If I might have a word with you, Lord Devlin?"

"Of course, Miss Jarvis," he said, following her down the hall to Gibson's dining room.

She stalked to the far side of the table before swinging to face him. "You know something you haven't told me. What is it?"

"Believe me, Miss Jarvis, this is the first I've heard of any link to the Prime Minister—if there is indeed any such link."

"So who is Max?"

"Max Ludlow. He's a hussar captain. Or he was. He's been missing since last Wednesday. Until recently, I thought it an interesting coincidence that he disappeared the same night as Rachel Fairchild fled Orchard Street. It may still be nothing more than a coincidence. On the other hand, he might well be the man she killed."

Miss Jarvis brought one hand to her forehead. "My God. What is this? Some French plot to assassinate the Prime Minister?"

"Hannah Green said the three men who hired them were gentlemen. She didn't say anything about them being French." Most men of their class could converse in French with ease, even after twenty years of war. But as the daughter of a French émigré, Rachel would have been fluent. "And we don't know they were talking about Spencer Perceval, after all. Perceval is a given name as well as a family name."

"Then why did they come back to kill those women? And why are they trying to kill us?"

"That I do not know, Miss Jarvis." He searched her face, noting the subtle signs of strain, the brittle way she held herself. He said, "Miss Jarvis, there are things we must discuss."

"I see no need to discuss anything," she said, gripping the back of the chair before her. "What passed between us was a bizarre aberration born of an unfortunate set of circumstances and best forgotten."

Only Hero Jarvis, he thought, could describe the loss of her virginity as a bizarre aberration. He said, "Nevertheless, I am honor bound to offer you my hand in—"

"Thank you, my lord, but that will not be necessary." Her cheeks darkened with what he first took for embarrassment, then realized was rage. "I have no intention of allowing a moment's weakness to lead to a lifetime of regret."

Sebastian could think of nothing more horrifying than finding himself united in unholy matrimony with the daughter of Lord Jarvis. But the code of honor he lived by was rigid in such matters. He said, "If we had died on cue as expected, it would have been unnecessary. Since, however, we did not die, it is now—"

"Lord Devlin. I told you before that I have no intention of ever marrying. What happened yesterday has not altered that."

She stared at him with her frank, faintly contemptuous gray eyes, and he found it virtually impossible to reconcile this icy, self-possessed gentlewoman with the frightened and very real woman he'd held in his arms less than twenty-four hours ago. He said, "There could be consequences."

Her head jerked up. "There is no reason anyone need ever know. My identity was never revealed to our rescuers. I was able to reenter my home without attracting undue attention. And I trust I may have full confidence in your honor as a gentleman that you will never speak of it to anyone."

"That's not what I meant."

Her eyes widened in a way that told him this aspect of yesterday's interlude had yet to occur to her. She said, "Fate would not be so perverse."

"Nevertheless, you will tell me?"

She brushed past him, headed for the door. He reached out and snagged her arm, pulling her back around. "Miss Jarvis, I must insist."

Fury and scorn blazed in her eyes. She dropped her gaze to his hand on her arm. He let her go.

She said, "I have no desire to speak of this again. I trust that you, as a gentleman, will respect that wish." She turned once more toward the door.

"Nevertheless, you will tell me. If there are consequences."

She checked for the briefest instant, but kept walking.

As soon as they were all once again assembled in Gibson's sitting room, Miss Jarvis said tartly, "Considering the fate of my wounded assailant, I don't think Hannah should stay here."

"What 'appened to 'im?" asked the irrepressible Hannah.

"Someone broke his neck."

Hannah's hand crept up to gently cradle her throat. For a moment, the animation seemed to drain out of her, leaving her bleak and frightened.

Sebastian said, "I can ask Jules Calhoun to take her to his mother. Calhoun is my valet," he added by way of explanation when Miss Jarvis threw him a questioning glance.

"You would send her to your valet's *mother*?" said Miss Jarvis, while Hannah Green let out a wail.

"I ain't goin' to nobody's bleedin' mother," said Hannah. "She'll make me feel like some bleedin' cockroach or somethin'. It'll be worse than the Quakers."

"You'd rather have your neck snapped?" said Sebastian.

Hannah opened, then closed, her mouth.

"Besides," said Sebastian, "I think Grace Calhoun will surprise you."

This time, Hannah's mouth fell open and stayed open. "*Grace Calhoun?* Your valet's mother is Grace Calhoun?"

"You know her?"

"Get on wit' you. Ev'rybody knows Grace Calhoun."

"Who is Grace Calhoun?" whispered Miss Jarvis to Paul Gibson.

But Paul Gibson only said, "Not someone you want to know."

Nobly volunteering to escort Hannah Green to Brook Street, Paul Gibson went in search of a hackney.

"Aw," said Hannah Green, casting a long, wistful look at the curricle and pair of blood chestnuts waiting with Tom across the street. "I was 'opin' maybe I'd get t'ride in yer curricle. I ain't never ridden in a rig like that afore."

While Miss Jarvis turned a laugh into a cough, Sebastian said to his friend, "Tell Calhoun I should be there shortly. And don't let her out of your sight until you turn her over to him."

"I ain't gonna pike off," said Hannah from the depths

of the hackney, both hands once again wrapped around her throat.

"Not if you want to live, you won't," said Sebastian, stepping back. Gibson scrambled in behind her and the hackney started with a jerk. "And I must say, I am surprised at you, Miss Jarvis," he added, turning to her. "Laughing at the enthusiasms of those who are less fortunate than we."

"I wasn't laughing at Hannah," said Miss Jarvis, opening her parasol against the noonday sun. "I fear I was overcome by the mental image of you driving that vision in pink-and-white stripes and burgundy plumes through the streets of London. It's why you sent her with Gibson, isn't it?"

"I sent her with Gibson because it is my intention to seek out Spencer Perceval and warn him of a possible plot to assassinate him. Just as soon as I drive you home."

Her smile faded. "Thank you, but I came by hackney, and I intend to return by hackney."

"I'm not sure that would be wise."

"Are you concerned about my safety, or my reputation?"

"Both. You don't even have your maid with you."

Miss Jarvis looked down her aquiline nose at him. "As for my reputation, I seriously doubt it would be enhanced by my driving through the streets of the City in your curricle—"

"You've done it before."

"While as for my safety—" She nodded down the street toward a loitering brown-coated man, who quickly glanced away when her gaze turned toward him. "I have my father's watchdog to protect me."

Sebastian studied the smooth line of her cheek, the proud angle of her head. "Nevertheless, you will take care."

Her hand tightened around the handle of her parasol. "Lord Devlin. There is no need for you to concern yourself over my safety. I have always considered myself an eminently practical and capable person."

"You've never before been involved in murder."

"Yet, in the past week, I have survived three separate attempts on my life."

"I know," he said. "That's what worries me."

Chapter 49

*H*e found Spencer Perceval at the Admiralty, walking rapidly toward Whitehall. "Lord Devlin," said the Prime Minister when he spotted Sebastian, "have you reconsidered your decision against taking up a position in the Commons?"

"I'm afraid not," said Sebastian, glancing at the huddle of clerks who'd followed the Prime Minister down the stairs. "Walk with me a ways. There's something we must discuss."

Perceval's smile faded. "If it's this business about that poor unfortunate Bellingham—"

"Bellingham?" With difficulty, Sebastian resurrected the memory of the half-mad merchant who had accosted Perceval on the footpath outside Almack's. "No. But there is something I believe you must be made aware of." The two men turned their steps toward the Parade. "Last Monday, someone attacked the Friends' Magdalene House in Covent Garden and killed all the women there."

Perceval nodded. "I'd heard you'd involved yourself in their deaths."

Sebastian studied the Prime Minister's open, congenial face. "Where did you hear that?"

"From your father."

"My father? What does he know of it?"

"He does concern himself with your welfare, you know. Your association with these types of affairs worries him."

"Because he considers my involvement in murder investigations beneath my station?"

"Because he fears for your safety."

Sebastian stared out over the company of infantrymen drilling before them, their backs rigid, their feet rising and falling in unison. "I spent six years in the Army. He didn't fear for my safety then."

"Only every minute of every day."

Sebastian looked at the man beside him. "I am sorry if my involvement in these matters causes Hendon distress. But this is something I must do."

"Because you enjoy it?"

"Enjoy it? I suppose I do enjoy the mental challenge of solving a puzzle," he admitted, considering. "But the swirl of emotions that inevitably surround a violent death? The hatred and envy, the grief and despair? No one could enjoy that."

Perceval's eyes narrowed into a frown. "You're certain the women in the Magdalene House were murdered?"

"Yes. But I'm afraid there's far more involved than that. The evidence suggests their deaths may be linked to a scheme to assassinate you."

"Me?"

"Last week, a party of gentlemen hired three young prostitutes to entertain them for the night. During the course of the evening's revelries, the men became incautious enough to discuss their plans in French. I suppose they thought it unlikely that any of the women could understand their conversation. But one did."

Perceval gave a sharp bark of laughter. "What are you suggesting? That Napoleon wants to see me dead? What would he think to gain by such an action? If the

Whigs were to come to power, they might seek to end this war. But the Whigs will never come to power. Not with Prinny as Regent."

"I don't claim to understand the motivation at work here. But two of the three women hired that night are dead, along with an uncomfortable number of the people they've come into contact with since. The one woman who survives says they were overheard discussing plans to murder someone named Perceval. Now I could be mistaken. They could be planning to kill someone else entirely. But the lengths to which they've been willing to go to silence everyone who has any knowledge of their plot suggests that something more serious is afoot here."

Perceval was quiet a moment, his gaze like Sebastian's following the troop of men as they wheeled to their right. "A man in my position makes enemies," he said at last. "It's inevitable. You saw that poor old sod Bellingham."

"Bellingham is an annoying gnat compared to these men. They're ruthless and brutal."

Perceval scrubbed one hand across the lower part of his face. "If they killed those eight women—"

"And that was only the beginning."

The Prime Minister turned to face him. "What would you have me do? Cower in Downing Street in fear? I can't do that and still properly run this country."

Sebastian felt the cold wind buffet his face, bringing him the smell of dust and damp grass. "I don't know what I'm suggesting you do. Only—be aware that someone wants you dead, and take whatever precautions you can."

The bells of the abbey began to strike the hour. "I must go," said Perceval, turning toward Carlton House. "I'm to meet with the Prince Regent at half past." He gripped Sebastian's shoulder for a moment, then let him go. "Thank you for the warning."

Sebastian stood for a moment, watching the slim, middle-aged man hurry away. Then he turned toward his own waiting curricle. And it occurred to him as he crossed Whitehall that in the past hour he'd said essentially the same thing to three very different people—Hannah Green, Miss Jarvis, and Spencer Perceval. He had the disquieting feeling that time was running out for all three.

"I can take her to my mum, no worries," said Calhoun, when Sebastian returned to Brook Street for a quick consultation with his valet.

"To the Blue Anchor?"

Calhoun shook his head. "Grace spends most of her time these days at the Red Lion."

"Good Lord," said Sebastian. If anything, the Red Lion had an even more shocking reputation than the Blue Anchor, but he couldn't see how he had any choice. "I'll order the town carriage for you."

Hannah Green caught her breath in shivering delight when she saw the carriage pull up before the door. "Gor," she whispered. "It's like somethin' out of a fairy tale, it is."

"As good as a ride in the curricle?" Sebastian asked, giving her a hand up the steps.

"Better!"

He cast a glance at Jules Calhoun. "Think your mother can handle her?"

The valet laughed and hopped up behind her. "My mum? Are you serious?"

"You ain't comin' with us?" said Hannah.

Sebastian shook his head and took a step back. He'd realized it was past time he paid another visit to the Orchard Street Academy.

Chapter 50

$\mathcal{L}$eaving Tom and the curricle at Portman Square, Sebastian walked the length of Orchard Street, the weight of a double-barreled pistol heavy against his side. It was early yet, the footpath crowded with last-minute shoppers. As he approached the once grand old house, he pulled his hat low over his eyes and turned up the collar of his driving coat.

If anyone could identify the men who'd hired Rose, Hessy, and Hannah off the floor last Tuesday and returned the next night to kill them, it was the abbess of the Orchard Street Academy, Miss Lil. The problem was going to be getting past the broken-nosed pugilist who guarded the brothel's door to talk to her.

The oil lamp mounted high on the Academy's front had already been lit against the gathering gloom, the flame flickering in the evening breeze to throw patterns of light and shadow across the house's stone facade. Sebastian mounted the shallow brown steps, his hand on the flintlock in his pocket as he prepared to either bluff or bully his way inside. But at the top of the steps, he hesitated. The door stood unlatched and slightly ajar.

His hand tightening around the handle of the pistol, Sebastian drew it from his pocket, every sense coming to tingling alertness. Drawing back the flintlock's first hammer, he used his shoulder to nudge the door open wider.

The familiar tang of freshly spilled blood hit him first, overlaying the scents of candle wax and dry rot and decadence. The hall looked much as he remembered it, the once grand carpet and soaring plasterwork illuminated by bronze sconces with mottled mirrors. The dim golden light showed him the doorman, Thackery, half sitting, half lying in a huddled heap against the wall just inside the entrance.

Stepping cautiously into the hall, Sebastian gave the man a nudge with the toe of one boot, which sent the pugilist flopping sideways in a heavy, slow-motion roll. His eyes were closed, his plump cheeks as soft and flushed as a sleeping babe's. His pistol held at the alert, Sebastian reached down with his left hand and felt the man's still-warm neck for a pulse. Then his gaze fell to the dark stain of blood visible beneath the edge of the man's coat. Flipping back the brown corduroy, Sebastian studied the neatly sliced waistcoat. It was the kind of cut left by a dagger aimed well and deep.

He straightened, aware of the unnatural quiet of the house around him. He threw a quick glance into the small room to his right but found it, mercifully, empty. He moved on, his heart pounding in his chest. *How many women would a house like this one employ?* he wondered. *Two dozen? More? Add to that their customers . . .*

He paused at the heavy velvet curtain of the arch, the polished grip of the pistol slick with sweat in his hand. At his feet lay a stout man of perhaps fifty with heavy jowls and graying dark hair. A customer, by the looks of him, at the wrong place at the wrong time. He sprawled on his back, his arms flung wide like a crucifixion victim.

Moving cautiously, Sebastian stepped past him, into the parlor with its fading emerald hangings, the tawdry splendor of moldering mirrors grand enough to have

graced the halls of Versailles in an earlier, less deca-
dent life. The light from the branches of candles on the
chipped marble mantelpiece flared up warm and golden,
showing him two more dead women.

The Cyprian lying near the settee was unknown to
him. Turning her over, he found himself staring into wide,
vacant blue eyes. Her hair was the color of cornsilk, her
teeth as small and white as a child's. A spill of blood trick-
led from the corner of her open mouth to pool on the
carpet like a misshapen black rose. Beyond her, near the
base of the staircase, he found Miss Lil.

Sebastian crouched down beside the Academy's abbess. She lay curled on one side, her hands thrust out as
if she'd sought to fend off her assailant. He touched her
cheek and watched her head loll unnaturally against her
shoulder. He didn't need Paul Gibson to diagnose the
cause of death.

Four dead. Sitting back on his heels, Sebastian lifted
his gaze toward the first floor above. Surely one of them
had cried out in alarm or terror before they'd died. Had
no one upstairs heard? Or were the inhabitants of this
house so accustomed to the sound of screams and shouts
that no one had paid any heed?

Pushing to his feet, he was about to mount the steps
when he became aware of another scent hanging in the
air, mingling with the odor of blood and decay. The hot,
pungent scent of a quickly extinguished candle.

His gaze shifted to the lacy alcove to the right of the
hearth. When he'd been here before, the alcove had
been lit by a candle that had shown him the wraithlike
silhouette of a woman and a harp. Now all was darkness
and silence.

He crossed the room with rapid strides to snatch
back the lace curtain. The alcove smelled of hot wax and
charred candlewick and raw fear. The harp stood abandoned in the center of the alcove, the low stool beside

it overturned. Just inside the curtain, a tall, gaunt-faced woman pressed her back to the wall, her hands splayed out beside her as if she could will herself to disappear into the paneling.

"I'm not going to hurt you," he said gently. "You're safe."

The woman's thin chest jerked with her ragged breathing. "God have mercy on me," she whispered, her voice cracking. "They're dead, aren't they? All dead."

Sebastian studied her pale face, the straight brown brows and sharply edged bones so obvious beneath the inadequate flesh of cheek and forehead. She looked to be in her late twenties or early thirties. Her speech was cultured, her gown rigorously high-necked and modest. And judging by the milky-white glaze that obscured her eyes, she was quite blind.

He said, "How long ago did this happen?"

"A minute. Maybe two. Not long."

Sebastian's gaze lifted to the stairs. He had walked the length of Orchard Street, the Academy always in his line of sight. If anyone had left the house a minute or two before his arrival, he'd have seen them. He felt his body tense. "Where did they go? The men who did this, I mean. Upstairs?"

Even as he asked the question, he heard a thump from overhead followed by a woman's high-pitched laugh and the lower tones of a man's voice.

"No," said the harpist, her spine still pressed flat to the wall. "Down the hall, toward the back of the house."

His gaze shifted to the darkened hall that ran along the back of the stairs. "What's there?"

"The kitchen," she said. Her head lifted suddenly, her face turning as a more pungent scent of smoke overrode the lingering wisps from the candles. "Do you smell that?"

He smelled it. He could hear it, too: the crackling of

flames, the roar of ancient timbers catching, flaring up. "Bloody hell," he swore, grabbing her wrist. "They've torched the place. *Come on.*" Jerking her from the alcove, he raised his voice to shout, "Fire! Everyone out! Quickly! *Fire!*"

"No," she said, squirming from his grasp to dart back behind the curtain. "My harp."

"Bloody hell," he said again as she struggled beneath the instrument's weight. "I'll bring the bloody harp." Already he could see the faint reddish glow from the rear of the house, hear the screams of the women, the excited shouts of the men, the thump of running feet on the stairs. "Just get out of here."

She refused to leave without him—or, more accurately, without her harp. "Be careful," she cautioned as he staggered beneath its bulk. Squealing, half-naked women and men with bare pink flesh that glowed in the lamplight pushed past them in a scrambling rush for the door. A middle-aged man with a hairy, sunken white chest and flaccid phallus kept bleating, "I say, I say, I say."

The clanging of the firebell reverberated up and down the street. Already a crowd was forming at the base of the house's front steps. Buckets appeared, passed hand to hand. Swearing softly beneath his load, Sebastian pushed their way through the shouting throng and turned toward Portman Square. "There's just one thing I don't understand, Miss—"

"Driscoll," she said, hovering protectively about her harp as the crush of men, women, and children rushing toward the fire increased. "Mary Driscoll."

"Miss Driscoll." The sounding board of the harp was beginning to dig unpleasantly into his back. "Why didn't those men kill you?"

"They didn't know I was there. I put out my candle

and quit playing the instant I heard them in the hall with Thackery."

"You know who they were?"

"No. But I recognized their voices. They came to the house the night Hessy Abrahams died."

Sebastian studied her gaunt, strained features. "You recognized their *voices*? How many times have you heard them?"

"Only the once." She must have caught the doubt in his own voice, because an unexpected smile curled her lips. "When you're blind, you learn to listen very, very carefully."

He could see his curricle now, Tom at the chestnuts' heads trying to quiet them as they sidled nervously, their manes tossing, nostrils flaring at the scent of the fire. Sebastian said, "Tell me about the men. How many were there?"

"Only two," she said. "The one was older, in his thirties, I'd say. He was the one in charge. The younger man listened to him, did what he was told without question or argument."

Like a good soldier, thought Sebastian. Aloud, he said, "What about their accents?"

She shook her head. "I couldn't tell much, beyond the fact that they were gentlemen."

He put out his hand, stopping her when she would have kept walking. "We're at my carriage."

"Gov'nor," said Tom, his mouth falling open, "you ain't never gonna fit that thing in the curricle."

"Yes, I am," said Sebastian, temporarily setting the harp on the flagstones beside the carriage. "Miss Driscoll here is going to hold it on her lap." He offered her a hand up and she took it without hesitation.

With the Academy in flames, he supposed she had no place else to go. But as he watched her settle on the curricle's high seat, another thought occurred to him. He said, "Do you know who I am?"

Again, that faint smile. "Of course I know who you are. You're Viscount Devlin. You came to the house last Tuesday. You had wine with Miss Lil, Tasmin, Becky, and Sarah. Then your questions made Miss Lil uncomfortable, and she asked you to leave."

"I never gave my name."

"No. But I heard Miss Lil and Mr. Kane talking about you later. People are strange in that way. If you can't see, they often act as if you can't hear, either. Or perhaps they simply assume I'm stupid."

She was far from stupid. He handed the harp up to her, grunting softly beneath its weight. "That still doesn't explain why you're willing to come with me."

She clutched the harp to her. "Those men were looking for Miss Lil. Once they'd killed her, they left." He saw her delicate throat work as she swallowed. "I don't want them to come for me."

Sebastian gazed up at her thin, plain face. Now that he had her in his curricle, he wasn't exactly sure what he was going to do with her. From the distance came a shout, followed by what sounded like a collective sigh as the walls of the Academy collapsed inward in a fiery inferno that sent sparks flying high into the night sky.

"Gov'nor?" said Tom.

Sebastian leapt up into the curricle and gathered the reins. "Stand away from their heads," he said, and turned the chestnuts toward Covent Garden Theater.

Chapter 51

Kat Boleyn might have been the most celebrated young actress of the London stage, but her cramped dressing room at the Covent Garden Theater was not designed to accommodate Miss Boleyn in full costume as Beatrice, a tall nobleman in a many-caped driving coat, and a blind woman clutching a harp.

She looked at Mary Driscoll's pale, strained face and said to Sebastian, "Could I speak to you outside for a moment?"

They crowded into a dimly lit corridor smelling strongly of greasepaint and orange peels and dust. Kat whispered, "Sebastian, what are you going to do with her?"

"I'm hoping she can identify the men who forced their way into the Academy tonight."

"She's blind."

"Yes, but she heard their voices. She'll be able to recognize them if she hears them again."

Kat looked at him. He knew what she was thinking, that while he might credit Miss Driscoll's ability to identify voices, no one else would. But all she said was, "And afterward? What will you do with her then?"

"Don't worry. I won't leave you lumbered with her forever."

"I'm not worried about that."

"I'm sorry, but I had no place else to take her where I knew she'd be safe." He couldn't see taking a woman like Mary Driscoll to the Red Lion.

"Sebastian, truly, it's all right." She reached out to touch his arm. A simple enough gesture, yet it sent a rush of forbidden longing coursing through him. It had been a mistake to come here, he realized, a mistake to allow himself to stand this close to her, to breathe in all the old familiar scents of a tainted past.

She dropped her hand and took a step back. "I heard someone has tried to kill you. Twice."

"Where did you hear that?"

She stood with her arms gripped across the stomach of her costume as if she were cold, although it was not cold in the theater. Instead of answering, she said, "You will be careful. Not just of this killer, but of Jarvis."

"I can handle Jarvis."

"No one can handle Jarvis."

To his surprise, Sebastian found himself smiling. "His daughter can."

Walking out of the theater a few minutes later, Sebastian found his tiger waiting patiently at the chestnuts' heads. The night had fallen clear and cold, with just the hint of a breeze that carried with it the sound of music and laughter and men's voices raised in a toast. Sebastian said, "Take them home, Tom. I won't be needing you anymore tonight."

The tiger glanced at the door of the nearby music hall, then back at Sebastian's face. "I can stay."

Sebastian's gaze lifted, like Tom's, to the music hall door. It was too well lit, too loud, too full of the exuberance of life. Sebastian intended to do his drinking someplace dark and earnest. He clapped the tiger on the shoulder and turned away. "Just go home, Tom. Now."

Chapter 52

"My lord? *My lord*."

Sebastian opened one eye, tried to focus on the lean, serious face of his valet, then gave it up with a groan. "I don't care if the entire city of London is afire. Just go away."

"Here," said Calhoun, slipping what felt like a warm mug into Sebastian's slack hand. "Drink this."

"What the devil is it?"

"Tincture of milk thistle."

Sebastian opened the other eye, but it didn't work any better than the first. "What the hell are you doing here? Go away."

"A message has arrived from Dr. Gibson."

"And?" Sebastian opened both eyes this time and clenched his teeth as the room spun unpleasantly around him.

"It seems the authorities have recovered the body of a military gentleman by the name of Max Ludlow. Dr. Gibson will be performing the autopsy this morning, and he thought you might be interested."

Sebastian sat up so fast the hot liquid in the forgotten mug sloshed over the sides and burned his hand. "Bloody hell."

"Drink it, my lord," said Calhoun, turning away toward the dressing room. "Nothing is better than milk thistle when you've got the devil of a head."

The milk thistle helped some, but not enough to encourage Sebastian to do more than glance at the dishes awaiting him in the breakfast room before turning away and calling for his town carriage. The day had dawned cool but clear and far too bright. He subsided into one corner of his carriage and closed his eyes. Gibson's autopsies were never pleasant, but Sebastian didn't want to even think about the kind of shape Max Ludlow's body would be in after ten days.

" 'E's in the room out the back," said Gibson's housekeeper when she opened the door to Sebastian. A short, stout woman with iron gray hair and a plain, ruddy face, she scowled at him with unabashed disapproval. "I'm to take you there. Not that I'm going any farther than halfway down the garden, mind you. It's unnatural, what 'e does down there."

Sebastian followed Mrs. Federico's broad back down the ancient, narrow hall and through the kitchen to the untidy yard that led to the small stone building where Gibson performed both his postmortems and his illicit dissections. True to her word, halfway across the yard Mrs. Federico drew up short. "Viscount or no viscount, I ain't goin' no farther," she said, and headed back toward her kitchen.

Sebastian had to quell the urge to follow her. He could already smell Max Ludlow.

"There you are," said Gibson, appearing at the building's open doorway, his gore-stained hands held aloft. "I thought you'd be interested in this."

Sebastian tried breathing through his mouth. "Where did they find him?"

"In Bethnal Green. Wrapped in canvas and dumped in a ditch along Jews Walk."

"I suppose it's better than the Thames," said Sebastian. He'd seen bodies pulled out of the river after a week. It wasn't a sight he cared to see again.

"There was water in the ditch."

"Good God," said Sebastian. He should have had more of Calhoun's milk thistle.

Gibson ducked back into the building's dank interior. After a brief hesitation, Sebastian followed.

Naked and half eviscerated, the body on the room's stone slab looked like something out of his worse nightmares. One glance at the bloated, waxy flesh and its resident insect population was enough. Sebastian stared at the ceiling. "Are they sure that's Max Ludlow?" Sebastian asked when he was able.

"Someone from the regiment identified him. In another day it probably would have been impossible. Parts of the body were already virtually reduced to bones, but thanks to the way he was lying, the face is actually fairly well preserved."

Sebastian held his handkerchief to his nose and resisted the impulse to take another look. "Any idea how he died?"

"As a matter of fact, yes." Gibson turned around to reach for a tin basin. "I found this in his heart."

Sebastian stared down at a bloody pair of strange, broken blades, handleless and oddly shaped. "What are they?"

"It's a broken pair of sewing scissors," said Gibson, setting the bowl aside so that he could demonstrate an upthrusting, twisting motion. "Whoever killed him must have stabbed him with the scissors, then broken them off when they hit a rib."

"So he was killed by a woman," said Sebastian.

"Not necessarily, but more than likely. Did Hannah

Green ever mention how Rachel Fairchild killed the man in her room?"

Sebastian shook his head. "She may not have known." He went to stand in the yard just outside the door to try to breathe. It didn't help.

Wiping his hands on a stained cloth, Gibson came out with him. "I heard about the fire at the Academy last night. That makes four more dead." He brought up one splayed hand to rub his temples. "I thought I'd left carnage on this scale behind when I got out of the Army."

Sebastian jerked his head toward the dark, foul room behind them. "That body on your slab was once a hussar captain, remember?"

Gibson's hand slipped back to his side, his eyes widening. "What are you saying? That you think these killers are *military men*?"

"It's what war teaches us, isn't it? Not just to kill, but to kill on a grand scale."

"There's a difference between killing enemy soldiers on a battlefield and slaughtering unarmed Englishwomen in a London slum."

"You mean because one is sanctioned by authority and the other is not?"

"Well, yes."

In the silence that followed, the endless drone of buzzing flies sounded both abnormally loud and oppressively familiar. It was the sound of death. Sebastian said, "Some men learn to like killing. Or at least, they learn not to shrink from it. And that can be just as dangerous."

Gibson squinted up at the clouds beginning to gather on the horizon, his face grim. Sebastian knew what he was remembering, the images that haunted both men's dreams. The Portuguese peasants shot down in their fields along with their mules and their dogs. The Spanish families burned alive in their farmhouses. Gibson said, "But for British soldiers—officers—to kill Englishwomen . . ." He shook his head. "I know that shouldn't make a difference, yet to most people it does."

"It makes a difference because most people have a tendency to see anyone who speaks a different language or has darker skin as somehow less human than themselves. But a lot of people see prostitutes as less than human, too. Their lives are considered cheap. Expendable. If it hadn't been for Miss Jarvis, the eight women who died at the Magdalene House would already be forgotten."

"But why would hussar officers want to kill the Prime Minister?"

"I don't know," Sebastian admitted.

Gibson jerked his head toward the dank room behind them. "If it's true . . . if Max Ludlow was one of the three men Hannah Green was telling us about, then who were the other two?"

"At this point, I'd put my money on Patrick Somerville being one of them."

"The hussar captain from Northamptonshire? Do you think Hannah could identify him?"

"She might not be able to remember names, but women in her line of work learn to recognize faces."

"Yet it won't be enough, will it?" said Gibson. "Even if Somerville was at the Academy the night Rachel Fairchild and Hannah Green fled, there's still nothing to tie him to the Magdalene House killings. Or to last night's attack."

"No. But Miss Driscoll might be able to do so."

Gibson looked confused. "Miss Driscoll. Who is she?"

"The Academy's blind harp player."

Gibson's frown deepened. "If she's blind, how can she identify him?"

Sebastian thought about explaining, then gave it up. "Never mind. Just lend me some paper and a pen, would you?"

Chapter 53

The difficult part, Sebastian realized, would be finding a surreptitious way for Miss Driscoll to hear Patrick Somerville speak. Much easier to first show Patrick Somerville to Hannah Green, he decided, and see if she recognized him.

Leaving Gibson's surgery near Tower Hill, Sebastian directed his coachman to Grace Calhoun's Red Lion Tavern in West Street. Lying just a few houses from Saffron Hill on the north side of one of the last uncovered stretches of Fleet Ditch, the Red Lion was well-known as the resort of thieves and the lowest grade of the frail sisterhood.

He found Grace in the tavern's back parlor, polishing pewter tankards. She was a tall woman, taller even than her son and just as lean, with a face that was all sharp planes and interesting angles accentuated rather than blurred by the passing of the years. At the sight of Sebastian, she turned the tankards over to a gnarled old man with a gray-whiskered face and a wooden peg for a leg, and came out from behind the counter.

She had bright, intelligent brown eyes and hair the color of storm clouds she wore neatly tucked beneath a fine lace cap. In her youth, she must have been striking. She was still handsome—and very, very astute. "So you're the fine lord my Jules has been telling me about," she said, looking Sebastian up and down without a smile. "It was never my intention to see the boy set up as a gentleman's gentleman, you know. I hired that old fool of a valet to teach him how to talk and act and dress like a gentleman. Not to teach him to be a gentleman's gentleman."

"He is a very good valet."

"It's not what I'd intended." She wiped her hands on her apron. "I s'pose you're here to see that young trollop Jules asked me to mind."

"I hope Miss Green hasn't been causing you any trouble."

Grace Calhoun gave a derisive snort. "That one. She's a taking little thing—I'll grant you that. Which is lucky, seein' as how she ain't got the sense God give a fence post." She cast him another assessing glance, then turned back to her tankards. "Last I saw her, she was in the yard."

He found Hannah Green sitting cross-legged in a corner of the cobbled yard near the dilapidated stables, the fitful sun on her bowed bare head, her arms full of three wiggling, squirming black-and-white kittens. "Do look, Lord Devlin," she said merrily when she saw him. "Aren't they just the sweetest things you've ever seen? I always wanted a kitten."

She was still wearing the spangled pink-and-white-striped gown, but without the rouge and the burgundy plumes, she looked even younger than before, no more than fifteen or sixteen at the most. Sebastian watched her laughingly peel one adventurous kitten off the top of her head, and it occurred to him that he was beginning to collect dependent females. He had no idea what he was going to do with either of them.

"If you can tear yourself away from the kittens," he

said, "I thought you might like to take another carriage ride."

Hannah scrambled to her feet, her eyes going round. "Honest? Oooh. Let me just get my bonnet."

Sebastian rescued the tumbling kittens and barely had time to restore them to the mother cat sunning herself atop a nearby moldering bed of hay before Hannah was back, the bedraggled plumed hat once more atop her auburn head, her reticule swinging from its fraying strings.

"Where we goin'?" she asked as she trustingly allowed herself to be handed up into Sebastian's town carriage.

He swung up to take the forward seat. "You said you recognized the man who came to your rooms in the Haymarket and strangled Tasmin Poole. That he was one of the men who also hired you off the floor last week?"

"Y-yes," she said, not sure where his questions were headed. "He was the tight-lipped one who picked us up from the Academy."

"Tight-lipped?" asked Sebastian, diverted.

"Yeah. You know. He has those thin kinda lips he always keeps crimped together." She held out both hands, thumbs pressed tightly to index fingers in what he supposed was meant to be an imitation of the killer's mouth. "Like he was afraid a bug might crawl in there when he weren't payin' attention or somethin'."

It was more than she'd said before. "And the man Rose Fletcher killed the next night, when the men came back—he was with the tight-lipped gentleman when he picked you up in the hackney?"

She nodded. She'd given up imitating the killer's mouth and had taken to gnawing a fingernail instead, her gaze on the crowded streets and shop windows flashing past outside the carriage.

"I'm interested in the third gentleman," said Sebastian.

She craned her neck around to continue watching a hurdy-gurdy player with a monkey, who stood on a street corner. "You mean the birthday cove?"

"That's right. The one who chose you when the men returned to the Academy the next night. Would you recognize him if you saw him again?"

Hannah swung her head to look at him, her eyes huge in an uncharacteristically solemn face. "I don't want to see him again. I don't want to see any of them again."

"But you would recognize him."

"Yes," said Hannah around the fingernail in her mouth.

"That's where we're going now. To see if we can find him."

She gave a startled laugh. "Go on with you. I hear tell there's a million or more people in London. How you going to find one cove in amongst a million people?"

"There's a coffeehouse in Cockspur Street called the Scarlet Man. Most officers in town—either active duty or half pay—wander in there at one point or another on a Sunday afternoon."

"How'd you know they was military coves?"

He regarded her fixedly. "You knew they were military?" She'd never mentioned it.

She twitched one shoulder. "Yeah."

"What else do you know that you haven't told me?"

It came out more sharply than he'd intended. Her eyes narrowed. "I didn't think it was important."

The horses slowed. She shifted her gaze to the glazed front of the coffee shop that stood near Charing Cross. "You reckon the birthday cove is in there now?"

The coachman drew the carriage in close to the opposite curb. "If not, he'll be here eventually. Can you see the door of the coffeehouse from where you are?"

She shifted her weight restlessly, her lower lip creeping out in the beginnings of a pout. "Aye."

Suppressing a smile, Sebastian drew from his pocket the note he had prepared and signaled one of the footmen. "Find an urchin and give him a couple of shillings to deliver this to Captain Patrick Somerville in the Scarlet Man."

"That's right clever," said Hannah, watching the footman turn away with the note. "What's it say?"

"Only that the Captain is needed at his regiment."

Her brows drew together under the strain of thought. "You reckon this Somerville is the birthday cove?"

"Does the name sound familiar?"

Hannah shrugged. "I don't pay no attention to names." Her frown deepened as she watched the footman hail a half-grown lad. "What if this Somerville ain't there?"

"Then we wait."

The lower lip came into play again. "We shoulda brought the kittens."

But in the end, they had no need to wait. A moment later, a tall, lean gentleman in the gold frogged, dark blue tunic of a hussar appeared at the door of the coffeehouse and turned to walk briskly toward Whitehall.

"That's him," said Hannah, shrinking back into the shadows of the carriage's interior. "That's the birthday cove."

"You're certain?"

" 'Course I'm certain. I told you, I don't pay no attention to names. But I never forget a face."

Sebastian regarded her thoughtfully. She was not, despite all appearances to the contrary, quite as lacking in sense as a fencepost. He said, "You wouldn't happen to know how Rose Fletcher killed the man in her room that night, would you?"

"She stabbed him," Hannah whispered, leaning forward as if someone could overhear. "Stabbed him with a pair of sewing scissors. Leastways, that's what she said." She sat back again, the anxiety on her face fading as her thoughts turned to a more pleasant topic. "Do you think Mrs. Calhoun would let me keep one of the kittens?"

Chapter 54

$\mathcal{A}$ slow drizzle fell that evening, glazing the paving stones and footpaths of Mayfair with a wet sheen that reflected the light of the wind-flickered streetlamps and passing carriage lanterns. Dressed in knee breeches and a white silk waistcoat with buckled shoes at his feet and a chapeau-bras tucked under one arm, Sebastian set forth for the ball being given that evening by Lady Burnham in her Park Lane home.

The rain had thinned the crowds gathered on the footpath outside to watch, but it still took Sebastian's carriage an inordinate amount of time to press its way forward, for some five hundred people had been invited to the ball. He had no doubt that Patrick Somerville's well-married sister, Lady Berridge, would be in attendance, with her reluctant brother in tow.

As he entered the ballroom, the first person he saw was his aunt Henrietta, who immediately gasped and groped for the quizzing glass she always wore around her neck, even when decked out in mauve silk and lace and a towering turban. "Good heavens. Devlin, whatever are you doing here? First Almack's and Lady Melbourne's breakfast, now Lady Burnham's ball?" She drew in a deep breath that swelled her massive bosom and gave him an arch smile. "Don't tell me you've finally taken it into your head to look for a wife?"

"No," he said baldly, his gaze raking the crowded ballroom beyond her. In actual fact he was looking for a murderer, but he wasn't about to tell his aunt that. His eyes narrowed as he spied Patrick Somerville talking to a pale-haired young matron near the bank of French doors that overlooked the rear terrace. "If I change my mind, believe me, Aunt, you'll be the first to know."

Excusing himself, he pushed on through the laughing, chattering crowd. But as ill luck would have it, he had only worked his way around half of the room when he came upon Miss Jarvis.

"Good heavens," she said in a tone that exactly matched his aunt's, except that Miss Jarvis was not smiling. "What are you doing here?"

"I received an invitation."

"Yes, but you never attend these things." She was wearing an emerald green silk gown that became her surprisingly well, and had crimped her hair so that it softened the angular planes of her face. But there was nothing soft about her expression. She frowned. "You're looking for someone, aren't you? Who is it?"

He deliberately turned his back on the row of French doors. "Perhaps I've suddenly taken it into my head to enjoy a bit of dancing."

"Nonsense." She cast a quick glance around. "We can't talk here. Escort me to the refreshment room."

He was too much of a gentleman to refuse her, and she knew it. Lending her his arm, he led her through the crush to a chamber that had been set aside for refreshments. He was hoping to find it crowded. It was nearly deserted.

"I want you to tell me what happened last night in Orchard Street," she said, accepting a glass of lemonade. "You do know, don't you?"

She would have read about the fire in that morning's

papers, of course. He picked up a plate and surveyed the delicate tidbits offered by their hostess to sustain her guests until supper. "I think the abbess was the intended target," he said as calmly as if they were discussing the orchestra or the silver streamers decorating the ballroom. "Do you like shrimp or crab?"

"Shrimp, please." He didn't expect her to know what an abbess was, but in that, he reckoned without the research that had embroiled her in this murderous tangle to begin with. She said, "They killed her?"

"Yes." He selected three fat shrimp, then added a slice of ham and some melon. "Along with a fair number of others."

"Because they thought she could identify them? Is that it? If she could, it's a wonder they let her live so long."

"I suspect she didn't know their names. She only became a threat as we began to circle around toward them." He let his gaze wander over the table. "Would you like an ice?"

"No, thank you." She took the plate he'd prepared for her. "Do you think they'll go after Hannah Green again?"

"They would if they knew where to find her. Fortunately, they don't."

She applied herself to the refreshments with a healthy appetite. "How is she, by the way?"

"Hannah? Last time I saw her, she was in rapture over the stable cat's litter of black-and-white kittens."

Miss Jarvis glanced up, half frowning and half laughing, as if uncertain whether to believe him or not. "Kittens?"

"Kittens." He studied her clear gray eyes, the delicate curve of her cheek. He considered telling her about the harp player and about Patrick Somerville, then changed his mind. The less he involved her in all this, the better.

She said, "What will become of her, when this is over?"

"Hannah?" He shook his head. "I'm not certain. In many ways she's still a child."

"But not in all ways." He knew she regretted her words the instant she said them. For one frozen moment, their gazes met and held. She set her plate aside. "Thank you for the refreshments," she said, and turned on her heel and left him there, looking after her.

By the time Sebastian made his way back to the ballroom, Patrick Somerville had disappeared. Sebastian prowled the conservatory and the rooms set aside for card playing, before finally wandering out onto the terrace to find the hussar captain leaning against the stone balustrade and smoking a cheroot.

"Nasty habit I picked up in the Americas," said Somerville, blowing a cloud of blue smoke out of his lungs. "My sister Mary keeps telling me it'll be the death of me, but I tell her the malaria'll kill me long before then."

Sebastian came to stand beside him and look out over the glistening wet garden. The rain had eased up, but the air was still chill and damp and smelled strongly of wet earth and wet stone. "I hear they've found your friend's body."

Somerville drew on his cheroot, his eyes narrowing. "Yes, poor old sod."

"I understand he had a pair of sewing scissors broken off in his heart."

The hussar turned his head to stare directly at Sebastian. "Where'd you hear that?"

"From the surgeon who performed the postmortem." Sebastian kept his gaze on the garden. "A man killed at the Orchard Street Academy last week was stabbed by a pair of sewing scissors."

Somerville drew on his cheroot, and said nothing.

Sebastian said, "How many bodies do you think have turned up in London in the past year with pairs of sewing scissors broken off in their hearts?"

The captain tossed the stub of his cheroot into the wet garden below, then pursed his lips, expelling a long stream of fragrant smoke. "You know I was there, too, don't you?"

"Yes."

Somerville flattened his hands on the wet balustrade, his back hunched as he stared out over the shadowy gardens. "I still don't understand what happened that night. First the girl I was with disappeared. And then, when I went looking for Ludlow, they said he'd already gone."

"You believed them?"

"Why wouldn't I? We were supposed to meet up later, at a tavern near Soho. I went there expecting to find him waiting for me. But he never showed up. At first I thought he'd simply changed his mind and gone home. It wasn't until he was still missing the next day that I realized something had gone wrong. I thought he'd been jumped by footpads or something. I never imagined he hadn't even left the Academy."

"Who else was with you that night?"

"No one." He pushed away from the balustrade. "What's your interest in this, anyway?"

From the ballroom behind them came the lilting chorus of an English country dance. Sebastian said, "I'm just doing a favor for an acquaintance." He studied the man's pale face, clammy with sweat despite the chill from the rain. "By the way, I've been meaning to ask: When's your birthday?"

"My birthday?" Somerville gave a shaky laugh. "Why do you ask?"

"It was last week, was it?"

A muscle jumped along the man's tightened jaw as

he considered his answer. "Yes," he said slowly, realizing the futility of denying it. "Why?"

"Happy birthday," Sebastian said, and walked off into the night.

"Unfortunately, you've no real proof," said Sir Henry Lovejoy. They were seated beside the cold hearth in the magistrate's simple parlor on Russell Square. A fire would have helped take the chill off the damp night, but Lovejoy never allowed a fire to be kindled in his house outside the kitchen after the first of April. Sebastian knew that for Lovejoy, it wasn't a matter of frugality so much as a question of moral fiber.

Sebastian poured himself another cup of hot tea and said, "Hannah Green identified Patrick Somerville."

"As a customer. There's no law against paying a woman for a moment's physical gratification, however morally repugnant it might be. She didn't see him kill anyone. And even if she had, who'd take the word of a soiled dove against that of a hussar captain wounded in the defense of his country?"

"He wasn't wounded. He has malaria."

"I think I'd rather be wounded."

"Frankly, so would I." Sebastian took a sip of his tea and wished it were something stronger. "There's still the harp player. She heard the men who attacked the Academy last night. If Somerville was one of them—and I strongly suspect he was—she would recognize his voice. If we can set up a situation in which she can hear him—"

"No jury would convict a hussar captain on the strength of testimony given by a blind woman who played the harp in a brothel."

Sebastian knew a welling of frustration. Lovejoy was right, of course. But there had to be a way.... "The girl who worked in the cheesemonger's shop across from the Magdalene House might recognize him. She noticed several gentlemen loitering in the street right before the fire."

"Did she actually see them go into the house?"

"No."

Lovejoy thrust out his short legs and crossed them at the ankles. "It's just all too convoluted and confused. Even I still don't understand it properly."

Sebastian leaned forward, his elbows braced on his knees. "A week ago last Tuesday, two men—Max Ludlow and another gentleman I've yet to identify—hired Rose Fletcher, Hannah Green, and Hessy Abrahams off the floor of the Academy as part of a birthday surprise for one of their friends—Captain Patrick Somerville. The women were taken by hackney to rooms someplace, where Somerville later joined them. It must have been decidedly awkward when he realized one of the women his friends had hired for the night was Rachel Fairchild, the sister of his childhood playmate."

Lovejoy cleared his throat uncomfortably. "Decidedly awkward, I should think."

"So awkward that I get the impression neither one of them let on about it. But Somerville must have said something to his friends the next day. And when it came out that Rachel's mother was French—that Rachel herself spoke French—they realized they'd been indiscreet. That she had overheard—and understood—a dangerous conversation the men had conducted in French, assuming none of the women could understand them."

"So they went back to the Academy the next night, planning to kill the women? Before they could tell anyone what they'd heard?"

"Yes. Except, of course, it all went awry. The mysterious third gentleman made his kill quickly, breaking Hessy Abrahams's neck. But Rachel Fairchild managed to stab Max Ludlow with a pair of sewing scissors, and then warn Hannah Green. I gather the three men were supposed to meet up at a tavern later. When Ludlow didn't show up, the others had no way of knowing what had gone wrong. It must have taken them several days to figure it out, and to trace the two surviving women to the Magdalene House."

"By which time Hannah Green had already fled." Lovejoy stared thoughtfully at the cold, blackened recesses of the hearth. "They killed an extraordinary number of people, simply to silence one woman."

"They're soldiers. They're trained to kill. And they're on a mission."

"To kill the Prime Minister?" Lovejoy stirred his tea, his features pinched and troubled. "You've told Perceval of your theory?"

"That someone is planning to assassinate him? Yes."

"And?"

Sebastian smiled. "He didn't believe me any more than you do."

Lovejoy laid aside his spoon with a soft clatter. "It just seems so absurd. No British prime minister has ever been assassinated. And by three of His Majesty's own officers? What possible motive could they have for doing such a thing?"

Sebastian shook his head. "I don't know. What can you tell me about the man found this morning? Max Ludlow."

"Nothing to his discredit. He's described as a model officer—loyal, brave, efficient."

"Which regiment?"

"The Twentieth Hussars."

The same as Somerville, thought Sebastian. Aloud, he said, "Where did he serve?"

"Italy, Jamaica, Egypt, the Sudan—just about everywhere. He even had a hand in the capture of Cape Town from the Dutch."

"Then he was sent to Argentina?"

"That's right."

Sebastian stared down at the dregs of his teacup. It had been nearly five years since the disastrous Argentinean campaign, when Britain had tried to wrest Spain's wealthy South American colony for its own. The expedition had been ill conceived and undermanned. Thousands of men from England, Scotland, and Ireland had left their bones in the Rio de la Plata, while many of the survivors returned home ruined and bitter.

"You've no idea who this third man is?" said Lovejoy.

Sebastian set aside his empty cup and pushed to his feet. "No. If I could find out who Ludlow and Somerville's associates are—who they served with in the past—it might tell me something."

Lovejoy nodded. "I'll set one of the constables to look into it."

"You'll—" Sebastian broke off as comprehension dawned. "So you've done it, have you? You've decided to accept the position at Bow Street."

Sir Henry permitted himself a small, proud smile. "It's not official until tomorrow morning, of course. But, yes."

"Congratulations."

Sir Henry's smile widened, then slowly began to dim.

Chapter 55

*H*ero slept poorly that night. Long after the house had settled down around her and the last of the carriages had rattled past in the street below, she lay awake staring at the satin folds in the hangings above her bed.

She'd thought, once, that if she could only discover who killed the women of the Magdalene House, and why, then she'd understand how Rachel Fairchild had come to be there—how the granddaughter of a duke could ever have fallen so low as to make the sordid life of a woman of the streets her own. Once or twice Hero'd had the niggling suspicion that Devlin knew more than he was letting on. But she couldn't begin to comprehend why he was refusing to tell her. Hero herself felt no closer, today, to understanding the riddle of Rachel's life than she'd been a week ago. And she knew a growing sense of frustration, a fear that she was never going to know, never going to understand.

Sometime before dawn she heard the rain begin again, pattering against the windowpanes. She thought of Rachel Fairchild lying in her cold, lonely grave beneath the pounding rain, and although she knew it was absurd, the rain unsettled her. When she finally drifted off to sleep, it was with the vague, half-formed intention of visiting the Friends' burial ground the next day.

She arose early that morning, little refreshed. The rain had stopped sometime after dawn, although the clouds still hung low and heavy. Armed with a selection of lilacs and lilies from the corner flower stall, Hero set forth shortly after breakfast, accompanied by her maid and traveling in her own carriage. She was aware of her father's servant discreetly shadowing her, but she had no need, today, to escape his watchful eye.

He followed her north, past Oxford Road to Paddington and the small hamlet of Pentonville that lay beyond it. She located the Friends' meetinghouse and burial grounds easily enough, for she had sought directions from Joshua Walden. Leaving her carriage beneath the arching canopy of an old elm growing at the side of the road, she entered the burial ground through a simple gate in its low rubble wall.

The graves of the eight women were easy to find, a sad row of freshly turned earth beside the far western wall, slashes of dark brown contrasting starkly with the green of the wet grass. As Hero walked down the hill, her gaze narrowed at the sight of a tall woman who stood beside the graves with her head bowed, her shoulders hunched. She was dressed in black silk, with her hands fisted around the strings of a large traveling reticule. At the sound of Hero's footfalls on the sodden grass, the woman turned, revealing the grief-ravaged face of Rachel's sister Lady Sewell.

"It's you," she said in a breathy whisper, one hand coming up to cover her trembling mouth.

Hero's step faltered. "I'm sorry. I didn't know you were here." She made a vague gesture with the flowers she'd brought. "I'll just leave these and go."

Lady Sewell nodded toward the row of unmarked

graves. "I don't even know which of these graves is hers. Do you?"

Hero shook her head. "No. I'm sorry."

Lady Sewell's breath caught on a sob. "She never told me what he was doing to her. You do believe me, don't you?"

"Yes, of course," said Hero, although she hadn't the slightest idea what the woman was talking about.

"All those years and she never said a word. But I should have known, shouldn't I?"

"You should?"

Lady Sewell clenched her jaw tight to keep it from shuddering. "We made a deal, Father and I. I would keep quiet about the shooting, and he in turn would let me marry Sewell." Her lip curled. "I should have known I couldn't trust him."

"The shooting?" said Hero.

A muscle bunched along the woman's jaw. "He killed her, you know. My mother. It was an accident. He was trying to take the gun away from her, and it went off. But he still killed her."

Hero remembered what Devlin had told her, about the death of Rachel's mother. "You mean, in the pavilion?"

Rachel's sister nodded. "Mama found out what he was doing to me. She knew he was spending the afternoon by the lake, working on some speech he was to give. She went down there, intending to kill him. I ran after her, begging her not to do it. She just told me to go home."

Hero studied the other woman's mottled, tear-streaked face. "Your mother was planning to shoot your father? But . . . why?"

Lady Sewell gave a soft, scornful laugh. "You still don't understand, do you? You have no idea what it's like. Lying in bed at night, afraid. Listening for the creak of the stairs. Your stomach clenching with the dread of hearing his footsteps in the hall. Knowing what's coming. The pain, the . . ." Her lip curled. "The shame."

Surely she didn't mean . . . Comprehension warred with incredulity and Hero's own ignorance. *Did fathers do that to their own daughters?*

A wry smile curled the other woman's lips, and Hero realized something of her horror and disbelief must have shown on her face. "See," said Rachel's sister. "You don't believe it. After he killed Mama, I told him I was going to let everyone know what he did to me at night—what he'd been doing to me for years. He just laughed at me. He said no one would believe me. They'd think I made it all up."

Hero hunched her shoulders as a damp wind blowing off the surrounding fields buffeted her. It wasn't cold, but she still shivered.

"So we struck a bargain, he and I. He promised if I left he wouldn't start doing to Rachel what he'd done to me all those years. But now that I look back on it, I realize . . ." She drew in a ragged breath. "He'd already started doing it to her, too. It's why she stopped singing. Why she buried her dolls. I thought it was because of Mama, but it wasn't. It was because of him."

Hero stared at the woman's tall, elegant frame and pale features, not knowing what to say.

Lady Sewell turned away to stare out over the surrounding fields. "I remember one morning not long after Rachel's betrothal to Ramsey was announced, I came upon her in the garden. She was singing, and I thought she was happy because she was in love. Now I realize she was happy because she thought she was finally going to get away from *him.*"

Hero's voice came out in a broken, raspy croak. "When she ran away, where did you think she'd gone?"

"I thought she'd gone to Ramsey. Secretly, to get

away from Father. I just—" She broke off, swallowed, and began again. "I don't understand. Why didn't she come to me? Why didn't she tell me what he'd been doing to her?"

"Perhaps she thought you wouldn't believe her," Hero said softly.

Lady Sewell gave a strange laugh that raised the hairs on the back of Hero's neck. "I went there to kill him, you know. This morning."

Hero shook her head, not understanding. "Kill whom?"

"Father. I should have done it all those years ago." Yanking open her tapestry reticule, Lady Sewell drew forth a heavy carriage pistol. Hero stepped back, her gaze darting to the road, where her father's watchdog lounged at his ease.

"I held the gun right in his face. But then I thought, if I shoot him, they'll hang me. And then what will become of Alice?"

"Alice?"

"My little sister. He swears he's never touched her. But I don't believe him. Not this time."

Hero felt a cool gust of wind caress her cheek, breathed in the familiar scents of long, wet grass and damp earth, and felt so fundamentally altered by what she was hearing that she wondered if she'd ever quite right herself again. In the last two weeks, she'd been touched by violence on a shocking scale; she'd killed, and very nearly been killed herself. And then there was that other incident—the one she was endeavoring to forget. Yet this . . . this was somehow worse. She'd known about violence and death and, vaguely, about what happened between a man and a woman. She hadn't known about . . . this. How could any man be so depraved as to do such a thing to his own child? How could any child ever come to terms with such a monstrous betrayal?

"So we made another bargain," Lady Sewell was saying. "Father and I. I let him live, and he will send Alice to live with me." She gave another of those wild laughs. "He worries people will think it strange. Can you imagine?" The laughter suddenly died, leaving her expression pinched. "I wish I could have killed him," she whispered.

"No," said Hero, reaching out to take the gun from Lady Sewell's hand. She expected the woman to resist, but she did not. "No. Your younger sister needs your comfort and support, and he's not worth hanging for."

"Yet if I'd killed him before, Rachel wouldn't be here."

Hero stared down at the row of unmarked graves. "Don't blame yourself. You can't be certain of that."

"You know it's true," said Rachel's sister.

Hero's fist tightened around the gun in her hand. "You can't blame yourself," she said again, even though she knew there was nothing she could say, nothing anyone could do that would ever take away the crushing burden of this woman's guilt.

It was several hours later that a lad playing catch with his dog on Bethnal Green stumbled across the decomposing remains of another body.

"Is it a woman?" asked Sir Henry Lovejoy, holding his folded handkerchief to his nose as he peered into the weed-filled ditch.

"Looks like it, sir," said one of the constables, standing ankle deep in the murky water, his hat pulled low against the drizzle. "What you want we should do with 'er?"

"Take the body to the surgery of Paul Gibson, near Tower Hill," said Lovejoy, his eyes watering from the stench. "And you—" He beckoned to the lad still hovering nearby with his dog. "I've a crown for you, if you'll take a message to Brook Street."

Chapter 56

When Sebastian arrived at Tower Hill, Paul Gibson was downing a tankard of ale in his kitchen. The surgeon had stripped down to his breeches and shirtsleeves, and even from across the room, Sebastian could smell the stench of rotting flesh that clung to him. Mrs. Federico was nowhere in sight.

"Is it Hessy Abrahams?" Sebastian asked.

"Could be," said Gibson, wiping his mouth with the back of his hand. "She's the right age. But she's beyond identification, I'm afraid."

Sebastian knew a spurt of disappointment. "How did she die?"

"Her neck's broken. But it's the way it's broken that's interesting. Come, I'll show you."

Suppressing a groan, Sebastian followed the Irishman down to the end of the garden, through a swarm of buzzing flies, and into a room so thick with the reek of death it made his eyes water. "Good God," said Sebastian, holding his handkerchief to his nose. "How do you stand it?"

"You get used to it," said Gibson, tying a stained apron over his clothes.

After nearly two weeks, Hessy Abrahams's body—if this was indeed Hessy Abrahams—was in an advanced state of decomposition, the flesh blistered and suppurating and hideously discolored. It took all of Sebastian's concentration to keep from losing what little he'd eaten of Madame LeClerc's delicate nuncheon.

"Do you know what happens when someone dies of a broken neck?" Gibson asked, picking up a scalpel and what looked like a pair of pincers.

"Not exactly, no."

Standing at the corpse's throat, Gibson peeled back some of the decaying flesh to reveal the bone beneath. "The top seven bones in your spine form your neck. Basically, they're part of your backbone, but they also serve to protect the spinal cord that runs through here—" He broke off, pointing. "You can break your neck and be all right as long as you don't damage your spinal cord. If you break the lower part of your neck and do injure the cord, you lose the use of your legs and maybe your arms, too, depending on which vertebrae you break."

Sebastian nodded. He'd seen a lot of men crippled by their injuries in the war.

"But if the neck breaks up here," said Gibson, indicating the first several bones, "and the spinal cord is injured, then a person basically suffocates. They can't breathe."

Sebastian took one look, then glanced away. "How long does that take?"

"About two to four minutes."

"Is that what happened to this woman?"

"No. You see, there's another way to die from a broken neck. If the neck is twisted so sharply the spinal cord is torn in half, it affects your heart and the circulation of the blood."

"And you die?"

"Almost instantly. You see it sometimes when a hanging goes well. Of course, they don't often go well."

Sebastian forced himself to look, again, at the desiccated form on Gibson's dissection table. "How was her neck broken?"

"The spinal cord was snapped. The man I was treating after he stopped Miss Jarvis on the way back from Richmond had his neck snapped in exactly the same way. I didn't attach much importance to it at the time, but after I saw this, I got to thinking. So I spoke to the surgeon at St. Thomas's who performed the postmortem on Sir William Hadley. He was killed the same way. So was the Cyprian found in the Haymarket, Tasmin Poole."

Sebastian raised his gaze to his friend's face. "This is significant. Why?"

"It's not an easy thing to do, to break a neck like this. It requires training."

"We already suspected these men were military."

"Yes. But learning how to kill silently with a quick snapping of the neck isn't part of most officers' training. The thing is," said Gibson, laying aside his instruments, "I've seen necks snapped like this before. Over the last three or four years, we've probably had a dozen or more cases."

Sebastian studied his friend's tight, worried face, not understanding at all. "And?"

"No one investigates those deaths," said Gibson. "Some are common people—government clerks, French émigrés. But some are more prominent. You recall when Sir Humphrey Carmichael was found dead last autumn? His neck was broken. Just like this."

The realization of what Gibson was saying spread through Sebastian like a strange numbing sensation. Sir Humphrey Carmichael and Lord Stanton, along with an East India Company man named Atkinson, had all died for the same reason. "And Felix Atkinson? He was killed the same way?"

"Yes."

Sebastian walked out of the dank, foul-smelling building into the sunlit garden. Last night's rain had cleansed the dust from the air, leaving the sky scrubbed so clean and blue it nearly hurt the eyes to look at it. "It makes no sense," said Sebastian, aware of Gibson coming to stand beside him.

"I didn't think so. But then I thought maybe I was missing something."

Sebastian shook his head. A hideous possibility dawned, that all of this—the attack on the Magdalene House, Miss Jarvis's interest in solving the riddle of Rachel Fairchild's fall from grace and subsequent murder, even that poignant brush with death beneath the ancient gardens of Somerset House—had all been a part of some diabolical charade designed by Jarvis to draw him into . . . *what*? And for what purpose?

There was only one thing Sebastian did know: While their deaths had never been officially solved, the men Gibson had listed—Carmichael and Atkinson—had both been killed on the orders of the same man.

Charles, Lord Jarvis.

Chapter 57

*S*ebastian slapped open the door to Lord Jarvis's Carlton House antechamber and strode purposefully toward the inner sanctum. From behind the closed panel came the measured drone of the Baron's voice.

"Sir!" A pathetically thin clerk with bushy eyebrows and a cadaver's pallor gasped and scrambled after him. "Lord Jarvis is dealing with important affairs of state. You can't just go barging in there."

Ignoring him, Sebastian thrust open the door to the inner chamber.

"As for the revenue—" Lord Jarvis broke off, frowning as his head turned toward the door. He sat at his ease on a settee with crocodile-shaped feet and plump cushions covered in brown-and-turquoise-striped silk. From a long table near the window overlooking the Mall, a second clerk occupied with the task of transcribing his lordship's words looked up, his eyes widening in horror.

"Just what the bloody hell did you do?" Sebastian demanded without preamble. "Get your daughter to lure me into one of your diabolical plots so you could use me as a stalking horse?"

Jarvis cast a frozen stare first at one clerk, then the other. "Leave us. Both of you."

Bowing his head, the man at the table scuttled away,

his papers clutched to his chest, the first clerk at his heels.

Jarvis leaned back against the silk cushions, his arms comfortably spread out along the settee's back, his big body relaxed. Far from being intimidated by Sebastian's angry, looming presence, the Baron looked vaguely amused. "My daughter approached you on her own initiative," he said. "If she employed some subterfuge to draw you into this investigation, it was not of my devising."

Sebastian felt the heat of an old rage course through him, blending with the new. "You expect me to believe that? When your henchmen have been killing everyone from Hessy Abrahams to Sir William Hadley?"

With deliberate slowness, Jarvis extracted an enameled snuffbox from his coat pocket and flipped it open. "And who, precisely, is Hessy Abrahams?"

"Don't your men even bother to tell you the names of the people they kill?"

"Only if they're important."

Sebastian resisted with difficulty the urge to smash his fist into the big man's fleshy, complacent face. "What precisely were their orders? To kill everyone connected with this incident in any way?"

Rather than answer, Jarvis lifted a pinch of snuff to one nostril and sniffed. He looked utterly bored and uninterested, but Sebastian knew it was all for effect. "What gives you the impression my men were responsible for the death of Sir William Hadley?"

"The manner of Hadley's death—and Hessy Abrahams's, and half a dozen others—is exactly the same as that employed to dispose of those individuals like Carmichael who have displeased you in the past. It's so unique it's like a signature. There can't be many men in England who know how to kill instantly with the simple snapping of a neck."

Jarvis closed his snuffbox with a soft click. He was no longer smiling. "If you want me to believe this accusation, you need to tell me what you have discovered."

"Why? So your henchmen can kill anyone they've missed?"

"*Have* they missed anyone?"

Sebastian thought of Hannah Green, and the blind harp player from the Academy, and realized the list was actually rather short.

Jarvis pushed to his feet and went to stand at the window overlooking the Mall. Watching him, Sebastian realized that his anger might have led him to misinterpret the situation. It was possible the plot to kill Perceval was Jarvis's own, but that the big man remained ignorant of both his hirelings' indiscretion on the night of Somerville's birthday celebration and their subsequent attempts to cover it up.

Fixing his gaze on Jarvis's face, Sebastian provided the King's powerful cousin with a succinct version of the past two weeks' events as he understood them.

But Jarvis never gave anything away. In the end, he merely said calmly, "Why would my henchman, as you call him, want to kill the Prime Minister?" The use of the singular—*henchman* as opposed to henchmen—was not lost on Sebastian. "There are far less spectacular ways of getting rid of Spencer Perceval," Jarvis was saying, "if that were indeed my wish. The Prince is easily persuadable. One need only whisper in the royal ear."

"You could intend to use Perceval's death to inflame public opinion. Or as an excuse to move against an enemy."

"I could," agreed Jarvis. "But I don't."

The two men's gazes met, and for one fleeting moment, Jarvis's famed self-possession slipped. Sebastian saw swift comprehension mingled with horror and the dawning of a fury so white-hot it swept away whatever lingering doubts Sebastian might still have had. And he knew in that instant that Jarvis would never forgive him for this, never forgive him for having been privy to the enormity of his failure.

"What are you saying? That your man is acting on his own for reasons neither one of us understands?" Sebastian gave a low laugh. "That's rich. You think you know everything and control everything. Yet your agent has nearly killed your own daughter three times, and may yet succeed in assassinating the Prime Minister."

Jarvis frowned. "*Three* times?"

Too late, Sebastian recalled the Baron's ignorance of the third incident. He flattened his hands on the surface of the table between them and leaned forward. "Tell me the man's name."

Jarvis's fist clenched around his snuffbox so hard Sebastian heard the delicate metal crack. "Epson-Smith. Colonel Bryce Epson-Smith."

Chapter 58

The rooms occupied by Colonel Bryce Epson-Smith were on the first floor of a genteel house just off Bedford Square. Sebastian arrived there shortly after four to find the former hussar colonel gone from home. A terse conversation with the Colonel's majordomo elicited the information that the Colonel was spending the afternoon escorting the family of a Liverpudlian friend to the exhibition at the Royal Academy of Art.

Turning south toward the river, Sebastian dropped his hands and let the chestnuts shoot forward. "If'n 'e's lookin' at pictures, at least 'e ain't killin' the Prime Minister," said Tom, clamping his hat down tighter on his head and tightening his hold on his perch.

Sebastian kept his attention on his horses, feathering the corner as he swung onto Drury Lane. He had a niggling sense that he was still missing something. A connection he should have seen, perhaps, or an implication that continued to elude him.

The Royal Academy of Art occupied rooms in the large neoclassical pile on the Thames that had replaced the Duke of Somerset's original palace. Pulling up on the Strand, Sebastian tossed the reins to Tom and hit the footpath running. He sprinted toward the vestibule, heedless of the shocked expressions and muttered *tut-tut*s, and took the steep, winding staircase two steps at a time. The Academy, like all the other societies and governmental departments housed in the building, occupied a vertical slice of all six floors. To take advantage of the natural light provided by a skylight, the Academy had placed their Exhibition Room in the high-ceilinged, nearly square space at the very top of the stairs.

Breathing hard, Sebastian burst into a chamber crowded with more than a thousand paintings, which climbed toward the ceiling in row after row hung together so closely that their heavy gilt frames nearly touched. At the sound of his hurried footsteps crossing the polished floor, the small party gathered beneath the central lantern turned. Sebastian had a vague impression of two wan-faced women in plain round bonnets and unfashionably cut pelisses, one clutching the hand of a half-grown girl, the other attempting to restrain a fidgety boy of perhaps eight. Beside them, Epson-Smith cut a dashing figure in his military-styled coat, shining top boots, and swooping side-whiskers.

His gaze fixed firmly on the former hussar officer, Sebastian walked up to the small group and executed a short bow. "Ladies, if you'll excuse us? The Colonel and I have something to discuss."

The men's gazes met, clashed. "This won't take but a moment," said Epson-Smith to his companions. "Some friends of one of my acquaintances from Liverpool," he told Sebastian as they moved away from the ladies. "I thought it would make a nice outing."

Sebastian kept his own tone low, conversational. "Lord Jarvis might be a powerful protector, but he also makes a powerful enemy. I've no doubt he'd be willing to overlook the murder of any number of unimportant people, but he's not at all pleased with your little plot to kill the Prime Minister. And as for your attempts on the life of his daughter . . . I'd say you've signed your own death warrant."

The man's complacent arrogance never faltered. "You've no proof tying me to any of this," he said, still faintly smiling.

"Not enough to convict you in a court of law," Sebastian conceded. "But then, you'll never see the inside of a courtroom. The only thing that matters is what Jarvis believes."

"True. Only, why should he believe you? You've threatened to kill him—several times, whereas I have served him faithfully for nearly four years now."

"Faithfully and efficiently," said Sebastian, dodging one of the pedestals topped with a particularly hideous set of bronzes that littered the Exhibition Room's floor. "It's a distinctive way of killing—just a quick snap of the neck. Where'd you learn it?"

The Colonel's smile hardened. "The Sudan."

Through the glass of the skylight, Sebastian could see the afternoon clouds building overhead, bunching masses of angry black turmoil. The room grew perceptibly darker. "What precisely is your argument with Perceval?" he asked.

Epson-Smith's lips pressed into a thin, tight line. "Thanks to the incompetence of his government, my regiment went through hell in Argentina. We were promised compensation, but Perceval deemed it an extravagant and unnecessary expense, and canceled the arrangements. Thanks to his damnable interference, the ambitions of the few men who survived have been shattered, while the widows of those who died are ruined."

"You would kill him over that?"

Epson-Smith pivoted to look back at the small party of women and children now clustered at the far end of the room. "Not me," he said calmly. "Perceval has made many enemies. A man driven by passion can sometimes be goaded to act in ways not precisely in his own best interest. Particularly when he's not in his right mind."

"Bellingham," said Sebastian, remembering the half-mad Liverpudlian he and Perceval had encountered on the footpath outside Almack's.

"You know him? Then what a pity you've just missed him. He was here with us, you know, but he had to leave early. Some business to attend to, I believe he said. At the House of Commons."

Sebastian swung toward the steps, but Epson-Smith put out a hand that closed on Sebastian's forearm in a surprisingly strong grip. "You're too late," said the Colonel.

Sebastian lunged toward him, trying to break the man's hold on his arm. But in a maneuver Sebastian didn't see coming, the ex-hussar spun Sebastian around, one arm clamping across Sebastian's chest to grip him by his right arm and draw him back into Epson-Smith's deadly embrace.

"You kill me here, now, and you'll never get away with it," said Sebastian.

The Colonel's free hand came up to grasp Sebastian's chin in an unexpectedly iron hold. "If Jarvis knows I tried to kill his daughter, I'm a dead man anyway."

One quick twist, Sebastian realized, and his neck would snap. Bucking against the man's hold, Sebastian slammed his head back into Epson-Smith's face, bone crunching cartilage. With a startled grunt, Epson-Smith loosened his grip on Sebastian just long enough for Sebastian to grasp the arm clamped across his chest and spin around, smashing the back of his fist into Epson-Smith's bloody face. Still holding the man's arm, Sebastian twisted it in and down, forcing Epson-Smith to pivot enough that Sebastian could stomp the heel of his right boot into the back of the man's left knee.

Epson-Smith went down on his knees, his left arm still held in Sebastian's grasp. Too late, Sebastian saw the flash of the blade that had appeared in the man's right hand. Slashing upward, he laid open Sebastian's fore-arm to the bone.

Sebastian stumbled back, slipping in his own blood, bumping into one of the Exhibition Room's pedestals. Whirling, he caught up the bronze statue of a satyr and hurled it. As Epson-Smith ducked sideways, Sebastian yanked his own knife from his boot and charged. With a sweep of his forearm, Sebastian knocked the wrist of the hand holding the blade aside and drove his own dagger deep into Epson-Smith's chest.

He became aware, suddenly, of a woman screaming, a man's harsh shout, running footsteps. Yanking his knife free, sliding in the spreading pool of blood, Sebastian hurtled back down the steep winding stairs. Sprinting across the vestibule, he set up a call for his curricle. If only Tom hadn't gone far—

" 'Oly 'ell, gov'nor!" Wide-eyed, Tom reined the chest-nuts in hard before the vestibule's entrance. "You're bleedin' worse'n a leaky bucket."

Sebastian scrambled into the curricle. "You drive," he said, yanking off his cravat to wind the long strip of linen around his throbbing arm. "The House of Commons. *Quickly!*"

Chapter 59

"What's all this, then?" Tom demanded, struggling to thread the curricle through the tangle of chaises, sedan chairs, gigs, and hackneys that clogged Parliament Street from Whitehall to far beyond the houses of Parliament and the Abbey.

"There's to be an inquiry this evening into the Orders in Council," Sebastian said as the bells of the Abbey began to toll five o'clock. Men shouted and whips cracked. A donkey brayed. Ragged urchins and barking dogs darted past, the boys whooping and laughing. "Looks like it's attracting the devil of a crowd."

"What time's the Prime Minister s'posed to arrive?"

"Five o'clock." From up ahead came the crash of splintering wood as a landau hooked one of its wheels with a coal cart. "Bloody hell," said Sebastian, grasping the seat rail with his good hand. "Pull up here. I can make better time on foot."

He leapt from the curricle and started running. Pushing his way up Margaret Street, he cut across Old Palace Yard to the small former chapel that stood at right angles to Westminster Hall and served as the House of Commons. Bursting through the double doors, he found himself in a dark, low-ceilinged lobby crowded with a throng of spectators queuing patiently for a spot in the galleries. He knew a surge of relief. He wasn't too late.

Glancing around, Sebastian snagged the arm of a self-important clerk bustling past and hauled him back. "Where is Perceval? Is he here yet? Tell me quickly, man."

"I say, sir," bleated the clerk. "You're not allowed here in boots." He blanched as his gaze traveled from Sebastian's bare neck to his bloodied, hastily bandaged arm. "And neck clothes are mandatory. Have you an introduction from a member? Because you really should have entered through the Hall, you kn—"

Sebastian resisted the urge to shake the man. "Damn you, I'm not here to gawk from the galleries. Where is Perceval?"

A movement to one side of the lobby caught Sebastian's attention. A dark-haired man had risen from a seat near an open fire and was now walking briskly toward the entrance, one hand resting conspicuously inside his coat. "Bellingham," said Sebastian. Then he bellowed, *"Bellingham. Someone seize that man!"*

Shocked faces turned not toward Bellingham, but toward Sebastian.

With an oath, Sebastian surged forward. The clerk latched on to his wounded arm and held tight. "Sir, I must insist—"

The slight figure of the Prime Minister appeared in the open doorway. He had his head half turned away, speaking to someone behind him.

"No!" shouted Sebastian, shaking off the clerk just as Bellingham walked up to the Prime Minister and fired a single shot into Perceval's chest from a distance of no more than three or four feet. As Perceval stumbled back into the arms of the man behind him, Bellingham turned calmly and resumed his seat beside the fire.

*   *   *

They carried the Prime Minister into the office of the secretary of the speaker. Someone called for a doctor, but one glance at the gaping charred hole in Perceval's chest was enough to tell Sebastian the Prime Minister was beyond any doctor's help.

Sebastian looked around. "You," he said, his gaze falling on the self-important clerk hovering nearby. "Run to Downing Street. Tell his family what has happened. *Run!*" he said again when the men hesitated.

Perceval's hand fluttered. "Spence? Is he here?"

"He's coming," lied Sebastian, grasping the Prime Minister's hand. Already, it felt cold.

Perceval sucked in a gasping breath that rattled in his throat. "I would like to have seen him one last time before I . . ."

Sebastian leaned forward, straining to hear his words. But the Prime Minister only stared up with blank, unseeing eyes.

Chapter 60

*P*aul Gibson thrust his needle through the flesh of Sebastian's forearm, stitching up the long gash left by Epson-Smith's blade. "You're lucky," said Gibson. "He nearly sliced the tendon."

Sebastian watched the Irishman work his needle in and out. "I think you sew better than my tailor."

Gibson tied off his thread and reached for a pair of scissors. "You keep me in practice."

Sebastian held out his arm to open and close his fist.

"It would be better if you rested it for a few days," said Gibson, turning away to smear salve on a bandage. "Not that I expect you to pay me any heed." He began wrapping the bandage in place. "What do you think they'll do to Bellingham?"

"Hang him, I should think. Probably before the week is out."

"The man is obviously insane."

"Yes. But I doubt that will stop them."

"One thing I don't understand," said Gibson, busy with his task, "is how the gentleman who stopped Miss Jarvis's carriage on the way back from Richmond fits into all this."

"He was probably another hussar officer. He obviously wasn't at the birthday debauchery, but he must have been involved in the plot to goad Bellingham into shooting Perceval. I suspect it was the four of them—Epson-Smith, Somerville, Drummond, and the Richmond assailant—who attacked the Magdalene House. Epson-Smith killed him to keep him from talking."

"You think there could be more mixed up in it?"

Sebastian thought about the men who had nearly lured Hero Jarvis to her death. But all he said was, "I doubt we'll ever know exactly how many hussars were involved."

"Particularly if the Crown continues to insist that Bellingham acted alone."

The sound of a carriage pulling up in the street outside drew Sebastian's attention. Even before he heard the knock on the door, before he heard the lilt of her voice as she spoke to Mrs. Federico, he knew it was Kat.

She came in, bringing with her the scent of the night and the promise of more rain. She wore a sapphire blue carriage dress with cream braided trim and a matching pelisse, and as she paused on the threshold to Gibson's front room, the exquisite peacock feather of her jaunty blue hat curled down from the brim to rest against her pale cheek. He knew she hadn't expected to find him here.

"I beg your pardon," she said, her gaze focused resolutely on Gibson. "I see you're busy. I'll come back later."

She turned to go, but Gibson said, "No, wait. Let me just empty this and I'll be back." Picking up the basin of bloody water and soiled cloths, he walked out of the room.

Her gaze fell to the bandage on Sebastian's arm. "I'd heard you were wounded."

"It's just a cut."

"You could have been killed."

"I wasn't." He slid off the edge of the table but made

no move to approach her. They stared at each other across the width of the room. "Do you come here often?" he asked. "To see Gibson?"

"Sometimes."

They fell silent. For one stolen moment he lost himself in looking at her, at the familiar childlike tilt of her nose and the full curve of her lips. He would have sworn that the very air quivered with an aching awareness of all they had once been to each other and all that they could never be again.

She said, "I must go." But still she lingered, her gaze on his. And he knew then with a quiet rush of despair that both this love and this pain would always be a part of him.

And a part of her.

Later that evening, Hero received a courteous note from Viscount Devlin briefly detailing for her benefit the day's events and the circumstances surrounding the Magdalene House killings. He told her of the quarrel between Rachel and Tristan Ramsey, but without the knowledge Hero had acquired from Lady Sewell, Rachel's subsequent flight would still have made no sense. She had no doubt that Devlin himself knew of Lord Fairchild's dark secret, and it irked her that Devlin had thought to protect her by withholding the information from her.

She held the crisp white sheet of his letter a moment too long, then resolutely thrust it into the library fire before her. She was still in the library, curled up in an overstuffed chair beside the fire and lost in the contemplation of the dancing flames, when she felt her father's gaze upon her. She looked up to find him watching her from the doorway.

"No book?" he said. His lips smiled, but his eyes were narrow with concern.

She shifted uncomfortably beneath his regard, as if

he might somehow detect the dangerous drift of her thoughts, just by looking at her. To forestall him, she said, "I heard Patrick Somerville is dead. Did you have him killed?"

"No. It was my intention to do so, but he managed to beat me to it. Quinine and arsenic can be a deadly combination."

"He killed himself?"

"Probably. Although for the sake of his father, it will be ruled an accident."

She tipped her head back against the seat cushion. "So many deaths," she said quietly. "Any decision yet on who'll replace Perceval?"

Jarvis snorted. "I left Prinny and the rest arguing over whether to offer the premiership to Canning or Castlereagh. A moot point, since neither man will take it. Between Bonaparte and the Americans, this is a damnable time to be without a prime minister. Perceval might have been an ineffectual idiot, but he was better than no one."

"Will there be any repercussions from today's events?" she asked with studied casualness. "To Devlin's killing of Epson-Smith, I mean."

"Hardly. Epson-Smith attacked him. Oh, there'll be some talk, of course. But then, there is always talk about Devlin. It will die down eventually." He stared at her for so long it took all of her sangfroid to continue holding his gaze. "Devlin said there were three attempts on your life. I am only aware of two."

His enemies credited him with such omniscience that she'd worried he might somehow come to learn of those disastrous hours in the vaults beneath the ruined gardens of the old Somerset House. It was a relief to know that he had not. Perhaps, with time, she herself would be able to forget for days at a time that it had occurred. "There was no third attempt."

"You lie well," he said, coming toward her, "but not well enough yet to deceive me."

Tipping back her head, she gave him a soft smile. "No one can deceive you, Papa."

"Not for long. Remember that," he said. Reaching out, he touched her cheek, briefly, with his knuckles. It was the closest he ever came to a gesture of affection. Or an apology.

It was the Earl of Hendon's habit every morning that he was in London to rise early and exercise his big gray in Hyde Park before breakfast.

On the Tuesday following the death of Spencer Perceval, the mist lay heavily on the rain-drenched grass. But the air held a new crispness, a promise of the vital energy of a spring too long delayed in coming. Turning his black Arabian mare through the gates to the park, Sebastian could see the Earl trotting briskly up the Row, his body rising and falling in rhythmic precision with his horse's easy action.

For a moment, Sebastian checked, the familiar drumming of the gray's hooves on the earth reverberating in the ghostly stillness. The urge to wheel the mare's head and simply ride away was strong. But still he sat, his reins held in a clenched fist.

Through the mist beyond the dark line of trees, he could see the spire of the Abbey and, beyond that, the towers of the ancient palace of Westminster. He kept remembering the helpless longing he'd seen in Perceval's face as the dying Prime Minister asked for his son with his last, gasping breath. Sebastian's anger was still there, burrowed deep. The anger and the hurt. But something had shifted within him, and he knew now what he must do.

Hendon had reached the end of the Row. When he turned, his gaze fell on his son's rigid, solitary figure. Sebastian saw the Earl tense with a cautious, joyous hope.

He felt the air damp against his face, the mare restless beneath him. Tightening his knees, he sent the mare flying forward across the park.

Toward his father, and toward a reconciliation too long delayed.

Author's Note

*F*resh from their conquest of Cape Town from the Dutch, the British did indeed attempt to conquer Argentina in 1806 and 1807. The expedition was a disastrous failure, although the lingering animosity toward Perceval on the part of the surviving officers of the 20th Hussars is my own invention.

On May 11, 1812, Spencer Perceval became the only British Prime Minister—thus far—to be assassinated in office. His death occurred much as it is portrayed here, although the proceedings at the Old Bailey (now available online, for those who are interested) uncovered no evidence of any kind of conspiracy. Despite his obvious insanity, John Bellingham was found guilty and hanged barely a week later.

I have altered a few other facts to fit my story. Prior to his fatal visit to the House of Commons, Bellingham did take the family of a friend to look at pictures, but it was to a watercolor exhibit at the European Museum rather than the annual exhibit at the Royal Academy of Art. According to a journalist present at the assassination, Perceval's last words were, "I am murdered!" It is likely, however, that the journalist was indulging in sensationalism, given that other witnesses testified the Prime minister said nothing before his death. I have therefore taken the liberty of also altering his last utterances.

Look for the next book in the
Sebastian St. Cyr Mystery series
by C. S. Harris

WHAT REMAINS OF HEAVEN

Available now.

An excerpt follows . . .

Tanfield Hill, Tuesday, 7 July 1812

*H*is breath coming in undignified gasps, the Reverend Malcolm Earnshaw abandoned the village high street and struck out through the lanky grass of the church-yard. He was a small, plump man, well into his middle years, his hair sparse and graying, his knees stiff. Looking up, he saw the belfry of the village church silhouetted dark against the white of the evening sky, and suppressed a groan.

"What have I done? What have I done?" he murmured to himself in a kind of chant. He never should have lingered so long with old Mrs. Cummings. Yes, the woman was dying, but he'd done what he could to ease her passing, and one did not keep the Bishop of London waiting—especially when one was a lowly churchman who owed the Bishop's family his living.

Hot and breathless now in his haste, the Reverend reached the sweep of gravel before the church. His step faltered, the small stones crunching beneath the leather soles of his shoes. "Merciful heavens," he whispered, his jaw sagging at the sight of the Bishop's carriage, its coachman dozing on the box. "He's *here*."

Swallowing hard, Earnshaw cast a searching glance around the ancient churchyard. Despite the lengthening shadows, the jagged piles of stones and aged timbers left from the demolition of the charnel house that once stood against the north wall of the chancel were clearly visible. But Bishop Prescott was nowhere in sight.

The Reverend hesitated, the urge to rush forward warring with a craven desire to duck into the sacristy for a lantern. He pushed on, his heart thumping painfully in his chest as he neared the gaping hole before him. The workmen had accidentally broken through the thin brick wall that afternoon. The wall had concealed a forgotten staircase of worn stone steps that led down to an ancient crypt far older even than the venerable Norman nave above it.

During his ten years of service here at St. Margaret's, Malcolm Earnshaw had heard vague rumors of a crypt, sealed decades ago for health reasons. But nothing the Reverend had heard had prepared him for the workmen's gruesome discovery.

Tugging his handkerchief from his pocket, he pressed the linen folds against his mouth and nostrils as the foul air of the crypt wafted up to him. He was near enough now to see the glow of lantern light on the worn steps coming up from below. The Bishop had indeed gone before him.

Again Earnshaw hesitated, not from indecision this time but from revulsion at the horror of what lay below. The Bible taught that the trumpet shall sound, and the dead shall be raised incorruptible. And again in Ezekiel it was written that God shall put flesh on the bones of the dead and breathe life into them. Earnshaw knew that. Yet still he found himself trembling at the need to confront once again a sight that might have been conjured from the vilest visions of Dante's *Inferno*.

Grasping the rusted railing that ran along one side of

the steps, he stumbled down the shadowy stairs toward the flickering light below. "I most humbly beg your pardon, Bishop Prescott," he began, his voice echoing back to him from that sepulchral vault. "I do hope I've not kept you waiting long?"

The oppressive silence of the crypt closed around him. Built of rough stone covered in limestone mortar and with a low vaulted ceiling supported by worn columns, the bays of the chamber stretched before him in shadowy phalanxes of death. Piles of coffins stacked five and six high were crammed into nearly every bay, their wood warped and split to reveal tomb-blackened remnants of tattered clothing and the occasional, unmistakable gleam of a skull or long bone.

But that clean scouring of time was rare. What truly horrified the Reverend and caused him to tighten his grip on the stair railing was the way the dry air had combined with the high concentration of lime to preserve most of the burials. All too often, what spilled from those crushed tombs was an arm or leg still recognizably human, or a hair-topped nightmare of a face, its flesh shriveled and tanned like that of a mummy brought back from Egypt.

"Bishop Prescott?" Earnshaw called again, his voice quavering. Misled by the gleam of lamplight, he'd obviously erred in choosing to come here directly. The Bishop must simply have abandoned his lantern in the crypt and returned to the sacristy to wait.

Devastated by his error, Earnshaw was turning back toward the stairs when his gaze fell on the far end of the chamber. A man lay facedown beside the last worn, spiraled column. Only this was not some ancient, desiccated corpse tumbled from its collapsed coffin. "*Bishop Prescott,*" said Earnshaw with a gasp, recognizing the man's tall, gaunt form, the distinctive purple cassock, the thinning white hair worn unusually long.

The Reverend staggered to where the Bishop lay with his head turned slightly to one side, his pale gray eyes open wide and blankly staring. From beneath the matted, crushed side of his head, a spreading stain of blood ran in a slow, dark rivulet across the ancient stone floor.

London, the early hours of Wednesday, 8 July 1812

The Circular Room at Carlton House was an inner sanctum reserved for the most intimate friends of His Royal Highness George, Prince Regent. Here, amidst the glitter of crystal chandeliers and the glories of blue silk draped in imitation of a Roman tent, those with the privilege of entrée gathered late into the night to drink wine and listen to music and bask in all the benefits of being in the royal favor.

But tonight, the Prince was in a petulant mood, his full, almost feminine lower lip thrust out in a pout. "I hear the Bishop of London is set to give a speech against slavery before the Lords this Thursday," said the Regent, snapping his fingers for another bottle.

Once, the Prince had been a handsome man. Now, in his early fifties, a lifetime of overindulgence in the various delights of the flesh had taken their toll. His face was flushed, his features blurred, and not even the talents of London's best tailors—or the use of rigidly laced stays—could disguise the corpulence of his body.

His stays creaking perilously, the Regent turned to frown at his cousin Charles, Lord Jarvis, the acknowledged power behind the Prince's fragile regency. "What say you, Jarvis? Surely there's some way to stop him?"

His cousin Jarvis was also a big man, standing more than six feet tall and fleshy. Jarvis's size alone would have made him impressive. But it was his awe-inspiring intellect, his formidable ruthlessness, and a true dedication to King and country that had combined to make him the most powerful man in the kingdom. He took a slow sip of his own wine before answering. "I hardly see what, short of killing him."

A nervous titter spread amongst the men gathered near enough to hear. Everyone knew that those Jarvis considered his enemies—or even merely inconvenient—had a nasty habit of turning up dead.

The Prince's pout grew. One of his intimates—a slim, hawk-faced exquisite named Lord Quillian—raised one eyebrow and said, "The man's on a bloody crusade. You're not troubled by it, Jarvis?"

Jarvis flicked open a gold snuffbox with one careless finger. "You think I should be?"

"Considering the fact that Prescott was largely responsible for getting the Slave Trade Act passed five years ago, I'd say so, yes. There's a growing piety in this country, combined with a mawkish kind of sensibility that worries me."

"It's easy to support abolition in theory." Jarvis raised a pinch of snuff to his nostril. "In practice, things become considerably more complicated."

A movement near the door drew Jarvis's attention. A tall, military-looking gentleman in a riding coat and top boots spoke in an low voice to the attendants, then strode across the room to whisper in Jarvis's ear.

"Excuse me, Your Highness," said the King's powerful cousin with a bow. "I shan't be but a moment."

Withdrawing to a secluded alcove, Jarvis snapped, "What is it?"

The tall, military-looking gentleman, a former captain in the 9th Foot, smiled. "The Bishop of London is dead."

In the cool light of early morning, father and son trotted their horses companionably side by side through Hyde

Park. Faint wisps of mist still hovered here and there beneath the trees, although the strengthening sun was beginning to burn off the fog rising from the nearby river.

"It's been two months now since Perceval was shot," grumbled Alistair James St. Cyr, Fifth Earl of Hendon. Mounted on a big gray gelding, the Earl was a powerfully framed man of sixty-six with a barrel chest, a thick shock of white hair, and vivid blue eyes. "Two months!" he said again, when his son made no comment. "And Liverpool is still acting more like an incompetent backbencher than a prime minister. This situation can't continue. We're already at war with half of Europe. The next thing you know we're going to have the bloody Americans attacking Canada."

Mounted on the neat black Arab mare he'd acquired during his years as an Army officer, the Earl's only surviving son and heir, Sebastian, Viscount Devlin, ducked his head to hide a smile. Even taller than his father, the Viscount was built lean, with dark hair and strange, feral-looking yellow eyes. "You're the one who turned down the Regent's invitation to form a government," he said.

"I should rather think so," said the Earl, who for the past three years had held the position of Chancellor of the Exchequer. "Why should I spend my days fighting Jarvis for the loyalty of my own cabinet? Once, I might have been persuaded to do so. No longer."

"I should think you'd jump at the chance," said Sebastian, "if for no other reason than to spite Jarvis." The King's formidable, eerily omnipotent cousin intimidated most men, but not Hendon. The two had been at loggerheads for as long as Sebastian could remember. Yet as powerful as he was, Jarvis would never form a government himself. The big man preferred to exercise his authority discreetly—and more effectively—from the shadows.

Hendon blew out a long breath. "I must be getting old. I find I've better things to do with my time."

Sebastian raised one eyebrow.

"You heard me," said Hendon. "I'd like to spend my declining years surrounded by a passel of lusty grandsons. Unfortunately, my only surviving son has yet to condescend to give me any."

"You have a grandson. And a granddaughter."

"Bayard?" Hendon dismissed the children of his only legitimate daughter, Amanda, Lady Wilcox, with a wave of one hand. "Bayard's a Wilcox, and half as mad as his father besides. I'm talking about St. Cyr grandsons. The kind only you can give me. Heirs. You're nearly thirty years old now, Sebastian. It's high time you settled down and started a family."

Sebastian kept his gaze firmly fixed between his horse's ears and said nothing. The estrangement that had arisen between father and son the previous autumn had eased these past few weeks, but Hendon was straying into dangerous territory.

There was a moment of tense silence; then the Earl grunted, his eyes narrowing as he stared across the park. "I see you're still employing that impertinent pickpocket as a groom."

Sebastian followed his father's gaze to where a sharp-faced boy dressed in the Devlin livery and mounted on one of Sebastian's hacks pelted inelegantly toward them, one elbow cocked skyward to hold his hat in place. "What the devil?"

Tom, Sebastian's young tiger, reined in hard beside them. He was thirteen years old, although he looked younger, with his gap-toothed grin and slight frame. Bobbing his head to Hendon, he said breathlessly, "Beggin' yer pardon for the interruption, yer lordship." He turned to Sebastian. "Ye've visitors awaitin' ye at Brook Street, gov'nor. Yer aunt, the Duchess of Claiborne, and the Archbishop of Canterbury!"

Devlin said, "The Archbishop of Canterbury?"

"Henrietta?" said his father, eyes widening with incredulity. "At this hour?" The Duchess of Claiborne was famous for never leaving her bed before noon. Hendon sniffed the air. "The boy is obviously foxed."

"I ain't been drinkin'," said Tom, bridling. "It's 'Er Grace, all right, sittin' up there in the drawing room with the Archbishop 'isself."

Hendon's suspicious frown deepened. "The last I heard, Archbishop Moore was essentially at death's door. Why, Jarvis is already maneuvering to line up the man's replacement."

"Well, 'e don't look none too 'ale, that's fer sure," agreed Tom. "But I reckon that's to be expected, given what's 'appened."

"What has happened?" said Sebastian.

"Why, someone's done gone and murdered the Bishop of London. Last night, in the crypt o' some church near 'Ounslow 'Eath!"